BREAKING CURSED BONDS

I0678117

Curses & Secrets Book One

A novel by Elisabeth Zguta

Copyright

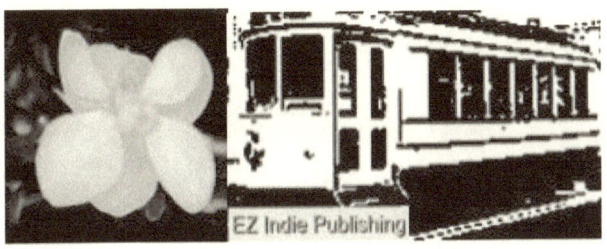

"A broken heart can never be perfectly mended, there are always scars."

— Mrs. Boniverre

CHAPTER ONE

Thaddeus Riley's heart pumped faster as he grabbed a tight hold to his satchel, protecting his precious cargo. Sweating now, the old man picked up the pace as best he could on the deserted, rain-slicked street. As he neared his home, he loosened his collar to aid his breathing. He glanced back at the man trailing him, the same man he'd seen at the pub on High Street earlier that night. The same man Thaddeus and his nephew, Jeremy, had both taken note of. *I'm sure he means no harm*, Jeremy had reassured him. Now, Thaddeus wished they both had been more mindful.

"Just another block," he said aloud to himself.

Refuge was near. Turning the corner, Thaddeus saw his front door with its old brass knocker, stark against the red paint of the old brick townhouse. A quick glance back confirmed the stranger still followed.

His throat tightened, swelling from adrenalin. Thaddeus pulled his keys from his pocket, fumbled for the right one, and continued walking. He found the correct key just as he arrived at his stoop. He inserted it and turned it in the lock with a quick jerk, then pushed the door with his shoulder. The door opened with a thump as it broke free from the swollen wood jamb. He entered quickly and closed the door behind him, latching the security bolt.

His entire body deflated. Taking a couple of deep breaths, he scurried to the window and peeked out the corner, moving the curtain just enough to view the empty street. He chuckled to himself as he combed back his disheveled gray hair with his fingers.

"Thad, you fool, you're letting your imagination run wild in your old age!"

He inhaled deeply once more, feeling like himself again now that he was safe in his home. He patted himself on his chest, then took off his scarf and weathered raincoat and hung them on a hook near the door. Thaddeus walked across the cluttered room and with careful hands, laid his worn satchel on the big roll-top desk where he stored his most recent work and research. He slid the book out and examined it with a triumphant smile.

It was a treasure: an old book, an ancient journal, and it had a tale to tell. A tale that would help him find the truth about his dear aunt's death so many years ago. Thaddeus admired the leather cover and the tattered spine, touching it with reverence. He remembered the story his friend had begun interpreting from this ancient journal. A tale about French seamen, Florida tribes, and aboriginal ceremonies.

He opened the book and made a mental note of the blue-inked emblem printed on the inside cover. It was a unique insignia, well worth investigation. His weathered hands turned the pages as he examined the primitive designs on the parchment, his excitement building. This new relic reminded him of his past, and the many other treasures he'd rescued during his long career as a history professor. He'd traipsed the globe seeking authentic and unusual documents, delving into the mysteries of the past, searching for his own family footprint.

He contemplated this new enigma, until something broke his reverie. Footsteps just outside his door, he thought. *Surely not a visitor this late?* His heart pounded, adrenalin pumping again. He stood. Before he could investigate, he heard the unmistakable sound of glass breaking in the back room. A split second later, the door slammed open, cracking against the wall with the force.

He swallowed past terror and the throb of his heart, pounding out of control now. He rushed across the room in a mad race for the phone but the stranger loomed in front of him, blocking his path. The man was common enough in height and build, it was his expression that unnerved

Thaddeus. The stranger's glare sliced through him, with soulless, dagger eyes. Thaddeus cringed at the handgun pointed straight at his head.

"What do you want? Who are you? How dare you break into my home."

The stranger didn't respond. His dark eyes shifted from one corner of the room to another, surveying the space, searching for something. The room was comfy and used often, decorated in warm colors and paisley prints, with odd relics on display. Piles of papers and books were stacked on every surface. Thaddeus knew there was only one book the stranger wanted, though: the ancient journal. Enraged that the stranger had violated his space, Thaddeus found his voice as his temper flared.

"Get out of my house before the authorities arrive."

He stretched his arm around the man and strained to pick up the phone. The threat of the police had no effect; the stranger tore the phone off the table, ripping the cord from the wall, and threw it across the room.

There was a loud thud and trilling of bells as the phone collided with the wall and crashed to the floor, knocking a hung picture off its hook on the way down. It was a framed photo of Jeremy as a boy, the son Thaddeus had never had. Glass shattered when it hit the hardwood floor, splinters flying like shrapnel.

Thaddeus whimpered, well and truly terrified. He swallowed hard, gulping for air, and turned to escape. Before he'd gone a step, the stranger caught his arm and pushed the old man into a nearby chair. There was nowhere to flee. The stranger strode to the desk and took the old book, then placed the journal into a cloth bag he'd extracted from his coat pocket.

"No, you can't take that!" the old man screamed. "I searched my whole life for that book. Get your hands off it!"

Thaddeus rose from the chair, focused on his prized possession. The sudden movement made him stumble, snagging his foot on the rug as he tried to reach the desk. The room spun, nausea overtaking him. He crashed to the floor. He felt no pain at first, just a heavy pressure in his chest. The old man struggled to roll over onto his back, gasping for breath. His heart thumped faster and faster, as if his chest would explode.

Please merciful God, please forgive me my sins. Please Lord, take care of my Jeremy. With one last gulp of air and a slight tremor that rocked his weakened body, Thaddeus lost the battle.

The stranger looked down at the old man, showing no trace of remorse. Taking the journal, he unlocked the front door and left.

At just past midnight that same night, Jeremy Laughton's phone rang.

"Mr. Laughton, this is Detective Mason from the Response Command. I'm at Markenfield Road. Sir, do you know a Mr. Thaddeus Riley? You're listed as the contact person."

Jeremy squeezed the back of his neck, his throat constricted. "Yes, why are you at my uncle's place? What's going on?" The words stuck in his mouth.

"Mr. Laughton, could you please come right over? There's been an incident."

There was a brief moment of silence.

Jeremy's gut sunk in fear. Something must have happened to Uncle Thaddeus. His blood shot through his veins in a heated rush. Thoughts of his Uncle Thad dead raced through his head, *incomprehensible, no, it's a mistake, maybe a heart attack?* He swallowed back the lump in his throat, pushing the panic from his voice.

"Sir, are you still on the line?"

"I'm on my way," Jeremy said.

Adrenalin kicked him into gear; he jumped into his Rover and rushed to his uncle's place. Everything flashed by in a blur as he drove on autopilot, arriving within minutes. He shoved the column into park, jumped out of his vehicle, and headed straight for his uncle's front door. There were constables all around, a cruiser with lights flashing parked in front of the house. The front door was wide open. A man pulled a stretcher from a yellow NHS ambulance's back hatch, and someone wheeled it toward the house.

Petrified by the surreal scene, Jeremy lost focus for a moment. *It must be a misunderstanding.* He breathed in deep gasps as he approached the house. A detective constable with tired sagging eyes, dressed in rumpled clothes, scratched his tilted head as he walked over to meet Jeremy.

"Are you Mr. Laughton?"

"Yes, how is my uncle?"

The DC hung his head as they approached the front door. He extended his arm, steering Jeremy into the house. The place was a mess. Jeremy scanned the room in disbelief as a gurney rolled close. The wheels crunched over splinters of glass. Jeremy looked down at a bleached sheet, fixated on the contrast of bright white against the darkened room. There was something beneath the sheet. He didn't want to know what. Didn't want to know who. The detective held up his hand and the men with the gurney stopped.

"Mr. Laughton, I'm very sorry about this. But we need to know for certain . . ." He pulled the sheet back. "Is this your uncle, Mr. Laughton?"

Jeremy's insides twisted, all hope sunk. He looked down and shook his head. "Yes, that's my uncle. Thaddeus Riley."

The detective covered Uncle Thad's face again. They rolled him into the truck, closed the doors, and drove away. Jeremy stood in the doorway and watched until the ambulance was out of sight. He turned his attention to the room. The place looked sad, depleted, without his uncle. He sat in a chair, quiet for a few moments.

Uncle Thad had been his support system; he'd helped his nephew believe in himself over the years. Even though he was an old man, Jeremy had never considered Thaddeus would die. He looked around the disheveled room. Something bad had happened. *Who was here?* He got up from the chair, checking the shelves before he moved on to the desk to rummage through his uncle's papers. The detective had already been looking through the clutter.

"Mr. Laughton, can you tell if anything is missing?"

Jeremy looked over his shoulder to answer as he searched.

"He had an old book he'd just acquired; he showed it to me tonight. He said it was a relevant find. He always put his current work right here, on this desk."

He moved more piles around, searching. "It was important, and now it's gone. I can't find it anywhere."

"Do you know anyone who would want to steal that book? Is it worth a lot of money?" the detective asked.

"I have no idea its worth. Like I said, he'd just acquired it. Maybe some of his friends would know? He did say it needed translating."

A sinking feeling settled in the pit of his stomach and a face flashed in his mind. Jeremy remembered a man from earlier that evening: he'd gawked at them while he and Thaddeus inspected the book. The man had clearly been eavesdropping on their conversation, and Jeremy caught him staring. The man had no manners and never averted his eyes, just glared back at them. Jeremy had dismissed it then, but now . . . He had learned from his uncle a long time ago to follow his instincts.

"Wait, Inspector, there was a man earlier this evening. He was staring at us and—"

"Do you know his name?" the detective said.

"No, never saw him before tonight."

The detective hung his head.

"Why do you think it was him?" he countered. "A complete stranger?"

"Something was off with this fellow. He was brazen, no, he was suspicious. I just have this gut feeling he's involved."

"Sorry, Mr. Laughton, that's not enough to go on. I work with facts, not gut feelings about staring strangers. Perhaps the book is just misplaced and will turn up somewhere in this mess. Don't let your imagination run away with you in your grief."

The detective patted Jeremy's back and lowered his head like a humble servant. Jeremy understood that the police needed evidence and motive; they needed facts. Well, if it was facts they wanted, he told himself, he would get that and more.

CHAPTER TWO

Another Memphis in May Festival had come and gone, and now it was back to work. The French business visitors had a great weekend trolling Beale Street with the other music lovers, but now the paperwork for the new merger for PDG Inc. needed approvals.

Emilie entered the large conference room and sat in the first empty seat. She kept to herself as she riffled through the documents, focused on the project instead of the others in the room. Stray strands of hair fell across her face and veiled her dark brown eyes. She gathered and wrapped tendrils behind her right ear with a hurried hand, but her fingers lingered and fell away slowly. She leaned forward, squinting to read the pages in front of her, but the dim lighting from the wall sconces wasn't sufficient. She appreciated low lights on most days, as they helped alleviate her frequent headaches, but today it was only a nuisance.

She heard laughter and pulled herself from her paperwork. At the other end of the long mahogany table, her older brother Robert was seated with a few other businessmen as they waited for the meeting to begin. Comfortable in the overstuffed leather chairs, they prattled on about nonsense that had no bearing on the business at hand. *Don't they realize how important this merger is?*

Irritated because she'd lost her concentration, Emilie rose to turn the lights brighter when her father, Pierre de Gourgues, walked into the room. He stopped for a moment in the doorway. His lean frame filled the entrance, and the light from the hall created a glowing effect around his silhouetted shape. He turned and switched on the overhead light. Pierre stood with command, dressed in a tailored Wain Shiell suit, his dark hair peppered with silver. Emilie found his presence at once intimidating and yet comforting. Everyone in the room quieted and looked his way. Emilie wondered if they respected her father for his business sense or feared him because of his power.

"I know I called this meeting to discuss the final points of the merger, but an urgent matter has come to my attention and we'll have to reschedule."

Mumbles filled the room. One of the men objected, speaking up in a French accent.

"But Pierre, our flight leaves this afternoon. We won't be able to make a trip again for some time. I was under the impression that we wanted to get this project wrapped up as quickly as possible."

Pierre moved into the room and leaned on the table, his weight balanced on his fists.

"I am sorry, Louis, it can't be avoided. We will continue with a virtual meeting at a later time. Please accept my apologies, gentlemen, but I must leave. *Meilleures salutations jusqu'à ce que la prochaine fois que nous nous rencontrons.*"

Pierre left the room. Louis and the other men bent their heads together and whispered anguished laments laced with French obscenities. Robert stood, and they turned their attention to him. Tall and lean like their father, he sported dark wavy hair and deep brown eyes that seemed to laugh at the world. He took a moment to adjust his suit jacket, a tactic meant to draw the men's attention toward him. Emilie admired his showmanship.

"Gentlemen," her brother said, using his hands to calm their chatter. "Please, don't worry. We'll schedule a virtual meeting when you get back to your offices. I promise no more delays, and I assure you that next time I will have all the pertinent information so we can finalize the terms. Get your things together, gentlemen, and I will take you out to lunch before you have to catch your flight." He turned to the man who'd protested before. "Okay, Louis?"

Robert's charm appeased them all. The men were smiling once again as they filed out of the room to gather their belongings, each acknowledging Emilie with a brief nod as they passed. Robert stayed back. He pulled out a chair across from her and sat down in one swift gesture.

"So, Em, what do you think of that? The old man is off his rocker."

He leaned forward, bent elbows on the table and his chin positioned snug in his hands. His dark brown eyes were just like Father's, except Robert mirrored a different kind of sadness. Emilie straightened the paperwork in front of her as she spoke.

"I'm surprised by Father's last minute cancellation just like you, but there must be a reason for calling it off. I'll talk with him and find out what's so important that he'd cancel such an important meeting."

Robert's forehead furrowed in doubt. "Why bother, the old man's lost it, let's face it. You and I can pool our resources and finish the deal ourselves. We don't need him."

Emilie clutched her files and stood up. It seemed there was a silent war between her father and Robert, and she felt the tension every time they occupied the same room. She wondered why her brother had bothered coming home to work for Pierre if he disliked him so much, criticizing his every step.

"Robert, you know things get dumped on Father all the time, and he doesn't know how to say no. After all the hoopla we've been planning, it must have been something important that came up. You should have more faith in him, after all, he's been running this enterprise successfully since long before we were born. The financial charts prove the company returns tripled since he took the helm right out of college. We owe a lot to Father."

"Humph. Well, maybe he's lost his Midas touch."

Robert stood. The chair rolled back and collided with the wall. He jerked his head a tick, then walked out without further comment.

A bad feeling snaked into Emilie's mind, and she knew there were other things besides Father that troubled her brother. Something had been off ever since he'd returned to Memphis to help run the family business, though she'd been unable to ask since Robert avoided any meaningful conversations about his personal reasons for coming home. Emilie welcomed him with open arms, of course, even though she'd been surprised at his decision. Over the years it had been difficult for her, being the only one watching over Father. Not that he was helpless, just mournful. Ever since Mother died, the entire family had been heartbroken—her father, her brother Robert, her sister Michelle, and Emilie herself, had all shared a deep loss.

She agreed with Robert's assessment that their father's behavior seemed odd. Curious now, she decided to learn the reason behind the abrupt cancellation of the most important meeting of the year. Emilie walked down the corridor, bound for her father's office.

She marched down the main hall of PDG Inc., her father's main holding company. The various businesses of his enterprise funneled into this core identity. Emilie enjoyed working for her father, it allowed her to remain preoccupied with projects instead of dealing with the dysfunction she experienced when around her family. At PDG, everything seemed so black and white, like watching an old noir movie, clicking away at life frame by frame.

Her step quickened as she neared the end of the hall, where it opened up to a reception area. Anxiety kept pace with her as she passed the doors lining the long hallway, portals to her father's various business interests. The offices that flanked the hall shrouded his employees, seated behind those doors as they finagled deals and maneuvered options. Emilie was an empath.

Her gift, if you could call it that, was experiencing other people's emotions, blind to the reasons behind them. Despite the doors that stood as barrier between her and her father's employees, she could feel their every doubt and suspicion, all the highs and lows. Now, the barrage of emotions assaulted her psyche.

Her pulse pounded against her temples. Sweat warming her brow, Emilie teetered on the edge of another paranormal break-in—what she called it when her mind soaked up the emotions around her. These episodes had plagued her since childhood, and no matter what she tried to prevent the force, her clairvoyant gift always resurfaced. Shielding herself remained the best hope, but proved to be a difficult task.

She breathed deeply and calmed herself, forcing her pulse to slow. She knew what would happen later: a pounding headache, worse than a migraine. She massaged her temples as she approached the open area where her father's secretary, Laura, sat at a desk pecking away on her computer. She looked up when Emilie approached.

"Your father is with someone and asked not to be disturbed," she said.

The woman snapped her gum, then bent her dark curled head and started keying into her computer once more, ignoring Emilie. That was fine with her, she'd never liked Laura. Emilie had heard stories about her from the other women in the office. She wasn't the type to judge on pure gossip or based on the unfortunate situation one was born into, but the innuendos she heard corresponded with what she had observed and sensed when she was around the woman. Laura flirted whenever there was a man around, to the point of embarrassment, and Emilie wondered why her father kept her as his secretary. Then again, he didn't seem to notice things like the behavior of the people around him, almost as if he'd turned his emotions off.

Emilie wished she could do the same, but instead seemed to have inherited more of her mother. Everyone said her mother, Bethany, had been special. She had been a comfort to people and had borne other's pain as if it was her own.

"There is no such thing!"

A loud voice disrupted Emilie's thoughts. Both Emilie and the secretary heard the shouting and turned their heads to her father's office door. Something banged, as if her father had slammed his hand onto the desk. Emilie heard more ranting, but couldn't make out the words; the stranger in there must have challenged her father somehow. She fought the urge to barge into the office to help. Laura slipped out of her chair and stood in her way.

"For real, he said no interruptions. Sounds like a war zone in there anyway, so you'd better stay clear," Laura said.

Emilie pushed her aside without a thought and rushed to the door. She leaned her ear against the dark smooth wood to eavesdrop.

"The package will be at your house later today. When you see the contents, you will believe me," a man said. "You will realize that the price I'm asking is a bargain."

"Get out," her father said.

Emilie jumped back from the door and turned to Laura.

"Sorry, I didn't mean to brush you aside. You're right. I'll just talk with him later when he's not busy."

Emilie turned and headed toward her own office. Walking away, she looked back over her shoulder and saw Laura watching her with an odd smile. The image of a sly fox came to mind, and Emilie knew she couldn't trust the woman. Then, from out of nowhere, panic clouded her mind. It was so strong it took her breath away for a moment. *Where was it coming from?* Her chest tightened, her vision funneled to only the area directly in front of her. She reached out for the wall beside her, steadying herself. *Was this her father's emotions she was sensing?* That sealed her decision to go home early for the day: she wanted to inspect that package before her father returned. Emilie needed to know what was happening to him.

CHAPTER THREE

Emilie stood vigil in the front parlor. She pressed her face against the cool window glass as she gazed out at the expansive lawn that gleamed bright green with new spring grass. The southern breeze touched the tree limbs, shaking the new leaves. The sky was painted pale blue, picture perfect. Distressed despite the peaceful vista, Emilie had a premonition of something going wrong.

She had left the office and driven straight home after overhearing her father arguing with the stranger in his office. It had been three hours since then, and she was tired of anxiously waiting for the delivery. Finally a truck crawled forward from the open front gate. She hurried to the entry hall and pulled open the front door before the messenger had a chance to ring the bell.

"Oh, hi there," he said. "Special delivery, and I need a signature."

The driver slapped a stylus on the electronic pad and held it out to her. He was lanky and wearing sunglasses, which he pushed up along his nose to keep them from falling off.

Emilie grabbed the clunky pad from him and balanced the thing in the air as she signed. Her long brunette waves dropped across her eyes, so she pulled the strands back behind her ear, away from her heart-shaped face. She looked up at the young man as she handed the pad back to him and forced a wide smile. Emilie noticed his quick glance up and down and blushed at his blatant consideration. The driver left the package, whistling to himself as he walked back to his truck.

Emilie closed the door and ran upstairs to her bedroom. Once inside, she laid the package on her desk. She checked around to see if anyone was watching her, maybe Evans, the house manager, who reported back to her father about everything. There was no one in sight. Her father would be angry if he learned she'd opened his mail, but she didn't care about that now.

Still, her stomach twisted. She took a deep breath, closed her eyes a second, and then returned her attention to the package. She opened it with care, trying to keep the flaps from getting torn, then slid her finger between the taped ends and pulled the folded edge up. The paper unfolded and she flattened the sides. Inside the packaging, she found a disc and another item inside a cloth bag. She opened the bag and found an antique book.

She examined the book first, taken by the beauty rubbed into the honed leather cover and rough parchment pages. Right away she was pulled by an attraction. Some kind of force emanated from the ancient book, and she experienced that force as waves of spiritual energy. She touched the cover, her hand shaking. Determined, she opened it and turned the pages. Her fingers tingled as if zinged with an electric shock. She flinched at the unexpected charge and pulled her hand away. Being a clairvoyant empath, she was used to strange sensations, but this feeling wasn't familiar. She chose to ignore it and pushed the sensation to the back of her mind. She continued her inspection.

Emilie appreciated the book's fragility, and realized it was a unique historical piece. A blue ink insignia marked the inside cover. She gingerly turned more pages, scanning the lines. It contained dated journal entries written in French script. Though fortunate to be fluent in the language, she'd need time to interpret a proper translation from the old handwriting. The yellowed parchment and faded ink made the task even harder.

She discovered strange hieroglyphics drawn onto some of the old pages, penned with brighter inks and more colors. The drawings had eerie faces with evil eyes, and what looked like disfigured animals. Picasso meets the ancient Aztecs. The more she gazed at them, the stronger she felt the madness that pulsated from the page.

A coolness chilled her skin and goose bumps rose on her bare arms. Darkness penetrated her thoughts and an old magic poured out from the sketches. The drawings described something otherworldly, she felt sure the book possessed an element of evil.

Intrigued, she wondered why the stranger thought this antique book would interest her father. Pierre, a superstitious man, despised anything that suggested the paranormal, refusing even to discuss his own daughter's clairvoyance. A flash of anger washed over her, as she wished her father would accept her true self. She breathed deep and exhaled slowly.

She closed the book and turned her attention to the disc. Opening her laptop, Emilie pushed the disc into its side slot. The file opened, showing a visual inventory of documents. Paranoid, she looked over her shoulder to make sure she was still alone, then copied the information from the disc to her hard drive. She then placed the disc and old book back into the box, and wrapped and taped it again without a tear. When finished she flew down the stairs so she could leave the package on her father's desk in the library.

Emilie opened the doors and surveyed the large, masculine room. Everything was in its place, no photographs or personal touches visible in the decor. She left the package at the center of the desk, careful not to disturb anything else. She backed out of the room and closed the doors, not making a sound. She turned to go back to her room.

"What are you doing in there, young lady?"

Emilie jumped. She put her hand to her chest and tried to stop her heart from bouncing out.

"You scared me to death, Nina." She laughed to cover her rattled nerves. "I just put a package on Father's desk. It was just delivered."

"I didn't hear no bell ring," Nina said.

Nina had a strange look on her wizened face, and Emilie knew the old cook was making some kind of internal judgment again. Emilie sometimes considered that Nina knew the family better than the de Gourgues's knew themselves. She'd been working for her family for years, but Emilie suspected Nina's intense devotion to her own religious beliefs as a Southern Christian led her to distrust the de Gourgues' association with the Catholic Church. Whenever Father Eddie stopped by to visit she looked at him with overt suspicion.

"Nina, don't worry. It's just a package, some kind of business," Emilie said.

"Monkey business, I bet." Nina left, laughing to herself as she walked away toward the kitchen. Emilie wasn't laughing. It was clear that something was wrong with her father. Since her mother's death, it was rare for her father to show any emotion, this library a perfect reflection of his apathy. He was a great man, handsome and brilliant, always groomed and proper, it just seemed that he was missing a heart.

Emilie pulled in another deep breath and exhaled, then went back through the foyer and up to her room. She opened her computer and scrolled through the items listed from the disc, anxious to understand what it all meant. Most of the images looked like old documents, PDF images of marriage certificates, death notices, postcards, letters, and statements made by people Emilie had never heard of.

According to the documents, a young woman named Rose Riley had married Emilie's great grandfather in 1935, and died within weeks. There were all kinds of clippings from news stories speculating about the mysterious death, and even more when her great grandfather married his second wife a few years later. Another odd statement came from a man living nearby in Fayette County, telling boyhood stories about conversations of curses long ago. His ancestors came to Tennessee from New Orleans, and had lived with a family on a big farm estate.

"What does any of this have to do with my father?"

Emilie, more perplexed than before, decided to read through every document and review every image until it made sense. She scrolled through the files, scrutinizing each one. It took some time, but eventually she recognized a pattern that established a grim timetable of sorts.

The files documented the deaths of the women who had married her father's ancestors.

It appeared that every woman who ever married a male de Gourgues had died young. Some lived long enough to have children, but always died before the children were full grown. Pierre, her father, had seemed to be the blessed one . . . until Mother died.

The files went all the way back to the sixteenth century. The deaths were tragic, the women just beginning their lives and families. Some of the documents were statements taken from observers, strangers and relatives who insisted there was a curse on the de Gourgues family.

Hours later, she finished.

Emilie stared at the wall with blank focus. A deep sadness filled her. "Impossible!" she cried to herself. "There is no such thing as curses!" The ornate toile wallpaper melted away as her eyes swelled with tears.

For as long as she could remember, Emilie had known something evil hovered around her family. She had told her parents years ago, when she was just a little girl, that something was wrong. Emilie remembered her mother laughing at her warning, then swooping her up into her arms as she hugged her. *Don't worry, Emilie, we're all perfectly safe,* Mother reassured her. Emilie had believed her . . . right up until the day she died.

Dread filled her thoughts, knowing there was truth to this preposterous claim. She wondered who'd sent her father this package, and why. This curse she'd just learned of could explain so much about everything she'd felt all these years. It wasn't all in her head, and if it wasn't all in her head, then there might be a way to actually do something. There was nothing she could do to bring her mother back, but she asked herself, *How can I change our fate and prevent this from happening again?* If there truly was a curse, she was determined to end it for good.

The last of the sun's rays streamed through the window into her bedroom. The glow warmed her face, and soothed her mind after the influx of information she'd just read and absorbed.

The grandfather clock in the hallway chimed eight. By the fourth bong, the sound registered. Emilie pulled herself back to reality, hurried to the bathroom, and splashed water on her face. She grabbed a towel to dry herself, and gazed at her image in the mirror. The reflection showed similarities to her mother, her face was heart-shaped like Mother's and they shared many of the same features. She didn't have the freckles, however. Emilie's coloring came from the French side, dark brown hair, and eyes like her father instead of her mother's blue. But she had the Irish spunk of her mother. She brushed the last wrinkles out of her skirt and left her room, dragging herself downstairs for dinner. After everything she'd read, all that she had learned, she was determined to get to the truth.

Emilie's stomach twisted in knots, her palms damp with perspiration. She wiped her hands on her skirt. Ever since Mother died, it was hard to converse with her father. Trying to get information out of him seemed like a tall task. She was certain that something bothered him, and wished he'd let her in so she could help him.

She approached the room with apprehension. The doors were open to the dining room, her father and Robert both seated at the table. She entered and slipped into a chair as they waited. When she pulled her napkin to her lap, they began to fill their plates with portions of catfish, black-eyed peas, and collard greens, all Southern specialties made by Nina. She had been a godsend. Mother had hired her shortly before she died because she'd known that simplicity in life, like dinner together as a family, was important. Nina provided a reminder of the family unit, which they all seemed to need from time to time.

Almost thirty now and still handsome as ever, Emilie noticed Robert had gained weight since he'd returned home, though he still looked good. She watched, nauseous, as he piled fried fish onto his plate. Never would Emilie eat a whiskered fish that trolled the bottom of a river. The room was quiet except for the light tap and scrape of utensils against the serving dishes. She wondered why there was never conversation at dinner anymore. Emilie took a piece of leftover king's bread from the pre-Lenten season and picked at her salad, searching for the best way to start this conversation. Why was it so hard to communicate with her own father? She looked at him and noticed the distance in his eyes.

"Good evening, Father. Robert," she said.

Perspiration shimmered on her forehead. She wiped the film from her brow with a napkin, then picked at her food again. An internal debate bounced back and forth in her mind as she sought the best way to start a conversation about the man in her father's office. *Do it quick, rip off that bandage,* she told herself.

"Father, after you canceled the meeting I noticed a stranger going into your office. Who was it?"

She tried to sound nonchalant, and hoped for a straight answer. He lifted his head to acknowledge her. *That's hopeful.*

"A lot of people came into my office today Emilie. I'm not sure to whom you're referring."

"If I knew who it was I wouldn't be asking. The man you met right after you canceled the meeting," she said.

"Humph. Remember the rule in this house, no business at the dinner table." He stared off, distant and disengaged. Avoidance. *Great, Emilie, that was real subtle!* She noticed Robert shaking his head and smirking.

The conversation ended, they sat in silence eating dinner. Only the sound of silverware tapping against the china filled the room. Emilie listened to the white noise. The clinking and scraping grew louder. She massaged her head and hoped to avoid another headache. Something else felt wrong.

Emilie sensed something off about the room. A shroud of negative energy loomed around her brother; the strange feeling crept across the table. It seemed like confusion. *But no, there's more to it than that,* she thought. She tried to read her brother's face, studying his expression, but he remained distant. He hung his head without slipping her a clue.

"Robert, how are things lately? Any new shows going on at the Orpheum? Any new conquests?" she asked.

He raised his head and smiled that fake grin of his. It stamped an invisible logo across his head: *I'm a great guy.* Emilie knew that look well, and wished he'd talk with her with sincerity instead of his staged facade.

"Come to think of it, I am dating someone you know."

A different grin touched his lips now. Emilie didn't recognize it, but it sent a chill up her spine. As though he was laughing, at her, and everyone around her.

"So who is this mystery date?" Emilie encouraged the topic.

"You remember Rachael La France? I believe you were friends back in grammar school, weren't you?"

A fond memory of her friend slipped into her thoughts, and she smiled. She and Rachael had been best friends years ago. They both loved to read, and spent hours together in the library. Theirs had been a quiet friendship, but a strong one.

"Of course I remember her. I had no idea you two knew each other."

Robert took another bite with gusto, and seemed to come alive. He wiped his mouth and continued the news.

"I met Rachael at a business party her father hosted at their place," he said between bites. "Her father is one smart businessman. He makes an ocean of money. Em, you should see their estate, it's all decked out, a fashionable home of the new South. It's colossal, built of brick with French design, you know, with the massive roof lines, copper details, beams, shutters, and extra-large windows that bow at the top, like they belong in a church. "

Pierre cleared his throat. "Robert, I don't think we should determine people's worth by their money."

Robert averted his eyes and a coldness descended over the table. Emilie felt sorry for him. After a moment, he cleared his throat and continued with more reserve.

"Anyway, I caught sight of her standing across the room. She wore a black dress that clung to her shape and accented her auburn hair, and she turned to me and gave me a look, so seductive." He winked at Emilie. "I couldn't help but notice her."

Emilie giggled. "Robert, I'm glad you like her, but please don't break her heart."

She hoped he knew she didn't mean to criticize.

"I hope she doesn't break mine," he retorted. "Honest, Em, I melted on the spot. Rachael is exciting." He shivered, as if warding off a chill. "I'm trying so hard to impress her, to win her heart. Rachael's not like the usual screwed-up pretty face that follows me around and hangs on my shoulder, wanting me only as a paycheck. She's vibrant and clever, not like those nauseating socialites who only want their faces smeared all over the society columns."

He took a deep breath. It sounded exaggerated to Emilie, but she didn't say anything to ruin his good mood. Robert was usually so closed-mouthed about the girls he dated, the outpouring, whether sincere or not, was unexpected. She looked up in surprise when he continued.

"Rachael is a complete daddy's girl and always gets what she wants. A real challenge for me to set my sights on. I hope she wants me, too."

Emilie tried to be happy for her brother. Maybe coming home and falling in love was his fate. Still, there was something brewing in the shadows that she was sure he wasn't telling her.

"I am happy for you, Robert. Just be gentle with her."

Robert shook his head. His face turned red when he replied. "She's a challenge for me, Em. I am serious about her; I've never tried so hard in my life. Just the pursuit of her gives me a rush."

Pierre squirmed in his chair, shifting his weight. He seemed uncomfortable with the conversation, though his expression remained unreadable.

"Rachael is an heiress to one of the greatest fortunes in America," he said, his voice stern. "Is that what entices you, Robert? Your obsession with money? Maybe you should concentrate on generating wealth, instead of spending the opulence and chasing innocent women. When will you learn there is more to life than being rich?"

Robert's smile vanished. The conversation ended. He took his last bite, wiped his mouth with the napkin, and tossed it on his plate. He left the room, not even mentioning where he was going.

"Goodnight," he managed to say as he walked away.

The mysterious mood went with him. Father nodded to him and then finished his own meal, moved away from the table, and headed for his library.

"I will be busy all evening," he said.

He turned and left the room.

Anger soared through Emilie. *Great! So much for a family dinner.* She pushed her plate away, sat back, and pulled her hair away from her face. She needed more information about that book and the stranger who'd visited her father's office, but it wouldn't be tonight. Father would be looking over the information from the package all evening, no doubt.

She needed to find out who had sent the package and why. This talk of the curse was bound to upset her father, and dredge up pent-up feelings surrounding Mother's death. Father was so superstitious, and if he believed the curse existed, then having Robert interested in a woman would cause even more anguish for him. Robert's future was at risk, more than that, though, Emilie was certain that Rachael was in jeopardy thanks to Robert's newfound obsession.

Emilie roused from her reverie, rushed to the parlor, and looked out the front window. She watched Robert's silver Jaguar as it shot down the driveway and neatly maneuvered around the corners. He'd fled the house anticipating another exciting rendezvous with his newest fling, Emilie was sure. She wondered if he truly was in love with Rachael, or if there was more to the story.

CHAPTER FOUR

The next day, Emilie went to work as usual, driving her small Z4 down the streets through Midtown. She parked in her designated spot and took the elevator up to the fourth floor, where her office awaited. The entire time, she racked her brain over the situation, and tried to recall her family's past in order to connect the dots. She'd sensed some type of evil all these years, and now she was justified. Still, she knew her family would never accept her precognition. Every time Emilie tried to discuss her ability, her brother and sister refused to listen. At first they thought it was a ruse to get attention; later, they simply didn't want her to be clairvoyant. Michelle had even gone so far as to ask her to shut it out, once. *If only it was that simple.*

She sat back in her chair and looked across her desk. She needed to get her work organized so she could afford time off to investigate further. Emilie was outraged at the realization that her father was being threatened, and possibly even extorted by this man. These were personal scars her family bore, and no stranger had the right to rub salt there. But maybe he knew more; maybe she could pry that information from the stranger, and stop the curse for good.

This curse on the family's lineage finally provided a nemesis she could blame for her mother's death, even if she still didn't understand it fully. Bethany, her mother, had only been thirty-six when she'd died. The actual cause remained undetermined. *Most probably Legionnaires'*, the doctors had reasoned. Emilie remembered the long year of suffering, the pain her mother had endured, before finally indulging in the painkillers. In the end, the morphine made her sleep most of the time as the infection attacked every part of her body, until there was nothing left.

The documents brought back memories of her mother's death, raw edges Emilie struggled with every day. She had only been ten at the time, but she had an understanding beyond her years even then of pain and suffering. Emilie's clairvoyant "gift" of empathy often felt like a curse. When she'd sat by her mother on the hospital bed, she had experienced her agony. In the end, Emilie had sensed her surrender, too.

After Mother died, Father tried to be brave, but he'd been so angry. It was hard to watch such a strong man crumble, a man with so much power at his disposal. Still, all the money and connections could not change fate. Emilie remembered the one time she'd seen her father cry—long, deep sobs that made his entire body tremble. Then he pulled himself together, as if drawing from some well of inner strength. He had said he would never cry again, and so far he'd been true to his word. Not only did Father never cry, he never showed any emotion again. Emilie couldn't remember the last time he'd laughed. *Did he ever laugh, or even smile?*

Emilie pulled herself from her thoughts and wiped her eyes. She inhaled and blew the air out slowly, then pulled a folder open and got to work. She spent the morning in her office mulling over the merger details. Her main focus was to line up the two independent-brand market campaigns, into a seamless voice that urged the customer to spend money. She excelled at her job, using her intuitive understanding of others to create compelling branding campaigns.

Hours later, Emilie rubbed her forehead and knew she needed a break, so she left her office and strolled down to the cafeteria. She poured herself a coffee and blew the warm steam away from her face as she gazed out the window that faced the building's front entrance. She noticed a man walking up the sidewalk. The same feeling came over her that she'd experienced the other day when she'd stood by her father's office door. The stranger from his office, she knew it was him the moment the man entered the building.

Something fluttered against her skin, some irritation, an itch from the inside, and Emilie knew she had to do something, and quick. She put down her cup and ran to the elevators. She'd just missed the one the stranger must have taken. Her impatience mounting, she knew she couldn't wait for the next lift. Instead, she decided to take the stairs. Her father's office was on the fourth floor. Emilie ran up the stairs, pushing herself. Without a warm-up, her thighs burned. She made it to the top floor a bit winded. Emilie opened the door and looked down the long hallway. She saw the stranger enter her father's office. In a rush, she ran down the corridor after him. When she reached the reception area just before his office, she noticed Laura sitting behind her desk.

"Who was that man?" Emilie asked quickly, catching her breath.

Her father's secretary snapped her gum, a habit that continued to irritate Emilie. Laura glanced up for a second, offering only vague acknowledgment.

"I haven't a clue who he is, your father never tells me anything. I just do as I'm told and put in my hours. You can't go in, either. Your father doesn't want anyone to disturb him, that much he did tell me."

She leaned forward and snapped her gum again, then turned away and resumed typing. Emilie got the distinct feeling she'd been dismissed.

"Thanks for your help," Emilie said.

Irritated, she walked away and turned the corner. The moment she was out of sight, she crouched behind a large potted fern. She planned to guard the door until the stranger left. She read a book on her iPhone and waited.

Laura sat in her chair, clicking the mouse, pretending to work. Emilie watched, knowing the secretary couldn't see her in her surveillance spot. The phone on the desk rang and Laura picked it up.

"Hey baby, I was hoping you'd call. Will I see you again tonight?"

Suddenly, the brusque secretary Emilie knew vanished, replaced with a coy, purring minx. Emilie resisted the urge to cover her ears. She so didn't want to be here for this. At the same time, though, she was strangely compelled to follow the conversation.

She stuck her head out to spy and watched Laura's head bop up and down, reminded of the bobble-head clowns mounted on car dashboards. Laura's face scrunched up as she appeared to listen with intense concentration. To Emilie she looked absurd. *Is she infatuated, or drugged? Maybe both.*

The next words out of Laura's mouth snapped Emilie back to reality, however. Suddenly, nothing seemed quite so amusing.

"Okay, Robert. Yeah, he's in there now and everything's quiet." Laura nodded in agreement to something else he said. "Right, I'll start it up again first thing tomorrow morning. You know how the old man loves his morning coffee." She giggled at her own remark, as if at an inside joke. "Oh, don't worry your cute ass, I've got it all under control."

Another phone line rang. "Sorry, hon, I have to take another call. Okay, see you later."

She ended the call with Robert and picked up the other line. "PDG, Laura speaking. Uh huh...uh huh. Okay, I'll be there in a minute."

Laura hung up the phone and left, walking in the opposite direction from where Emilie hid.

It had to have been her brother on the other end of the line, Emilie was sure of it. But what had they been talking about? And what about Robert's claim that he was head over heels for Rachael now?

Curiouser and curiouser, Emilie mused.

Emilie wondered about the conversation she'd overheard, but soon realized it was pointless. There were too many other secrets in this family, she didn't have time to worry about who Robert was or wasn't sleeping with. She returned to contemplating her father's mysteries instead. The stranger still hadn't left his office.

Emilie's blood boiled. She turned her wrist to see the time on her Omega watch. Half an hour had gone by already. Tired of waiting for the stranger to leave, she jumped to her feet and, in a flare of gumption, strode to her father's office. She tapped on the door and burst right in, only to find her father alone in the room. He slumped behind his desk, haggard and weary.

Fearing her father was ill, she ran to him. His pain stopped her in her tracks, it was palpable, a physical force that she could barely stand. Her father was terrified, that much was clear. Emilie hadn't felt any emotion emanating from the man in years, and this kind of intensity was definitely not a change for the better. Overcome as his despair swept over her, Emilie doubled over in pain. The room spun. She stood still and took a deep breath, trying to regain balance.

Reaching out her hand, she touched her father's cheek. The greatness her father had once exuded, the love he'd had for her dear mother, seemed nothing but a memory now.

Her parents had met at a Harvard Business School mixer back in the '70s. They'd come from different worlds, but together had woven a bond held by true love. They had married shortly after college, with a big reception in Boston before they'd settled into the family homestead in Memphis. Pierre took over responsibility for the family estate. Bethany was a straightforward and honest woman with a less superstitious nature than Pierre, who feared the unknown. Emilie recalled the stories her mother used to tell her about their early years together. The couple had been opposites in many ways, raised in different areas of the country, different social circles, but they had the Church in common and Emilie knew their union had been blessed by God. They conceived three healthy children, the fruit of their love.

Now Pierre was a lost soul, devastated since his wife's death. His obligations to the family forced him to continue, but he wasn't alive. Emilie knew that deep in his soul, Pierre was proud of his children and wanted so much to show his love, but he would not allow himself. He had closed his heart, in fear of reliving the pain of his wife's death. Emilie felt his internal conflict. The stranger who'd come to him with the documents about a family curse tormented him.

"I should have saved her, Emilie," he mumbled. "I should have known that something ominous threatened my family."

"Father, how could you have known? Please don't, we'll work things out."

Pierre looked crazed as he rebuked himself. "I should have asked questions instead of hiding from my haunted childhood. No more hiding from the past."

Worry stung her. "Who was that man in your office, Father?"

Pierre shook his head. Emilie couldn't tell whether he was trying to clear his mind of memories, or he was in denial.

"I don't know who you're referring to. I was alone all morning," he said.

"Father, I saw him enter your office. Please be honest with me, tell me what's happening. I'm concerned about you. You've been so stressed, ever since you received that package."

Pierre flinched in alarm. His eyes bulged as he looked up at her. "What do you know about that? Please, Emilie, stay out of my affairs, do you hear me?"

He stood and pushed the chair back so hard it rolled and slammed against the wall. Like father like son, Emilie thought. Then, her father rushed for the door, flying past Emilie as he stormed out of his office.

"Please, Father, wait!" she called after him. He never looked back at her, but just kept walking.

Emilie panicked, her heart tight in her chest. Nothing made sense. Why had her father kept the stranger's visit a secret? *What is he hiding from me?* She needed answers. How was she supposed to find them if no one would talk to her, though? She considered the question for a moment before she realized she needn't be quite so alone in all this. Robert might know about father's secret visitor, or remember some family history that could shed some light. Emilie turned with resolve and hurried toward her brother's office.

She opened his office door while knocking, and entered the room. She realized Robert was on the phone and raised her eyebrows, an invisible question. He motioned with his hand for her to come in while he finished his conversation.

"Yes, proceed as planned. Send me an update when he pays you."

She took a seat and waited in a big leather chair, tugging her hair and fussing with her skirt. He glanced her way and took notice of her fidgeting, and she realized she had given herself away.

"I have to go, but I expect that update." Robert finished his call and turned his attention to her. "Hi, Em. What's up? You look worried."

There was humor in his voice. He always seemed more alive when he was away from the house. Emilie noticed he had that look in his eyes, as if he was laughing at the world. His smile was aloof, so carefree right now, and she hated dragging him into this matter.

"Who was that on the phone?"

Robert chuckled and shrugged. "Nothing of concern, believe me."

Emilie felt like a child. She wanted to believe her brother, but she was certain he was hiding something from her. "I was just with Father. He didn't look well, and he's keeping a secret. I want to know what it's about. Robert, do you know what's going on?"

"What in God's name are you talking about, Emilie?"

Now she had his serious attention.

"I heard Father talking with someone in his office, upset and screaming, literally shaking with fear!"

Robert rolled his eyes while she talked. Emilie knew he assumed that she was overreacting, this wasn't the first time he'd used that look on her. She knew it well. She slapped the corner of his desk.

"Listen to me, I'm not exaggerating. I saw a stranger go into Father's office right after he canceled the meeting. They argued. And today the same man visited him again, but when I asked Father about him, he pretended nothing was wrong, and denies he was ever there, but he lied, the stranger was definitely there, I saw him. The man went into his office and when he left, Father was distraught."

Emilie hoped her brother would take serious interest, but he played like it was a joke. Robert folded his hands on the desk. He had his peacemaking face on now. It amazed Emilie how easy it was for her brother to change his mood, his gestures, and his voice. He'd missed his calling in life; he should have been an actor.

"Em, calm down. Maybe nothing is wrong. You know how tense the old man gets going through new product launches. Plus, we have this merger dangling."

He began moving papers around on his desk, behaving like he had no concerns in the world.

"No, Robert, it was more than that. This was different. I heard them mention Mother."

The room went silent, except for the air conditioning that blew cool air from the ceiling vent. Robert let go of his papers and sat up straight, his face impassive. He swallowed hard. Emilie watched the muscles twitch under his eyes. Beads of sweat appeared on his forehead. His eyes clouded with anger, and she was entrenched in his rage.

"Leave this alone. This is not your concern, Emilie," he said.

"What do you mean, not my concern? She was my mother, too. Robert, please tell me, what is going on? Do you know something about this?"

He turned away from her, got up from his chair, and headed for the door. "Leave this alone. I will talk with Father myself, please don't consider this for one minute longer. I mean it, stay out of this affair."

He walked out and left her standing there alone, just like Father had done. The anger oozed from Robert. She was baffled; his rage seemed somehow directed at her.

Since Robert and Father wouldn't discuss it, Emilie decided to find the truth on her own. It was time to get answers.

CHAPTER FIVE

Home again, at last. The family estate was an old mansion built in the 1800s, back when the de Gourgues family owned major interests in the local cotton trade. It lay between the Wolf and Mississippi Rivers, where quick storms had always threatened the area. The estate wasn't affected by the rage of these storms, however, even though a tributary of the Wolf River touched the back of the property. The homestead sat on high ground, protected from the riverbank's overflow.

Set back from the road, the red brick mansion featured grand columns in the front facade, supporting porches on both the main and upper floors. A unique stone water fountain was displayed on the front lawn, acquired by Robert during one of his trips to Florida. He had shipped it home as a memento. An old magnolia tree stood prominent in the front yard, with large, fragrant white blooms nested on the shiny green leaves. The tree was surrounded by a colorful array of pink azalea bushes below. The skies were bright blue and the temperature a humid eighty degrees, the moisture keeping everything fresh.

Emilie took a deep breath, inhaling the sweetness of the Southern air. *Memphis in May, what a wonderful time and place.* A bird sang in a nearby tree. Emilie closed her eyes and listened. She left her car and walked, deep in thought as she passed the new ferns on the wide open porch without notice, ignoring the wicker furniture. Instead, she plodded inside to the parlor, where she dropped herself into the overstuffed gold velvet sofa. Kicking her shoes off, she pulled her hair up, laid her head back, and closed her eyes. She needed to develop a plan of action.

Within a few minutes, an idea came to her. She ran to her room to search her father's documents again. Her mother's death had been the most recent, so Emilie called for her medical records first. The voice on the other end of the line informed Emilie a copy had recently been sent to their address. It seemed someone else had been checking, too.

The victim before her mother had been her grandmother, Claudia, who died in 1962 from some type of lung disease. Emilie had never met her grandmother, and only knew of her from a few old photographs in an album that Father kept in the bottom drawer, down in the parlor. Her father never mentioned his mother, and she never thought to ask. Emilie did the math and realized that Pierre had only been ten when he'd lost his mother, too. *He must understand what we felt. Why didn't he ever say anything?* Searching her memories, an idea popped into her head.

With a rush of excitement, she opened her computer and searched for websites that specialized in tracing family lineage. She answered some basic questions and provided as many names as she could recall, which weren't many. Her grandmother's death record came up quickly as an available document. Agreeing to the terms and payments of the site, she clicked on the icon to read the public inquest report. According to the report, Claudia de Gourgues's cause of death had never been substantiated. Emilie continued reading more results, as icons popped up with documents available. The fragments found by the website matched some of the documents in the files listed on the disc sent to her father. The genealogy of the family traced back to France in the sixteenth century. They were ancestors of the famous Captain Dominique de Gourgues.

Emilie learned more about her lineage from the disc and website than she had known her entire life living at the family estate. She read about the de Gourgues family of centuries ago.

> In the sixteenth century, Captain de Gourgues sailed to Florida to reestablish Fort Carolina, which was just north of St. Augustine, at the mouth of the St James

River, formerly May River. Approximately
five hundred Frenchmen had settled near the
river at Fort Carolina, where they were
subsequently massacred by the Spaniards, who
had a stronghold on the entire area.
Meanwhile, Europe was embroiled in the War
of the Religions, which pitted Catholics
against Protestants. As a result, the King
of France refused to send aid to the
survivors at the fort, fearing the Catholic
Church might cause monetary problems for
France if they supported the Protestant
Huguenots. The French people, horrified by
the brutal attack, reached out to help.
Captain de Gourgues, a Catholic himself,
sold his personal assets and used the
resulting funds to travel to Florida with
hired soldiers and seamen to avenge the
brutal deaths of the original French
Huguenot settlers. When the Captain arrived
on the shores, he made a pact with the local
tribe's chief, Chief Saturiwa, and the
Timucuan tribe helped the effort to regain
Fort Carolina and push out the Spanish.
The French took back the fort and raised the
French flag again. Captain de Gourgues and
the French seamen returned to Europe, not
having enough military power to take over St
Augustine, the Spanish stronghold. The
Captain became a hero to all Frenchmen,
Catholic and Protestant alike.

There was much more about the exploits while in Florida,
but she understood the main idea: her ancestor had been
successful in the liberation of the fort with the help of the
natives. Emilie searched the remaining documents and found
PDF images of letters, including one that mentioned the
captain's wife and her early death. Another letter spoke of a
son's wife, who died during childbirth at only twenty years
old. None were proof of a curse on their own; all the early
death accounts found were plausible, however, considering
the mortality rate of those times.

But it suggested a pattern, particularly since the same phenomenon that had happened to Emilie's ancestors also happened to her mother. It had begun so long ago.

Something must have happened while Captain de Gourgues was in America, something that started this whole curse. That's when the deaths began.

Her nerves were as worn as the rug she paced. Emilie tried to sort the obscure facts in her mind, to clarify the situation, but she was left with more questions than answers. The old feelings she'd experienced as a child resurfaced, that deep shadow she had always sensed. It must have existed for centuries. Confused by the history, she decided a new approach was necessary. She wanted to concentrate on information about curses, in particular, the kind inflicted upon the captain so long ago. The curse that now threatened to revisit her brother and any potential wife.

A rush of anxiety flooded her. For a moment, she stopped breathing. *Rachael is in danger if Robert is truly serious about her.*

She had to take action. The statement she'd found on the disc, made by the local man in Fayette County, seemed worth checking into. The man had claimed to be an ancestor of a family from New Orleans who had handed down stories about curses and an old magic spell believed to have the power to curse family bloodlines. There were no facts, just rants of random boyhood memories. Emilie wanted a face-to-face conversation with the man. Looking his name up in the web white pages, she found his current address and decided to pay him a visit. She grabbed her scarf and handbag, ran down the stairs, and headed for her car.

CHAPTER SIX

Emilie drove her car north to Route 64 and then headed east to Fayette County. She watched as scenery whizzed by until farmland occupied both sides of the road. Gazing in her rearview mirror, she admired the beautiful pink and gray skyline as the sun began to set. The GPS and road signs directed her to the middle of nowhere, leading to a small, obscure dirt drive in the tiny southern town. Trees grew to the very edge of the road. Spaced between them were gloomy, scum-covered swamp areas, most likely infested with creatures. A dark, creepy place.

Emilie's hands trembled like an electrometer needle. She gripped the steering wheel tight to stop the trembling. A split-second streak of regret made her question the reason for coming to this awful place. Although she liked nature hikes, she preferred the open areas and had never been much for the back country. She slowed down and held her breath as she drove on. A moment later the road opened up, revealing plowed fields laid neatly between a few houses that dotted the road. Her grip eased, and she took a gulp of air and exhaled.

She found the correct address on a mailbox that stood sideways at the end of a driveway. The house was a small ranch made of brick and gray clapboard siding in need of paint, though the place seemed homey enough. The yard was in order, the bushes trimmed and brush cleared away. The smell of the fresh-cut grass tinged with wild onion hung in the air. The side yard revealed a garden with even rows of sprouts jutting from the soil, piled into raised beds. A workshop in the back displayed tools hung on pegs screwed into the sideboard. The cicadas and bullfrogs began their nightly song. The serenade soothed.

Emilie got out of her car and walked toward the porch. A vibrant yellow rose bush climbed a trellis tilted against the railing. The flowers emitted a subtle sweetness in the warm, moist evening breeze. She tried her best to stay calm.

Meeting new people made her anxious, and this conversation was bound to be awkward. She even experienced people's emotions when shaking their hand, usually elusive sensations, but still uncomfortable, as if she intruded on their privacy. It had been that way for as long as she could remember.

No matter how difficult this would be, however, she needed to get answers. She walked to the front door, determined. Her small hand knocked against the hard wooden panel.

The door opened. *Breathe, breathe*, Emilie chastised herself. An older gentleman stood in the doorway. He was tall and thin, with a bald brown head and big dark eyes. He welcomed her with a pleasant voice.

"Can I help you, Miss?"

She recovered her manners with an ingrained response. "Good evening. My name is Emilie de Gourgues, and I'm looking for a gentleman by the name of Mr. Labue."

His eyes opened wide with acknowledgment, and he opened the screen door so he could shake her hand. Taken by surprise, his benevolence warmed her spirit, and she sensed that Mr. Labue was a kind man. She felt the smooth dark brown skin of his hand, and noticed his weathered face and the wrinkles in the corners of his eyes. His smile, bright and youthful despite his years, reflected a happy soul.

"You found him, Miss Emilie. A pleasure. Now, please go home. I already gave all the information I can. Don't be bothering with this anymore."

He closed the screen door and waited for her to leave.

"What do you mean, sir? I just got here. Who else has been here asking questions?"

"Your brother was here the other week," he explained, his head bobbing left to right as he spoke. "He asked me all kinds of questions about curses and spells. I told him I didn't know anything about your family curse. I do know something about Voodoo, things my folks used to mention, but curses like what he talked about is more like a spell, or some kind of made up hoodoo, there's no such curse in Voodoo, anyway. Why don't you kids just leave all this alone!"

There was finality to his tone. Startled to learn that her brother had been there, Emilie pressed for more information. "Whatever you told Robert, you can tell me, too."

"I told him the same thing I'm telling you, leave it alone! There's no good from this kinda talk. Only bad things happen when people start gossip of curses and spells. Please leave it alone, Miss de Gourgues! It is what it is."

"Please, Mr. Labue, let me tell you why it's so important." Frustrated, tears stung her eyes. "My mother died because of this curse, and I miss her every day. She was so beautiful. She used to read to us underneath the wisteria tree in the backyard. I miss the walks we took to the stables, and I miss watching her trot her favorite Paint Horse around the track. Sometimes I go to the barn, and try to visit her spirit there. Sometimes I feel her presence lingering, like she's trying to connect with me, but it fades away. She always brightened me when I was little, and I could feel things when I was near her, like she was an antenna trapping waves of verve for me."

"Miss Emilie, I am sorry for your loss. But what do you think I can do?" The old man's face filled with sadness.

"You still don't understand. One afternoon she fell asleep, while my little sister Michelle and I were reading poems to her, Robert Frost, her favorite poet. Mother never woke up again. She was so young. I was so young. It was because of the curse, the curse on my family. I need answers. I need to stop whatever is plaguing my family."

She poured her heart out to this man, and connected with his wonderful old soul. He could help, she knew it. Finished with her plea, she wiped her eyes with the back of her hand. The old man opened the screen door again and stepped onto the porch to join her. He looked down at her with concern.

"I don't know anything about this family curse of yours, but I can help you get to the right person, someone who might know a thing or two about spells. Like I mentioned to your brother, my great granddaddy came here from New Orleans. They had been what you call Choctaw Freedmen. My ancestors worked as slaves for the Folsom family, on their farm. But after the Civil War, they were accepted as Choctaw. You know, from the tribe."

Mr. Labue's voice cracked. He cleared his throat. "There was a girl with them who messed around with spells and such foolery. They all thought it was Voodoo, but it wasn't. She liked to fool them and keep them afraid of her, so that no one would take advantage. No pretty girl was safe from the boss back then. My granddaddy said she had secrets. Claimed she knew of 'spirit spells' that wuz handed down to her from her grandmammy, who learned them from the native people who lived in the woods near the old plantation they worked in Mississippi. It's supposed to be the oldest of all magic and spells."

Emilie was hopeful. This sounded like a good prospect to get answers. "Oldest of all magic spells. Are spirit spells the same as a curse?"

"Some people call it hoodoo because it's all mixed up. Me and most folks call it just plain silly and wrong. I still say you should leave it alone. No good comes from spells and curses. Once a person starts believing, it grows like a cancer."

Emilie was obstinate. "What's her name, please?"

"Their family name is Boniverre. I think they still have some folks left down in New Orleans."

"Thank you, thank you so much. I promise your name will never come up in discussion. You don't need to be afraid of getting involved. Sir, thank you."

Emilie was tripping over her words, ecstatic with hope. Mr. Labue covered his heart with crossed hands and looked up to the sky.

"Miss Emilie, I am not afraid for me. I have received the good Lord in my heart. I'm a Christian with a clean and happy soul. Jesus is my Savior. Amen."

His eyes turned down to Emilie. "It's you I'm worried about. Now don't go telling your sad song to everyone down there in New Orleans. You be careful, you promise me, girl." He shook his finger at her.

"I promise." Emilie smiled back.

They embraced for a moment. Her spirit lifted at the strength and purity emanating from the old man.

"Thank you, Mr. Labue."

Satisfied with her progress so far, Emilie continued her search. A trip to New Orleans to visit the Boniverre family was in order. She turned the ignition key and the engine ramped up to a hum, and idled. Squinting through the windshield, she evaluated the steel sky. Eerie shadows of trees cast across the road like long dark fingers, illuminated by the slivers of light coming from the lamppost outside the house.

She pulled the car away, taking her time going down this country road, one wrong turn could send her off course and into the swampy ditch that ran alongside. Once she found her way back to the highway, however, her relief only lasted for a moment. From nowhere, a blinding downpour pelted the road.

Her insides jittered at the sudden change. Her pulse raced and she squeezed the steering wheel. The sheets of rain roared louder than the engine as they battered the car's roof. Emilie turned on the wipers and slowed to a crawl. The rain had nowhere to go and flooded the pavement in front of the car. The water churned up into the wheel wells, causing the car to pull back, echoing a swooshing sound from beneath the wheels. A warning of possible tornado activity interrupted the music on the radio.

"Great, a storm and I'm here in the middle of nowhere!" she said aloud.

The stress of the day and now the sudden storm took their toll on her nerves. She just wanted to get back to the house. Agitated, wary of hitting a tree or getting sucked up in a wind funnel, she used the streaks of lightning to guide her way along the road as the car crept forward into a black hole. There was nothing but darkness ahead.

The wind shoved the small car, pushing it sideways as it thrust against the door. A disquieting mood permeated the space around. Her nerves unraveled; vulnerable to an extrasensory episode, she felt it creep into her head.

Chills ran down her spine. Alarmed, she tightened her entire body and held her breath. A presence was there, in the car, as if someone else was sitting right beside her. *Is a spirit trying to visit, or send a message?* She pulled the car to the curb, put it in park, and turned on the flashers. Seconds passed. Some unknown tragedy crowded her mind. She rubbed her forehead and tried to physically push the vision from her mind, shielding herself, not wanting to see, hear, or feel anything. The sensation consumed her.

Is Mother trying to send me a message or premonition? No, she scolded herself, *things like that don't happen.*

Lightning cracked across the dark sky, then a loud thunderous boom roared. The vibration rattled the car. Like a jumpstart to a battery, she flashed back in time. A vision from years ago, she stood alone when just a small child, warning her family about the evil forces at work around them, but no one believed her.

The car rocked in a rapid torrent of wind. Emilie pulled herself from the groggy haze, as if waking from a bad dream. She closed herself up, shielded herself, and ignored the weirdness in the car. The ugliness would not get in; she wouldn't allow it. With great strength of will, she pushed them into her subconscious. *I will deal with them later.* If only she could just erase these feelings with one swipe, and be done with it all. Emilie took deep breaths, letting the oxygen calm her, and then she put the car back into gear. She concentrated on driving home, determined to ignore these impressions, this curse of hers.

On the drive home, Emilie remained cautious. The feeling finally receded. She told herself all she needed was rest. The car rolled up to the house, but an unfamiliar sedan parked in front blocked the entry. Wondering who was visiting so late, she turned the steering wheel and parked on the other side. She jogged to the porch, trying not to get drenched with rain or zapped by the persistent lightning. Dripping wet, she entered the foyer. The door closed behind her with a slam, aided by a gust of wind.

Emilie bolted from the door, startled. Water dripped from her clothes as she stood for a moment and regained her bearings. She'd barely gotten her breath before darkness descended once more—that unbearable pain, terror, she'd experienced before. *Father's terror.*

She turned. The stranger stood at Father's side, the two men frozen at the entrance to the room. Everything she'd learned, everything she felt, swept over her in an instant. She rushed toward the men, unable to hide her agitation. Father held up his hand, and Emilie stopped in her tracks.

"Emilie, this is Mr. Pierce, the man you saw with me. Please excuse us, we have business to discuss."

Before she could respond, both men turned and walked into the library, closing the door behind them.

Her stomach knotted in worry, and a rush of blood made her face burn. She imagined herself bursting through the doors and demanding to know what was going on. Emilie shook her head, rain dripping down her face and neck. She walked over to the doors and stood with her hand in midair, not sure if she should knock. Instead, she turned her ear to the thick wooden door, but could only make out a few words, not enough to make sense of the conversation. She didn't dare act on her desire to disrupt them; Father abhorred impetuous behavior.

She took a deep breath and resigned herself to the situation, then hurried to her room. There was a trip to plan.

Determined to follow the Boniverre lead in New Orleans, and with no time to waste, she called her sister. Not being street savvy when it came to scouting out new places, Emilie didn't want to wander by herself in the unfamiliar city. Michelle loved New Orleans, though. Besides, they hadn't seen each other in a while.

Emilie called and Michelle readily agreed, saying she'd been wanting some time off. The spontaneous trip gave Emilie hope.

CHAPTER SEVEN

Emilie left the house for work as usual, but with much more optimism than was typical. She went straight to her office and pressed through her paperwork, anxious to clear her desk as early as possible. Her sister was due to arrive later, in time for dinner. It had been a while since they'd spent quality time together, and Emilie wanted to connect with her again. She intended on telling her about the weird things going on lately.

Robert stuck his head in the doorway. "Time for the meeting, Emilie." He smiled. If she didn't know him better, she'd have thought it was with genuine happiness.

"Thanks for getting me. I'll walk with you."

She grabbed her folders and followed her brother to the conference room. This time, Robert turned on the ceiling light. The room was bright, and she heard the hum from the fluorescent fixture above. Emilie focused on the noise, hoping it would keep her from feeling the emotions of the others in the room. Many of their coworkers were high strung lately. She knew everyone was anxious to get this merger finished. Others followed them in for the meeting, and within minutes there were twelve of them seated around the table. Everyone made a point of saying good morning to Robert, and nodded their heads at Emilie.

Someone rang her father, then dialed the call to France. They got Louis and his crew on the line and a few niceties passed around the room. Then they discussed business details, and prepared to close the meeting. They only needed Pierre to give his approval. Robert buzzed him again. A minute later, Pierre walked into the room. He appeared off balance and staggered to his seat. He sat down, slumped into the chair, and took a moment to look around the room, dazed.

"What is this about?" he demanded.

His voice seemed foreign, harsh but not slurred, so Emilie brushed away her silent fear of stroke. A few people in the room dared to mumble to each other. Emilie got up and approached her father, whispering in his ear. "What's wrong?"

Pierre groaned and then stood, leaning on the table. "I am fine, just leave me alone."

He spoke a bit too loudly, uncharacteristic of him, and everyone turned their attention on them. Emilie went back to her seat, concerned and embarrassed. Then her father made his big mistake: he started speaking in French, so half the room didn't understand a word. They looked at each other with puzzled expressions. Those on the other end of the line understood perfectly, despite the fact that his pronunciation was off, something virtually unheard of for Pierre de Gourgues.

"C'est la fin. Nous sommes tous maudits. Oubliez cette entreprise. Prenez soin de vous. Rentrez chez vous et profiter de vos proches que vous pouvez."

This is the end, we're all cursed. Forget about this business. Take care of yourselves, go home and enjoy your loved ones while you can, Emilie translated in her head. *What the hell is he doing?*

When he finished, Pierre leaned against the table as he tried to find his balance. For a moment, Emilie thought he'd fall on his face. Then, he turned toward the door and left the room, mumbling to himself. She worried her father may be having an attack of some kind, or a mental breakdown, hell, *something* had happened to him.

Robert's face was red, and he looked like his head might pop off from the pressure. *Great, this is all they need in their relationship.* She got up from her chair and went to her brother, whispering, "Finish the meeting and make it right. I'll back you one hundred percent. Let me see what's wrong with father."

Then she left the room to follow her father to his office, her brother already beginning apologies on her way out.

"Gentlemen, I am sorry for that episode. It seems my father is not well, but we'll finish this today. You have my support and my sister's, too."

Emilie hurried down the hallway and caught up with her father. She touched his arm and he turned toward her. His eyes looked far away. A deep sorrow burdened her spirit with more pain than she had ever known, and tears stung her eyes. They walked together to his office, and she helped him onto the full-grain leather sofa, which was soft and molded perfectly to his form. She grabbed a pillow from the chair and put it under his head, and covered him with an afghan throw. Then, she sat on the floor next to him and rubbed his hand with hers, speaking to him with her softest voice as she stroked his hair back with her other hand.

"Father, I know what you're feeling, it's making me sick. Why is this happening? What can I do to help you? Let me help you."

He groaned and tossed his head. "Emilie, I don't want you involved in this. I don't want you to know this sorrow. Leave me if you want to help, let me know you are spared from this curse."

His voice drifted off as he fell asleep. Emilie wiped back her tears and took a deep breath, knowing full well she'd help even if he didn't wish her to. She stood and went to the desk, where she found the doctor's number in her father's Rolodex, a resource which contained years of his contacts' information. She called Pierre's doctor on his private cell phone.

"Doc Hannigan, hello, this is Emilie de Gourgues."

"Hello, my dear. I hope everything is all right, how are you?"

"Yes, I'm fine thank you. I am calling about my father. He just had some kind of episode at a meeting. He was off balance, and — "

"Tell me, had he taken some of the pills I prescribed? If so, best for him to sleep it off," Doc said.

"What? Yes, he's sleeping now. He's under medication?"

"I gave him something to help him sleep. Maybe he took them during the day. They do have a calming effect. How many are in the bottle?"

"A sleeping aid? Let me check."

Emilie put the phone down and opened the top drawer of Father's desk. She found a bottle of sleeping pills, opened it, and counted them out.

"Doc, I count twenty pills."

"Good, that means he only took one. I gave him a three-week supply. Let him rest, I think he needs the sleep," Doc said.

"Yes, he's resting. Please promise me you'll check on him later today."

"Of course, my dear, don't worry. It will be late afternoon, but I'll be sure to make a point of stopping in. Will that be all right?"

"Yes, but I'm going out of town, so please call me if anything turns up."

"I will call with an update. Have a safe trip."

"Yes, I will. Thank you, Doc Hannigan."

She hung up the phone; confused by this new information. Emilie had never heard of anyone acting this bizarre just because they'd taken a sleeping pill. Her father had never been one to take medication, either. She would force him to discuss this when she got back, and make sure he stopped taking the pills. Maybe after the doctor saw him later today, he could prescribe something milder. Still, something felt wrong, and she had a feeling there was more to this situation. Another thing to worry about. Maybe Michelle would have some insight, or at least a fresh view on it all. Her heart went out to her father. He wasn't the most lovable figure, but she knew he loved them deep down, where it counted most.

A bit relieved knowing the doctor would check on her father later that day, Emilie headed for her office to get those details completed, more than ready to take off for a few days. Putting the trip to New Orleans on hold was not an option.

Finding out more about the curse was vital. Her brother's future, her family's future, depended on learning more, so she could eliminate the threat for good. That would be the best way to relieve her father's stress, too.

Emilie left her father's office so he could rest, as the doctor had ordered. She went back to work.

Emilie sat at her desk and couldn't get rid of the nagging thoughts about her father and the curse. She knew the reason her father needed sleeping pills: the stranger, Mr. Pierce. Father blamed himself for Mother's death, though his blame was unwarranted. Emilie knew he hadn't done anything wrong. The torment he felt, losing his mother and then his wife because of this strange curse . . . He teetered on an edge, close to giving up on life itself, and something had to soothe his mind before she lost him altogether. The thought gave Emilie a chill.

Inspiration struck. She picked up the phone and called Father Eddie. He was their parish priest, and a close friend of her parents. He had counseled them all for years, and she hoped he wouldn't mind her leaning on him once more.

"Hello, Father Eddie please. Yes, this is Emilie de Gourgues." She waited.

"Miss Emilie, how are you dear?"

She swallowed hard, and hoped that he'd understand her strange plea.

"Father Eddie, my father is not well. His behavior today was erratic, he shows symptoms of depression, more than I have ever seen before. He needs our help."

"Tell me exactly what's happening," he said.

Emilie explained to him about her father's bizarre behavior; about the documents and curse, and how Mr. Pierce taunted her father. She hoped he didn't think she was over the edge herself. To Emilie's surprise, the priest listened. He asked a few pointed questions, murmuring in response, and she pictured him nodding in agreement.

"Emilie, I am glad you called me. Your father did come to me in confidence, but I hadn't realized the severity of the situation. Pierre told me about your impromptu trip. Since you're going to New Orleans to vacation with Michelle anyway, maybe you can stay a few hours longer and meet with me before you return home. I think I know someone down there, from my old church, who can help."

Emilie blinked, trying to imagine how this could help her father. She trusted Father Eddie, so decided to go along.

"I have no idea what you have in mind, Father, but I will be there. I will call as soon as Michelle leaves," she said.

"You're a good daughter. I will be in touch."

Father Eddie hung up, and Emilie sat at her desk wondering what she had just agreed to.

CHAPTER EIGHT

Later in the afternoon, Emilie and Robert finished the paperwork for the merger. Her brother expressed his satisfaction with the terms, and Emilie smiled with relief. She went back to her office. The phone rang as soon as she walked through the door. It was Doc Hannigan, with good news: her father only needed rest and would be fine. A weight lifted from her shoulders. She locked up her desk and files and headed home.

Once there, she went up to her room and packed a few things. Ready to go, she strolled to the porch off her bedroom and looked out over the backyard, watching the horses grazing in the field near the pond. The pleasant sight tempted her to ride her favorite horse, Rex. Emilie remembered watching her mother ride when she was a young girl. Even now, she felt close to her mother's spirit while riding and working in the stable. A quick glance at her watch and she realized her sister was due soon, no time to ride today. Emilie settled for a walk down to the back porch instead.

Standing on the porch, already with a drink in his hand, Robert stared off at the cloudy southern sky. Emilie noticed him and felt a warm tenderness. She walked over to stand by his side, and looked up at him with a smile.

"Guess what? Michelle will be here any time now. Isn't that great?"

Robert smiled back. "Peaches."

"Oh come on, now, we can have fun together. It will be like when we were kids. How about you join us in New Orleans for a short vacation?"

Emilie wrapped her arm around her brother and gave him a gentle hug. He smiled again and kissed her on the top of her head.

"Tempting for sure, but I couldn't leave right now. You see how unreliable Father is lately. After you spoke to me about the mysterious stranger, I asked him questions about the man, and he's definitely hiding something from us."

Emily let go of her brother and stepped back. She remembered the phone conversation she'd overheard her father's secretary having the other day, and what Mr. Labue had said about Robert visiting him. *Why is he going behind my back and not sharing information with me?* Turmoil surrounded him, and she realized that as much as she loved her brother, she distrusted him.

"I heard you did a little investigating yourself, Emilie."

She smiled half-heartedly. "You mean Mr. Labue? Yes, I needed to know what's going on."

"How did you know to go to him?" Robert looked annoyed, his aggravation slipping from beneath his veil. Emile hated playing games. *I will not hide the truth like everyone else.* She cleared her throat.

"His name came up on a document I saw on Father's desk."

"What, you went through his things?! You are a brave soul, Cherie." He grinned, that same smirk he often got when it seemed he was secretly laughing at her. "And what did you find out? Please, Emilie, tell me everything so we can figure this all out together."

Robert flashed an odd smile, an expression Emilie didn't quite understand.

"Rob, Mr. Labue told me exactly what he'd already told you. That's what he said, anyway." Choosing to let her guard down, she told him about the package.

"His name was listed with other information that I saw in the package sent to Father. Someone delivered information about a curse on our family. It was from that man who was here last night, Mr. Pierce."

Robert's face turned red. "Emilie, it's not wise for you to go any deeper with this stuff. It seems someone is just trying to make a quick buck off of Father. You know, appealing to his grief-stricken heart, that is, if he even has a heart. Please, just stay out of this. I will take care of Mr. Pierce, okay? Promise me, Emilie, that you will leave this alone. I don't want our family paying off swindlers left and right."

She shivered from an icy chill that ran down her back. Robert turned and started to walk away, still speaking. "Have fun with Michelle in New Orleans. Try and have a real vacation, Emilie."

The coldness melted when a tender smile spread across his face, as he gave a last glance over his shoulder.

"Okay, we will. Thank you, Robert."

She smiled back, but an internal alarm continued to sound inside her head, telling Emilie that all was not well with her brother. Something twisted and warped resided in him, deep inside. She didn't know what or why, but her instinct cried danger zone. She stood quiet, eyes downcast. Maybe the trip to New Orleans would lead her to an answer. Emilie wanted to understand what was happening in Robert's life, but her first priority was understanding the phenomenon that threatened her family, because her big brother was next in line for the curse.

Later in the evening, Emilie heard a ruckus. Michelle had arrived and the house burst with jubilant noise that drifted all the way to the back porch. Emilie opened the screen door, ran through the house, and greeted her sister in the front hall, where everyone gathered sharing hugs and kisses. Michelle bubbled with life and Emilie drank in her happy mood.

"Good Lord, it is so good to see you home again, Miss Michelle." Nina hugged her tight; her laugh sounded like bells ringing. Michelle struggled to get out of her hold.

"I miss you too, and something smells good. You made something special?"

"Nina made your favorite," Emilie said. She made her way to Michelle, kissed her cheek, and hugged her sister.

"Well hello, dear sister."

Robert boomed into the foyer, and they all turned their attention to him. "Michelle, my bell, what's happening in Beantown? You miss me?"

He gave Michelle a bear hug. Emilie smiled as she watched, thrilled to see them both so happy.

"Of course! There's plenty of people asking about you, too. Cindy said to say hello."

"Cindy? Cindy who?" he said.

"Cindy Hahn, of course. You remember. She said to say 'hello, big boy,'" Michelle giggled.

"Oh, that Cindy." He rolled his eyes with a smirk. Obvious to Emilie, Robert and Michelle shared an inside joke from a previous romp together up in Boston.

"Your old roommate, Jackson Bennett, was at a party last week, Robert. I had a nice talk with him," Michelle said.

Robert twitched, a nerve in his face pinched at the mention of Jackson's name. Emilie felt a jolt, like an emotional slap. Some days she couldn't keep her feelings straight from his. Whatever secrets he harbored, it had to stop, for her sake as much as his. She couldn't take this invisible assault much longer.

"How is he doing these days?" he said, recovering smoothly.

"He said you haven't been in touch for a while, and he wondered when you'll come up north for a visit. Seems his father invited you to their home for a weekend visit. Anyway, he asked for you to call ahead and make sure he's around this time. I guess he missed you the last time you visited the house. Did you fly up to meet with his father, Tom Bennett? I don't remember you visiting lately, Rob. Did you come up north without seeing me?"

Michelle faked a pout on her petite face. Emilie noticed her sister watching him. She was fishing for something, and Emilie wondered what mystery Michelle hid or sought. Blind to the reasons, Emilie knew something important had just gone on. She shook her head and scolded herself. *I have enough to think about without imagining more.*

61

"Of course not, Michelle," Robert said. "I don't know what Jackson told you. Why would I visit Tom Bennett, anyway? I haven't been up to New England for almost a year now. Besides, you know I'll always stop to see you first, you know where all the great parties are! It would be a wash without you."

Michelle smiled back. "Of course, you're right." Unable to keep a straight face, Michelle laughed aloud.

Robert showed an outward smile, but the blood rushed to his cheeks; he was either red from embarrassment or he was angry. Emilie couldn't tell which. He turned his head quickly and caught Emilie watching him. The tension between them thickened. She couldn't understand these intense emotions surrounding him, almost as though he hated her. She turned away, determined to stop watching him. He would explain what bothered him when he was ready to talk.

"Let's go to the dining room for dinner," Emilie said.

Robert's expression changed and a new mask emerged. "Well, girls, I love you both but I've got to go," he said.

"Rob, I just got here. Can't you stay in one night?" Michelle frowned. Being the youngest, that pout often got her what she wanted, but not tonight.

"Sorry. Next time give me a little lead time to clear my schedule."

Nina laughed. "Yes, don't you know his majesty has important business? Out every night! Acting like a cat in heat. Robert de Gourgues, may the good Lord bless you. You be needing it." Nina shook her head, but still smiled. Robert turned and gave her a big squeeze.

"Stop your teasing now, Nina," he said. "I am no king, but I do have much on my plate. You have no idea. Just ask Emilie, she knows."

Robert gave his sisters a hug, and waved as he went out the door. "Have a fun trip and a drink for me."

Emilie knew he was in a hurry to see Rachael again tonight, *or is he seeing Laura?* He was still insisting that Rachael had bewitched him, and he hoped they'd be happy forever, which meant the curse was her official first priority. She needed to stop it before he made any drastic decisions, like marriage.

With just the two sisters left for a late dinner, they decided to eat in the kitchen with Nina. The housekeeper smiled widely, jubilant that the girls were together, and her contagious excitement lifted Emilie's mood.

"You know, Miss Michelle, you need to come home more often. You look too skinny and I miss you. Your sister misses you, too. We need more whooping and hollering around here. She has no one here. Miss Emilie is all alone most evenings. Maybe you could find her a man to hitch up to."

A pang of regret shot through Emilie, despite the knowledge that Nina was only teasing. "Oh, funny. Thanks, Nina, but I don't need a man."

"We all need a man or two or three!" Michelle said.

They all laughed until their sides hurt. Emilie hadn't realized how much she had missed her sister. Her expectations soared, and she was suddenly anticipating a great trip to New Orleans.

CHAPTER NINE

Emilie and Michelle left early in the morning on the family's private jet to New Orleans, and landed within an hour. A car whisked them to the hotel and they settled into a luxurious suite at the Ritz-Carlton on Canal Street, in the Warehouse District. Their rooms had a view of the Mississippi and the French Quarter.

Emilie indulged in a relaxing stone massage. She let herself find some release as the warm stones soothed her frazzled nerves. Then, she and Michelle went out to lunch. Catching a cab, they drove to a small local spot along the trolley line at the edge of the French Quarter. The hostess seated them without delay.

The spring sun filtered through the massive restaurant window. The warmth of the sunbeams cast across her face. She noticed the sparkle in her sister's blue eyes, just like Mother's eyes. Michelle talked about her friends in Boston, and her job as a writer with the *Boston Common*, a popular magazine at the heart of the city, and finally about their Aunt Victoria, who was Mother's only sister. Michelle's vitality seemed bottomless, and Emilie enjoyed every upbeat moment.

Then, like hitting a wall at forty miles per hour, Michelle's good mood changed. Emilie jerked her head back, closed her eyes, and tried to understand what had just happened. The conversation had been pleasant, and then Emilie had asked about the conversation with Jackson, that Michelle had mentioned to Robert. Is that what changed her mood? Michelle reacted harshly, and Emilie didn't understand why that would trigger such a strong reaction. Her head hurt, so she rubbed her temple. *All the results from the massage therapy, gone in a flash.* Something clearly bothered Michelle, and the conversation stalled. Then Michelle leaned forward and, in a softer voice, asked Emilie an odd question.

"Has anyone from up north been down here to visit with Robert lately? You asked about my conversation with Jackson. Well, Jackson told me his father talks about Robert all the time. I think it's kind of weird. Have you noticed anything wrong?"

Emilie harrumphed. *Of course I've noticed something wrong, but what to say to Michelle?* "Well, Robert gallivants all around town at night with all kinds of people, but he never drops names to me. I'm not sure if any friends from Boston stop to visit, but I suppose it's possible. I assumed he was spending most nights lately with Rachael, his new flame. Do you remember her, my old friend, Rachael La France?"

Emilie waited a moment for Michelle to respond, but she didn't appear to be listening any longer, already thinking of something else. She returned to the question Michelle had just posed. "Why would his friend's father ask about Robert, anyway? That is odd," Emilie said.

Emilie didn't doubt the merit of this new tidbit, especially because of the unusual vibes Robert projected lately. Michelle leaned forward again. This time, she lowered her voice as if she needed to speak in secret.

"All I can think of is that he wants Rob's money somehow. I know that sounds strange. This, of course, means he wants our money, too."

Michelle dropped her hand onto the white linen-covered table. Emilie shivered, suddenly sensing something evil in the room. She looked around. There weren't many people, and no one seemed to be paying them any attention. She sighed with frustration, unable to figure out where the feeling had come from. Quiet for a moment, she mulled over her sister's words.

"Honestly, Michelle, Robert does seem off lately. He and Father are often at odds, and Robert's despondent most days. Lately I've sensed creepy moods surrounding him, and something peculiar is going on."

Michelle's face lit up with interest as she waited to hear more. "I told you they want our money," she said.

"A man came to see Father with some documents and an old journal, and he's extorting money from him, but I'm not worried about the cash. It's something about a curse on our family. Robert—"

Michelle couldn't hold back her laughter. "You have got to be kidding! I am definitely taking you out of the South. You're more superstitious than I remembered. Before you know it, you'll be just like Father!"

Emilie was quick to defend. "Crazy girl, just listen for a minute. I found out there's a family down here in New Orleans who may know something about this curse. That's the reason I chose to come here, to look up the family and see if someone can talk to us."

"Us? Listen to yourself, Emilie. Talking like this could even be real."

"Just hear me out. I know you don't believe in curses, but Father does. If we can get some background info, or find a way to stop this or show him there's nothing to worry about, whatever . . . then maybe Father will stop listening to this man. It's not a joke! Robert told me, no, he *demanded* that I stay out of it, which only makes me wonder what he's hiding."

Michelle raised her eyebrow, clearly intrigued at this latest news. Emilie saw a twinkle and nod, and knew she'd played the right card. "Well, if Robert says don't investigate, I say let's go for it! I hate it when people try to control us. Okay, let's check out your lead and see what happens."

Relieved that her sister was on board, Emilie explained the plan. "I checked the addresses of the Boniverre families in the area yesterday, and after considering everything, I determined there was only one good prospect. It's an address in the Garden District, one of the oldest neighborhoods around, so that's our best shot at the eldest living relative."

"Listen to you, girl, sounding like a detective." Michelle's voice almost sang the words. "Just don't start getting all superstitious, and no more talk of your clairvoyant gift, either.

I don't like getting freaked out. If you get any weird vibes from Rob, please keep them to yourself." She slapped her hands on the table to stress her point. "Just give me the facts, you know, the who, where, and what. I suppose this might be fun."

"Okay, we'll go after lunch and get it over with."

The waitress handed them menus.

Emilie, though happy her sister had agreed to go to the Boniverre home, was still upset. It was hard pretending she wasn't different. Her special connection with the paranormal had always made Michelle nervous, and her sister never hesitated to let her know it. Once again, Emilie couldn't be open about her nature, but at least she wasn't hiding anything. Michelle knew everything, even though she refused to accept.

The two sisters ordered and feasted on a Cajun crawfish dish, then had another drink to wash it down. Finished with lunch, they left the restaurant and took the St. Charles Avenue streetcar. They sat side by side on the wooden seats. Emilie enjoyed the clanging and the movement of the old train. The sun was bright and the faces of the other people around them became a blurred haze. Emilie felt lightheaded, either from their drinks or another break-in edging her thoughts.

Emotions of the other passengers crept up and surrounded her own, taking over. Something painful emanated from the poor older man who sat across from her, withering away. Hatred, from the girl sitting in the back who sported a black eye that she tried to hide behind sunglasses. Self-loathing and doubt spilled from the young man who sat hunkered down next to his domineering dad, a few rows down from them. Emilie closed her eyes and, with effort, pushed those feelings away. She shielded herself, a task that increased in difficulty with each new episode.

Determined to enjoy the ride, she concentrated on the surroundings in the Garden District, mindful of the souls who still filled this old neighborhood. The essence of the spirits here rang strong, however, and their turmoil proved difficult to ignore.

The streetcar had just passed Bordeaux Street, the air humid and the emotions of those around weighing her down, when a pang jolted her from her reverie. She opened her eyes, searching the faces of those around her for the source of the evil that now permeated her very being. A man two rows down stared at her, but quickly turned away. She hadn't noticed him before. Ordinary, dressed casually, dark hair, medium build; he looked typical, but she was sure, suddenly, that he was anything but. She knew he had been watching them. Her instincts warned her to be careful.

She and Michelle got off at the next stop to walk a few blocks, enjoying the stroll past the elegant houses with their yesteryear facades. Emilie looked over her shoulder, but no one followed them. *Letting my imagination run wild.* She recalled some of her favorite fictional witches and vampires, who lived behind Victorian doors in this very neighborhood in books, and wondered if the inspiration might have come from real people. Maybe she and Michelle could learn about this curse in a neighborhood with so much superstition surrounding it, or maybe her imagination truly had gone wild.

They reached the Boniverre house, blue with white trim and columns. Shutters hung on the windows, some of them closed. They entered through the black wrought-iron gate and approached the house. Emilie inhaled the rich scents from the fragrant yard, with dozens of rose bushes and lilies blazing a pink and yellow path. The blooming southern magnolias released their citrus perfume, and a flowering pear tree shed its last petals, falling in the breeze like a gentle snow.

Butterflies fluttered in the garden, and stirred in her stomach too, as Emilie walked up the wooden steps.

With so much at stake, she hoped to learn something helpful. She sensed that something important was about to happen, and not soon enough if her brother's relationship with Rachael took a serious turn. If the curse truly was to be believed, her old friend's life was in danger.

Michelle reached over and pushed the button, ringing the doorbell. An old woman, near to a hundred by Emilie's best guess, opened the door. She appeared feeble, but an amiable disposition flowed from her. Her small wrinkled face sagged, covered with dark brown patches, indicative of years of sun exposure. Her eyes sparkled like deep brown jewels. Small in stature, she stooped with her back bent from osteoporosis. Her gray hair was slicked back into a ponytail. She wore a pink flower-print housedress, crisp, clean, and ironed, snapped up the front.

Emilie made introductions and told the old woman that they wanted to know about the rumored old magic spells and family curses.

"Please come in, we can have some tea. Just straight through to my parlor," Miss Boniverre invited. "There's plenty of stories to tell."

CHAPTER TEN

Miss Boniverre escorted the girls through the narrow hall, the wall covered with framed photos of children of all ages. The parlor opened up, homey and decorated with pale hues of pinks and blues. The air smelled like lavender soap, the kind Emilie used to use when she was a young girl.

"I'm glad to have your company, I'm alone most days."

She served them jasmine green tea and ginger cookies that a young girl, who seemed to be her helper, brought in from the kitchen.

Miss Boniverre's skin was paper thin, her hands fragile. They wobbled as she carefully handed each of them a precious bone-china teacup, embellished with dainty painted red roses. The old woman managed not to spill a drop. She settled into her blue velvet wingback. Small as a child nestled between the arms of the chair, she began to tell her stories. Miss Boniverre recalled with clarity some of her family history, and confirmed that her ancestors claimed knowledge of magic spells from long ago.

"Lots of people thought the secret was a Voodoo spell. They didn't understand Voodoo doesn't use curses or spells, only blessings. They were afraid to get on my family's bad side and they always stayed clear of causing us any trouble, fearing the power of the *old magic*. That was fine by us."

The old woman chuckled as she recalled her memories.

"My grandma told me about the *old magic* when I was just a child, many years ago, too many to count. You see, my ancestors were part of the Choctaw tribe. They were what the tribe called colored folks back then, Choctaw freedmen, all of us descended from slaves emancipated after the Civil War. The Choctaw had lots of land down here, and all the way up, pretty much covering the entire Mississippi Valley. Those Choctaws were smart people, and spiritual too.

"Legend says the Choctaw came to this area following their medicine man, who was guided by the Great Spirit, pointing the shaman's red pole in the right direction. It was a long journey and many folks died along the way, but they kept the bones of the loved ones with them. When a tribe member died along the trail, the bone picker scraped them dry, so they could carry the bones as they traveled.

"When they arrived in Mississippi, they buried all the bones of their loved ones at Nanih Waiya, and performed a big ceremony. Then they settled, and as time passed, they planted and took in workers and slaves too, to harvest the crops, just like the white folks did. They wanted to be equal with the whites."

Miss Boniverre chuckled in a soft tone, shaking her head, enjoying her own private joke. Michelle raised her eyebrow, and Emilie knew she had no desire to be there, but Emilie had no intention of leaving yet.

"Well, a few hundred years ago, some other people appeared at the special ceremonial place called Nanih Waiya, too. They walked out from the ground caves. Since everyone believed that place had magical powers, they figured these people were special. Turns out they were from the Timucua tribe. Their chief had been Saturiwa, but he'd already died."

Emile raised her head, alerted by her last words as she recalled the research she'd read earlier. A hopeful spark of curiosity welled. "Excuse me, Miss Boniverre, did you say Chief Saturiwa?"

The old woman smiled. "Yes. These people were a few stragglers left of his tribe, and they asked the Choctaw to let them live and work with them, to escape the persecution of Spanish soldiers, who'd taken over Timucuan lands . . . Where we call Florida today."

Miss Boniverre sipped her tea, picking the cup up slowly. Emilie tried to remember the facts she'd read about her ancestors, back in the days of Captain Dominic and Chief

71

Saturiwa, to determine if this piece of the puzzle fit, and if so, how.

"They had different ways about them, but the Choctaw gave them refuge, and in return for safety the Timucua shared their special spells. Many years later, after the Treaty of Dancing Rabbit Creek, most of the Choctaw tribe were forced off the land, and moved to the Indian territory that's now the big reservation in Oklahoma. The Choctaw were the first tribe to begin the migration called the Trail of Tears. Many died from exposure and starvation, even though the government promised ample supplies and safety. Afterward other tribes, also forced to the reservations, suffered with people dying along the way. After years of being loyal citizens, and fighting and defending their country in the Independence War, the Choctaws had been betrayed by the government."

The old woman shook her head as if in pain, and tears rimmed her eyes. Emilie felt her deep sorrow and started to tear, too.

"Sorry, children, it makes me sad. The government took most of the Choctaw lands, and let only a few people remain, but those who stayed in Mississippi were abused and tormented, their fences torn down and houses burned. They struggled. It was genocide dreamed up by the government."

A slicing pain split in Emilie's head as the old woman's feelings wedged into her space. Miss Boniverre wiped the corner of her eyes with a handkerchief, and maintained her decorum. She seemed to want to finish the story. Emilie massaged her temples, determined to listen to it all.

"When the emancipation happened after the Civil War, the Boniverre clan, my family, stayed working at the plantation, as Choctaw freedmen for a long time. The legend of the old magic spell was handed down through my family for generations, serving as a reminder of the old way, and the last Timucuan memory. Now there's no Timucuan people left, only the legends."

Michelle squirmed in her chair. This conversation was clearly unsettling for her, but Emilie wanted to hear more. She craved more details about the curse.

"Miss Boniverre, what was the *old magic*, a spell or a curse?"

The old woman beamed. "Finally, someone wants to hear the story. For years I've tried to get the younger folks to listen, but they have no time for my stories. They're too busy living their modern life." She cleared her throat and continued her tale.

Emilie noticed Michelle rolling her eyes, her patience wearing bone thin.

"The Timucuan people used magic spells and made offerings to the Great Spirits to keep them healthy and safe. They made a potion called *White Drink*, used in ceremonies just before a battle or hunt to cleanse their bodies and purify the soul."

Miss Boniverre chuckled. Emilie had no clue what seemed funny.

"They were spiritual even though they weren't religious yet, that came later, with the missionaries. There were lots of superstitions, and one special drink they feared called ooooold maaagic."

The old woman stretched out her last words, and said them in a low, menacing voice. Michelle's eyes widened, and Emilie suppressed the urge to giggle.

"That *old magic* spell had been used only once according to legend, by Chief Saturiwa himself, centuries ago when a sea captain came to help his tribe. The chief had learned the secret potion from a Caribbean traveler from the Arawak tribe. This potion makes a person one with the spirit world, and is supposed to help the soul travel into other dimensions."

The theme from *The Twilight Zone* stuck in her head. Emilie tried to focus on the old woman's words.

"When they swallowed the *Yopo*, the chief and the captain traveled to *Coyaba*, which was their version of heaven. Their spirits connected to both sides, the earth world and the heaven world, at the same time."

Miss Boniverre sat back and stared straight ahead. She looked peaceful as she spoke, as if she read from a ghostly text only she could see. Her voice sounded eerie, like a younger version of herself, as she told the legend.

"In the spiritual world anything is possible. This drink joined Saturiwa's fate with the fate of the mighty sea warrior. They formed an allegiance, fought together, and won a battle against the Spanish soldiers."

A teacup clattered. Emilie turned and watched as Michelle placed it on the table in front of her. Emilie had no intentions of stopping. "Miss Boniverre, please tell us more."

The old woman nodded yes. She held her old-fashioned handkerchief tight, her knuckles taut. Emilie noticed the detailed lace edging and wondered how old it was, as well as the age of the woman. She considered that Miss Boniverre may suffer from Alzheimer's and was having an issue remembering, but after a few moments, the old woman continued her recollections in a calm voice, proving her wits better than many.

"The legend tells us that the chief's tribe fought side by side with the warriors from the sea. Together they won a battle against the Spanish invaders. The night before the battle, the tribesmen dressed disguised as animals, wearing the skins of wolves and panthers over their heads. They became skin walkers, a frightful sight, able to scare the devil himself. By wearing the animal skins they gained the instincts of that animal. The chief and the bravest of the warriors wore panther skins, using its masterful hunting skills to track. They traveled by night through the swamps, fighting off the mosquitoes, pests, and gators that lived there in the wetlands. In the early morning, they crept out of the swamp and ambushed the Spanish soldiers. By high noon they'd won the battle."

"So were these warriors Frenchmen?" Emilie asked. "Was the person who practiced the old magic with Saturiwa named Captain de Gourgues?"

The old woman looked confused.

"I don't know names, child, other than the chief. The men from the sea left and went back to their homeland, and then more invaders came. The tribe tried to defend their people, but they had no chance in hell against the Spanish soldiers all by themselves. Then they got sick with disease. Others became slaves and were tortured. Some left the tribe and fled to the Franciscan missionaries who set up settlements nearby. They taught them religion and then they lost their traditions and spiritual beliefs, replaced with Catholic ideas. A few strayed, escaping to join up with other tribes, like those who lived here with the Choctaw in the Mississippi Valley."

Emilie believed the sea warriors had been the French sailors who came with Captain de Gourgues; history had documented his allegiance to the tribe and the chief himself by name. *The truth about the curse is wrapped inside this ancient legend, and somehow generated by this old magic spell*, Emilie thought.

Miss Boniverre started speaking again. "They trusted my family with the secrets because we had great respect for the spirit world, too. We cannot forget these strong, brave people." She stopped and smiled.

"Well, since my family's newest generation isn't so keen on their responsibility to keep the story alive, maybe telling you girls this legend is part of our fate. Here is what I remember, told to me about that frightful night of the spirit bond.

"Remember, the spirit world controls all in our lives. The chief and the captain drank a secret potion and cleansed their souls. Then their spirits leaped through the veil, and into the shadows of the other world, joined together in the journey. The entire tribe had witnessed the dark night sky change and light up with bolts of spectral energy, flashing from the heavens. They saw the mystic power of the other world shine down on both men. They merged that night in the boundless world, and forged a spiritual bond. Their fates on earth also intertwined, but somehow the arcane bond became cursed. Maybe it happened when the sea warriors left the tribe on their own. After that, the tribe died away into the ghostly hereafter. Because their fates were connected, the sea warriors' tribe was also doomed to a shadowy existence. The lineage was cursed in the abstruse realm."

Emilie glanced at her sister in concern. Michelle was rattled. She knew her sister hated this kind of thing, so Emilie tried to soak up her anxiety to protect her from the intensity of the story. The edge softened, and Michelle smiled again.

"My ancestors had a hard life too," Miss Boniverre continued. "We struggled but worked hard over the years. We faced bigotry and cruelty at times, but we never faced trials like the Timucua tribes'. Their entire culture died. Years later, the Choctaw saw their children die, too. They were helpless walking the Trail of Tears, a literal death sentence. This was a crime of genocide, and yet few people today even remember because it's not taught, or they prefer to be ignorant. The Choctaw survive today and have a great community on the reservation; many are dedicated to keeping their heritage. But tribes like the Timucua are gone, completely wiped off the face of this earth."

The old woman wiped her eyes, and blew her nose into her hankie.

"We still haven't learned the lessons. We hear in the news about horrible things happening, killing women and children. In this past century, our supposed intelligent society is blinded to the truth. We allow too much killing."

Miss Boniverre's mind was in another place, filled with doom. It seeped into Emilie's head; the old woman's emotions rang strong but Emilie held back her tears, swallowing hard.

Suddenly, something thumped across the room from behind them. Emilie's heart jumped, her pulse racing. She turned her head to the other side of the room and saw a cat sitting on a tabletop; it had knocked a candlestick to the floor.

Emilie realized she had been holding her breath, while feeling the horror the woman emitted. She snapped her head back, took in some air, and exhaled.

"I can't give anything more than legends, but I'm glad that someone else knows the story," Miss Boniverre continued. "The Timucua tribe is extinct and we should remember what others' greed and arrogance did to them. We need to be tolerant if we are to survive as a race."

The old woman looked tired as she dried her tears. Emilie needed an answer to one more question before she wore the old woman out completely.

"Thank you for the information about the tribe but, Miss Boniverre, is there any other part of the story that talks about a cure or reversal of the magic spell, to break the spiritual bond between the lineages?"

"Girls, you both look like you're educated, I wouldn't think you'd believe in curses." She smiled. Her voice sounded hoarse when she continued. "Yes, there was a concoction made from the poisonous leaves and roots, using holly and cassava, and most definitely a ceremony was part of it all. I'm sure of that, but no spell could ever truly cross souls to the other side and curse two bloodlines. And even if there was something like that, how would it concern such pretty young women?"

Miss Boniverre slipped a grin. The old woman had humored them, and Emilie wondered how much she really knew. It was time to leave, Emilie's mind overloaded with the old woman's emotions. Smiling at her sister, knowing Michelle was probably scared to death, she stood. Michelle stood too and, as if on cue, crossed the room, bent, and gave the old woman a hug. Emilie followed her lead.

"Goodbye and thank you, Miss Boniverre, for the afternoon tea. God bless."

They walked back to the trolley stop. Emilie was drained and thankful Michelle remained quiet, but she still looked worried.

Emilie wondered what her sister was thinking about, and, more than that, what Father Eddie had planned after Michelle left. Emilie sensed more metaphysical experiences yet to come, here in New Orleans. She had no intention of sharing that information with Michelle, or the next step planned with Father Eddie to help their father. Her sister was better off not knowing.

CHAPTER ELEVEN

Emilie imagined they both needed to unwind after that heavy session of storytelling by Miss Boniverre.

"Let's go down to the French Quarter, find a nice spot with good music and lots of people. We'll have some fun. I need to get that legend out of my head," Michelle said.

Exactly what I need, Emilie thought.

"Yes, let's enjoy the rest of this weekend together. I vowed to myself that I'd open up to new people and experiences, and get out of my cocoon."

"It's about time! I'm going to hold you to that promise, starting right now. I know a great place just down the street."

Michelle grabbed Emilie's hand and led the way. They wandered into the Bombay Club, enticed by the aroma of nouveau Creole cuisine and the slow piano music that flowed into the street. Michelle picked the best table for viewing the entire room, and they settled in as the server brought the menus. They both ordered, deciding on martinis to drink.

"Now for the people watching. Let the fun begin. Who looks like trouble?"

"That would be you, Michelle."

Her sister waved her hand, dismissing Emilie's remark, moving her head back and forth as she scouted the room.

Emilie smiled, happy with her little jibe. She watched the young performer playing a subdued piano tune. The crowd was still thin, and consisted mostly of young lovers sitting cozily, secluded in booths. Their drinks arrived, and Michelle chatted away as Emilie gazed around the room. A man caught her attention. He stood out from the others as he leaned his body against the back of a chair. He smiled, showing off deep-set dimples and white, even teeth from clear across the room.

A rush of excitement shot through her, and a tingling sensation traveled all the way from her head to toes. Emilie raised her hand to her neck; her throat tightened with excitement. She drew in a deep breath. He was the most gorgeous man she'd ever laid eyes on. He returned her gaze and she dropped her eyes, her face burning with embarrassment. Michelle was in the middle of a story about her exploits in Boston. Emilie interrupted, tugging at her sleeve.

"Hey, Michelle, that guy is checking you out." She pointed her finger toward the other side of the room, but kept her hand low. He stood alone, tall, fit, and handsome, against the wood-paneled wall.

"What guy?" Michelle swung her head from side to side, searching the room.

"It's the man standing against the wall near the leather wingback chair."

Emilie hung her head lower still, blushing with humiliation, trying to stay as inconspicuous as possible, most difficult with Michelle's obvious gawking.

"I hate to tell you this, but he's checking you out, Sis," Michelle said.

"I don't think so. You're the one men check out, not me."

"Emilie, Emilie, Emilie, you're so naïve! You still don't get that you're a damned knockout. Men love to look at you and your gorgeous curves. And let's not forget that sweet face. You can protest all you want, but I know better!"

"Thanks, Michelle," Emilie said, still blushing deeply.

The handsome man with ash brown hair, hazel eyes, and that dazzling dimpled smile still looked their way. Emilie secretly hoped he had noticed her, unable to deny her intense attraction.

A waitress approached the table with the next round of drinks and Emilie pulled herself from her daydream. A moment later, she sensed a change in the room. She looked up and noticed the man was gone, and felt a loss.

Her disappointment didn't last long. Michelle grabbed her hand and pulled Emilie to her feet. She led her through the room, which had started filling with people. Michelle smiled, saying hello to everyone they bumped into, pausing at every table they passed. She played the crowd and Emilie absorbed her sister's good humor as it chased away all the negativity of the day.

Emilie let her guard down as the crowd got larger and the room filled with laughter. At a table toward the back, a young couple sat swaying to the music and Emilie caught their eye. The woman nodded to her.

"Dreamy music, isn't it?" she said, half shouting to be heard over the noise.

Emilie rarely spoke with strangers at home. Here, she was liberated, freer than she had in a long time. It was nice to see young love blossoming.

"It is," she replied. "You look like you're having a good time."

"We always do," the man said, as he placed his hand over his girlfriend's. "We're getting married soon and came back here where we met, in this very spot, one year ago."

"Isn't he romantic?" the young woman said.

"Congratulations," Emilie replied.

The room grew louder as Emilie moved away from the couple, warmed by their affection. She was nearly across the room before she felt another change, a sudden chill, and a jolt of fear as someone tugged on her shoulder from behind. She spilled some of her drink as she turned.

"What is it?" she demanded when she realized it was only Michelle. Then, she noticed her sister's frown.

"Emilie, there's some goon watching us. I noticed him earlier following us here, but I didn't think much of it. But now he's creeping me out."

Emilie followed the line of her sister's stare. An icy sensation ran up her back. The big shadow of the man Michelle pointed out was definitely a problem; she sensed the same danger she'd experienced with the man on the trolley earlier that day. He stared right at them. Emilie turned her face away.

"He's probably just security," she said.

"Or a stalker," Michelle replied.

Emilie turned her sister around so her back was to him too, and whispered close to her ear. "Okay, let's pretend we didn't see him. Just act normal."

"Us normal?" Michelle laughed in the middle of a sip and choked. "Em, my drink came out my nose."

Emilie smiled and handed her sister a napkin from a table nearby. Michelle wiped her face, giggling.

"You know what I mean," Emilie said. "Let's head to the ladies room, acting casual. When we're out of sight, we can sneak out the back. Okay?"

Michelle shook her head and smiled. They both turned around and danced in the crowded room. When the song finished, they walked away. The man watched them. His stare burned into her back. Pretending not to notice him, they strolled toward the ladies restroom. Once through the doorway, they ran to the window that happened to face the back alley. They tried to pull up the sash. It was stuck.

"Pull it harder," Michelle said.

"I am pulling hard." Emilie tugged with all her strength. Finally, the old window jerked free from the swollen sill, making a nasty screeching sound as it scraped against the layers of paint on its way up the jamb. Two other women in the restroom turned their heads to see what was going on.

"What the hell are you doing?" one of the women said.

"Oh, don't mind us," Michelle said, "We're just getting fresh air."

Michelle bent her head near the open window and inhaled a deep breath. The two women turned and left. Emilie laughed hard, holding her belly, suddenly more daring than she'd ever been before. Putting her leg over the window ledge, she yanked her body out. She fell sideways and landed on her ass in the alley, banging against some crates and making a racket. "Ouch."

"Shit, Em, what the hell are you doing?"

"Ow. Don't worry, I'm okay," Emilie laughed.

"Good thing you're drunk, otherwise that might have felt as bad as it sounded," Michelle said.

"My butt is just a bit sore."

Michelle climbed out the window next. They looked at each other and burst into more laughter.

"Shush!" Emilie held her fingers to her mouth; Michelle stifled her giggles.

"Okay, let's get out of here. I know another great place," Michelle whispered loudly.

Emilie held onto her sister's arm as they stumbled down the alley together. They found a place to haunt, still hiding from the big shadow man. The night went on and Emilie soon forgot about the stalking stranger, and the gorgeous man that had stood in the corner. They bar hopped most of the night, the bands in full swing. The jazz melodies swept Emilie into a carefree world, sorrowful but beautiful at the same time. She fed off the emotional highs that her sister radiated, and everything else slipped away. Sometime after midnight, they took a taxi back to the hotel and called it a night.

Emilie crawled into the queen bed with her clothes on. The room was quiet. Relaxed by the booze, she embraced the freedom, liberated from the negativity in her head. She wished she could follow her sister around more often. *Maybe I should start drinking as a habit.* The tradeoff, a spinning room, was well worth it.

Michelle stirred. "Emilie, are you awake?"

"Yeah. How are you awake, Michelle?"

"I keep thinking of that man who followed us."

"Big shadow man?"

"Yeah. Do you think Robert had us followed?"

Surprised by an unexpected shot of fear, Emilie opened her eyes, now wide awake. She wondered why her sister was afraid, and of what. The nagging suspicion that Michelle knew something echoed in the back of her mind.

"Why would you think that, Michelle? Besides, Shadow Man was a creep, just one of those ogling types. He wasn't following us, after all."

Once again, Emilie remembered the evil feeling she'd gotten from the man on the trolley earlier in the day in the Garden District. *Could someone be following us, though?*

"What does Robert have to do with things?" Emilie asked.

Michelle turned onto her side to face Emilie from the other queen bed. "He did tell you not to go to the Boniverre's place, right? Maybe he was having us followed to be sure we didn't. Maybe Robert is hiding something from us."

"Well, there is something wrong with him, that's for sure, but I can't think of why he'd have us followed. It's no big deal that we went to Miss Boniverre's and asked a few questions. I mean, what's it to him? Besides, would he hire a dumbass so easy to get away from?"

Michelle laughed, but then got quiet. "Robert has so many secrets."

Emilie thought about that for a moment. "You know, I feel bad things around him. Hateful emotions, or some kind of deep resentments, and I have no idea why."

"There you go again. Please, Emilie, stop talking about ESP stuff. You promised."

The covers rustled again as Michelle turned away. Emilie closed her eyes and tried not to feel hurt. She wished Michelle accepted her for her true self. If she could turn this gift off, she would for her sister's sake if not her own. They were both quiet until sleep found them.

The next day, the sisters went shopping on Royal Street in the French Quarter. Michelle bought some antique jewelry at M.S. Rau Antiques, more than her fair share of bling for herself, and a gift to take back for Aunt Victoria. Then they devoured an omelet at the Court of Two Sisters restaurant, and relished the spring blooms in the warm late morning sun. Happy being with her sister, the tranquil setting eased Emilie and she wished it could last forever.

"This has been a great weekend together," she said.

Michelle twisted her wrist, admiring her new antique bracelet. It reflected the sun's rays and bounced small rainbows onto the white tablecloth.

"Let's do this more often. I miss you so much, and I worry about you, too. You spend too much time alone in that big house, and Father and Robert aren't exactly good company."

"Michelle, I miss you too, and I am happy for you. I get jealous that you see so much of Aunt Victoria, I wish I knew her better. But if I were to leave, who would be here for Father?"

"Father! Be there for him? You're crazy. He doesn't give a damn about any of us, Em. I mean, I know he loves us, but caring is not part of his makeup. All these years since Mother died, he barely sees us. We went up north and he just forgot about Robert and me. He is nothing but self-serving, Em. You would understand if you had left, too."

"You don't understand," Emilie said, gulping back her frustration. "It's more like self-preservation, not apathy toward you. Father loves us all, and he keeps tabs on you, Michelle, he always has. I know he's hard on Robert, but maybe he needs it."

Emilie watched her reaction, and noticed a glint in her sister's eyes when she mentioned their brother. She could tell Michelle knew more about Robert than she let on.

"Michelle, what was it you wanted to say to me about Robert?"

"Oh, that. It was nothing. I just let my imagination run wild, besides you're right. Why would he have us followed? That goon was just another creep in the crowd."

There was more she wasn't saying; an ice cube would have been warmer than the feeling Emilie got from her sister. She let it go, and decided to wait until Michelle found the right time to share.

From there, the mini vacation ended abruptly. Michelle took a direct flight back to Boston, leaving Emilie on her own once more. As soon as she was gone, Emilie called Father Eddie. He picked up right away.

"Miss Emilie, I have been waiting for your call. Let's meet in the lobby in half an hour."

CHAPTER TWELVE

Emilie saw Father Eddie sitting in the lobby. A big man who seemed to fill the room, he could have been the brother of Pavarotti. His clerical collar was an indicator of his true benevolent self. Emilie walked up to him and gave him a friendly hug.

"Hello, Father Eddie."

"Miss Emilie, thank you for meeting me. We have an adventure ahead of us today," he said.

"What exactly are we about to do?" Emilie asked.

Eddie smiled, but she noticed his hands clasped in angst. "Pierre came to me about this presumed curse," he said. "I get a sense that he's in trouble and he needs something that will protect him."

"Like what, a gun?" she said.

"No. No, more like a blessing."

He led the way out of the hotel lobby and to his rental car, parked in front. Emilie noticed a valet attendant standing nearby and gave him a tip as Father Eddie got into the driver's seat. The valet helped Emilie in and closed the door.

"I think a visit to my old congregation might help," Father Eddie said. "I know some folks down here who still use the old practices of curses and spells. Even though I always denounce such superstitious beliefs, they still use Voodoo anyway. I thought someone might help us."

Emilie turned and looked at Father Eddie, surprised by his intentions. It almost seemed like a betrayal, giving in to any belief other than Catholicism. A streak of guilt colored her words. "So if you denounce the practice, then why are we pursuing it? I don't mind telling you, the thought of Voodoo sends shivers up my spine. I'm not so sure about this idea of yours," she said.

He drove off, heading toward his old parish. "Don't worry, Emilie. I don't claim to understand these beliefs, but these blessings seem to work. And who knows, maybe they can give us something to cancel the curse. You know I'd do anything for your father. He's been a good friend over the years."

Emilie surrendered, deciding not to second-guess the priest. Her parents had always trusted him, so she did too. She watched out the window as they passed other sections of New Orleans that weren't so well off.

"I haven't been here in a while, I am ashamed to say, and I miss the Sunday picnics of my old church. I used to enjoy cooking the recipes we conjured up, my mouth waters at the thought."

He gave a slight laugh, and a side glance at Emilie. She smiled back, but still felt uneasy.

"Are you ready for some home Creole cooking? Maybe they have a few bites left from today's bounty."

Emilie nodded. What was she was getting herself into? He pulled the car into the parking lot, and rolled into a spot. Some of the people approached to greet him as he labored getting out of the car, pushing his large frame out of the little compact. Combing back his dark hair with his fingers, he smiled to everyone as they gathered around him.

"Father, you haven't forgotten us. We are so happy to see you," an old man said.

Emilie watched, amazed. Everyone appeared to love Father Eddie. He had a formidable presence, but his sensitive demeanor and calming words drew people to him. He introduced everyone to Emilie, but with so many new faces she couldn't keep their names straight. They walked to the church's backyard together like sloths, sweating in the humid late afternoon air. Pecan and oak trees surrounded the perimeter, too far off to offer shade. They reached a tented area where more people awaited them, and Father Eddie once again introduced Emilie.

Most of the congregation was older, and seemed to appreciate his kind recognition. Emilie found a chair and sat down, preferring not to open herself up to so many people and emotions. She made a conscious effort to shield herself.

Some of the old men led Eddie to the cooking pit to inspect the big kettles that held seafood gumbos and steamed vegetables. Eddie raised the lids and released the heated seasonings of the Cajun cooking. The steam from the pots blended with the afternoon humidity, the air heavy with the spiced aroma of pepper and garlic.

"My mouth is watering," Father Eddie said.

He closed the lid that held the flavors in, and took out a handkerchief and wiped his brow, patting himself with a nervous hand. The men milled around Eddie, filling him in on the latest parish news.

A tremor of regret stirred Emilie; she remembered what Miss Boniverre had said and chastised herself for not doing more for these people. This was a poor neighborhood. Many were still trying to recover from the devastating hurricanes the region had experienced in recent years. They spoke about new construction going on in other neighborhoods, and the houses still in need of repair in their tiny corner of the world. The hot topic shared with Eddie was who had the best prices on salvaged lumber. Most of the gossip led to stories of families leaving for a new start. Emilie eavesdropped as Father Eddie asked about certain people.

"I will keep them in my prayers," Emilie heard Eddie say.

Eventually, Father Eddie took a break from his socializing and sat down next to Emilie. She felt heat pouring from his body. He handed her a plate of food, and the two ate in silence. A lone old man walked over. Dressed in his best Sunday clothes, he took off his hat and twirled it in his hands. Eddie looked up.

"Hello, sir," Eddie said. "Do I know you? Sorry, but I don't recall your name."

"Reverend Eddie, you don't know me none. There is someone else who wants to be seeing you, but she can't be here at the picnic today, so I come for her. She's asking for you to stop by, before you leave town. Come after this get together. If you want to help your friend, you will make the visit," the man said.

Paranoia gripped Emilie. *How does anyone know about Eddie's intentions to help my father?* The old man shook Eddie's hand.

"Thank you, Father."

"No, thank you, sir."

The old man walked away. Eddie opened his hand to reveal a small scrap of paper with an address scrawled on it.

"Who was that man?" Emilie said.

"I don't know, but this address is to one of the Voodoo followers' home. Eat up, we need to leave."

Eddie looked anxious as he finished his food. Emilie wondered how a priest could be so open to this road they were following.

They finished the meal and Father Eddie said his goodbyes to his old friends, leaving the picnic early with excuses of a long drive home. When they were back in the car, Emilie buckled up, anxious to get the next part over with quickly.

"Can I see the note?" she asked.

He pulled the scratched message from his pocket and gave it to her, then started the car. Emilie's curiosity peaked as she touched the piece of paper with the scribbled address in blue ink.

During the drive, they passed empty lots, then a cluster of small shotgun shanties littering the neighborhood, some lived in, others abandoned. Very few were new or refurbished. They arrived at a very old section of St Bernard Parish, and Father Eddie parked the car. While Emilie was still lost in her thoughts, he got out and walked across the street, intent on the faded street sign. Emilie got out and followed him.

"Do you know this place?" she asked.

"Yes, these back streets, let's say I am aware of the mistrust in this area, and I don't blame them. So many people were just forgotten after Katrina."

They walked past a group of houses. Some young men hung out on the stoops, talking in their own thick, local drawl. Their conversation was filled with half-spoken words pronounced with a musical inflection, and Emilie could understand little of what they said. She looked back over her shoulder, suddenly anxious, but no one followed. Despite that, she still felt edgy.

"I really don't like the idea of asking for help from Voodoo worshipers," she said.

"Don't worry, Emilie," Eddie said. He patted her hand. "It's dangerous here, but the people won't bother us, they have respect for the collar I wear. Most of the people in this area either believe in, or have a healthy respect for, Catholicism and Voodoo. For many, the two intertwine."

"Just what exactly are we here for?"

"We're here to help your father. No matter what happens, keep an open mind and be brave. We may just be able to save your father's life, Emilie. Here we are."

The house, designed in the old Craftsman style with handcrafted woodwork embellishments, was the only original home left standing on this street, as though something had protected it all these years. *Maybe the occupants inside do have some old magic working in their favor.*

She climbed a few steps up to an open porch, following Father Eddie's lead. Stepping up, the boards squeaked under his weight. Emilie felt the floor dip beneath her own feet. Why would a priest go to these lengths to help a friend, she wondered? Didn't he worry about his soul? Sweat dripped down Eddie's face. He loosened his collar a bit, took out a handkerchief, and dabbed his face dry. Emilie wiped her forehead with the back of her hand, and then pulled her hair away from her face, tying it back in a knot. Eddie pulled the knocker in the center of the door and let it drop. He looked down at Emilie.

"Have courage," he said.

Emilie sighed. The door opened and a pretty, petite brown girl, just a child in braids, wearing a flowered summer dress, stood there. Without saying a word, she opened the screen door and motioned for them to enter.

The house was a shotgun layout with a hallway that ran from the front of the house to the back. It was furnished with old-style furniture that made everything seem as though time had gone backwards.

"This place could have been my grandmother's," Father Eddie mumbled to Emilie.

They followed the little girl to a large bedroom in the back of the bungalow, where an old woman rested in a large antique bed. The metal headboard and footboard were painted white, stamped with floral designs. A homemade quilt covered the bed, the type frugal people created years ago from recycled coats.

The old woman sat awake and smiling, her skin dark and wrinkled. She motioned for them to enter and sit near the edge of her bed. Father Eddie lifted the crucifix that lay around his neck and kissed it, then crossed himself. He prayed with the old woman. Compassion flowed from him, and Emilie felt his sincerity; her confidence in him grew.

The woman mimicked his motions, making the sign of the cross too. Her gray hair glistened as if wet, combed back in a bun away from her thin face. Emilie tried to feel the old woman's emotions, but got nothing. That had never happened before. Emilie couldn't remember anyone ever blocking her gift. The woman looked up at Emilie, nodded, and smiled, as if she understood the young woman's thoughts.

"Thank you for coming, Father Eddie." Her voice was clear, soft and heavily accented in French Creole resonance. "I was expecting you. I saw in a dream that you would be here seeking an answer. You hope I have one. Am I right, Father?"

Father Eddie nodded, but his eyes were wide with wonder and the color drained from his face. "Yes, I do need some information." His voice was faint. "You see, I have a good friend, an old friend, who is afraid he has a curse on his family, on his lineage."

Eddie stopped. The old woman showed no reaction to his words, and after a moment's pause, she spoke, her voice low.

"I can't help with the curse. What you need is a gris-gris bag. We'll make a special one for him," she said.

A creaking sounded in the room and they turned to see the young girl, entering from the door behind them. The girl went to the old woman's other bedside, took her hands, and they rambled on in a language Emilie had never heard before. They chanted something together, swinging their heads back and forth in rhythm, but it wasn't a prayer she recalled ever hearing. The chant turned into song that sounded like an old Negro spiritual, but in a strange language.

"Gematria notarikon duppie Loa come. Gematria notarikon Loa come."

They repeated the words over and over again. As it grew, the room swerved and shook. The chandelier on the ceiling swayed, and the pictures on the walls rattled. The noise thundered; Emilie buckled over as her gift kicked in and she experienced Eddie's emotions. He was sick with fear.

A chill ran through Emilie and her skin prickled. She looked over and saw Eddie's face go pale. Looking queasy, he held his stomach.

The daylight that had shined through the window disappeared. The room was plunged into darkness, the nearby white candles the only visible light in the room. The candles flickered, stationed on a table near the bed.

White linen covered the tabletop, which resembled a small altar. Statues of Christ and the Madonna and various pictures of saints were arranged between them. An incense burner placed in front smoked with a frankincense sillage. To the right sat a bowl of water, Emilie presumed holy water, vital for any blessings. Other items lay on the tabletop: a black feather, some sprigs of weeds or herbs that looked like lemongrass and bay leaves, a piece of torn material stained with what appeared to be someone's blood, and a lock of dark curled hair. The hair reminded Emilie of her brother Robert. Right in the center of it all, impossible to miss, lay a claw from a dead blackbird. The sight of it sent shivers up Emilie's spine.

She looked up at Eddie, seeking his strength, but he just stared into the dark emptiness, deathly afraid. She sensed something eerie around him. Some unknown force of nature that she had never experienced before materialized in the room. Her fear spiked with his.

The woman's face appeared to age in front of them, the glow from the candles emphasizing every line and wrinkle. It was as though her face shriveled before their eyes. Father Eddie moved his thick lips in a mumbled prayer. Emilie closed her eyes, listening. Something moved. When she opened her eyes, the young girl held the old woman's trembling hands. They kept singing the chant, the words louder, more erratic now.

"Gematria notarikon, duppie Loa come."

Eddie covered his ears with his hands; the sound pierced Emilie's soul. The temperature soared, and the darkness became a vacuum as the severe sound of the chant rose until she feared her eardrums would burst. Emilie followed Eddie's example, and covered her own ears. The room quaked with more rigor, and they swayed off balance. Still, the chant did not cease.

An overwhelming grief took hold of Emilie, so profound she wanted to die. Just when she could not bear it a moment longer, it was gone.

Everything stopped.

The spinning sensation ceased, and the rattling of the chandelier quieted.

The chant was done.

Eddie reached out to steady himself with his hand on the wall, until he regained his equilibrium. He looked at Emilie, and she knew just how he felt. After a few seconds her ears stopped ringing. The darkness slipped back into sunshine and streamed through the window. Eddie raised his arm to shield his eyes from the sudden brightness.

"I have what you need," the old woman said.

Emilie turned her attention back to the old woman, who was smiling as though nothing had happened.

"My grandchild will give it to you. Just take this to your father. I know who you're here for, I saw him in a dream. Mr. de Gourgues needs the spell to protect him."

Emilie swallowed back the lump in her throat. People shouldn't need protection spells, it just wasn't normal. The old Voodoo woman looked at Emilie with an intensity that seemed to burn right through her.

"There are forces around your father that are trying to destroy him. He needs the protection more than you know. Take what my little sweetheart gives you. Have him place it in his home near something he treasures... This is the only way I know how to help."

Then, as quickly as everything else had happened in the room, she closed her eyes and was sound asleep. Emilie and Eddie looked across at the young girl.

The girl opened up a small cloth sack. She took the bird's claw, spit on it, and dipped it in holy water, then sprinkled some kind of oil. Then, she sifted red brick dust on it, making it look bloody, before she placed it in the bag. She waved the piece of cloth over the incense smoke and then added it to the bag. Last, she placed the hair and some twigs of herbs into the bag. She turned and held out her hands to Father Eddie, revealing the small twill bag. Father Eddie took it from her.

"Thank you. Can I give you anything for this gift?"

The little girl shook her head no, and then pointed to the door. Eddie shifted his weight from one foot to another, apprehensive.

"Can't we give you something in return for your help? We have money." Emilie said.

The girl pointed to the door again, frowning. Emilie and Eddie left and walked back to the car without another word.

The return trip to Memphis seemed long. Father Eddie returned his rental car and flew back with Emilie on the Cessna. Exhaustion helped her drift in and out of sleep as she rested in the seat. On the occasional bump from turbulence, she opened her eyes and saw Father Eddie praying, mumbling words for his friend. *Maybe he's praying for his own soul as well.* She knew he was conflicted by the episode they'd just experienced; she felt that way, too.

They landed in Memphis and returned to the house after a quiet ride home from the airport. Emilie followed Father Eddie across the wide porch. He stopped before opening the door, turning to search her face. Emilie knew he was confused.

"Will God forgive me for believing in this supernatural direction I took today?"

He sought some kind of reassurance from her, but she didn't know the answer herself. "We will all find out someday. Father Eddie, just remember God gave you your intellect to make the choices you deem correct. Keep goodness in your heart and everything will be all right. A great priest told me that when I was a little girl."

She smiled. "Now, go give that thing to my father. I know exactly where he'll put it, he'll place it on his bookshelf next to the volume of poetry by Robert Frost. My mother's favorite poem was 'North of Boston.' She used to sit near the window in his library and read that book over and over."

"Your mother was a wonderful person. She had a loving soul," Father Eddie said with a smile, seeming more relaxed at Emilie's reassurance.

They walked into the house. The familiar scent of the oil soap that was used to wash the wood floors filled her nostrils. God, it was good to be home. Eddie went to her father's library. Emilie intended to go upstairs, she needed some rest. The trip to New Orleans revealed much, but there had been a cost; the strange experience had tipped her over the edge mentally, and she just wanted to retreat for a while. Before she reached the stairs, her brother hailed her.

"Emilie, hold up! I want to hear about your trip."

Recalling her conversation with her sister in New Orleans, Emilie had no idea what to tell him. How much, if any, of the truth should she share?

CHAPTER THIRTEEN

Emilie turned around and saw her brother walk out from the shadows of the other room. She met him in the middle of the foyer.

"So, how was the trip?" Robert smiled down at her. She forced herself to relax her shoulders, and smiled back.

"It was great, Robert. You should have come with us, we had the best time. We heard great music, ate good food, and laughed our heads off. We had fun. Life is much easier with Michelle around."

Robert shuffled his feet, uneasy. "Sounds like I missed a great time. Things here are okay... Father isn't crazy yet."

"I am sorry you have to be his watcher," she said.

"No problem. It comes with the job, I suppose." Negativity emanated from him. "You stayed away from investigations, right? Like I asked?" His expression hardened with the question. She felt like a scolded child, flashing back to Sister Antoinette's fourth-grade class.

"Robert, I'm going to be honest with you," she said, deciding on the spot that she had no choice. She wouldn't be bullied by her brother and his mysterious moods. "We did go to Miss Boniverre's home in the Garden District, and asked about the curse. She had stories to tell that her family passed on, but I'm not so sure—"

"I told you to stay away from this. What do you think you're doing, Emilie?" he demanded, his voice rising. "You have no understanding of what you're getting involved with. Can't you just listen to me, just once? You are such an instigator. You need to mind your own business."

Emilie wilted. Until recently, she'd never been afraid of Robert. Now, with his fists clenched and his jaw tight, she wasn't sure what he was capable of. The sudden change confused her. More than that, it frightened her. "Don't you think you're overreacting?"

She swallowed hard and stood her ground, planting her feet.

Before he could respond, there was a noise behind them as someone stepped into the room. Robert and Emilie both turned and looked at the man now standing in the doorway. He was a stranger, yet he looked and felt familiar to Emilie.

"Excuse me," he said. "I've just spoken with Mr. Evans and he suggested it was easier to leave through the back entrance. Can you point the way?"

Robert lowered his head, his face red. "Emilie, I'm confident you can help this man find his way out. I have places to be." He straightened out his shirtsleeves as if he had done physical work, not willing to show defeat.

The man sauntered across the room and stood between brother and sister. Robert didn't say another word. He turned and walked away, clearly not happy with how their argument had ended.

Not even home five minutes and the family is falling apart. Emilie wasn't sure if it was the curse she was afraid of at this point, or her own family.

She realized the man still stood by her side, and sensed goodness flowing from him. She recognized his soul somehow, almost as if a glow surrounded him. She looked up and met his stare. Time stopped as they gazed into each other's eyes. There was softness there, something that spoke to her. Suddenly, she remembered why he was familiar: he was the handsome man she'd noticed watching her in New Orleans.

Her face flushed, her entire body reacting to his closeness. Embarrassed by her thoughts, she looked away. "Thank you. You have just saved me from what could have been a bad situation. I don't like arguing with my brother. I am in your debt, sir."

She bowed her head. He smiled at her, showing off his deep dimples, and gazed at her with sparkling hazel eyes.

"You're welcome. I argue with my siblings from time to time, too."

He nodded to signal good night and turned around, moving toward the front door. His British accent just added to Emilie's attraction to him. *Not fair*, she thought.

Question after question arose: Who was he? What was he doing here? She sensed good in him, knew intuitively that he was no danger, but she couldn't dismiss such a wild coincidence as first seeing him in New Orleans and now, less than twenty-four hours later, in her own home. She forced herself to set the questions aside for the moment. *All in due time*, Emilie, she told herself.

"Please don't go yet," she called after him. "I could use some company. Would you like some coffee?" She didn't wait for his reply, but just turned and walked toward the kitchen, expecting him to follow. "Do you like Columbian? Or would you rather have tea? "

She opened the kitchen cabinet door and pulled out two cups. He sat down and introduced himself.

"My name is Jeremy Laughton. Hello." He held out his hand to shake, and she placed her hand in his. When she touched him, her intense yearning was heightened, his positive energy pushing her toward euphoria.

"Emilie de Gourgues," she stumbled, barely getting her own name out.

"I'm here working on a local environmental project as a contractor," he said. "I'm documenting the recent storm damages. I spoke with your house manager, Mr. Evans, about the project, and was leaving when I heard you . . . I'm glad I was able to help."

He smiled, showing his dimples again. Emilie, lost somewhere in the clouds, didn't comprehend what he'd said. Her mind wandered to his inviting lips, sensual smile, and firm body. Her face burned with embarrassment, knowing she looked a smitten fool.

"Are you okay?" he asked.

Emilie cleared her throat, and snapped herself back to the moment. "Yes, fine. So what's the project you're working on?"

"I'm assisting with an ongoing project along the Wolf River. A tributary backs up to your land here on the estate, and I will be accessing your property to document noticeable changes from the spring storms, erosion damage, the wildlife eco-cycle, migrations, and any impacts on the aquifer in the area, that kind of thing. I'm working for a commissioned environmental group assigned to work alongside the U.S. Army Corps of Engineers." He explained all of this with a smile, his natural ease making him that much more attractive. "And tea will be fine, thanks."

"Wow, that's an important undertaking. It sounds fascinating."

He laughed at her response.

"What's so funny?"

"You're the first woman who ever thought my work could be fascinating. Even my own mother makes fun of my job. She calls me a glorified muck walker." The smile they exchanged this time was warmer. For a moment, even the seemingly cool and collected Mr. Laughton seemed disarmed. "I am sorry for sounding so forward, but you seem so familiar to me."

"I know what you mean. Were you, by any chance, in New Orleans recently, yesterday, perhaps?" she asked.

It was his turn to blush. *He did notice me,* Emilie thought, gratified.

"I was there, yes. I didn't think you'd noticed me. This is such an odd coincidence. I didn't follow you here, honestly. When I got this assignment, I decided to take the opportunity for a quick trip to New Orleans, I've always wanted to see it. I took the train down on a whim, and just returned late this morning."

She could feel his sincerity and knew his intentions were honorable, thanks to her empathic gift. Once in a while it came in handy. The tension evaporated and the awkward moment passed.

Emilie handed him his herbal tea, and sat in a chair at the kitchen table, across from him. She sipped hers as she studied his face. His deep smile lines made it seem as if happiness had been permanently stamped there. She could use a bit of that these days.

"So what do you do?" he asked. His eyes were intense, and seemed to look deep into her soul. No one had ever been that interested in her, unless they were after money. That had been an issue years ago when she'd attempted to date. But that wasn't this man's story. A compassion for life flowed from him like a breath of fresh air.

"I work at PDG Inc., my father's company. I'm brand director for new product development."

She smiled and hoped she wouldn't have to explain more, but her answer only paved the way for more questions. Finally, after what seemed like an interrogation, she drew up short.

"Jeremy, you're so inquisitive," she said. "Are you always so curious about strange people you just met?"

"First off, you're not so strange," he smiled, "and I have to admit, I find you more interesting than most. I know it sounds sappy, but I want to learn everything about you."

There was a moment of silence. She looked at her tea, but sensed his eyes on her. Her body tingled as her pulse pounded and her throat tightened.

"I like sappy," she said softly. "Tell me more about you." She turned the table on the questions, happy to be out of the spotlight. "Where are you from? And why take this job?"

He chuckled to himself. "Well, not much to tell. I'm a simple man, grew up in Surrey. I have my mum and da and a sister and brother. I love nature and the science behind it all. I know it's not the most profitable line of work, but my great uncle always told me to chase after the things in life that are important to me. I want to be part of taking care of this planet, and I want to understand all of its mysteries."

His gentle nature moved her; the more he spoke, the more she wanted to know. She had a thirst for his words, and yearned to be close. The table that separated them felt intrusive. She nodded as he talked about some of his favorite places on earth, and she imagined she was there with him, walking the beaches, hiking the woods.

"So do you believe in fate?" she asked him.

"My mother always said life unfolds the way it should. Maybe that is fate, or maybe just the law of nature. Either way, I know I'm glad we crossed paths."

He winked. *He actually winked!* To her it seemed like an old-fashioned way of flirting, but she found it so endearing the way he did it. Emilie drew in a breath, totally smitten.

"Me, too." Emilie looked down at her tea, embarrassed that she felt such a deep attraction so quickly. She hoped he hadn't noticed, yet she wanted him to know exactly how she felt. She looked up at him again and their eyes met.

Time stood still at that moment.

The Black Forest cuckoo clock on the kitchen wall chimed midnight; she heard the soft dongs and the music box played *Edelweiss* while four small wood-carved people twirled in a waltz. Something special flourished between them, she knew he could sense it, too. Laughing and sharing their pasts, a new beginning had emerged.

"I'd better be off, but I'd like to see you again, if that's agreeable with you. Miss Emilie, will you have dinner with me tomorrow? I mean tonight."

Emilie smiled. "Yes, of course. Call me later today and we'll meet up. I'd like that, very much."

She handed him her card. Jeremy kissed her cheek softly. His lips hot against her skin.

"Cheers," he said as he walked toward the door.

Emilie watched as he walked to his truck, and knew she'd never be the same again. An emptiness she had endured for most of her life was suddenly filled.

"Life is wonderful!" she exclaimed to an empty room.

In bliss, she forgot all about her short argument with Robert. She leaped up the stairs, retreated to her bedroom, and climbed into bed. Falling into a deep sleep, she dreamed of things that had never been allowed before tonight.

The silent burden she'd endured since her mother's death began to lighten.

CHAPTER FOURTEEN

Emilie woke the next morning happy and relaxed, a new feeling that she hoped would last. The visit to New Orleans had been just what she'd needed: catching up with her sister, finding some insight into the curse, and, most surprisingly, meeting the most handsome man she had ever seen. Despite everything else in turmoil around her, Emilie's good mood persisted. She hummed as she washed and dressed, throwing on a pair of jeans and an old shirt that was loose and baggy. Today the house was empty, not a soul around, so she turned up the music until the tunes blasted through the house. She went downstairs and grabbed a cup of coffee and then headed back to her desk, opened her laptop, and went over the information she had copied, just one more time.

She remembered the old magic Miss Boniverre talked about, used by the sea warrior and the Chief Saturiwa. Captain de Gourgues had to have been the warrior from the sea, she was sure. History books stated he was an ally to the Timucua tribe, and since her ancestor was the sea warrior, then probably the bond between the two men in the ceremony had been the beginning of the curse. Something had gone wrong and the legacy of death began with the captain, or more accurately the captain's wife.

She shivered, feeling a sudden draft. Looking around, she saw there were no open windows, but she felt some kind of cold invisible trail in front of her, a presence leading her forward. She refused to worry, but instead allowed the spark of curiosity to guide her. *That old book is still in father's library. I bet it will hold answers.* She needed to get it back and translate it, and with no one in the house today, it was her opportunity to do so.

She noticed when passing the grandfather clock that it was already mid-afternoon. The library doors were closed. She grabbed the handles, pulled the large doors open, and went straight to the elegant Louis XVI desk. It was a beautiful piece of furniture with gold-leaf accents and a smooth leather top that was soft from years of use. The drawers pulled open with ease. She loved the old desk and checked all the drawers, taking her time, appreciating the whiff of tobacco that permeated the air, dispersing as she drew them open. She found nothing.

Next, she rummaged through the stacks of books on the table, feeling guilty going through her father's stuff, and again came up empty. Her attention turned to the large bookcase behind the desk. She scanned the shelves visible at eye level but found nothing that resembled the old journal. Looking for a stepladder to reach the top shelves, she noticed something that stood out as if placed there mistakenly. The old song from *Sesame Street* played in her head: *one of these things doesn't belong.*

Emilie felt the cold draft again. Her skin sprung goose bumps. Looking up she saw the small lightweight cloth bag that the little girl had given Father Eddie. Tied with twine and marked with a symbol designed like Poseidon's pitchfork on the outside, the bag sat there on the shelf. Some sort of force pulsed from it. She snatched it up and opened the bag cautiously. She found the strange ingredients inside.

Something odd came over her, a sensation she had never experienced before. "What the hell did we do?!" Her stomach tightened and her head spun. It took everything she had for her to stay on her feet. "What's happening to me?"

She panicked. She picked up the bag using only two fingers, pulled the string closed, and placed it back on the shelf, half tossing it to minimize the need to touch it. Whatever was in the bag was doing this. It was Voodoo. She realized now that she had invited these dark forces into their home, that perhaps she and Father Eddie had opened something they had no right to go near. Feeling ill, she barely made it out of the library to the guest powder room, before she vomited. She needed fresh air, and headed for the door.

Once outside, she sprinted away from the house, rubbing her hands frantically against her jeans, trying to erase the awful feeling on her skin. She breathed in erratic gasps, swallowing the needed fresh air to clear her lungs. Still in the grip of fear, Emilie ran toward the stables, her favorite place to think. Stopping, she leaned against a weathered fence post to catch her breath. She hated panic attacks almost as much as she hated Voodoo bags.

Her horse, Rex, walked over to see her. Emilie rubbed his face gently and said, "I can always count on you." Rex whinnied.

Now that she was away from the house, the bizarre feeling was gone. She tried to understand why it had happened.

There had been some kind of spiritual essence in that bag. A flash memory of the previous night and all the strange happenings in the room came to mind, the old lady, as the candlelight appeared to shrivel her face right in front of them. Emilie shook her head, pushing that image from her mind, and then she remembered Miss Boniverre had said Voodoo was for blessings.

The curse on her family had nothing to do with Voodoo, and definitely was not a blessing. Emilie needed to talk things out with someone, to clear her head and get a handle on which direction to go. For a brief moment, she considered of calling Robert, but right away realized that would be a mistake. He was already so angry with her. Michelle was a better choice for a friendly ear, but her sister hated stuff like this. Still, she had a clear head about things. Emilie tugged at her jeans, pulled the phone from her pocket, and hit speed dial. All she got was Michelle's voicemail. Instead, she left a text message: *Call me when you can, need advice.* She hit send.

"Now what should I do?" she asked herself aloud.

She envisioned Jeremy; he had shadowed her thoughts all day. His voice alone would make her feel safe again, she imagined. Even though they'd just met, Emilie felt in some ways like she had known him forever. Time was playing tricks on her, but she didn't care. All she wanted was to be with him again, she needed someone to talk with. Her phone rang. Looking at the display, she recognized his number. Jeremy's timing was perfect.

She hesitated a second, wondering how much she'd reveal to him, family curses and hex bags were definitely not first-date material. He would think she was crazy; normal people didn't have those things hanging around their house.

"Hello," she said.

"Emilie? Hi, it's Jeremy, I suppose you recognized my number from caller ID."

She smiled to herself, happy to hear his nervous voice. "I did see your name pop up, and I'm glad to hear from you."

"I'm glad you're glad." He cleared his throat. "Look, I just finished logging in my work notes and hoped we could grab that bite to eat. Wait a minute, let me try that again."

Emilie almost giggled, hearing the smile in his voice when he spoke.

"It would be my honor to take you to dinner. Can I stop by for you, Miss Emilie?"

His voice was calming. She was better already, as if everything in her life was suddenly manageable. "That would be perfect, Master Jeremy."

"See you in thirty minutes, if that is okay?"

"Sounds great."

Thinking about her secrets, she wondered if sharing the knowledge of her clairvoyant gift with Jeremy was a good idea. The gift had always been a part of her life, her ability made her feel alive, though at times it also made her suffer. To be completely honest with him, she should explain this critical part of who she was, but it just wasn't the kind of thing that popped up in normal conversation. But then, when had her life ever been normal? *Maybe I should try to keep my secret after all.*

Eager for her date to begin, she sprinted back toward the house to freshen up. Water splashed all over the mirror as she rinsed her face and brushed her teeth. She picked up a towel to wipe it clean, and saw her reflection. Her eyes seemed brighter, somehow, her smile wider, all thanks to Jeremy. She realized with a start that she looked like a woman in love. The thought made her grin.

Emilie rushed, in a hurry to see him, so she grabbed the first outfit her hands reached. A blue-print Oscar de la Renta sundress hung on a hanger that dangled over her door, along with the rest of the dry-cleaned and freshly washed clothes. She pulled it over her head, smoothed it over her body, and zipped the back, then pulled on a fresh pair of panties that she snatched from her drawer. She hopped as she slipped on a pair of satin Manolo Blahnik flats. Ready and excited to see Jeremy again, she dashed out of the house.

Exactly thirty minutes after the call, Emilie sat in the passenger seat of Jeremy's truck as they headed toward Germantown, a small city east of Memphis.

"I thought we could eat Italian. I found a cute little family-owned restaurant in the historic part of Germantown. Funny, let's have Italian in Germantown."

She glanced over at his smiling side profile. Jeremy kept his eyes on the road as he drove. He was handsome in his casual way, dressed in dark indigo jeans and wearing a green dress shirt and matching satin basket-weave tie, topped off with a slim-cut dark Moleskin sport jacket.

"That sounds perfect," she said.

He smiled. "It's your soft Southern twang that's perfect."

CHAPTER FIFTEEN

They arrived at the quaint restaurant, located in the historic section of town. A dozen or so tables were scattered in the space, the lights soft. A whisper of Italian music created an intimate atmosphere. They ordered lasagna Bolognese from a simple menu and a good red California wine. Plumes of garlic and herbs floated from the kitchen each time a waiter opened the swinging door.

Jeremy did most of the talking about the project he worked on, but the light conversation about the events of their day didn't last long. Soon, a silence strained Emilie's anxiety, and butterflies whirled in her stomach with each glance she stole. She noticed Jeremy raise his head a few times as if about to talk, then lower it back down, until finally he spoke his mind.

"I notice you're preoccupied tonight," he said, breaking the lull. "We've only been talking about my day. Conversations about migrating ospreys, headcutting and floodplains, it's not that interesting." He smiled. "What's on your mind? I'd be flattered if you decided to trust me."

He leaned across the table, his face inches from hers, and whispered, "Tell me your secrets, Emilie."

Emilie's face warmed, flustered. She could construe his meaning in many ways. She had tried to conceal herself, yet he read her so well. He knew she was keeping something from him, ultimately, his honesty compelled her to be truthful, too.

"I really don't know what to say. I'd rather not get into my family's deep dark secret, I'm afraid I'll scare you off." She smiled, trying to make light of things. Jeremy pulled his head back just a tad, continuing to watch her. *He's not convinced.*

"Well, if you don't trust me with your deepest thoughts, I suppose I'll have to live with that, but I am here to listen if you need me."

Emilie struggled internally. He sounded disappointed and hopeful at the same time, as if he was daring her to have faith in him. *Should I share my secrets or not?* She swallowed hard.

"This will sound insane, trust me, I know. I wouldn't even believe it myself . . . except I do believe it, because I've always sensed it, you know, felt that something was just...wrong." She pulled up short, her face flaming. Jeremy continued to watch her, a faint hint of amusement in his eyes, but more compassionate than any she'd glimpsed before. She took a deep breath.

"My family is cursed," she said. "Well, not me, don't worry. But supposedly the male members of my family are cursed. Any woman they marry dies young."

"It sounds like the women they marry are the cursed ones, then," he said, smiling.

"Exactly." She fidgeted, pulling her hair behind her ears and tugging at the strands. He was watching her so she stopped, dropping her hands to her lap. Did he think it endearing, or was it revealing? Jeremy was reading her again.

"There must be more to the story than that," he said. "More than just this strange curse that kills young women." The look in his eye told her that the curse was still unreal to him, a fairytale.

"Here's the whole story," she said. She took a moment to sort through the facts, the reality of her world and how it tied to the de Gourgues legacy. "Someone is extorting money from my father, selling him information about this curse that has been plaguing our family for generations, hell, centuries. It may be the reason my mother died, and it really has my father shaken up. My brother Robert is acting strange, too. You met Robert, the one you saved me from having an argument with last night."

Jeremy tilted his head to one side, processing what she said.

"You don't believe in any of this, do you?" she asked.

"Emilie, I don't get it. You sound like you're worried about a curse, but there's no such thing. Right? I wonder what my Uncle Thaddeus would think. He loved a good mystery. Give me the whole story, because I really want to understand what's bothering you. And I don't mean to be disrespectful, but if your brother ever raises his voice to you like that again, well . . ." He stopped and caught himself before finishing the sentence. "He has no right to speak to you in that tone," he finished.

"Well, this is what I know," she said, quelling butterflies stirred by his protective display. "A stranger visited my father and I'm pretty sure he's extorting money from him in return for the information, though I never witnessed it. He gave my father information about our family curse, and our long history of unexplained deaths. The women who married into our family died very young, usually shortly after the wedding. It might be a coincidence, but it seems too many to disregard the claim. I checked out the history myself, and the deaths are there, no exceptions. It's a curse, Jeremy, I'm telling you, I have no other explanation."

She took another breath. Jeremy continued to listen, riveted now. "The issue now is how much all this bothers my father. He's acting crazed. You see, my mother..." She stopped. Her eyes welled. "My mother died when she was only thirty-six. I remember it like it was yesterday. It was the worst day of my life."

She lowered her head and tried to push away the memory of the last words she had said to her mother, while sitting beside her on the hospital bed, reading a poem from the book *North of Boston* by Robert Frost.

I shall laugh the worst laugh I ever laughed.
I'm cursed. God, if I don't believe I'm cursed.

Emilie swallowed back her grief. She had known her mother's agony, and in that last moment, she experienced her mother's surrender as her spirit left her body. That horrific vision of her mother, all the life and strength drained from her limp body, remained with her still. She hated this part of her gift the most. She had known her mother's pain all too well.

"I'm so sorry you lost your mother," Jeremy said.

He gently touched her arm. Emilie felt a goodness seep into her being, and realized his touch alone brought her back to a balanced state of mind. *He is a godsend.* She looked up to meet his eyes and continued, hoping he'd be able to accept this bizarre family situation.

"This stranger showed my father legitimate documents and an ancient book, really more of an old journal of some kind. They met behind closed doors, as if hiding a deep dark secret. The whole thing is creepy. How's that for family secrets?" She wiped the corners of her eyes. "I told my brother and sister about the stranger and the curse, too. Michelle and Robert don't believe in it either, but that's why Michelle and I went to New Orleans, to visit someone who knew about the legend of a curse. This old woman said curses aren't real, but she spoke of an old magic potion and a legend handed down through generations. I want to believe she's right and there are no curses, but I just know it's there. I can feel it."

"What do you mean, you feel it?" he asked.

Emilie's face burned. She closed her eyes, wishing she hadn't said so much. "I sense things," she slowly admitted.

Jeremy stared straight ahead, his eyes blank, as if his mind had wandered to a different place. She chastised herself for telling him the truth about her gift. A plate dropped in another corner of the room. Jeremy flinched, and then wiped his mouth with his napkin. Emilie sensed he was gathering his thoughts, after being far away for a moment. *This whole conversation is freaking him out,* she thought.

"Emilie, I'm sorry this scandal is upsetting you and your family. I'm not sure if there's such a thing as a curse, but I am sorry that it brings back bad memories of your mother's death. Who is this person scamming money from your father? Do you know his name?"

Emilie didn't know why he asked or what he was thinking, but he definitely seemed concerned. Considering how much she'd already told him, it seemed pointless to hold anything back now. "His name is Pierce, a Mr. Hugh Pierce."

Jeremy choked on a sip of water and coughed a second, his face gone pale.

"Hugh Pierce, you're sure?" he said. They exchanged a searching regard. "You're not going to believe this, but I'm looking for this man."

Jeremy reached across the table and took Emilie's hands in his. "Hugh Pierce robbed my Great Uncle Thaddeus, and caused him to have a heart attack. My uncle died, and I vowed at his grave to find this man, and retrieve the book he stole. Uncle Thad said the old journal was essential to solve a mystery about a death in our family. That had been his goal in life, he called it his 'little mystery.' I took this project to be here in Memphis, so I could track Hugh Pierce down. "

Jeremy exhaled and slumped back in his chair. He looked relieved of a burden that he had carried all the way from Surrey. Somehow it all made perfect sense to Emilie: they were on the same quest, their paths intertwined. She understood now, fate had brought them together to help each other.

"Jeremy, an ancient book was delivered to my father. That man, Pierce, must have stolen it. Let me describe it for you, it was definitely very old. Worn at the edges and the spine was tattered. The pages were fragile, made of old parchment and written in a French script. I was afraid to open it. The pages almost fell from the dried binding."

Swallowing hard, she remembered the shock she'd felt when she'd touched the pages with the evil-faced drawings. She decided not to share that with Jeremy. It would only confuse things. "I remember hieroglyphic designs on some of the pages," she added.

Jeremy leaned forward again. "Tell me, Em, did the inside front cover have a blue mark drawn?"

"Yes, an insignia in a blue ink or dye of some sort."

Jeremy knocked on the table. "That sounds exactly like the journal stolen from my Uncle Thaddeus."

He sat back, placed his hands behind his head, and closed his eyes for a moment. He was thinking, or letting it all soak in, and Emilie hoped he was able to process all this. Most people found it difficult to absorb these bizarre things, but for Emilie it was too easy. Her life had been one big freak show.

"Today I was looking for the book in my father's library," she said. "It's linked to this curse somehow, and I want to translate it. I stopped searching, though, when I got spooked."

Jeremy covered her hands with his. "What could be worse than a curse? What scared you?"

Suddenly she was aware of her clammy skin. This was it, the moment of truth. If she told Jeremy any more of this crap, he may fly out the door and never look back. This was the final test. How much faith did she have in fate? Determined to trust her instincts, she cleared her throat and went for it.

"On a shelf in my father's library there is a hex bag. It scares the hell out of me, I don't like Voodoo stuff around the house, it's just freaky. But I was the one who went to get it, with a family friend."

"Why do you need a hex bag for your father?"

"I was told he needed its blessings to keep him safe."

They both stared at each other a moment. He didn't run away screaming, but stayed holding her hand. Reality returned when the waitperson interrupted to serve them their entrees.

For the rest of the evening, they avoided any further serious conversation. Emilie assumed Jeremy needed time to process everything. Hell, she still didn't have her head wrapped around it all, either. First her father's strange behavior, then the mysterious package being delivered, followed by a stranger fleecing money from Father, and then her brother acting out. Top that off with a warning from Mr. Labue and a legend from Miss Boniverre, followed up by chasing Voodoo bags with Father Eddie.

Each step of this puzzle seemed crazier than the last, but somehow fate had brought them together and now they were on the same path.

Emilie was determined to finish this jigsaw and end the damned curse that had thrown her entire life into a tailspin.

CHAPTER SIXTEEN

They finished dinner and left the restaurant. Jeremy drove west, to a nearby park at Shelby Farms. They parked and found a bench where they sat quietly for a while, avoiding the subject of the curse. The only sounds were the birds settling in for the night, and the cicadas beginning their nightly serenade. They watched the ducks swim on the small manmade lake, little ones squawking as they followed the momma.

Jeremy gazed down at her and said, "You belong outside with the flowers and trees, you smell so sweet and clean, like a fresh summer breeze carrying a jasmine current."

Emilie smiled. She hadn't heard sweet words in a long time, and he said them with a purity she rarely felt from people. Jeremy pinched a strand of her hair and froze for a moment. Then he traced the profile of her face with the back of his hand, barely touching. Her skin tingled at the slight contact, and she shivered. He wrapped his arms around her and snuggled her close to his chest. Emilie breathed in his scent, saltiness from his sweat, mixed with a subtle herbal hint of thyme.

Bending his face to hers, he gently kissed her lips. His mouth was moist and warm. She melted, lost all thoughts of anything else except his presence, and kissed him back but with more vigor. She soaked in the heat from his body. She raised her hand to his chest; it felt muscled and firm. She reflected how wonderful it was that he had such a strong body, not being a stranger to work, yet could be so gentle when he touched her.

"Please, take me to your hotel. I want to be with you Jeremy," she whispered.

Jeremy pulled back, and caught his breath. "We have something special, we both feel it, but I don't want to be too forward, too soon. Part of me says wait, but the other part wants you, right now, too." He kissed her again, this time with more urgency. "I don't care. I want to be with you, too."

Emilie kissed him back, then got up from the bench and walked toward the truck, pulling his hand. They didn't speak on the drive to the hotel. The silence was charged with anticipation. Emilie watched as if disconnected from the physical world. The streets flew by her window as they headed downtown. Jeremy parked the truck in the hotel garage, got out, and went around to open her door for her. They walked through the back entrance's glass doors and headed for the bank of elevators with brass doors.

"Staying at the Peabody, my, you are special," Emilie said. She smiled, giving the most seductive look she could muster. It had been a long time since she'd had sex, but it was like riding a bike, right?

Jeremy shrugged. "The project must get a special deal."

He took her hand in his, and pushed the floor button with the other. Emilie's stomach swirled as the elevator rose. A bell tinkled and the doors opened. They exited the elevator and walked down the long dimly lit hallway to his room. Jeremy took the key card from his jacket pocket, but before he could use it, Emilie grabbed his hand and reached up on her tiptoes. She kissed him, pressing her lips firmly against his, then using her tongue, traced his upper lip. He smiled, and she felt his immediate response, his body hard beneath his jeans. He leaned into her until her back was against the wall.

Emilie reached out and held him tight around his waist, reaching to kiss him again. He returned her intensity and slipped his hand up to her breast, giving her a gentle squeeze. Emilie's nipples hardened from his touch. Her entire body tensed and yet relaxed at the same time. Then she heard a click and realized Jeremy had slid the card in the lock, and opened the door to the room with his foot. A sudden sense of danger clouded her thoughts.

"Stop, Jeremy. I think someone is in there."

He turned toward her, his eyes questioning.

"I have the same feeling I did when the stranger was in with my father. I think someone's in your room."

"Why would anyone be in my room? Emilie, don't worry so much. Watch, we'll go in slowly and you'll see, the room will be empty."

The door swung open and they looked in. Light from the street filtered in through closed sheer drapes, casting a seductive ambiance in the room. Jeremy took a few steps past the threshold and raised his arms. "See, nothing to worry about." The soft light hit Jeremy's face, playing with his contours and dimples. Emilie followed him into the room.

"Hello, Mr. Laughton."

Jeremy jumped. "Who the hell are you?"

Emilie was confused and looked at Jeremy, his jawline clenched. She looked over to the far corner of the room, still dark. Sitting in a chair in the shadows of the room sat a motionless man.

"I said who the hell are you? Emilie, call 911." Jeremy moved toward him. The man switched on the table light and stood, still not saying anything.

"It's you," Jeremy said. "Bloody hell, what are you doing here? Speak!" His face burned red.

Emilie turned and recognized Mr. Pierce, then remembered she was supposed to be calling for help. She picked up the phone on the bedside table. The front desk responded.

"Peabody, front desk. How can I help you?"

"I heard you were looking for me, Mr. Laughton. Put down the phone. I want to chat."

Emilie looked over her shoulder and saw Pierce had a small handgun pointed at Jeremy. She said into the phone, "Sorry, my mistake." She hung up the receiver. "Why are you here, Mr. Pierce?"

"I am here to speak with Mr. Laughton, not you, Miss de Gourgues."

"Well, whatever you want to say to me, say it now, spill," Jeremy said angrily.

"All I want to say is stop looking for me. If you don't stop your hunt, I will file a complaint of harassment," Pierce said.

Jeremy shook his head. "You've got some nerve. I know you're the one who robbed my uncle's place. You killed him! And I intend to make you pay."

"You have no proof," the man said smugly. "There is no proof. So keep your distance or you will be the one arrested. Consider yourself warned."

In a flash, Jeremy lunged forward and wrestled Pierce to the floor, overpowering him. He knocked the gun from Pierce's hold, and it flung to the floor. He then immobilized Pierce by wrapping his arm around the man's neck, his forearm pressed to Pierce's throat. The small handgun had landed a few feet away, and Emilie snapped it up.

"Call the desk again. Tell them there's an intruder."

Emilie backed up to the phone and dialed the front desk once more. This time when they answered, she blurted out, "Get someone up to room 505, there's an intruder and we need help."

Pierce didn't struggle, but Jeremy refused to loosen his hold as he pulled him off the floor.

"You will regret this," Mr. Pierce said. "I won't be detained long, and then you will see me again."

His threats sent shivers up Emilie's spine, and she wondered what else was going on. She knew there was no reason for him to be so concerned about her family. Someone else had to be paying this guy, someone with a twisted agenda.

"Who sent you here, Mr. Pierce? Who are you working for? Is it my brother?" Emilie held the gun toward him. The man just sneered. The door opened.

"Drop the gun," a security guard said when he'd taken in the scene, his gun trained on Emilie.

Emilie threw the pistol on the bed.

"Not her, this is the guy."

Jeremy shoved Mr. Pierce toward the security guards and then walked around the bed and hugged Emilie. "It's all right. Everything will be okay."

The night dragged on. Questions were answered, and forms were filled out and signed once the police arrived. They took Hugh Pierce away in cuffs, but his threat still rang in the back of Emilie's mind. She realized someone was going to pay the bail and set him free, and Jeremy and she would need to track him again. The threat unnerved her.

"Jeremy, can I still stay here with you? I don't want to go home," she said.

"You never have to ask. You can stay with me as long as you want, no strings attached."

They stripped to their underclothes, then cuddled under the sheets. Jeremy held her in his arms and gave her a gentle kiss, then closed his eyes as Emilie closed hers. She fell into a deep and needed slumber.

Emilie's morning began with tenderness as she and Jeremy woke up together.

"Please, go ahead and shower first," Jeremy said. He kissed her head, but her phone rang before she could go anywhere.

"You go first and I'll take this call."

He rolled off the bed and retreated to the bathroom as Emilie answered her phone. A boisterous voice echoed on the line.

"Hey, Em. What do you want to talk about? Did something happen?"

It was her sister. "Hi, you. What do you mean, what are you talking about?"

"You left a text message yesterday, remember? So, big sister, what's up? You need my advice on what?"

Emilie smiled to herself. "I called yesterday because I felt some mojo from a hex bag sitting on Father's bookshelf. I didn't know what to do about it, but today I don't think I care. I'm so happy that I can't be bothered with it all."

"Wow. Okay, what's really up? You sound different. You sound happy. Oh my God, you got laid!"

Michelle, always a quick thinker. "No, I haven't. Not yet anyway," she amended, blushing.

"Listen, I can't talk right now. He's in the bathroom and he might hear me talking about him. I'll call you later."

"Just tell me who," Michelle pressed.

"Remember the man across the room at the Bombay Club?" Emilie whispered.

"No way, Mr. Gorgeous! I told you he was staring at you. He's hot for you, Em. How did you meet? Did he follow you to Memphis? He's not a stalker, is he?"

"Slow down, Michelle. He's not a stalker, there's not a bad idea in his head. Believe it or not, it's just a coincidence. I guess it's a small world after all, or else it's just fate."

"Well, I don't believe in fate, but I know you can feel these things, so I wish you the best. Keep me updated, okay? No going off doing anything stupid," Michelle said.

"Did I hear you right? You actually acknowledged that I can feel other people's emotions?"

They laughed and Emilie promised to call her sister later.

Her head whirled. So much to do, so much to sort out. All these new feelings were happening so fast, yet it seemed like she had known Jeremy forever. Finally, she was happy. They worked well together, and they were definitely physically drawn to each other, too. Last night proved at least that much, before they'd been so rudely interrupted. She couldn't imagine what it would be like when they were able to actually consummate their growing attraction.

When Jeremy came out of the bathroom, she was proud of herself for resisting the sight of him with only a towel wrapped around his lean hips. Determined to remain focused for just a bit longer, she took her turn in the shower and got dressed. From the hotel, they went to a cafe for coffee.

Jeremy handed Emilie her tall hazelnut with cream. "Careful, it's hot."

Emilie blew the steam away from her face, watching Jeremy as he added two sugars. "Sweet tooth?" she asked.

He only smiled as he stirred his coffee. "I think we need to put our heads together regarding this curse business," he said.

Emilie took a sip, but it was still too hot. She looked around. It seemed eerily quiet for a Starbucks in the morning.

"Yes, our common quest is quite the mystery to unravel."

"Emilie, I did a background check on our friend, Pierce. The man was originally from New Orleans, and he has a long arrest history. Promise you'll use caution if that man shows up again at the house or office."

She recognized the concern in his eyes, and smiled. "I will, don't worry. Listen, I've been thinking," she said. "Someone from Memphis must have hired Pierce to steal the book, but I'm stumped about the why. We need to find out who's behind this scheme. I have a hunch there's a bigger agenda going on here. Someone wants my family to suffer. It's not money they're after, it seems more about my father's emotional state. Bringing the journal forward made the curse feel too real for him, and dropped him into a deep depression. He's reliving my mother's death."

Tears stung the corners of her eyes. Emilie quickly wiped them away. Jeremy reached over and took her hands in his. "Who would have a reason to torment your father? A business rival, perhaps?"

Emilie hung her head. She let go of his hands and wrapped her hair behind her ears.

"It seems more like a personal grudge and assault, not a fiscal trap. Listen, the journal is safely stuffed away in my father's library, somewhere. How about you come over for dinner tonight, and after everyone is asleep we'll find it. Then we can translate the journal. I'm betting we can get some insight about this curse there."

"And then we'll plan a course of action to end the curse, and hopefully add charges against Hugh Pierce, too. I want him arrested and out of the picture for good. Retribution so my uncle can rest in peace, as well."

Not long after, Jeremy dropped Emilie off at the house. He kissed her gently goodbye, and promised they'd meet later in the evening. Emilie rushed up to her room as soon as he was gone and got ready for work. Nina wasn't at the house yet. Pleased she didn't have to answer any uncomfortable questions, Emilie knew it would be impossible to disguise her true feelings from the family this time...especially Nina.

Emilie was ecstatic to finally have someone in her life. For so long her soul had been in a pit so deep, she thought she had fallen into oblivion. Everything was different with Jeremy in her life.

"Snap out of it, girl," she said to herself aloud.

She changed and left for work, content to be alive and in love, but in the back of her mind she wondered if she was fooling herself. *Can I remain this happy while a black cloud haunts my family? When will the rug be pulled out from under me?*

CHAPTER SEVENTEEN

Emilie engrossed herself in her work, hoping to finish things early.

"You never came home last night."

Her stomach flipped, startled by Robert's stealthy entrance. He stood beside her desk, looming over her.

"Were you out with your knight in shining armor last night?"

"I don't know who you mean. And even if I did, it's none of your business, Robert," she snapped.

She looked away, irritated by his smirk. Besides that, she was still upset over the tone he'd used during their last confrontation. She'd planned on simply avoiding him.

"You know who I mean, that rather protective man who broke up our little disagreement the other night. I bet you were with him."

He rested his fists on the edge of her desk and leaned forward to get her attention. Emilie looked up and met his stare.

"I am happy for you, Emilie, really, but please be careful. According to Evans, your friend returns to England soon. I don't want you getting attached to the guy only to be hurt when he leaves. Of course, I doubt you'd listen to my warnings."

The split-second thought of losing Jeremy scared her. She hadn't considered the idea of him going back to Guilford. She closed her eyes for a moment, and his smiling face flashed before her. There was nothing to worry about and she forced herself to stay calm; they'd make it work, somehow.

"No," Robert continued. "Even after you assured me you would only have fun in New Orleans, I find out you decided to play detective, and dragged Michelle into it, too."

Robert's voice pitched louder with each word.

"Did you have us followed?" she said.

"What are you talking about? Why would I do that? Emilie, seriously, let's not encourage Father. Please, stay out of this curse business, for everyone's sake."

Robert straightened, glaring down at her. Emilie watched his brooding face and decided that he was not going to sway her into retreat, not today. She stood and scowled back at him.

"Listen, Robert, I know you don't believe in the curse, but Father does. This Mr. Pierce is extorting more than money from Father. Pierce is torturing him. He agonizes over Mother's death and blames himself, I feel it. I imagined that the information from Miss Boniverre could help explain it to him, and then maybe he'd realize that Mother's death wasn't his fault. We were both there, and saw how sick she was; it had nothing to do with him. I had hoped you would be the one to talk sense into the old man."

Robert stood there, quiet for the moment, darkness infusing his spirit. Petrified by the hate exuding from him, she froze. Her throat tightened as she watched his face change. For a moment, Emilie didn't recognize her own brother. His emotions were like the raw jagged rocks of a northern shore, and his soul cold, like icy waters. A shiver trickled down her back.

"Emilie, you think Father is a poor lonely soul just pining away for Mother, but he's not what he seems. There isn't a warm sentiment in the man, he's coldhearted, and deserves to feel some pain regarding Mother. She was a wonderful woman and loved us all. How did he reward her? With deceit! You think you know him, but you don't. I am glad if he feels some pain, he deserves it, for God's sake!"

"You're not making any sense, Robert, what are you talking about?" she demanded.

"Let's say that you and I agree that Father believes in the curse. My concern is the same as yours, but for different reasons. I don't want our family extorted, but please, spare me with the compassion for Father, okay? You're trying to find the reason behind the curse, well, it will only make things worse. Just stay out of this business, Emilie, like I asked. It doesn't concern you."

Robert spun around and, without saying another word, headed for the door. His fists clenched tight with his flaring rage. The room rattled when he slammed the door on his way out.

Emilie sat back in her chair and closed her eyes, trying to shut out all the hurt from the venom that spewed from her brother. His words were so harsh. Then out of nowhere, a picture flashed in her mind of the strange man who'd spied on her and Michelle in New Orleans. *Maybe Robert did have us followed.* Her heart sank.

Robert's return to Memphis had been a ruse of some sort, and he was definitely not here to help Father. He obviously despised him. She wondered about Robert's agenda, and his ulterior motive in returning. The happy family she'd envisioned for them all melted in front of her eyes, washed away with her tears. At least she had her sister, she consoled herself. And now Jeremy, too. *To hell with my brother!* Still, deep inside, Emilie wanted Robert to be happy.

CHAPTER EIGHTEEN

Jeremy and Emilie had planned to meet at the house for dinner. She arrived home early and went straight to the kitchen to tell Nina there would be a special person joining them, and to set an extra place. Nina wrapped her arms around Emilie and squeezed her tight.

"I am happy for you, Miss Emilie," she whispered. When Emilie left the room to go upstairs to wash and change, she knew Nina was smiling, glad for the excuse to make something special.

Emilie had never brought a man home before. She couldn't deny that she was nervous, not that she cared about Robert's opinion of late. Still, she couldn't help but want her family's blessing. She breezed downstairs to the parlor and took up a post at the front window, staring outside. Another sunset revealed shades of peach and salmon against the darkening blue sky. A moment later, she saw Jeremy's truck blaze up the driveway. Her pulse raced, and her entire body heated. She met him outside on the porch.

"Hello, beautiful."

He smiled, leaned down, and placed a gentle kiss on her lips. She responded in kind, and Jeremy pulled himself away.

"I've been thinking of you all day," she said.

"Me too. I'm crazy about you, Emilie. I daydreamed all day about your warm eyes." He looked into her eyes with want.

Her face grew hot as she blushed. "You should consider writing poetry."

"Oh, here, I almost forgot." Jeremy handed her a bouquet of wildflowers he'd been holding behind his back. Daisies and lilies tied together with a soft ribbon.

"Thank you. They're wild and perfect."

He smiled. "I picked them near the edge of the woods."

The grandfather clock in the hall chimed eight. Emilie tugged Jeremy to follow her. "Time for dinner. Hope you're hungry."

They strolled into the dining room and found Pierre pacing alongside the Louis XV mahogany buffet, a Krieger design topped with Carrara marble. Her father's appearance was sophisticated and refined, blending with the décor, but his eyes seemed vacant. Emilie felt a twinge of anxiety.

"Father, I'd like you to meet my friend, Jeremy."

Pierre looked across the room. *A miracle, there's life in his keen eyes.* Happy to see that flicker of intelligence in her father's face again, she hoped he was finally feeling better. Pierre assessed Jeremy from head to toe, making a meticulous and quick judgment of the younger man. Without pageantry, he acknowledged Emilie's guest.

"It is nice to meet you, Jeremy. Welcome."

That was the extent of the conversation. After that, Pierre seemed to lose his energy, and his attention wandered elsewhere. Emilie turned and started a conversation with Jeremy, hoping he hadn't noticed her father's strange detachment. It seemed lately that her family embarrassed her more than not.

She and Jeremy stood off to the side, deep in conversation and just beginning to relax, when a loud clang echoed through the dining room. A silver chafing dish cover had fallen to the floor, landing on the hard wood, and spun like a top. Nina bent to pick up the lid, mumbling to herself. The noise had drawn father's attention back to the others in the room; up until then, he might as well have been on another planet.

"I hope you all enjoy your dinner," Nina said. "I made something special."

"It smells delicious," Robert said as he entered the room. "Nina darlin', your food tastes like it came straight from heaven."

"Well, you're always callin' me an angel, hon. Guess this just proves it," Nina said. She laughed as she left the room.

"Emilie, have you introduced Jeremy to Robert yet?" their father asked.

"Yes, Father," Emilie assured him. "They were introduced the other day by Evans."

"Great, great. Good to see you made it home from the office, Robert." Pierre leaned on the arm of his chair and then sat slowly, looking a bit dazed. He picked up a serving dish and lethargically filled his plate, one spoonful at a time, with careful navigation. Emilie ate in silence, watching her father raise his fork as if every move was a great effort. She traded glances with Robert, and wondered if her brother even cared that Father appeared so peculiar. She decided not to make a fuss, but instead extended an olive branch.

"So, Robert, are you familiar with the project Jeremy is working on?"

"Yes, I am aware of the work. Evans gave me a heads-up. Glad you were able to travel all this way to work on the project, Jeremy. Tell me, will it be lengthy? How long will we have the pleasure of your company?"

Emilie dropped her fork, and it fell to her plate with a clatter. Robert smirked at her, well aware that his comment could cause problems. *Why is he such a bastard lately?* Nina entered the room with more food, fussing over Jeremy before he had time to respond.

"Jeremy, I hope you like how I spiced up the food tonight," she said. "If you don't like it hot, just let me know, and I can bring you something else. I wuz told you English like your food bland."

Jeremy smiled, his hand flying up to cover his mouth before he laughed aloud.

"Who on this great earth told you that?" Emilie said.

"Thank you, and this is delicious as is, I assure you. I like a little spice and you're a great cook. Thank you for your kindness, Nina," Jeremy said.

"I like this one, Miss Emilie. He has manners and charm. " She smiled and left with a few last words. "You all eat up, and enjoy your evening."

Robert called out, "Bye, Nina. See you tomorrow. Don't wait up for me, I have cat business again tonight."

They heard Nina laughing as she walked away. Robert smiled at his joke. They ate in silence after that, everyone stealing side glances at one another. Only the ticking of the grandfather clock in the hallway and the scraping of silverware against the china plates could be heard.

Pierre seemed to be functioning better, now that he had food in his system. Emilie gave herself permission to stop worrying; she was determined to have a nice evening with Jeremy.

After dinner, Father excused himself and retreated to his library, closing the doors. The others went to the parlor, where Robert played host.

"Would you like a drink?" her brother asked her and Jeremy.

"Yes, thank you. Whatever you're having is fine," Jeremy said.

He was so carefree, a trait that Emilie found endearing. Robert seemed irked with Jeremy's mood but he lingered regardless, pelting him with impertinent questions.

"So, Jeremy, are you married? Any kids running around we should know about?" Robert smiled mischievously.

"No, Robert, but thanks for asking," Jeremy replied, unruffled. "I'm just a single guy in Surrey, that's in England." He smiled, and for a second Emilie thought he'd burst out laughing. "I've lived there my entire life, along with my parents and siblings. A sister and brother, just like you and Emilie and your sister. I travel with my job, but I suppose someday I'll settle down. Most likely very soon. Maybe even get a dog."

Jeremy winked at Emilie.

"So then, you're serious about my sister." Robert stated it as fact.

"I am," he said simply. The look in his eye told Emilie everything she needed to know about just how serious.

Robert grunted. "Wow. You certainly are sure of yourself, or maybe I should say full of yourself? So, what about you, Em? Are you serious about this Englishman? Remember he has no French in him, and you hardly know the man."

Emilie felt her face heat. Robert loved taunting people, but lately he went over the line. "Sorry to disappoint you, Robert, but I'm not some schoolgirl. I like Jeremy. He likes me. The rest of it is frankly none of your business."

Emilie looked into Jeremy's eyes while she spoke. They both knew her words only touched the surface of what they felt for each other. Smiling, she looked back to Robert. He wore that stoic face that she couldn't interpret.

"What? Aren't you happy for me, Rob?"

He stood in place, swirling his drink. Turning his attention, he acknowledged her and cleared his throat. "I'm very happy for you, Em. It's just so sudden. You two only just met, but clearly you're both adults, and know your own minds. If you're happy, I'm glad for you. Just let me know when you're ready for something permanent, so I can prepare myself."

He walked over to Emilie and kissed her on her cheek. He turned and took a few steps, and then led the conversation in an entirely new direction.

"I have some news for you, too. I was going to wait until Michelle was home, but Lord knows when that will be. Anyway, since we're all sharing our feelings this evening, I want you to know I plan to propose to Rachael. I trust you two can keep it secret for now."

Emilie was too stunned to speak. Just then the clock chimed nine o'clock.

"Well, congratulations," Jeremy said awkwardly.

He walked over to Robert and put out his hand to shake. Robert looked down at his hand and waited a moment, then slowly extended his.

"Congratulations, Robert," Emilie said. Her voice sounded feeble. "Rachael is a wonderful person. I haven't seen her in years. When can we get together? "

"Very soon," Robert said.

"You'll tell her about our family history, won't you? So she's aware of the potential problem."

Robert laughed aloud. "Emilie, I don't believe in any curse, so there's no point. This will show your precious father that there is no such thing, and everything will be just fine."

He put his glass down on the table, smiling. He gave his sister another kiss, this time on her forehead, then tapped the tip of her nose playfully.

"It was nice talking with you, Jeremy. I have to run now, Rachael is waiting. Please remember, secret for now, understood? See you two later."

Robert whistled as he left. After he was gone, Emilie sat for a moment, shocked at the news. Jeremy sat beside her on the sofa. She turned her attention back to him.

"Do you think it's sincere? My brother isn't exactly the marrying type. Rachael is beautiful, but not exactly the match I envisioned for Robert. What do you think?"

"Maybe she's exactly what he needs. Maybe he wants to settle down. I am happy for him, and frankly, rather glad I'm not the center of his attention right now."

He smiled. She had to look away, otherwise all her concentration would be lost.

"What if he knows something? What if he believes in the curse, just like Father believes?"

Jeremy grabbed her hands and held them to his chest. "What if the sky falls? Are you crazy, Em? Of course he doesn't believe in it. No one in their right mind would believe in it."

He leaned closer and looked into her eyes. "You don't seriously believe in a real curse, do you? I considered maybe it was just a legend, like the story that old woman told you." He paused, considering everything she'd said. "If he doesn't truly love Rachael and want to marry her, what could possibly be an ulterior motive for your brother, anyway?"

Honesty had become the precedent for them since their first conversation, Emilie wasn't about to change that now. "I know there is a curse, I feel it all around here," she said. "And if the curse is real, that means Rachael will die if they marry. This sounds awful, I know, but if she died then Robert would be far wealthier than he is now. Her family comes from a long line of mega-millionaires." She paused again as she considered her own words.

"Robert isn't exactly hurting for money, though," she continued. "Maybe he just wants to make our father squirm over the idea of Rachael dying from the curse? He is so angry. You should have heard him this afternoon, he sounded like he hated Father. If Robert wants Father to suffer...but I don't understand the reason why he would."

Emilie dropped her head in defeat. Jeremy's brow rose in surprise at the proposed scenarios. "That would be cruel and hateful. Do you think he's truly that spiteful?"

A few moments lapsed as she deliberated the question, but she couldn't see anyone being that evil.

"We need to get that journal," Jeremy said suddenly. "We need to finish my uncle's work and translate the contents. Then we can figure out this mysterious legend of the family curse. Are you with me?"

"Absolutely. Let's get it from my father's library tonight after everyone is in bed."

CHAPTER NINETEEN

The clock struck midnight. Father had retired hours ago. Robert had returned to the house and gone up to his room. A dimmed lamp in the front hall that always remained on through the night was the only light. The house was silent except for the occasional tapping, as the walls cooled in the damp spring night. Emilie and Jeremy snuck into the library.

They slipped in quietly and closed the doors behind them. The floor squeaked. Emilie froze. Her heart was beating like a racehorse in the last lap. They listened, but no one roused. Jeremy turned on the flashlight in his phone and shined it toward Pierre's antique desk. The gold leafing reflected in the small beam. Emilie pointed up to the bookcase behind it. Right there in plain sight was the gris-gris bag.

"Look, there's the hex bag," she whispered.

"Don't touch it," Jeremy replied. "Let's just find the journal before someone wakes up, okay?"

They turned their attention to the other shelves. Scrutinizing the case, they found the journal on the very top. Jeremy was tall enough that he could simply reach up and grab it, bringing it down to the desk with care. It was heavy, and the book landed with a thump. They both went still for another second before Jeremy opened the brittle pages.

Emilie noticed he was holding his breath. The crackling of the page sounded like dried leaves brushed up against pavement in the wind, reminding her of how fragile and important this book was. On the inside cover was the blue-inked insignia that Jeremy had asked about. She pointed to it and he nodded. He slowly turned the pages. They were written in faint script, dulled with time, and the sketched images had horrific faces of distorted animals.

Her nerves caved, buried in the intense anguish that emanated from the drawings. She lost her breath for a moment and pulled her arms inward, hugging her body. Dizzy, she wanted to regain control before the feeling consumed her. Emilie closed her eyes and concentrated. She pushed the agony away and shielded her mind.

A moment later, she opened her eyes. She had forgotten how powerful the images were. Jeremy hadn't noticed her episode, too engrossed in the book. Relieved, she joined his inspection of the pages.

"What did your uncle uncover so far in the translations?" she asked him. "Did he tell you what he knew about the journal?"

Jeremy tilted his head in reverence for his uncle, then answered.

"He showed me this very book the day he died, but he didn't tell me much. Only that it's a story about French seamen, some Florida tribe, and ancient ceremonies that somehow related to his aunt. Thaddeus had fond memories of her from when he was a child. She died shortly after she married and left home. The entire family was upset. I believe Uncle Thad was no more than ten or so when she died, so that means it was the late 1930s or early 1940s."

A lump lodged in Emilie's throat. When her mother died, she had only been ten, too. She understood only too well the effect death had on someone so young.

"Uncle Thad stumbled across a reference in this journal to the family that his aunt had married into. That's why he said it held the answers to his quest. He was convinced that she died under mysterious circumstances. I can remember all my life his searching for clues and answers. I loved the old man. He was supportive of me and believed in me when no one else did. And I believed in him, I was the only one who paid any attention to his stories. That's why he left all his treasures to me, I suppose."

Jeremy cleared his throat, caught up in his emotions. "I remember the day he died, he was so excited. I can still see his face all lit up because of this journal. At the pub he was almost dancing." Jeremy smiled while recalling his memories. "That's when I noticed that Mr. Pierce gawking at us. I knew then he was bad news."

He tapped the book gently with his pointing finger. "Thad said he'd had a breakthrough, and I know this book was it. Unfortunately, it isn't translated, but I am hoping that together, we can discover the meaning behind it all."

Emilie put her hand on his shoulder. "It sounds like Thaddeus was a real character. A caring person too, to never forget your great great aunt." He nodded, and she continued in a whisper. "Jeremy, when the old woman in New Orleans told us the story about the old magic spell that linked the destiny of two men's spirits, she was talking about a tribe chief and a great sea captain. Maybe it is connected to the tribe you said was mentioned in this journal?"

She reasoned for a moment, still working something out in her head.

"And another weird thing, the women in my father's family all died young, just like your aunt. You said she died at a young age after marriage. How young? Your uncle's story sounds like my family's curse. My mother and the rest all died young, too young. Maybe they're connected somehow. Maybe your great great aunt married one of my ancestors?"

Emilie envisioned the puzzle coming together.

"Her name was Rose Riley," Jeremy said. "I have to be honest, I don't remember the name of the family she married into, and I'm not sure of her age at the time, just that she was young and had just been married."

Emilie felt the blood rush through her body in her excitement. "Hold on!" she said.

Jeremy moved his finger to his mouth suddenly, a shadow crossing his face. He hushed her to be quiet, then pointed to the door. There was a thump in the hallway.

Her pulse raced even faster. She squeezed his arm, then turned to look at Jeremy, his eyes large and alert. He turned off his phone light and they crouched down behind the desk, motionless for a moment. Someone was on the other side of the door. They waited a few seconds, listening. There was a click as someone opened the door, and then a moment later, it closed. All was quiet. Then there was a noise again: the swishing of slippers dragging on the wood floor on the other side of the door. Soon, the sleepwalker's steps faded away.

It took several more moments with Emilie's heart racing, acutely aware of the warmth of Jeremy's body beside her, before she remembered what she'd been thinking before they were interrupted.

"Jeremy, about your aunt, well, I remember a mention of a Rose in my family history. I saw the name when researching last week, doing an ancestry search. Let's go to my room. We can match up our information, and see if they're connected. Do you think your Great Great Aunt Rose died because she married one of my ancestors?"

Jeremy didn't answer. He closed the book and held it tight to his body as they headed out of the room. Emilie opened the doors slowly and peeked out. The hall was empty. They scuttled up the stairs. Closing her bedroom door, she leaned against it and exhaled. Jeremy smiled, his free arm hugged around her shoulder.

"I could crack all kinds of jokes right now, rushing me up into your bedroom like this. You devil." His dimples sunk deep as his smile spread. "But, I am too interested in where this aunt business is heading. I can't even think about having my way with you right now, well, okay, I'm thinking of it a little, but not too much."

He laughed low and intimately. Emilie took the book, blushing. "Not now, Mr. Sexpot. But hang on to that thought."

She hurried to the desk and opened her laptop. She searched for the folder containing the information from the family-tree web service. Emilie considered the possibilities and smiled.

The keypad softly tapped under Emilie's fingertips. Jeremy stood by her side as his gaze roamed the room. Her family was indeed wealthy, not just slightly wealthy, but old-money-and-a-great-deal-of-it wealthy.

The room revealed much with its original vintage decor. There were gold-gilt frames on the artwork decorating the walls. He recognized some as original Impressionist masterpieces, including a Monet and Degas, right here in her bedroom.

The Memphis he'd experienced so far had been littered with a host of McMansions owned by newly wealthy Southerners: local corporate executives from major businesses who flaunted their money with large brick estates that sported high ceilings, crown molding, pools with outdoor kitchens flanked by designer lawns and gardens.

The de Gourgues home was different. The house was older, set apart from the neighbors in the newer estates. Jeremy hadn't contemplated the implication until now.

He was hit suddenly by the same feeling he'd had as a boy wearing last year's track shoes while his well-off friends flaunted their newest trainers in the locker room. *Who am I trying to kid?* He was in love with an heiress, and what could he offer her? No wonder Robert was concerned.

Emilie jumped in her seat, pulling him from his trance and back to the computer.

"Here, look, this is what I mean," she called out. "There was a Rose Riley who married my Great Great Grandfather de Gourgues. They were only married for a short time. Looks like it adds up to only two weeks by the dates, and then she died. He later married again, and had one child. That would have been my great grandfather. Look, it's all here on this family-tree diagram. Your uncle's little mystery about Aunt Rose is right here."

She pointed to a spot on the screen, her fair skin paling even further. "It's all connected to this curse that was placed on my family. Oh my God, Jeremy, it's true. The curse is real, and it's touched both our families."

She looked up at Jeremy with tears in her eyes, and he saw the terror there. For the first time, he considered the de

Gourgues curse as something other than a fantasy dreamed up by this strange yet wonderful woman who'd so quickly captured his heart. *What if it is real?* He felt a deep need to take her pain away, and stop the curse. Uncle Thaddeus had certainly thought enough of the whole business, he'd spent his entire life searching for an answer. And if the curse was real and Emilie's brother planned to marry, soon there would be another casualty.

"Jeremy, we have to finish this. We have to decipher this book," she said.

He took a deep breath, reconciling his opinions. "You read my mind."

Now that he was considering the idea of the curse being real, the imminent danger of their situation became clear for the first time. Emilie reached up and traced the side of his face with her finger, and his skin tingled from her soft touch. She frowned as she touched his forehead, now wrinkled with worry.

Jeremy watched her eyes and saw the moxie there. There was no way he could keep her from pursuing the curse, it would never happen. It was too important, and Emilie wanted to finish this no matter what he thought or said. The best he could hope was to go along with her. If they investigated this together, then maybe he could keep her safe.

"Listen, Em, please don't take this the wrong way, but this could be dangerous. I think—"

"Don't tell me to stay out of this," she interrupted, showing her first bit of temper. "Not when it concerns my family."

Jeremy smiled, shaking his head. *I was right, she won't step out of this.* "No, that's not what I was going to say, Emilie. I know you're in this until the end. What I'm really concerned about is your brother. I hope you don't take this the wrong way, I know he's your family and I hardly know him but, Em, I don't trust him. I'm afraid that if he knows about this book and that we're translating it... Well, I am afraid for your safety. I'm not sure why, but there's no doubt there's something off about Robert in all this."

She gave a heavy sigh, her shoulders slumped. "I know, you're right. I'm concerned too, that's why this engagement business is bizarre to me. I'm worried for Rachael. I don't want her to be hurt by him, and I surely don't want her to be cursed."

He noticed how she weakened with the truth about her brother. It was hard to accept ugly truths about loved ones, he knew. They gradually steered the conversation in other directions, and he sat with her through the night discussing their next move. They planned to go to the local university library, where Emilie could translate the old French script with dictionaries and resources nearby. Then, they would research its history in the anthropology department and find out more about the tribe. It was a beginning to search for the end.

Emilie yawned. "Excuse me."

Jeremy looked at his watch. It was nearly two in the morning, time to leave.

"I think that's my cue. Someone needs her beauty sleep, though if you get much more beautiful, I won't be held accountable for my actions."

She smiled, her cheeks coloring lightly. "I guess I am a little tired." She hesitated. "I don't... I mean, I don't want you to leave. Even though we haven't known each other for long, I like being with you. It's not about sex, we're both tired so clearly it wouldn't be . . ." She stopped, blushing more deeply now.

Jeremy thought he'd never seen anything quite so endearing.

"I'm babbling. I just wondered . . ."

"If I'd stay with you tonight?" he asked. He stepped forward, brushing a hand down her cheek. "Beautiful Emilie, you never have to ask if I want to stay. Give me a few days, and you'll need to beg me to leave."

Tired after the roller coaster of emotions, they fell asleep in Emilie's bed, embracing each other contently. As they lay in each other's arms and dreamed, again it all felt so right. Jeremy couldn't remember why he'd had any doubts. They loved each other.

Something dangerous was happening, and he prepared himself to be there to protect Emilie, no matter what.

CHAPTER TWENTY

The next morning, they went to the university library to translate the journal. Emilie had doubts about her ability to capture the true meaning of the old text but tried her best, hoping the reference materials nearby would assist her efforts. They spent half the day working on the interpretation, and uncovered substantial revelations.

They monopolized the library table, littered with reference books and dictionaries. Emilie tugged at her dark strands, twisting them around with her fingers as she read the journal and conferred with the reference books. She let the information soak into her mind, and then wrote everything into a simple black spiral notebook. Her worst fears were real: the curse truly had come from that ceremony. This was a new state of weird for her, worse than anything else that had ever invaded Emilie's mind. Something was creeping into their lives, trying to end her family, and it had to be stopped.

The author of the journal had given a fanciful account, revealing the events with color and authenticity. The captain had interacted with the local natives, and parlayed with Saturiwa, the Timucua chief. They'd exchanged gifts and come to some agreements. Shortly thereafter, they fought against the Spanish soldiers, their common enemy, together. A celebration and a spiritual ceremony had taken place before the battle. The journal described the event, and how the two men's spirits were unified.

They both drank from a shell filled with the white tea, which caused them to sweat profusely and vomit, releasing the sickness that spouted from their mouths, and their souls were cleansed. A circle was drawn in the sand, and magical carved idols in the shapes of a panther and owl were placed in the center of the circle.

The tribe believed gods from the spirit world could possess the soul through these idols, known as zemi. They drank a second tea, stronger and more powerful.

The Captain trembled and spoke in a strange language, surely he was possessed. The Timucua Chief held out a sharp knife and spoke loudly in unknown words. The other warriors were now silent, heads bowed. The Chief took the knife and sliced a small wound on his forearm and dripped his blood into a bowl carved in wood that sat in the center of the circle on the ground. The Chief did the same to Captain de Gourgues, slicing his arm and with a firm hold, he squeezed the Captain's blood so it dripped into the same bowl. Saturiwa added the other tea to the mix and created a potion. Like a witch or shaman priest, he took the bowl from the ground and raised it above his head, speaking loudly in some unearthly language.

The clouds covered the moon and stretched the darkness across the sky. The night was eerie and quiet. Then the Chief and the Captain both took turns drinking of the potion. Once the Captain took the drink, he gagged and held his hands to his throat as if he was choking. His eyes grew large and he exploded with pain. His entire body contorted as if he were changing his form. Then the clouds separated and the full moon shone on the Captain and Chief, casting a shadow of their image on the ground. The sky became illuminated as bolts of a lightning storm, appearing from nowhere, chased the shadows.

The Captain fell to the ground moaning with a strange sound I had never heard before - it was a growling, monstrous voice, deep, guttural pangs. He sounded like a strange new kind of wild animal, or was this the Devil's voice spewing from his body?

The Chief chanted, and then pulled the Captain to his feet. The two men embraced. All the warriors stood and cheered loudly. The night sky returned to normal. Everyone became serious again, preparing for the next day's travel and attack against the Spanish.

The Chief shouted these words: "Our spirits pledged their lives to each other."

Jeremy read over her shoulder, raising his eyebrows.

"I'm trying hard to picture this all in my head," he said.

"And it's hard for me to decide whether the author of the journal was embellishing the events out of his own fear," she said. "It's apparent that the two men's spirits joined in an alliance of some kind. This could well be the beginning of the curse."

Jeremy put the pages down and listened to her explanation.

"I think that somehow the pledge of two warriors turned into a curse and has followed the de Gourgues lineage since," she said. "Jeremy, this ceremony happened, that's a reality, and I think that it either created or warped into this curse all those years ago. Do you believe in it now?"

Jeremy picked the papers up again, shaking his head. "I don't know what to think. I've never heard of anything like this before. I wish my Uncle Thaddeus was here so I could ask him his opinion, he was the historian, not me. I do know that the Church believes in possessions and strange things, supernatural things, that can happen, but this? I wonder if something this supernatural exists in a context that we can even try to end."

"Let's go visit my friend in the anthropology department," Emilie suggested. "Maybe he can shed some light on this bizarre story. Maybe there is a scientific explanation." After a second she added, "So that means we're both Catholic?"

"Yes, I guess we both are. Most English are Protestant, but my family held on to our Catholicism. My mother's side, the Rileys, are originally from Ireland and definitely Catholic." He pondered for a moment. "Do you by chance know a priest in the area who might be knowledgeable about this kind of thing? It's not the usual subject that comes up in conversation, but maybe one of the locals could help us at least determine if this could be real, on the spiritual level, I mean. The Church must know about curses."

She smiled. Father Eddie immediately came to mind, and she knew he could illuminate more about the curse. He did after all know all about the Voodoo in New Orleans, so why not curses, too?

"It's getting late. How about I visit my friend Steve, in the anthropology department, and you go to the rectory of my church and ask to speak with Father Eddie? This way we can get more done. I'll just call to make sure he's available, but I'm sure he'll make time."

"Sounds like a plan."

He gave her a gentle kiss and they both left in different directions.

CHAPTER TWENTY-ONE

Jeremy drove to the address Emilie had given him and parked his truck in front of the church. He took a moment to appreciate the warm day and the beautiful, late-afternoon sunshine. He wasn't used to so many sunny days in a row. He got out and climbed the porch steps of the rectory, then rang the doorbell. He was greeted by a proper-looking woman, her attire plain and businesslike, her hair pulled back neatly. She had a pleasant smile and a soft Southern voice.

"Can I help you, young man?"

"Yes, thank you. I'm here on behalf of Emilie de Gourgues, my name is Jeremy Laughton. I believe Emile called Father Eddie. He should be expecting me."

An instant smile crossed the woman's face at the mention of Emilie. "Yes, yes of course. Why didn't you say so? Please come in. I'll let the Reverend know you're here."

Jeremy waited for Father Eddie in the front hall, which reminded him of his youthful days in Jesuit school. Images of waiting in line at the confessional crowded his mind. He wondered if the third degree he should have gotten from Emilie's father would be in store for him now, delivered by her priest instead. He straightened out his khaki pants and tucked in his golf shirt, then paced uneasily. Moments later, Father Eddie entered the room.

The Reverend was a formidable-looking character, a big man who could have passed for a mobster if not for his collar. The priest held out his hand in greeting. Swallowing hard, Jeremy willed himself not to sweat. He reached his hand out and met the older man's grip.

"Hello, Mr. Laughton," Father Eddie said with a smile.

Jeremy realized right then why Father Eddie was Emilie's favorite priest. His voice sounded of benevolence. "Good afternoon, Father, thank you for seeing me without notice."

Eddie chuckled. "I've been waiting to meet you. My friend, Pierre, mentioned you to me. I hear you're a special friend to our Miss Emilie. I am a little surprised she's not with you today."

Father Eddie escorted Jeremy through the first floor to a nice breezy screened porch in the back of the house. The woman who had answered the door brought out a tray with cold sweet tea and homemade pastries.

"So you Englishmen like tea, right? Does it matter if it's cold?"

He motioned for Jeremy to be seated and, still smiling, handed him a cold glass of sweet tea. The condensation on the glass dripped and Jeremy grabbed a napkin. He sat back in the chair and tried to get comfortable. To him, sweet tea wasn't the same as real tea at all, but only an excuse for a sugar rush. He sipped the drink anyway, and aimed to be sociable.

"So what brings you here today, Mr. Laughton? Emilie didn't give any details, just mentioned you'd be stopping by. What can I do for you?"

Father Eddie smiled attentively as he waited for Jeremy to answer. Jeremy wiggled uncomfortably in his seat, still not completely at ease with his task.

"To be honest, I'm not certain how to begin. First, I realize how much Emilie's family means to her, and you may have gathered that I've become very fond of Emilie in the short time that we've known each other."

He paused. The depth of what he felt for her, in fact, still surprised Jeremy. He wiped his forehead with the napkin. He was sweating more than usual, and not only because of the humid air. He decided to be blunt.

"Father Eddie, I am concerned for Emilie. When it comes to her family, well, she appears to bear the emotional burden of keeping them a family. I know I haven't been here long, but

I haven't seen any of them return her affections. In fact, they seem rather mean to her, and dismissive. Emilie is intuitive, and she feels their issues deeply. She worries about them all. I'm honestly concerned for her happiness."

Father Eddie's eyes widened, clearly surprised by Jeremy's candor. He sat quiet for a moment in contemplation, digesting his words.

"You're very observant, Mr. Laughton. Emilie feels the emotional burden of her family, as well as others. She always has, even as a little girl. She's brimming with empathy, a rare gift, much like her mother, who was also very gifted spiritually. You're correct about the traumatic weight she carries. I have known the family for a long time, and I see it, too.

"I knew their mother, Bethany. She was a wonderful person, so full of life and pure of heart. When she died, a big part of Pierre died too, and the children . . . well, they were traumatized, of course. But Emilie, she's the only one who stayed near her father. She appreciated his pain and wanted desperately to reach his heart. Now that Robert has come home, she's trying to mend bridges between her father and brother. I'm not sure if her endeavor is even possible."

Father Eddie sipped his drink and took a moment to think. Jeremy could tell he was choosing his words carefully, wanting to express something important.

"A broken heart can never be perfectly mended, there are always scars," Eddie said in a soft voice, as if revealing a secret. "That is what Emilie will have to accept one day." He smiled. "I am hopeful for her future now that she has a friend like you, though, Jeremy. I can see that you'll be very good for her. Like Pierre, her father, you respect the Church and I can see that you believe in love, but I think that's where your likeness ends. The possibilities for you both are infinite, if you uphold your faith together."

Jeremy felt a renewed confidence, now that a priest had validated his feelings.

"Thank you, Father. I want to be there for Emilie and I think we could have a great future together, but right now there is something holding her back and she needs time to work her way through. I hope you understand."

"Yes, I do," Eddie said.

A few quiet moments passed as they sipped the tea. Jeremy shifted nervously, uncomfortable in his chair, thinking about the curse and wondering how he should broach that bizarre topic with a priest.

"This is great tea, Father. I hope you don't mind, but I'd like to talk to you about something else, too. I'm not sure how to say this."

"You haven't had a problem so far, young man. Start from the beginning. That's always best."

Jeremy jumped in, allowing the pieces to fall where they would. "Emilie and I are working on this project of sorts. Not really a project, well you see, it started with my uncle. He had acquired an ancient journal, that's why Emilie's not here. She's translating it now, it was written in French and it's dated back to the 1560s and is a little difficult to read due to its age. Sorry, I digress."

He laughed at himself. "At any rate, this journal describes a special ceremony performed back in 1565. It seems probable that this ceremony may have turned into a curse of some sort, and that curse is now hanging over the de Gourgues family."

Jeremy noticed the look on Eddie's face, and stopped talking. *Is he shocked?* No, his expression is more like fear. The priest's eyes stared off, dazed, and his skin was chalk white.

"Father, are you all right?"

Jeremy's face burned, embarrassed that he had said such a preposterous thing to a priest. Father Eddie turned to Jeremy and studied his face. *He must think I'm crazy.*

"I know about the book. What exactly does it say about the curse? I need to know everything."

Instantly, he was relieved when he heard the priest's interest. Now he could talk about all of this with Father Eddie openly. Memories of his Uncle Thaddeus surfaced, and he wondered what Thad would have done with the translation.

Jeremy explained everything they had uncovered so far about the ceremony that took place and the supposed crossing into the spirit world. He told the story as best he could, and mentioned the wooden carved idols used as talismans. Father Eddie listened, fixated.

"Emilie's father is my good friend," Eddie said. "Pierre came to me and asked for my help when that stranger, Pierce, came to him extorting money for information." He took a deep breath, and hung his head as he exhaled.

"I'm afraid this whole situation is a bit too real for me. Some of my parishioners in my old parish, St Bernard's . . . well, they still practice Voodoo. Despite my attempts to lure them away from it, they speak of the curses. I'm ashamed to say that I was the one who opened the door to the possibility of the supernatural, and asked for their help. I had no choice, I needed to protect Pierre somehow. Being a man of faith, I should never have given credence to such superstitious beliefs, but this curse business scares the hell out of me."

Jeremy noticed Father Eddie held onto the chained cross that adorned his neck, rubbing the crucifix with his thumb.

"The Church believes in possession and evil spirits, so I figured why not curses too? These poor women's souls were cursed, only because they loved their own husbands. Their marriages were sanctioned in the Church's sacrament, yet the Church had no protection for them. Curses will devour a person's soul if not stopped."

Jeremy struggled to understand. Deep down he had hoped that a priest would have grounded them somehow, but Father Eddie encouraged this vein of speculation. "Father Eddie, you're a scholar, how can you leap to this extreme?"

Beads of sweat covered Eddie's brow. "My friend, the human mind can create reality, when something is believed in the heart. I am questioning my own beliefs here too, and pray for spiritual guidance. I need to confirm whether or not this is a curse, and if so, it must end now. Years have passed since the death of Emilie's mother, but it's still very raw for me, too. We can't allow this to continue now that we are aware of its existence."

Morbid sadness filled the silence. Jeremy didn't know what to say or do.

"Robert will be facing this lethal legacy someday," Eddie continued. "If we can fix this, then he'll be able to marry Rachael without concern for her premature demise. I owe the family that much, as their friend and servant."

Just at that moment, a much-needed cool breeze swept through the porch. The screens rippled as the wind skimmed the surface. Jeremy relaxed, sinking into the porch chair cushion. He was thankful he had met with the Reverend. Now there was someone else working with them on their quest. Father Eddie clearly wanted to help, and if he believed in this too, then maybe they weren't crazy after all.

"Jeremy, let me explain some of the rituals that members in my previous congregation shared with me. When it comes to curses, they're usually broken with a counter-spell, or a strong gris-gris. But this is not just an ordinary spell we're talking about. It was a bond in the spirit world, a pledge. In this situation, the best thing we can do is make sure that all the parties involved with the spell or curse are gone. I mean completely gone." He sliced his hands through the air.

Jeremy was bewildered again. "Father, they are gone. They died centuries ago."

"Ah, yes they're dead, but maybe we need to burn the bones or what's left of them anyway. Maybe the threat is still here in this world because of the wooden idols. If the effigies you mentioned that were used in the ceremony are gone, maybe it will erase the curse, which may still cling to the objects associated with it."

"So, you think that will work? All we need to do is destroy the bones and idols? It sounds so . . . so . . . so . . . ."

"So morbid?" Eddie finished. "Yes, I think it is too, but that is all that's left of them in this world. If all elements of them are expunged, then maybe the curse will uproot also . . .

It's the only possible solution I've been able to think of, so far."

Jeremy considered the idea. Memories sprang to mind of old movies he'd watched as a kid, where cursed mummies and zombies raged in a frenzy against prospectors digging for artifacts around them. The idea bothered Jeremy, but he had no alternative plan to pitch, so he agreed to go along with the one Eddie proposed. Still, he couldn't help but wonder if the priest might have swampland in Florida to sell, too.

"Very well, Father Eddie, you've sold me. It sounds like the idea has farfetched possibilities. First we'll figure out where the chief was buried, and then the captain. Then if we can locate the wooden idols used, maybe we can end this madness for good. We have a lot more research to do, but Emilie and I will get cracking. I certainly miss my Uncle Thaddeus, now more than ever."

"There's just one more thing. Please don't spill a word of this to Robert."

"Not a problem, Father. I don't trust him anyway."

CHAPTER TWENTY-TWO

Emilie carefully wrapped the old book, gathered her research, and headed for Manning Hall, which housed the anthropology department on campus. At the front desk, she signed in and asked for her friend and old classmate, Steve, to be paged. Recently bestowed the title of professor, Steve worked on the third floor, home to the research area. He had completed casework on digs and was considered a national authority in Mayan writings.

Steve entered the reception area, greeting Emilie warmly. He towered over her, and wrapped his long arm around her with a hug, sporting a wide smile that complemented his large dark eyes. He had the body of a basketball player but had always claimed he hated the sport.

"Oh my Lord, look who's gracing us with her presence. It's been ages. How have you been, Miss Emilie?"

"I'm great, thanks. I hear you're engaged these days. Congrats."

"You know I had no choice, since you won't have me," he laughed. He teased with his familiar Southern drawl, just like always. The sight of him brought back warm memories of their college years together, study groups that rolled into late-night talks over wine and beer.

"Seriously, I'm happy, Emilie. My girl loves to go on digs, too. I know you'll love her too." He beamed.

"Soon we'll get together, I promise. But no time for fraternizing now, I need your expertise. A friend of mine owns a precious artifact. It's a book, and we need to decipher some designs and drawings. I hoped you might have some insight."

"No problem. It sounds intriguing."

They moved up to his office, taking the elevator. Emilie placed her bag down and carefully slid the book onto his desk, then reverently unwrapped it. Steve stared, mesmerized.

"This book is in pretty good condition," he said.

He snapped on some rubber gloves and carefully touched the volume, rambling on about possible tests for the page material and inks, to verify an exact date when it had been penned. As he examined the artifact, Emilie conveyed some of the story she had translated from the text in the journal.

"So, do you know anything about the journal's subject? And check out the drawings," she said.

"The true Timucua language and culture are extinct," he said, "so there's no real way to know anything for certain. The early Europeans tried to document what they observed, but there's a strong chance they misinterpreted much of what they witnessed because they didn't understand the language well."

Steve scratched his head, deep in thought. Emilie noticed the mood in the room changing; a covetous emotion radiated from him. Even someone as down to earth as Steve could be tempted by the possibility of notoriety.

"Here is the interesting part, as far as I'm concerned," he said. "There's a theory that the Timucua tribe traded with tribes from the West Indies, and that they were heavily influenced by them. They imitated some of the same ceremonial drinks and customs. You see, there were many trade routes among various tribes before the Europeans colonized the area. Recent theorists in the anthropological world speculate the Timucua tribe had customs that actually originated in South America and worked their way north to the Florida region. Just leave the book with me for a bit, and I'll see what I can uncover, this may prove to be the link that could substantiate that theory. This is a significant piece of evidence."

Emilie held up her hand.

"Let's not get ahead of ourselves, Steve. I just need some help understanding these hieroglyphics. Look at these drawings. I think they may be demonstrating something about a ceremony the Timucua performed."

Emilie pointed out the pages of the journal with the drawings and showed him her notes translating the ceremony.

"Very interesting," Steve said. "It sounds like a ceremony practiced by the Arawak, a Caribbean tribe. There are still descendants left, living up in the hills, where they fled to survive invasions centuries ago."

"I interviewed a woman who spoke of a legend involving the Timucua, and she mentioned the Arawak tribe in her story. Supposedly they traveled to meet with Saturiwa, a Chief of the Timucua," she said.

Steve's face glowed with enthusiasm. "This stuff is my specialty. The Arawak were a very spiritual tribe, and believed in many earthly gods. They were known for their deadly brewed tea, using the cassava, a toxic plant that produces cyanide. Some of the Arawak were enslaved by the Europeans, and many decided to use this potion to commit suicide." Steve's words came faster in his excitement. "They preferred death over life as slaves. Can't say I blame them. Anyway, they thought they'd finally be at peace in their version of heaven. They also believed people could be possessed by these brewed potions and enter the spirit world. But chances were, anyone who took this concoction would die and never come back."

He took a deep breath and stared at the book again. Emilie grew concerned about his emotional craving to keep it and considered leaving, but she still needed more of his insight. She continued, reading to him the translations about the use of the wooden idols in the hope that he had some insight to offer.

"Some artifacts that have been discovered near ancient middens resemble animals," he told her. "A common theory is that Timucua people believed owls signified evil. If they used the owl and the panther as idols during the ceremony, then there was probably an evil element to it. The panther would have represented cunning strength. It sounds like the French had no clue what the tribe was really up to, and the whole ordeal probably distressed them quite a bit. Religious people of the day totally feared black magic. If they were truly horrified by this ceremony, they may have believed they were being cursed. They may have brought the bad luck to themselves, through their own magnified imaginations."

"You mean by believing they were cursed they actually caused the curse?"

"I just mean the power of suggestion is great." He smiled down at her.

She felt better; his covetous mood seemed to have lifted. Steve bent for a closer look at the hieroglyphics on the page, using a small magnifying glass to scrutinize details.

"I've seen something like this before. These drawings are pretty basic representations of animals," he said. He pointed to one in particular, the one that spooked Emilie the most.

"This drawing here is like a summons to the gods. You need to imagine this from their perspective: they were a polytheistic society, they believed in all kinds of gods. These designs were probably traced in the sand on the ground, an altar of sorts, to help summon those gods. The ceremony was most likely to forge a bond, calling to the spirit of the animals to intervene on their behalf. The author of the journal was just documenting what he saw drawn in the sand, and then he jumped to his own conclusions."

Steve carefully turned the pages. His face brightened with each new revelation.

"The owl was considered bad luck, so I don't understand why it was used. To see the two together in a ceremony is unique. I wonder if this ceremony was some type of deception. Maybe they didn't trust the French and wanted them bound to them, like they were trying to control them by casting this spell."

The idea made too much sense to Emilie. "Do you think this spell was real, and that Captain de Gourgues and the

Chief Saturiwa were joined as one spirit, and linked to each other's survival? Is it possible?"

Steve looked away and pondered, deep in thought, before he answered. "I do believe it's possible. You have to remember, these people were close to nature, and very superstitious. They may have had some kind of extrasensory perception that we no longer utilize today. Yes, I think it was possible then . . . and there's no question that they believed it was."

Emilie was amazed that the one person she regarded as the most rational and scientific could believe in a curse. She knew firsthand about extrasensory perception, frankly, most days she wished she could just shut it off. Steve read aloud some of her translation:

They uttered words mere men were incapable of understanding. We witnessed our Captain become possessed by a demon. His fiendish voice called out as if he were a wounded animal. The wooden effigies dropped into the center of the circle, and glowed from hell fires. Silence swallowed us, even the frogs of the swamp and the cicada of the trees were still in the void. What was this trickery? There was some kind of black magic being done this night. The Chief bellowed words. What happened here I can only guess, but surely such a supernatural occurrence cannot be blessed. We witnessed something from the spirit world, and I pray my God will forgive me for exposing myself to such blasphemy.

"Emilie, this was serious stuff here, and probably some of the best documentation we can hope to find on this tribe. I really want to keep this book here and study it more thoroughly."

He was smiling, but an alarm went off in her head once more; his words grated against her better judgment. Emilie covered the book with her hands protectively.

"Sorry, Steve, I told you, this is my friend's personal property. It can't be shared with anyone, not yet."

He took a step back, surprised by her defensiveness. "Sorry, it's just that it should really be handled properly."

Her pulse raced, her heart pounding. "You need to keep this a secret. Promise me, Steve. No one can know about this yet. My family's future is at stake."

"Whoa, hold on Emilie," he said.

"I'm serious. No one. Once my friend decides what to do with it, we'll let you know, I promise. I'm certain he'll be happy for you to verify the journal's authenticity, and of course give you the credit, but not until it's time."

Steve looked down at the floor, but Emilie could still feel his disappointment. It was all very confusing and seemed far too real.

"I am going to keep bothering you about this, you know," he said, "and I want to meet this friend of yours."

His voice sounded intimidating. *Time to go.* Emilie gathered the journal and her notes in a rush. The room grew stuffy; she felt claustrophobic. She needed to get out of there.

"Goodbye for now, Steve. I have to go." Emilie hurried out the door and called over her shoulder, "I promise to be in touch soon."

Once in the corridor, she pushed the button for the elevator. As she stood there waiting, feeling she was being watched. She looked both ways, but didn't see anyone. Her frustration mounted. She couldn't wait for the lift any longer. She turned, pulled open the door and took the stairs, scrambling down three flights in the narrow stairwell. The walls seemed to cave in around her, and she was nearly panic-stricken by the time she reached the ground floor. She needed air. Another strange feeling assaulted her as she burst through the door into the front hall entrance. She took deep breaths.

Feeling shadowed, she turned to look down the hallway. Behind her, she saw the same man she'd noticed in the trolley back in New Orleans. Ordinary-looking enough, yet something about him was wrong. *No, it can't be him, it must be a coincidence.* She turned to the front doors and bolted from the building. He followed. *Is someone after me, or is it the book they want? Who is he?* Gasping, she sprinted with a new sense of urgency toward the street.

She realized going to Steve had been a mistake; someone might try to convince him to talk about the book. Suddenly, she felt guilty for putting her old friend in such a precarious situation.

Jeremy pulled his truck up to the curb just as Emilie barreled out of the building. She saw him parked and ran, jumping into his truck. "Hurry. Let's go," she said. "I think someone followed me." She had her hand on her chest, gasping for breath.

"Are you all right?" he said.

"Yes, just get us away from here."

He pulled away from the curb and drove off.

"Sorry, it might have been my imagination, but I thought someone was following me. Maybe I'm just tired, but I'm not sure why, it's just that things are getting scary."

Jeremy drove back to his hotel, keeping his eyes on the road. Emilie noticed his face twitch, his jaw tightened.

"Do you think your brother had you followed?" he said.

"I sincerely hope not. If he did, I have no clue why." Emilie didn't say anything about it being the same man who had shadowed her in New Orleans. She didn't want to add to Jeremy's worries, particularly when she wasn't really sure whether it was the same guy or not. Besides, they needed to focus on their next step.

They arrived at the hotel and Jeremy unlocked the door. Emilie was still in emergency mode and pushed past him, then dropped her bundle of paperwork on the desk. Oblivious to her surroundings, the information she'd gathered from Steve ran through her mind.

"Em, listen to me," Jeremy urged.

She turned when he snapped his fingers.

"Earth to Emilie," he said.

She smiled despite herself.

"Listen to me," he continued. "Father Eddie believes in this curse business, too. He thinks our best chance to get rid of this thing is to totally eliminate every trace of the two men and the idols." He ran his fingers through his hair, and paced while speaking. "That means we need to burn their remains, or rather their bones, until nothing is left, if there are any bones to be found. We need to destroy the wooden effigies, too."

She wondered once more how a priest could believe in Voodoo and curses, but after everything she'd experienced with Father Eddie in New Orleans, she didn't question it. Emilie stood up and blocked Jeremy's pacing. He stopped. She gazed into his eyes, searching to see if he really believed all this mess now.

"Eddie's idea is better than no plan at all," she said. "I agree the effigies definitely need to be destroyed."

"Yes, well that's all fine, but we have a lot of research to get on with to discover their resting spots."

She returned to the desk, pulled back her hair, and twisted it into a ponytail, thinking faster than she spoke. "Then let's get to work. We'll start the fire and burn the bones!" She laughed.

Jeremy shook in agreement, biting his lower lip.

"Most important of all, though, we need to destroy that wooden owl," she said. "I have a feeling it was the channel that infused the ceremony with evil."

CHAPTER TWENTY-THREE

Emilie and Jeremy spent the next few days clearing their desks and workload, even into the weekend, with spare time spent exploring the possible burial sites. Emilie promised to keep it to herself, and Jeremy had no one to share the plans with except Father Eddie. They used Jeremy's hotel room as a place to work, and he switched his room a few times, being careful just in case someone decided to break in again or maybe plant a bug while they went out for food and coffee, they had become that paranoid, and were taking no chances. The Peabody Hotel was very accommodating after the episode with Mr. Pierce, and Jeremy got a questioning eye only once.

Tuesday evening, barely a week after being officially introduced to Emilie, the two worked together in his room. Jeremy sat at the table, with many books scattered about, which he used to research the possible burial locations. He was jotting down important information in his laptop. He stopped for a moment and rubbed his tired, itching eyes, then raised his head and gazed over at Emilie. She sat on his bed with a book in her hand. Her long legs were folded, knees bent to support the thick volume. He watched as she did that habit of hers, twisting her hair. She always played with her stray strands, or pulled her hair back when she was nervous. Jeremy loved watching her. He smiled to himself, remembering it was exactly one week since he'd interrupted her argument with Robert.

True, he hadn't known her long, yet he was comfortable in her company, as if they had been friends since birth. They worked well together, too. He enjoyed the quiet company as they sat in his room reading, sharing pertinent information that they stumbled across. She inspired him, but at the same time tested his patience. She seemed bent on saving the world, which was endearing, but also meant he had to share her attention. He wasn't sure where this quest was leading them, but he knew he wanted to be there with her, and protect her. Drawn to her, he hated that such a beautiful woman was plagued with so much negativity in her life. With that contemplation, he felt the need to say something.

"Em," he said.

She looked up from the page she had been reading. "Yes?"

"With all this secrecy going on, well... I know you love your brother and the rest of your family...but I don't trust Robert. What can we do to keep him from finding out what we're doing?"

"Don't worry about him. I've been careful when he's around," she said.

"Then what's the story you'll be giving him once we start our trek?" Jeremy pursued.

"I've got a great, spur-of-the-moment vacation planned. Didn't you know?" She laughed.

He smiled, captured by her eyes. When she was happy, her face lit up and her eyes enlivened, like a spirited child looking at the world in awe. He hated that there were supernatural forces in the world that took that innocence away from her. The thought brought him back to some news he'd learned earlier that day, news he knew he had to share. It might as well be now.

"Em, I know we've talked about your brother, but I'm also concerned about Mr. Pierce."

She put down her book to listen.

"He's a threat, too. I called the courthouse this morning before you arrived. It seems as soon as he was arraigned, he was out on bail, just as we feared. He paid in cash, so there's no trail to follow. Then I was told that Pierce talked his way out of the charges altogether. He had some hotshot lawyer do a backroom deal, and the man doesn't have to go back. All charges dropped. Now he's gone with the wind."

"That's not good," she said. "Don't worry, we'll find him somehow. Maybe we should hire a detective."

"Maybe, but first we have to get a handle on finding the burial sites. Look at what I configured here."

Emilie rose from the bed and joined Jeremy at the table, which was up against the window. The sunlight glared across the screen, so she bent over and pivoted the screen of the laptop until she could see it clearly. Jeremy caught a whiff of her perfume; she smelled like jasmine. It was a gentle fragrance that suited her well. He moved the books and papers, and leaned over to pull a second chair near his, for her to sit.

"Look," he said when she was seated. "I've been inputting information from the historical data available of the area where the Timucua tribe resided back in 1565. The original fort was built here, at the mouth of the May River near Jacksonville, Florida, now it's called St Johns River."

He pointed to a spot on a map. Emilie bent her head to see, and then nodded for him to continue.

"Then I added the descriptions in the journal, hoping the burial midden for Chief Saturiwa was close to the tribe's reported area. From there, I added information from these historical accounts documented by the settlers and missionaries."

Jeremy clicked a few more keys on the computer as he finished his thoughts. "I'm aware that the scenery descriptions must be significantly different from today's landscape, so here's my brilliant solution."

"What are you up to?" she said.

He was a bit nervous suddenly, and hoped this was going to work. Not just because he wanted to impress her, he honestly had no other ideas about how to locate the secret midden. That jasmine scent washed over him again, as her leg brushed against his. She had wonderful legs: long and shapely, with slender ankles and . . . *Stop!* Cursing himself internally, he cleared his throat, and continued with the subject at hand.

"It's a simulation program that I helped develop while doing contract work with Halcrow for the (NCERM) project, National Coastal Erosion Risk Mapping. Our team did the work for England and Wales. Anyway, I mapped the distinguishable points into the program, and estimated possible locations for the tribal burial site today, using an erosion reversal simulation. Look."

He pushed the last button and locations popped up in a list. He quickly reviewed them and deleted positions that were obviously not good candidates, like Tick Island, another midden had been found there already, but the location was too far south for Saturiwa's tribe.

"Now let's zero in on the best possibilities for that area, in present day. The results lead us to this refuge area here." He pointed to a map. "It's a natural preserve. The grave may still be undisturbed after all these years, since it's in a protected area."

"Wow, this is magnificent," she said. Emilie turned to face him and gave him a big smack on the lips. "You're so smart!"

Jeremy was pleased with himself, and smiled back. She kissed him again, this time on his forehead. He got another chance to smell her when she drew close, her breast at eye level as she reached up to place her warm lips on his head. His blood rushed. He ached to take her to bed and have his way with her, but he knew it wasn't the right time. There was still so much to do. Hoping that all this work would fix her problems, he resigned to drop his fantasy, and follow the lead as quickly as possible. Maybe then they could concentrate on themselves.

"Okay, I'm booking us on a flight to Jacksonville. We'll leave first thing tomorrow morning. Sorry, it's coach." Jeremy cracked a smile.

"That's fine by me. Here's hoping for the best." Emilie held up a glass of water and tapped it against his bottle of Coke. "I'll call Father Eddie, so that at least one person knows where we are."

"Good idea. He would never give our true intentions away, especially to your brother. Tell him that our story is a short vacation on the beach," he said. "I wish it wasn't just a ruse."

CHAPTER TWENTY-FOUR

Landing mid-morning, Jeremy and Emilie rushed from the gate to the rental car area. The sky overhead was vivid blue, with white clouds slowly floating with the wind. It looked too perfect to be real. Emilie reflected of how ideas were as vague as clouds, unable to be touched, but there just the same. Just like this curse that followed her lineage, it was invisible but so real.

The humidity brought a heavy feeling that slowed their every movement. They found the car, set the GPS, and Jeremy wasted no time driving to the Fort Caroline National Memorial. They visited the park, hoping to get a sense of the Timucua tribe and of what their lives and landscape had looked like in 1565. The park made a good attempt to show the history surrounding the St John River and the events involving the French Huguenots and the Spanish, but after half an hour, Jeremy and Emilie decided to move on.

The best place to begin a physical search for the burial remains of Saturiwa turned out to be Big Talbot Island State Park, according to the reverse mapping Jeremy had done. It was their best hope.

Back in the car, Jeremy drove east on Heckscher Drive toward the reserve. They enjoyed the warm moist heat of the late morning. It was impossible to be anything but positive here, the waterway views along the route and the vivid blue of the sky created a surreal setting. A feeling of peacefulness overtook Emilie. She had never felt so free, with nothing tugging at her emotions. All she sensed here were her own thoughts.

Is this what heaven is like? she wondered. Unhindered, she dreamed of her newfound happiness with Jeremy; her spirit filled with an uplifting optimism. A sensation filled her soul, like sunshine reaching the corners of a cellar after the doors had been opened to the outside air.

They arrived at the reserve. Jeremy parked and grabbed a backpack that held some needed gear from the trunk. He hurried, anxious to get going with the search. They rented a kayak. Jeremy helped Emilie into the boat and they began paddling their way through the streams and wetlands. They looked for anything resembling the landscape markers mentioned in the journal.

They lifted the oars in smooth rotations, and propelled themselves across the mirrored surface of the water, moving the kayak forward in sync with each stroke. Enjoying the tranquility of the day, comfortable in the silence, they floated downstream. Watching the sun's reflection on the water was a calming experience. The small ripples of water sent echoes of reflected light out to the extruding bank's foliage.

They assumed Bone Yard Beach was the line of oak and pine trees written of in the journal, it fit, considering the years of erosion. The older trees were weathered, taking on the look of bones bleached from the sun and salt. So far, they were confident in their direction. They paddled south past Horseshoe Creek and into the Sister's Creek area, looking for anything that might be a sign. A line of old oaks edged along the western marsh banks, their limbs bending with the breeze and their leaves gently rattling a soothing jingle. So many birds nested here along the banks, blue herons and egret fishing in the shallow waters.

For the first time in a long while, Emilie was comfortable inside herself, without being bombarded with unwanted emotions that belonged to others. Even though the day's heat was almost at its peak, the breeze off the water made it all seem comfortable and dreamlike.

Emilie spied a white ibis not too far from the other birds. She watched amazed as it carefully regarded the other birds, making sure they kept their distance. He was like Emilie, a solitary soul. Most of the birds took no notice of her and Jeremy as they paddled by, indifferent to human disturbance with so many fishermen coming to these waters. Jeremy pointed to the east bank.

Emilie's attention turned in that direction, her excitement for the chase returned. She noticed the small area of high ground that Jeremy had indicated. They paddled their way across and looked for an open spot along the shoreline. It was marshy, and what appeared to be ground was not fit to stand on, in most cases. They laughed as they clumsily maneuvered the kayak and tried to find a spot to park. Finally, they found an area worth docking.

Emilie tried to stand first, but sank into the muck. She watched as her boots disappeared, her feet swamped with mud. She pulled them out of the sludge, making a sucking noise as the pressure released. She fell back into the boat and they paddled the kayak to the next open spot. This time Jeremy tried, and narrowly escaped falling completely into the marsh waters but was saved as Emilie pulled him back toward the boat. She laughed while pulling him up, helping him steady himself. Finally, on the third try, they managed to find a small patch of solid ground, and pulled the kayak out of the water, laughing together at their clumsiness.

"Let's not try that again." Emilie said.

Jeremy's face turned red, but he laughed aloud too.

"I owe you a pair of boots," he said.

Looking around at their surroundings, the foliage consisted of mostly old oaks with some scrap palms. The soil underneath their feet became more solid as they moved toward the center of the small island, until they reached a clump of trees dead center. Here, hidden away from all of humanity and the race of everyday life, stood a pile of hardened shells, covered with creeping weeds. They had discovered a midden.

"Jeremy, do you realize what this is? I can't believe it's really here!"

Emilie was excited, but also concerned. She wondered if they were doing the right thing by destroying a midden. It was a substantial anthropological find. Land developers in

Florida had destroyed middens in the past, without thinking of the implications. Many roads, railroads, and homes had been built at history's expense. Emilie knew they should do the proper thing to maintain the site's integrity, but they had no choice. They were no better than the previous pillagers.

"First things first, let's determine if this is the spot we are looking for," Jeremy said.

"I hope this is it. It would be awful if we destroyed the midden for nothing," she said.

"Emilie, I really feel we have a chance. We did the research. Either the bones are here or they aren't, let's just look. We can always contact the authorities later so they can properly excavate the remaining site. For now, we'll be as careful as possible and work our way down one side only, the way they usually do it, to see a slice of the midden, okay? I promise to preserve the integrity of the site, just in case we're wrong."

"Okay, I'm with you. Let's do it. We really don't have a choice if we want to end the curse."

They set straight to work, hoping they were uncovering the right bones.

The two of them dug for the rest of the afternoon, silently concentrating on the work. They had hand tools with them, including various-sized trowels, picks, and bone brushes, to use to uncover the mound. The midden they'd found was small, and most of the ground underneath the creeping foliage consisted of hardened shells that formed a tight cement-like bond. It was difficult work as they carefully chipped away.

Something in the nearby foliage grabbed Jeremy's attention. Emilie watched him as he broke away from his work. He looked like an excited little boy as he reached over and picked up whatever it was on the ground that had caught his eye. Using a bristle brush, he worked on the thing in his hand, dusted it, and then rubbed it with a Bergeon polishing cloth that he pulled from his pocket. He whistled to himself.

She smiled while watching him, curious but unwilling to interrupt his magic mood.

"Emilie, close your eyes a minute," he said

She stopped working to appease him, curious about his playfulness, and closed her eyes.

"Okay, now open your hands," he said.

She did. Jeremy dropped something into her hands.

"Open your eyes."

A small, perfect spiral shell, smoothed and shined, lay on her glove.

She looked up, Jeremy beamed. Emilie started to cry. He looked confused.

"What's the matter? Is something wrong?" he said.

Emilie shook her head. "I think it's so beautiful, and you make me so happy."

She reached up for Jeremy and hugged him. This small token touched her so deeply, and she knew that right now, with him, she was the happiest she had ever been. "Thank you."

She took off her glove and wiped her eyes. "I'm sorry, I'm not crying, not really. It's just that I think you're so sweet. I love you and your tenderness," she said.

Jeremy smiled. "I'll have to remember what a red spiral giant eastern murex does for you in the future."

He laughed in a low soft voice. His face was burnt from the sun and hid his blushing, but Emilie felt his warmth anyway. She put the shell in her pocket and hoped to feel this ember of love always. She pecked a kiss on his cheek, and they got back to their task.

Working for hours in silence, they carefully excavated. They scraped away the hardened ground until the reward underneath was revealed. The bones that had been lying there for centuries, hidden from the world, were finally exposed.

"There's only one person buried here. With only one set of remains, it stands to reason they belong to Saturiwa. Only a chief was allowed their own private burial midden," Jeremy said.

He examined the bones. "Based on the indicators I remember from years of studying old bones with my uncle, and of course anatomy class, I believe these remains belong to a male. Occasionally I stumble onto old bones when I work, too. Though they usually belong to animals, not a human."

Emilie wiped her brow, and considered his words. Jeremy was right: this had been a person, a living, breathing person, a long time ago. The entire quest took on a more personal tone for her.

"This skeleton is hardened, so size and bone density can't be used to determine much, but there are other markers. Look at this sternum," he pointed to the area. "The longer thorax doesn't necessarily mean anything, but the pelvis is deep and narrow. The sciatic notch is narrow too, look here." From the pelvis, he shifted his attention to the skull. "The external occipital protuberance at the back of the head, here, is larger and more pronounced. These all point to a man."

She smiled up at Jeremy. "You are a smarty pants," she teased.

"I wouldn't go that far, but let's get back to work. I can't wait to finish this up."

Jeremy chipped a bit more away, looking for the effigy. Near the bones was a small piece of carved wood, petrified until it was as hard as rock after being in the ground all these years. They took turns with the chisel, and brushed away as much of the packed ground as possible, until it was finally exposed. The primitive design they revealed looked like a carved panther.

"This is it," Jeremy cried aloud. "We found the grave of Saturiwa and the effigy. This is priceless! My God, I can't believe we did it, we found it."

He jumped up and pulled Emilie into a hug. She swam in his happiness until a bird cawed as it flew overhead. It was an omen. They both looked up as it flew away. Emilie's attention returned to the find. She bent down and touched the panther effigy. Her fingers trembled as she examined the calcified figure, rubbing her fingertip up and down its rough ridges.

She sensed something deep and very old from this artifact. It didn't frighten her, but instead it revealed an ancient sadness. There was a story being told to her. Tears welled in her eyes as she experienced the sorrow. Her extrasensory intuition told her they were on the right path, and they needed to complete their task. Too many souls were held hostage in the spirit world. They were crying to be released, she heard them in her mind, felt their anguish.

She pulled herself away and looked up at Jeremy. His face was riddled with wrinkles that showed his concern, a question in his eyes.

"I know this panther carving is a treasured relic of their culture, but we need to burn it with the skeleton," Emilie said. "They're crying for us to end this limbo. It does have something to do with the ceremonial spell. I hate defacing all this history too, but we need to finish this properly so we end my family's curse," she said.

"Emilie, my Uncle Thaddeus searched for historical finds like this his entire life, but even he would approve of burning it, if it meant an ending to his *little mystery*."

"Then let's get this done, before we overthink things."

Jeremy cleared the rest of the area so nothing else would burn, and soaked the remains and the panther effigy with a special lighter fluid he had made himself, using an acetylene base to create a high burn temperature. He lit a match and ignited the midden. The remains burst into a tall plume of flame, and quickly blazed. The dancing flames were bright blue and white at first, and then a full spectrum of color, like the most wild of sunsets. The salt from the water and sand that had encased the midden all these years gave off a brilliant show, with exquisite shades of yellow and blue. Emilie stepped close to Jeremy and he wrapped his arm around her. Together they watched it burn.

When the blaze died down, a thick smoke began to fill the air with a pungent odor. It was a heavy sweet and earthy trace, like the incense burned in church during a funeral. The scent tugged Emilie's memories, and she visualized her mother lying dead in her coffin at church. She missed her mother so much, no matter how much time had gone by, the pain was still raw. She figured Jeremy was thinking of his Uncle Thad and feeling the same way.

It was silent, except for the occasional pop from the stones near the fire. The flames withered to a glow, then died down to embers. Deep in somber thought, she reflected on the day, relieved knowing that half their task was accomplished.

"All we need now are marshmallows," she joked.

"What are you talking about?"

"You know, marshmallows. Toasting them around the campfire. Don't you do that back in Surrey?" She teased him, hoping to lighten his mood.

"Oh, now I see what you mean. And yes, I have had my share of toasted marshmallows around a campfire, but mostly when I'm here working. Americans as a culture love campsites and marshmallows."

He laughed and affectionately tightened his grip around her. It worked, and the gravity of the moment was lightened.

"Okay, next stop France, right?" Emilie said. "Let's get back to civilization, get a room, wash up, and start planning the rest of this curse-breaking mission."

"Yes, next stop France. But before we leave, I want to pick up these ashes. I promised Father Eddie we would send them to him; he wants them just in case. I'm not sure what that means, but whatever the reason, I promised him."

"That's a strange request, but it's Eddie. Whatever makes him happy."

Exhausted, Emilie helped to clean up the midden area as much as possible. Jeremy brushed the ash remains into a metal container he had carried in the backpack. They were both covered in sweat, dirt, and soot by the time they headed back to the kayak. It was late, the sun just beginning to set. The sky in the west was splashed with a glorious orange array of color, with peach layers that painted the sky. It was spellbinding. Together they shared a few quiet moments, mesmerized by the scene in front of them. Jeremy pulled her close again.

"I love you, Emilie."

She reached up and gave him a kiss for a reply. He sighed. Emilie melted and wanted to please him, but took a deep breath instead, and pulled herself out of her fantasy. *Best left for later.* "We need to get moving before it gets dark. There's lots of critters here at night," she said.

Back in the kayak, they paddled as fast as possible, wanting to reach the park's shore before it was complete darkness.

"There are alligators and snapping turtles in these waters, and they're more active at night," Jeremy said.

Emilie wasn't afraid. Instead, she embraced the evening. "Listen, did you hear that?" she asked.

"It's fish jumping, their splashes echo," Jeremy said.

The evening air held more sounds: the occasional branch snapping, a splash as a snakebird landed atop the water, and a rustling sound from a small creature creeping through the underbrush along the nearby shore's foliage. The cicadas were a choir in the background that filled the open scape with noise. While she and Jeremy paddled and enjoyed the glorious twilight, they took comfort, sharing this wonderful vista together. It was a spiritual sharing, a harmony between them, and a bond of fate that tied them to each other.

The night sky, a miracle onto itself, just like our new love, Emilie thought.

CHAPTER TWENTY-FIVE

They were exhausted by the time they reached the hotel. The first thing Emilie wanted to do was wash up and feel human again. She dropped her things on the floor and headed for the bathroom. "Do you mind if I go first?" she said. She looked over her shoulder and noticed Jeremy was watching her. Realizing she must have looked like a disaster, her face blazed hot with embarrassment.

"No problem. Ladies are always first in my book," he flirted.

Emilie hurried into the bathroom and closed the door. She leaned against the sink, feeling a bit lightheaded, and hoped that his smile meant something. *Why would an amazing man like Jeremy be remotely attracted to me looking like this?* Still, she knew he was drawn to her, she felt his attraction, yet he still kept his distance, ever the gentleman.

It was a last-minute find, a hotel near the airport, but to her surprise, it included a newly renovated bathroom. Stripping her filthy clothes, she turned on the water and stepped into the large walk-in shower tiled with marble. She sighed with relief as the waterfall spout rained on her. She washed her hair, enjoying the thick silky lather between her fingers, and then she let the water rinse the dirt away.

The day's events spun through her head, but she kept skipping back to the vision of Jeremy and his face as he handed her that shell. His eyes, the way they gleamed with warm hazel flecks . . .

Emilie was confused. She wanted him to make love to her tonight, but at the same time, she was uncomfortable pushing him into an intimate relationship before he was ready to commit. The more she thought of him, the more urgent her need became. She kept washing the smooth suds over her body as she imagined his smiling face and his muscled body.

Suddenly she heard something. She turned down the water to a light spray and listened. Another loud thump sounded from the bedroom area. She called out. "Are you okay? Jeremy, is everything all right?" No answer.

She slid open the glass shower door. Her body tingled with goosebumps as the cold air washed across her skin. She couldn't hear anything. She called out to him again. "Jeremy. Are you okay?" She shouted, loud enough to be heard in the other room. She worried something was off. *Were we followed?* Then she heard the door squeak open, slowly. She held her breath, her heart pounding in her chest.

"Do you need something?" he said.

She jumped when she heard his voice. Her heart skipped a beat. She flung a hand to her chest and, with the other, grabbed for a towel. Her foot slipped on the soapy shower floor and she landed on her ass with a thud.

"Ouch! Dammit!" She lay naked under the running water's mist.

His eyes widened and she noticed he swiped a quick glance up and down her sprawled out body. She was mortified. Then his eyes met hers, his face red. She definitely had his attention, but not exactly how she had imagined.

"Are you okay?" He rushed to help her up, handing her a towel.

They were both in the shower, the water's gentle mist covering them. He looked into her eyes as he bent to help her. She forgot about her awkward moment and could only think of his hazel eyes, warm and inviting.

The heat between them flared. She felt his intense yearning and blushed, her cheeks hot from her own desire. Her body registered every touch, his hand on her arm, his fingers wrapped around her bicep, his thigh against hers. She swallowed her saliva.

"Yes, I'm fine now. Just embarrassed."

He smiled, but his eyes stayed riveted to her own.

"Let me help you up," he said.

He wrapped his arm around her waist and pulled her up. They stood there facing each other. The water trickled down her body as he gazed into her eyes, and the combination made her tremble. She basked in his want. Suddenly, the strength of the primal attraction they'd denied for too long, won.

"Maybe you should take off your clothes too," she said, with her best attempt at a sexy voice. "You're already wet."

Jeremy disrobed in seconds, and threw his dirty clothes on the floor. He stood in front of her, displaying all his masculinity, but still appeared conflicted.

"What's the matter?" she asked. Emilie was confused. His physical attraction was more than obvious, but something troubled him.

"I don't want to take advantage of you. You're vulnerable right now," he said.

Emilie drew in a deep breath, and met his eyes. "I'm not thinking of my family or of curses, and not worried about my gift. I am thinking only of you. We have a connection, we both feel it, there's no hiding it. Let's make it real. I want to be with you now."

Jeremy was so close, but still not touching. Emilie grabbed a washcloth and added a squirt of shower soap, and started wiping the grime off his body, slowly rubbing him in circular motions, appreciating his chest muscles, as she touched his bronzed skin as gently as she could. He closed his eyes.

He turned around, his back to her, turned up the water pressure, and then snatched a bottle of shampoo. He squeezed some out, and lathered his scalp, then bent his head back as he let the bubbled soap rinse away. She smelled coconut as the suds rolled down his body, and reached out to place her hand on his back. Her mouth watered when she touched him. His body felt lean but firm, and his skin supple and smooth.

She moved her hands to his arm, and tugged to turn him around and face her. Making eye contact, she recognized his need. She leaned her body closer and felt him, hard against her stomach. With closed eyes, she gently kissed his warm lips.

He returned the kiss then nibbled a trail down her neck and up to her ear. "I love you," he whispered.

She gave him a gentle kiss that turned into a frenzy of passion when their lips met, and within seconds, his warm mouth and tongue melted with hers. More shivers. Emilie couldn't hold back as the pent-up longing surfaced. She kissed his lips more fervently, then his neck, his chest, and she traveled lower still. She heard him moan.

He massaged her shoulders, reaching spots that turned her longing into burning lust. He stopped, pulled her up straight once more, and held her face in his hands, focused on her eyes. Tilting her head, he kissed her eyes, her nose, her cheeks, and her neck.

Emilie melted, any inhibition long gone. His lips kissed her hardened nipples and she soared. Squeezing his arms, she craved for the moment to last forever, but he broke away yet again.

He turned off the water, picked her up, and carried her to the bedroom, gently dropping her on the bed. Emilie pulled more of the covers back, and opened her arms wide.

"Come here, then," she said.

Jeremy lay down beside her, rolled her onto her side to face him. He touched her back again, running his finger up and down her spine gently. She moaned, closing her eyes, feeling as if floating in air.

"You drive me crazy doing that," she said.

He smiled as he put his finger to her lips, shushing her from talking. Then he kissed her again, passionately. Together they enjoyed exploring each other's bodies. They spent hours learning about each other intimately.

After they quenched their attraction, glowing from each other's magic, they lay in bed together, smiling. Jeremy played with a strand of her hair, wrapping it around his finger. Her arm was around his waist as they faced each other, completely satisfied.

"Thank you for the best day of my life," he said. He kissed her head.

"I think the pleasure was mine, as well," she replied. "I never worked so hard in my life as I did today, digging up the midden. I've never loved so deeply as tonight, either." Emilie leaned her face up to meet his and kissed his lips warmly, just one soft goodnight kiss, then she laid her head back down on his chest, and fell asleep to the beat of his heart.

Emilie woke the next morning in the happiest mood she could remember. Peeking across the pillow, she saw Jeremy watching her, seemingly wide awake.

"Have a good show?" she asked.

"You snore," he quipped.

She gave him a gentle punch on the arm, and then a kiss before she rose and scurried to the bathroom. After a good night's rest and a morning shower, Emilie and Jeremy drank their morning coffee in a cafe downstairs off the lobby of the hotel, while researching on the web with a laptop. Now that half the mission was completed, they wanted to keep the momentum going. They racked their brains looking for the possible location of Captain Dominique de Gourgues's burial site.

"I booked a flight, we're all set to leave in three hours," Jeremy said.

"So, we land in France, and then what?" she said.

"Then we find the captain's burial site and finish the deed. There's no turning back now. We can use Church records to find the location. I called Father Eddie while you were in the shower and he gave some direction over the phone, and he promised to assist us with the Church's red tape once we're in France."

Emilie nodded, but some things still bothered her.

"Do you ever wonder about Father Eddie? You've been getting chummy with the man, what do you think of him? I mean, I love him, he's been there for my family over the years, but ..."

"Well whatever his story is, he's all we've got, and I am very thankful. Besides, just think about it for a minute. If the Church believes in things like possession and exorcisms, then why not believe in curses and the burning of bones?"

It was a rhetorical question, but Emilie still wondered about it a little. However, there was no time to waste. A few minutes later, they were in the rental driving back to the airport on their way to France. They went through security check and made it to the gate just in time to board. Together they traveled in quiet companionship.

Emilie was reading a book, but her mind wandered. She considered her feelings for Jeremy and their developing relationship. When she was with him, she understood what it meant to be cherished. Jeremy respected her and inspired her to be a better person. She admired his positive attitude toward life. After years of loneliness, finally she felt accepted by someone's love.

She glanced at his profile while he rested. A thrill coursed through her body, remembering his warm touch playing on her skin. She slipped her hand into her purse and found the red spiral shell he had given her, and rubbed her finger against its smooth surface.

The seatbelt light rang. Her attention returned to the present. They were near their destination: France, so lovely, despite the gravity of their task.

CHAPTER TWENTY-SIX

When Emilie and Jeremy's flight landed, they took the train to Tours, a beautiful thriving city in central France that sits along the Loire River. They were staying at the old Hotel de l'Univers, a resting place in the heart of the city since 1846, three minutes away from the train station and just a ten-minute walk from their first destination.

"Perfect!" Emilie said when they arrived.

They stood in front of the old hotel, a building designed with Parisian flare. Large windows with iron gates protected anyone from falling to the street below. The clock above the hotel's name, fixed in stone, rang the noon hour.

"Come on, let's check in," Jeremy said. He led the way into the old-world lobby. It was filled with lavish gold leather sofas and soft palms that stood tall in the corners of the room, but they still looked small in the vast space. Midriff-height, wrought-iron railings held back other guests, who strolled the floors above.

Jeremy and Emilie signed the register at the front desk and were led to their room. Jeremy offered American dollars for the tip, and received a grimace in return. "Sorry, we didn't pick up any exchanged currency," he said.

"We can get some when we go out," Emilie said.

She explored the suite, amazed at its modern design. Compared with the public area of the hotel, the bedroom furniture here was sleek, with colored fabric patterns and contemporary design.

"Check out this shower, it's beautiful." She tugged Jeremy's hand and led him into the bathroom.

"It is," Jeremy agreed. "Why don't we just stay here the remainder of today and start our search tomorrow?"

He studied her with a frown, and Emilie glanced down at herself.

"I don't look that bad, do I?"

He grinned. "Of course not, you're beautiful, but I don't want you to get worn out. Maybe a nap first. Besides, we have this wonderful shower to test out." He raised his eyebrows at her suggestively, and she laughed. "But seriously, you need to keep your strength up. I have a lot for you to do later on." He gave her a kiss on her forehead.

She smiled at his teasing. "I don't think we should waste time, lover boy. We need to get this done quick, before anything happens to Rachael."

"Em, she's only dating your brother. We have time."

"Maybe so, but I'll be more relaxed once this is finished."

"I like relaxed," Jeremy said.

Every time he smiled at her with that look, it made her shiver with anticipation. Emilie disregarded those thoughts, for the moment. "I think we need to be adults."

They settled into the room and took a brief nap, but then both agreed it was too nice to stay indoors. By two in the afternoon, they were strolling away from their hotel to the center of the Old City, the area known as le Vieux Tours. It's an energetic neighborhood still boasting the original half-timbered buildings, famous since the medieval days. The cathedral rested on Rue Lavoisier.

"Come on Jeremy, we're almost there. Look, it's Saint Gatien's Cathedral."

Pointing to the cathedral, Emilie took off for the front doors. She gawked up at the huge towers embracing the entrance. The architecture amazed her. She had read up on this place.

"You know, the process of constructing this cathedral took four centuries of labor," she said. "See the different architectural influences, the Romanesque and Gothic design."

"Wow, this sanctuary is overwhelming."

She nodded. "I wonder how such an imposing presence could have been built by mere men. This craftsmanship is impeccable." She pointed up at the doorways and windows. "They look as if they're held together by lace made of stone."

Jeremy opened the door and together they walked down the aisle, admiring the wood-carved organ that was displayed above the main floor, with colorful windows as its backdrop. When they reached the pews closer to the altar, they sat. Emilie yanked Jeremy's sleeve and pointed up at the artistry of the stained glass above, mesmerized by the colors. They sat in silence, in awe of the rainbows that reached to the lofty heights of the arches, leaving shadows of color like a kaleidoscope on the objects below. Encouraged by this majestic cathedral, she reflected on the fact that they now shared this experience. Filled with joy, a new resolve occupied her soul.

They knelt and prayed, and then Emilie made the sign of the cross and sat down once more on the wooden bench. She placed her hand on top of Jeremy's, and he instinctively wrapped his around hers. She sensed that her touch gave him a new experience, too. They sat together for a moment, appreciating the surroundings.

There was a leaflet left on the seat. Emilie picked it up and read the weekly bulletin, and found the names of the priests for the congregation. Tugging to get his attention, she accidentally ripped Jeremy's sleeve at the seam. He turned with a smile.

"I love you too, Em," he whispered, his eyes gleaming. "But tearing my clothes off in church? What would your father say?"

"Sorry," she said, blushing. "Can you call Father Eddie and see if he knows any of these priests? The two of you seem to have hit it off, talking with each other on the phone almost every day lately."

She handed him the bulletin and he made a quick call to Eddie. Luck once again struck: Father Eddie was friendly with Father Lefevre. They waited on the line while he contacted his old acquaintance, and after hearing about their dilemma, the priest agreed to meet with them.

They waited in the church for another ten minutes before a sole priest walked down the aisle. He reached the bench where Emilie and Jeremy sat, and held out his hand. Father Lefevre was an elderly, gentle-mannered man, slightly built and thin, conveying a peacefulness that immediately put Emilie at ease. She shook his hand, and then Jeremy did the same.

"Nice to meet you," the priest said in broken English. He leaned his head toward the exit, and invited them to his office. They walked down a short hallway and turned right, into a small room lined with bookshelves stuffed with paperwork and folders. Only a small window of tempered glass let in light, with no discernable view. The room smelled of old paper with a tinge of mildew.

"*S'il vous plaît se asseoir*, please, sit," he said. He bowed his body, with his arm out toward the center of the room. They sat down in the indicated wooden chairs, situated around a large round wooden table.

Emilie said something to Father Lefevre in French and he smiled and nodded. He went to an old wooden desk and started keying at a relatively new computer sitting at the edge of all his work.

"I told him we need help locating my ancestors' resting place, and that I think it may be here, in Tours," she said to Jeremy.

The priest turned his head and spoke again. Emilie listened carefully, nodding, as she translated in her mind his words, then she turned to Jeremy. "He's checking any Church records that have been logged into the computer system," she said. "The Church scanned thousands of old documents, including burial information. He's looking as far back as possible."

Father Lefevre rattled off more, his French tongue rolling through a long story. Emilie listened and conveyed the message to Jeremy.

"He says the only prominent grave in the Church from the 1500s documented in this area was for the children of

Charles VII and Anne of Brittany. Nothing recorded from this cathedral references the de Gourgues family. But, he suggested another church nearby, the Basilica of Saint Martin. Apparently, it was a popular church in the 1500s because Saint Martin was the patron saint of the city. Pilgrimages were very common back then."

Jeremy shifted his weight, looking uncomfortable in the chair. "Okay, we'll look there next," he said.

Father Lefevre nodded, his aged face revealing a few wrinkles that deepened with his concern. He rattled off more conversation, and Emilie leaned forward to take in every word.

"What's he saying?" Jeremy asked.

"He says that unfortunately, the Basilica of Saint Martin had been attacked by the Huguenots back in 1562 during the wars of religion. The saint's tomb was destroyed, but the church was still used until 1793. That's when it was completely demolished during the Revolution. Since then it's been rebuilt, and there's only a slight possibility Captain de Gourgues was buried near the old remains of the original basilica."

Jeremy ran his fingers through his hair. "Sounds like it's a shot in the dark."

"Wait, Father Lefevre is searching the records from Saint Martins," Emilie said.

The priest shook his head and responded.

Emilie listened and translated. "He says the records for the other church at that time period were all destroyed. Let me ask him if there's any other source, maybe the Vatican's main records."

Jeremy nodded his agreement.

Emilie spoke in French, asking the priest to check any other sources available.

The priest turned back to his desk and typed away, performing one last search, directly into the Vatican records this time. Emilie stood beside him, reading aloud, as he scrolled through the records.

"Again, nothing comes up in the Tours area for the de Gourgues family," she said, "but the name did surface in the Vatican records in the Bordeaux area. That's where the family lived for centuries. They were well-known in society there for generations."

Emilie, mumbled to herself as she squinted at the screen, thinking through the translation. "The records don't reveal the specific name of the captain, Dominique, but still there's hope. These documents are so old. They appear to be incomplete. I remember reading about a commission working on deciphering the land ownership of the family, going back centuries. Maybe they can help."

"I'm not sure we have time to get involved with that kind of pedigree paperwork," Jeremy said. His lips were tight, his face worried.

The priest looked up at Emilie and spoke again.

"Father Lefevre suggests there may be some burial records available in Bordeaux that may help us," she said.

"You know, Em, over the years these places have been riddled with so many wars and destruction, that lost records and artifacts are unfortunately a commonplace occurrence. It's possible that Dominique de Gourgues was buried with his family, even though his name isn't listed. I wish Uncle Thad was here, he was a master at this kind of research, his little mysteries." His smile returned.

"Well, we'd better be going then, we have work to do," Emilie said.

"*Adieu Révérend. Merci pour votre aide.*" Father Lefevre smiled and bowed his head, just slightly. Then he raised his arms and gave them his blessing, with the sign of the cross. They crossed themselves, smiling, and took their leave.

"His last advice was to visit the Basilica of Saint Martin before leaving for Bordeaux, just in case. It sounds like a wonderful church," she said.

Emilie felt hopeful. They headed for the Basilica of Saint Martin. If their luck continued, they might find something in the ruins. If not, she still held out hope for Bordeaux.

As they walked away from his office, Emilie noticed a man who looked a lot like the guy who had shadowed her at the university the other day, and on the trolley in New Orleans. She stared, trying to get a good look. He noticed her, turned around, and was gone. *Your imagination is going wild again,* she said to herself.

Emilie drew in a deep breath, and exhaled.

"Do you think this could work?" she asked Jeremy.

"I do. Let's check out the Basilica of Saint Martin, just to see if our luck holds out," he replied. "We might find something in the ruins. If not, we'll go straight to Bordeaux."

A chill run up her spine, still feeling as if they were being followed. She looked over her shoulder, but no one seemed interested in them, so she dismissed it. Everything that had been happening, visiting Mr. Labue and Miss Boniverre, conjuring Voodoo hex bags, translating the journal, and then the burning of the bones in Florida, it was all taking a toll on her nerves. She didn't trust the reliability of her senses any longer, after they had been so heightened and taxed by recent events. She hoped she was right, and she and Jeremy were truly in no danger.

They walked through the vibrant city of Tours, filled with colorful shops and displays of beautiful art. They meandered until they arrived at the front entrance to the new basilica via Rue des Halles. The facade of this church was different from Saint Gatien's. The Saint Martin's Basilica was built with a Neo-Byzantine influence, ornate but an entirely different type of appeal. Built over the original site of St Martin's tomb, the original church was now only ruins beyond. Only the tower of the old basilica survived, along with a Renaissance cloister, which was located on the grounds. If the captain had been buried there, the remains would be near the original ruins.

They walked toward the front entrance. The huge columns on either side of the building were a strong force that supported the bulky strength of the structure. The ornate trim at the edge lent the fortress some ornamental distinction and conveyed the building's importance. Hopeful, they entered the basilica.

The interior pillars on either side of the aisle space were massive anchors, and held up the prominent wood-beam ceiling above. The glass windows told the story of Saint Martin in brilliant blue and red colors, a vibrant legacy of miracles. Together, they walked to the front of the church and genuflected with a quick prayer and sign of the cross.

Emilie noticed that a stream of light from an opening in the center dome above shone down upon Jeremy's head. His expression looked angelic in the beam. She worried she may be corrupting him with all this curse business, and hoped she wasn't destined to hell for warping him. He finished with the sign of the cross, and then they left through the back entrance.

Just beyond the back wall, they noticed the tall old tower at the end of the street, with its crumbling walls and ragged edges. The exposed brick that remained was like a jagged razor edge against the blue spring sky. The rawness of the fragmented structure was softened by the moss and greenery spreading around the base.

Jeremy let go of her hand. "Search the ground for any hint of a burial structure or evidence of an old cemetery plot or tomb," he said.

"There seems to be nothing here." Emilie walked within the ruin itself, imagining where the original altars and burial vaults might have been. She looked with a keen eye, not exactly sure what she expected to find.

"Em, over there." Something had caught Jeremy's eye, and he pointed across the ruin's span.

"What? I don't see anything."

"There, see that piece of cracked marble jutting out from the ground. It's possible that it's an old marker." His face lit with excitement. Jeremy looked around to check for tourists milling about as they both moved closer for a look. He squatted, balancing on his heels, and wiped clean the visible surface, making what was left of the engraved markings more legible.

"Can you read this?" he asked.

"I'll try, but it's hard to decipher any words." Emilie looked over his left shoulder and scanned the marks on the stone, but they were smoothed by centuries of weathering, the crevices stained with mildew.

"Wait a minute," he said. "Let me pull away some of this ground covering the bottom of the stone. There, this part isn't as worn." He brushed more dirt away with his hand, revealing inscribed words on the section of the thick marble.

"Are there more words below?" Emilie asked.

"Yes." He leaned in for a closer look.

Emilie's anticipation rose. She was surprised when the name appeared, despite it being the reason for their journey. "Dominique de Gourgues," she said aloud. She froze for a moment, staring at the engraved name. Her throat tightened and tears threatened. The idea had seemed impractical from the start, but maybe this was her destiny, her part to play in the de Gourgues story. She glanced at Jeremy, and noticed that his gaze was on her. She leaned down and kissed him. "Thank you."

Appearing pleased, Jeremy took off the backpack he carried, opened it, and pulled out a trowel.

"Do you see anyone around?" he asked.

"You're safe. No prying eyes."

He cleared more ground from the marble slab. A date appeared, along with the French inscription sculpted into the hard, cold stone. Emilie lightly stroked her fingers over the etched words and read them softly to Jeremy as she translated:

'In honor of a man who lived helping others in their search for freedom and liberty before God, and a spirit brother with men of the new world.'

"Is this a grave? It sounds more like a marker recognizing his efforts aiding the Huguenots in America," she said.

"There's only one way to find out," Jeremy said. He looked around and noticed a group of tourists who had entered the area, standing about twenty yards from them. He pointed at them. Emilie looked up and nodded.

"Discretion is impossible right now, with so many tourists," she said. Her gaze spanned the lawn, and she saw a man standing there watching them. She stared back at him, trying to determine if he was the same man she thought she'd seen repeatedly since the trolley in New Orleans, or if he just reminded her of him. It couldn't be. She pulled on Jeremy's sleeve and pointed, but when he looked up the man was gone.

"You have a thing for my sleeves, or what? What is it?" he asked.

"Never mind, he's gone."

"Who's gone?"

"Just a man. He was standing on the other side of the lawn, it doesn't matter."

"How are we going to do this with so many people strolling around? We aren't even sure if this is a grave. As you said, it could be a monument or plaque of some sort. Do you have any ideas?"

"Maybe we should ask for permission from the church? Father Lefevre seemed reasonable, maybe the same will hold true of this basilica's priest, too?"

"I don't know if we dare," Jeremy said. "What if they turn us down? I have a better idea. How about I come back at night when it's quiet. Don't worry, I won't get caught, promise. I have no desire to spend any time in a French jail." He laughed at the idea, but Emilie didn't think it was funny.

"I think *we* will come back tonight is more likely."

Ignoring her retort, Jeremy started digging beneath the stone marker. "I'm checking if there is even room for a grave underneath." A moment later, "I found something hard. It might be a stone box for holding remains. More likely, it's part of the old foundation."

He pulled his hand out of the hole and brushed away the dirt as he continued. "For centuries, family plots had one large stone flush to the ground bearing the family name and crest.

One person's corpse was buried right on top of another's. The beginnings of the concept of 'family togetherness.'"

Emilie made a face as if revolted, then smiled. "But that couldn't be the case for the de Gourgues family because the plot is in Bordeaux according to the records. I think we need to change our plans."

Jeremy stopped for a moment, and squinted his eyes with his head raised just a bit. He looked adorable when thinking, she thought.

"Okay, I agree this is probably a monument rather than the actual grave. I hope his remains were sent to his family's plot in Bordeaux, because that's all we've got. Sometimes local written records have more information than what's listed in digital archives. We should check down there, it's not that far from here."

Emilie nodded her agreement. "Yes, it's best to be certain before we start a major dig here. Besides, I don't have any particular feelings about this spot."

"I agree it's better to be sure." He chuckled softly with relief before a look of confusion crossed his face.

"What's wrong?" she asked.

"These feelings you get when you know something is right, is that something that usually happens to you?" he asked.

Emilie cleared her throat. "Not always, but often. I'm an empath. I can't read minds or anything like that, but I can feel people's emotions, instead. I get a sense of what they're going through. The only problem is, I most often don't know the reason for the emotion in the first place. It drives me crazy not knowing why I am feeling something. At times it's downright painful, and it's hard to keep my spirits up when I'm near depressed people. I've been trying to learn how to block negative things. But, other times it's a little different. I can just tell when something is off, or if it's in sync. Just like I know you were meant for me." She looked up at him, grinning, and searched his face for a response. She felt like a fool until he smiled back at her.

"Jeremy, when you touch me, I feel like I'm in heaven."

He leaned in and kissed her. "That's a nice thought."

Jeremy gathered the tools, stood, and pulled Emilie up too. They left and headed back toward the hotel.

Emilie didn't notice whether the man still lurked nearby spying, she was too wrapped up with Jeremy right now.

They stopped at a wonderful restaurant on the way back to the hotel, where they shared a French dinner with a delicious local wine at a restaurant off Place Plumereau. The evening turned magical. They enjoyed swapping stories with each other, as they talked away the evening. The past two days of this trek had given them the opportunity to become familiar with each other's joys and heartaches. The more they discovered, the closer they became.

"Em, I can't wait for you to meet my family. They're going to love you. I think my kid brother William will fall in love with you first."

Jeremy's face lit up when he told stories of his family. Emilie wanted to meet them all. It was clear that family was important to him, that was one of the things she loved most about him.

"As soon as we get this mess over with, I think a trip to meet your folks will be perfect," she said.

Jeremy beamed. "I hope you like Surrey. I loved growing up there. Maybe someday we'll have kids of our own." He glanced at her and watched for a response.

Her face burned with embarrassment, not knowing what to say. His warmth was so overpowering she couldn't help but smile back. *Maybe there is hope for a normal life and a family of our own.* Still, she had doubts that shadowed her and the idea that she could ever have that kind of happiness.

Emilie remembered her younger years before Mother died, which held many good memories, and she'd never let them go. She shared a few stories with Jeremy. He listened, and laughed, and made her world feel warm again.

"Excuse me," Jeremy said as he wiped his mouth with the napkin, "I'll be right back." He left the table. Emilie sat a moment glowing in her happiness.

"Hello, Miss de Gourgues." An unfamiliar baritone voice addressed her, abruptly pulling her from her reverie. Emilie looked up. The speaker was a tall, dark-haired man with an olive complexion, a straight and pointed nose, and peering eyes. He was well dressed, in a fashionable suit. He extended his hand.

"Do I know you?" she said.

"We met once, many years ago. I'm Tom Bennett, my son was your brother's roommate in college."

She smiled even though she felt as if she should start running. "Yes, that's right. How are you, Mr. Bennett? Visiting France for pleasure, or on business?" She took his extended hand. A sudden uneasiness filled her. She watched his eyes grow dark. He grinned at her, but the smile never touched his eyes.

"I am always doing business, Miss de Gourgues. I noticed you sitting here, and wanted to stop by and give my regards. Your brother Robert said you were upset these recent days, over a family curse?"

Emilie pulled her hand free, startled by the mention of her brother, who was obviously sharing family confidences with a stranger. Then she remembered Michelle expressing concern about Jackson's father. Something was definitely amiss. She recovered her manners.

"I'm sorry, Mr. Bennett, you have caught me off guard. You spoke with Robert about me? Why in heaven would he do that?"

His smile morphed into disdain. Emilie swallowed the lump in her throat. He leaned in closer.

"Perhaps I've spoken out of turn; you'll have to forgive my presumptuousness." There was no apology in his tone. "It was an unexpected pleasure to see you. I'm sure we'll run into each again soon, Miss de Gourgues." He bowed his head and touched her hand again.

Immediately, an evil like nothing else she had ever experienced before, poured from him. She jerked her hand away. He bowed his head again, still leering unapologetically, and then walked away without another word.

Jeremy walked past him on his return to the table. "Who's that?" he asked, clearly reading the disturbance on her face. "What did he want? Are you okay?"

Emilie closed her eyes for a moment, and recovered when Jeremy placed his hand on hers. "I'm fine now that you're here. That was Tom Bennett. His son went to college with Robert."

"So, what did he want? How did he upset you?" he said.

"No worries, he just stopped to say hello. It's just that he seems so . . . evil. When I held his hand, I felt threatened. Never mind, it's crazy. All is well, so why should I try to jinx things?" she said.

Jeremy got up and helped Emilie out of her chair. "Come on, let's go rest a while. Tomorrow's another big day."

They walked back to the hotel hand in hand. Emilie wondered what was going on in Memphis while they were gone, how her father was holding up, and what her brother was up to. Bumping into Tom Bennett had jarred her resolve, and made her anxious to get the task finished. She hoped Bordeaux would hold the answers.

CHAPTER TWENTY-SEVEN

The next day, Emilie and Jeremy rented a car and drove to Bordeaux. Jeremy navigated traffic on the A10, while Emilie researched on her laptop. Centuries ago, the de Gourgues family had been aristocrats and so were most likely affiliated with St Andre's Cathedral, the church most prominent in the years of Dominique's life. Entering the city limits, they parked at a reserved spot and found the Petit Hotel Labottiere, a unique bed and breakfast. Emilie managed a last-minute reservation for one of the two guest rooms. She wanted an out-of-the-way place just in case they had been followed.

They entered the front doorway, and right off noticed what looked like a priceless wall clock in the entry hall, made of dark wood and exquisitely accented with gold leaf. Emilie had already learned that Jeremy loved looking at antiques, he said it reminded him of his treasure hunts with Uncle Thaddeus. Emilie was charmed by the place too, but not by the treasures. Instead, the spirits in the old converted mansion greeted her.

After signing the register, they retreated to their room and took their leisure, settling into the small suite that was quaint and homey, a refreshing change from the ordinary chain hotel or the fuss of more prestigious accommodations. They both agreed that a little downtime was in order before they trekked across the city looking for the grave.

The owner gave them a tour of the mansion, telling them stories as they examined the antiques throughout the house. There was a large harp displayed in the salon and many odd paintings hung on the plastered walls, eclectic pieces of furniture throughout.

Emilie began feeling emotions that still emanated from the room. Centuries of heartache lingered from abandoned lovers and fevered revenge, as well as loathing that left a residue time hadn't been able to wash away. She didn't enjoy these kind of interruptions, and pushed them from her mind.

She turned her gaze to the other side of the room, pleased that Jeremy hadn't noticed her distraction. He was busy talking with the owners, and complimenting them for their wonderful restoration efforts with the home. He walked back across the room and took her arm.

"Enjoying this old place?" he said.

Emilie nodded, reassured by his kindness. Jeremy led her to the terrace, where they would have afternoon tea in the hedged courtyard. Emilie sat down in a garden chair and unfolded and straightened out a tourist map she had taken from the lobby. She studied it, searching for walking directions to the cathedral. Keeping busy helped her to stay focused instead of being absorbed by the life forces haunting the place.

The sun was warm, so Emilie pulled her hair up away from her face to keep cool. She raised her face toward the sky with closed eyes, to let the sun soak into her skin for a moment. Ignoring Jeremy for the moment, she knew he was watching her. He finally turned and pulled out his phone. Emilie heard the buzz of the dial tone. Jeremy called Father Eddie and asked about his connections in Bordeaux, then chuckled softly at Eddie's response.

He finished the call and disrupted Emilie's meditation. "Father Eddie knows a deacon from the nearby cathedral. They were friends from seminary years ago."

"He's our rabbit's foot. We're lucky he's helping with this part of the trip," she said.

"How about we contact the deacon later? Let's take a day off," he said.

Emilie was more than happy with that plan.

They began their day by exploring the nearby public gardens, and then ventured into the city streets to enjoy the sights. They had a romantic and elegant dinner in the French bistro Jean Ramet, located near the River Garonne. They were served a seasonal meal of bright red peppers and dark green beans infused with spices, accompanied by a lively local wine. The area was famous for great wines. They enjoyed an evening stroll after dinner, and then ambled back to their room, where they retreated for a romantic night together, and then a restful night's sleep.

The next morning they woke early and wandered down to the hotel's long gallery for breakfast. The morning light bounced glittering sunbeams that shined off the three crystal chandeliers that hung from the high ceiling. Emilie watched the colored reflections playing on the white tablecloth, dazzled, and forgot all about eating her breakfast. Lost in a cloud of whimsy, of Jeremy running through a field with her as the warm sun soaked into their skin, she dreamed.

"Em, eat up. We have a long day ahead of us, you need the energy."

Jeremy pulled her out of the fantasy. They were served omelets, fruit, and croissants with their juice and coffee. Soon, they were ready to start another day's journey.

They walked a few blocks to the St Andre Cathedral, a church of varied styles. The front, referred to as the Royal Gate, was built in the thirteenth century and constructed in front of what remained of the original Romanesque edifice. The steeples were taller on either side of the entrance, trailing high into the sky, slimming as they reached the top. The sides were from a later construction, finished in the fourteenth and fifteenth centuries, and decorated with gargoyles designed to protect the place from evil. The north entrance had a high, large center window that looked like a lace doily filled with glass.

This older center doorway was grand, with floral details in the stone that arched up toward the spires. Passing through the large wooden doors, they met the deacon in the entry. A stout man dressed in black robes with red sashes, he was polite but nervous as he spoke to Emilie and Jeremy in English, explaining the church was busy this time of year, due to Bordeaux's International Organ Festival. It was to begin shortly. The best organists from all over Europe attended every year. Since they were expecting a crowd, he suggested that they go directly to the old cemetery.

"Father Edward already called and explained what you're looking for, so I searched the records and, although there is no mention of Dominique in the files, I did find something. The oldest known de Gourgues family members from this church were laid to rest in a very old cemetery, in the outskirts of the city."

He handed them a hand-drawn map with directions for how to find the old cemetery. "Take this, and I hope you find the answers you're seeking."

The deacon wished them luck, then made the sign of the cross and blessed them. Jeremy and Emilie returned to their parked car and sped down the roadway, heading west, away from the city's center.

"Okay, follow Rue Georges Bonnae. Look, there's a cemetery on the left," she said.

"That can't be it, we still have quite a ways to go."

"Right. Okay, follow this road, it turns into Avenue d'Ares." They traveled ten more miles and ended up on D213. "After Passage de Marchegay turn left, that's right down this street," Emilie directed.

"Was that a left or right?" he quibbled.

"A left, smartass. Yes, now another left." They followed the directions until they reached their destination, and parked the car. They walked for a mile and found the spot. It was a sparse area with no houses nearby, and block walls fenced off sections along the road. Hidden to the street with overgrown bushes, almost invisible, was a very old church graveyard, tucked away from all the city turmoil.

They found an entrance and walked down the old time-forgotten road, now so overgrown with grass that it more closely resembled a path than an actual road. To either side lay graves, the weather-worn headstones cracked, some just lying flat on the ground partially covered with moss, others barely distinguishable. Crowded together, it looked more like a potter's field of pauper's graves than a respectable cemetery.

The road was lined with big old trees with roots bumping into the gravestones. Lilac bushes were in full bloom, now reaching high into the sky from many years of growth. Oddly, this old cemetery filled with decrepit stones seemed peaceful as the sun filtered through the tree branches, bringing serenity to the place.

The trail ended at an iron gate that was tilted off its hinges and half stuck in the ground, buried in the dirt that had accumulated over time.

"Emilie, can you climb over the stone gate post without hurting yourself?"

"Please give me some credit. I climb higher to reach the horses I ride!"

She laughed the remark off, and felt his regret for mentioning it. Clambering over the gate post they found themselves in an even older section of the cemetery, confirmed by the dated stones. Larger family stones carved of marble filled the central area. Mausoleums fortified with massive doors crafted of wood and iron pins established the perimeter of the overgrown field, keeping the dead in and the living out. It reminded Emilie of the cemeteries in New Orleans, filled with grand statues and graves, only this church plot was definitely forgotten, neglected and overgrown with brambles, wild grass, weeds, and thorny bushes.

"Ouch! Great, just great, this isn't going to be an easy feat, walking through all this! And trying to read the stones at the same time!" Emilie said.

"Are you okay?"

"Just a thorn, is all." She pulled out the barb and sucked her thumb, tasting her own blood, as she thought about the spirits that now dwelled here. They had all been alive once, too.

Jeremy picked up a stick, long and strong, a perfect hiking staff. He used it to push back the overgrowth, making a small path they could walk through without too much trouble.

"Keep looking as best you can, try to make out any names on the headstones. We'll find it here somewhere. According to the deacon, all the old graves of the wealthier families are here. Chances are the de Gourgues family of those days had a larger mausoleum, seeing as they were one of the most prominent of the day."

"That makes sense," Emilie said. "Let's start with the larger ones first to save time."

Jeremy pointed toward the largest mausoleum in the old churchyard. A statue of an angel stood on each side. The one to the left held a cross and the other's hands were folded in prayer, both carved in white marble. The mausoleum snuggled into a slight hill, the ground protecting its rear like a sheath made of earth and grass. The wall was crumbling. An intricately carved wooden door was at its entrance. Its massive thickness kept it from decay, although the dark corners exposed to persistent shade had begun to soften. Shady moss and ground vines covered the tomb and permeated an earthy smell.

As they walked closer, the illusive inscription became salient. The name engraved above the doorway on the front facade, although weathered and stained from years of exposure, clearly read 'de Gourgues'. Jeremy stopped thrashing the pathway, and leaned on the staff.

"Do you see that?" Emilie stood motionless, her finger pointing up to the inscribed name. She turned and looked at Jeremy. He returned her gaze and smiled, then he turned away for a moment, and gave Emilie a quiet moment.

Overwhelmed with a sense of belonging, hot tears stung the corners of her eyes and gently rolled down her cheeks. She wiped them away with the back of her hand, and turned away. Emilie felt providence, astounded with the site. It was her family, her descendants, her history. *How many of my ancestors are buried here, forgotten in time,* she wondered. Flooded with emotion, she stared straight ahead in deep reflection.

Suddenly, spirits overpowered her mind, and her body turned into a pathway for rushing streams of energy. She heard the voices, and sensed the echoes of yesteryear's emotions. They assaulted her with pain, anger, and happiness, all at once. The vibes filled her mind so quickly she was unable to hold onto her own thoughts.

Emilie was stunned by the multitude of voices reaching out to her. Her body jerked, seized by the temperaments of the spirits, and she opened her mouth wide but was unable to mutter a word, only strange sounds gurgled. Inside herself, she screamed and pushed, making way for her own mind to take control again. Emilie used every ounce of strength to regain her reason.

Jeremy noticed the change. He rushed to her side and grabbed her arm. Immediately his strength radiated into her, and restored her balance. They stood in front of the gravesite, still for a moment.

"Are you all right?" he asked.

His brow was furrowed, and she realized this kind of episode must be scary for him. She was thankful he tried so hard to understand, but he'd never fully comprehend the bloodcurdling fear and emotional trauma that hung in this place. They needed to get this done quickly, before she collapsed again from the haunted spirits that resided here. She drew in a deep breath.

"I'm fine. We need to finish this now."

Emilie struggled to make sense of the past uncovered so far: the tribe, the ceremony, the chief and the captain, she and Jeremy had brought all of that here, carried it to this place. She knew she had to finish this. Looking up, she saw Jeremy looking back at her.

"I'm more than worried about you," he said. He stood beside her, patient, caring, and lovingly faithful. She knew him, as if they had been soulmates together for eternity. His face reflected his tenderness; strength radiated from him and recharged her resolve. He was saving her life and he didn't even know it.

"Thank you so much for being here with me. All this curse business is bizarre, I never could have done this without you. I just want you to know I love you dearly. And I am fine."

Jeremy smiled back.

"Good. I love you, too. So, right, let's get this over with as quickly as we can."

He used the staff to clear the remaining weeds leading to the door of the crypt. Ferns and small trees sprouted from the crevices in the building. The mausoleum stood ignored for centuries, not even a lock on the door to show that anyone cared for the contents of the tomb. No glass in the windows, just tall and narrow openings to let in minimal light.

Yanking at the old rusted iron latch, Jeremy pulled and tugged until the door started to budge within the weather-swollen doorframe. Slowly he opened the door, gaining purchase with each try, until there was enough space for him to squeeze through. Once inside, he pushed the door out until it was half open and some light exposed the inside wall. An unpleasant earthly smell escaped from the tomb, released from the enclosed vacuum of time. Looking back at Emilie, Jeremy said, "Here we go."

CHAPTER TWENTY-EIGHT

They entered the tomb together. Regret spiked through Emilie. It took only a moment for her to understand it wasn't her own emotion she felt, but the spirits from the tomb.

On the far side, a crevasse carved into the wall held an altar, once used but now only crumbling pieces of stone. Compelled to go over, she walked to the corner breathing in the stale, muggy air. She covered her face with her sleeve and adjusted to the heavy atmosphere. Emilie bent down and picked up a piece of rubble.

Waves of energy emitted from near the old dais, where superstitious beliefs lingered. It was difficult for her to think in this space, assaulted by continuous emotional turmoil that endured through time.

She returned to Jeremy and inspected the side walls for a trace of the name Dominique, or for anything with the date 1593 etched in it. Lined on the walls were large marble tile squares. Each hoary square had a sullied brass metal plaque etched with a name. Jeremy groped the wall with his fingers, brushing away the dirt and vines to read the plaques.

"Emilie, look. Dominique de Gourgues—we found it!" Jeremy said.

Emilie noticed his weariness as she returned to his side. "Are you all right?" she asked.

"I'm fine. Let's get this done." He took off the backpack and pulled out a small crowbar. Perspiration from his exertions dripped down his face and back. Every move inside this space was amplified by the lack of fresh air. Jeremy firmly gripped the bar in his wet hands. His breathing was heavy, so he took a few deep breaths, adjusting to the room's environment. Turning his attention back to the wall with determination, using the tool, he leveraged it into a space between two abutting tiles.

Carefully but forcefully, he pushed with his weight until the stone popped out. Jeremy dropped the bar. It clanged to the floor and then he grabbed the heavy marble tile, absorbing its weight with his legs before it could smash to the ground. He laid the heavy marble stone down and dragged it across the hard floor. Returning their attention to the wall, Jeremy and Emilie moved in closer to scrutinize the space. The opened grave exposed a thick, tarnished metal handle.

Some kind of force was released into the space, joining the other lingering spirits already hovering. A stream of emotions whirlpooled into rivers of feelings and flooded Emilie in a rush. Her energy drained away in the tide as she struggled with the haunting waves that threatened to drown her. She grabbed Jeremy's arm again for strength.

They looked at each other. Emilie realized he was in trouble, too. With questioning eyes, he held up a finger to let her know he needed a moment. He panted for more air, and grabbed hold of his knees as he leaned forward to catch his breath.

"I'm not sure what's in here, but it's got to be what we've been looking for," he gasped. "Are you ready?"

The walls closed in on her, but she pushed back the feeling and took control. "Ready when you are, let's do this quick," she said.

They took hold of the oxidized handle, its edges rusted, brittle, and rough. Shaves of iron dust littered the floor, as they moved the handle up for a good grip. Pulling hard, like tugging a file drawer filled with lead, the tomb slid open. Slowly it pulled forward, crowding the crypt with a cloud of dust. Gagging at the smell, they covered their faces and tried to acclimate to the transformation.

"Are you okay?" Jeremy choked.

Waving her hands in the air, Emilie tried to breathe. The dust was smothering her. "I'm fine, are you? This stench is so strong."

"Let's give it a minute," he said.

He grabbed the sleeve of her cotton blouse, now smeared with dirt, and led her out of the mausoleum. They coughed out the putrid air, and took a few deep breaths to clear their lungs.

"My God, the air in there is so thick," Jeremy said. He coughed some more.

"Not only is it stifling, but I sensed so much turmoil in there. It's like swimming against a tide of black doom."

Jeremy watched her as she took in deep breaths and cleared her lungs. Suddenly she was embarrassed, afraid he wasn't pleased with what he saw. Had he noticed the stress on her face, and in her eyes? Noting his obvious concern, she smiled, hoping he'd be comforted. He gave a smirk back as he took in a few more deep breaths of fresh air before he spoke again.

"Okay, let's try this again," he said. He pulled two disposable teal colored masks from the backpack. "But first put on this pollen mask for some protection."

"You're quite the boy scout. You seem to have everything in that bag."

They snapped the elastic strap around their heads and trudged back into the death den to finish their awful task. The dust had settled a bit, but a heavy smell still permeated the space. The narrow windows on either side of the doorway offered little light and even less air flow. Looking into the box, they saw the petrified corpse. The conditions had preserved the captain's body like a mummy.

Emilie was curious and reached in to touch the discolored cloak that wrapped the leathered corpse of the captain. It crumbled under the slight touch of her fingers, so dry from years of confinement. Some bones penetrated through the frayed wrap, now visible between the cracked folds of the dried cloth. A brooch made of gold caught Emilie's eye, as it reflected the single sunbeam that peeked through a small gap in the doorway. It was etched with a design that looked like a coat of arms, and adorned with colorful gemstones.

"This trinket must have been important," Jeremy said as he carefully removed the treasure. "Emilie, here, take this. It's an heirloom, you should keep it. There's no sense to leave it here to burn. It wasn't part of the ceremony. Take it, put it in the backpack."

He handed her the jewel. She took it in her shaking hands, repelled. "I'm not sure I want it. I'll feel like I robbed the grave."

Jeremy tilted his head. "We are robbing a grave." He smiled and tapped her shoulder playfully, trying to relieve the tension. "Just kidding. Relax, okay? Really, if it is left here, it will only be destroyed by the fire. This is the one piece of history we can salvage. Besides, this can be proof to your father."

He paused. "Wait a minute, look, Emilie. There, in the corner. Shine the torch down there to see what it is."

Emilie placed the heirloom into the backpack and grabbed the flashlight, turned the beam on, and pointed it into the crypt.

"Okay, there it is. See it? Something is wrapped up and pushed into the far corner."

Jeremy stretched his arm into the depths of the tomb and began pulling on the cloth wrapping, slowly inching it forward with his fingers. When it was finally within reach, Emilie picked it up to examine it under the flashlight's beam.

"It's heavy," she said.

She placed it on top of the corpse and gingerly pulled the cloth away, exposing the artifact. They both gasped.

Relief rushed through Emilie. Her voice trembled softly when she spoke, shocked as the truth sank in.

"Oh, my God! Jeremy, it's here. It's really here, look. It's the wooden owl. I honestly thought it wouldn't be here after all this time, but it is. I can't believe it."

"We've done it," Jeremy said. He met her eye, his smile matching her own. "Emilie, I'm so happy for you. The curse will end. You've saved your family."

Jeremy leaned back against the dark marble wall, resting his head against the cool stone. He closed his eyes. Emilie understood, he was weak with relief after all the stress this quest had caused. This venture had affected him, too.

"We should do as Father Eddie said and get rid of it all. Let's finish this right now, get it done and behind us," he said.

"Yes, let's do it now," she agreed. "I want to be done with this all. I want things to be normal."

"Yeah, whatever normal is supposed to be." He laughed.

Motivated once more, Jeremy covered the inside of the tomb drawer with a lighter fluid they'd made from acetone and hydrogen peroxide, making due with ingredients they'd purchased in a drugstore. He squeezed the bottle until every drop was gone. He checked that the owl effigy was soaked along with the bones.

Emilie snatched a small box of matches from Jeremy's backpack, and took out two sticks. "One for you, one for me."

"Wait, I think we need to step back. Get behind the door just in case," he said.

"Really, don't you think you're being overly cautious? Just light the damn thing."

He stepped back, moving just a foot away from the door, then took the box from her. "I don't think this will work," he said, and threw the matches aside. He took out a silver lighter, opened it, and clicked. The small flame brightened the dark vault.

"Please, you do the honors for us both," she said.

Jeremy threw the burning lighter about ten feet into the grave's drawer, a perfect throw. The contents instantly ignited. A loud puff exploded in the confined space. They jumped back as a sudden burst of flame erupted. Jeremy grabbed Emilie's hand and yanked her through the doorway and away from the tomb.

"Thank God we were close to the door, you were right," Emilie choked out.

They brushed themselves off, making sure there were no sparks left on their clothes.

"Emilie, I'm so sorry. I wasn't thinking straight. I figured we were far enough away." He coughed. "Are you burnt?"

"No, no burns, but I smell singed hair. You're covered with soot." She brushed his clothes and they both hacked a few more seconds while a thick smoke poured from the mausoleum. "What was in that concoction you made?"

"I'm so sorry. I had to make it with a flashpoint high enough to burn bones. I guess being enclosed, well, I didn't calculate it right. I am very sorry."

"Don't feel so bad." Emilie coughed, her lungs aching. "The worst is over."

As she calmed down, Emilie became aware of the same feeling that had haunted her these past few days, the shadow that seemed forever behind her. She looked up and saw the man again, the same person she'd seen on the New Orleans streetcar and so many times since. There was no doubt in her mind now that he was following her. She turned and looked at Jeremy. He looked back at her with questioning eyes.

"Over there," she said. She twitched her head in the direction of the man. Jeremy turned. This time, he saw the man too. The stranger had a camera pointed in their direction, the shutter snapping in quick pulses as he took photo after photo.

"Bloody hell! Who's that?" Jeremy said.

Before Emilie could reply, Jeremy bolted toward him. The man turned and ran, and then stopped just long enough to pull a small motorbike from behind a tree. He fled. After a few yards, Jeremy gave up the chase. He stopped and leaned over, grabbing his knees, and drew in deep breaths. Emily ran to his side.

"Who the hell was that?" he gasped.

"I'm not sure. I've noticed him a few times, following us."

"Why didn't you say something? Who is he?"

"I'm not sure. I wasn't even positive he was following us, until now. I wonder what his game is. Why did he follow me to New Orleans and now here?"

"He was in New Orleans, too?"

"Yes, and Michelle spotted another man, too. She assumed Robert had them follow us."

"Well, I agree with your sister. We need to figure out your brother's game."

"I asked Robert if he had us followed and he seemed genuinely surprised. But maybe it has something to do with Mr. Bennett's appearance yesterday."

"Well, let's get this completed so we can get the hell out of here." Jeremy straightened and turned to go back to the gravesite, clearly agitated. The fire was burning hot, scorching the marble tiles with a thick black residue. The flames filled the mausoleum with a dense suffocating smoke, forcing them to stay outside the tomb. They waited until the fire died down, hoping no one would come to investigate the smoke.

Emilie dropped to the ground, her body too tired to stand any longer. She sat on the grass and watched the fire burn. Jeremy settled beside her with his arm around her shoulders. They leaned on each other as they watched the fire do its work. It burned hot and fast. Once the smoke dissipated, the flames burned bright with orange, yellow, and blue hues, like the fire that had consumed the bones in the Florida midden.

"What a show," Jeremy said. Emilie nodded in agreement, but stayed quiet. They sat without talking until the fire died down completely. It took hours.

Emilie finally allowed herself to feel relief. All her fears caused by this curse could hopefully be replaced with a promising future. If Father Eddie was correct, this would free her father and brother from the curse forever; the family legacy was saved. She only hoped that they'd finally make peace with each other, too.

Jeremy held her more tightly. She felt accepted, her gift and all. He knew it was sometimes a burden, but Jeremy still freely offered his help to her. Emilie appreciated his support more than she could possible show.

Jeremy gently brushed some soot off Emilie's clothes.

"Give it up, Jeremy. We're both so dirty there's no help for us except a long bath."

"Sounds about right. How about a shower with a friend?" he said.

She laughed, drawn in by his sparkling eyes. The cloud that hovered over them lifted.

Hours later, the fire was extinguished, and the embers finally cooled. Jeremy brushed the warm ashes into a metal container, and would send them back to Tennessee as Father Eddie requested, just as he had with the chief's ashes. They were ready for that shower, both covered in dirt and sweat.

It was dark when they returned to the hotel, so they snuck in through the back entrance to avoid having to invent lame excuses for their appearance. They wasted no time getting cleaned up, then booked a flight from Bordeaux to Boston. Emilie insisted on stopping to visit her sister before going back to Memphis. She wanted to explain these events, even if Michelle most likely wouldn't recognize the truth about the curse. Besides, something was up with Robert, and Emilie had a feeling that Michelle knew more than she had shared. Once it was all explained and things were out in the open, they'd go back to the estate and let everyone else know the curse had been lifted.

They took the red-eye from Paris. As they sat side by side during the flight back to the States, Emilie reached into her bag and felt for the small shell. She pulled it out and admired the red spiral design on the small memento. Of all the treasures in the world, this small shell made her the happiest. It reminded her of the most peaceful day she had ever experienced in her life: the day she spent with her love, on the warm sunny shoreline.

Now that the curse was wiped away, everything could begin with a clean slate. *So why do I still feel some kind of peril waiting in the shadows?* she wondered.

Something was still wrong, not finished. Uneasiness lingered, but she refused to listen. She wanted to be happy.

CHAPTER TWENTY-NINE

The plane landed at terminal E in Logan Airport early in the morning. Emilie sent a text message to her sister checking to see if she was awake. Michelle replied, telling them she was awake and on her way to pick them up.

Emilie and Jeremy walked blindly through customs, retrieved their bags, and then waited a few minutes on the sidewalk until a shiny black BMW pulled up. Her sister was behind the wheel, a beautiful young woman with long legs, short spikey hair, and a mischievous face. She jumped out of her car, ran to Emilie, and hugged her excitedly.

"Em, I am so happy to see you." Michelle let go and looked her sister up and down. "You look terrible."

Emilie side glanced at Jeremy. "Thanks, Michelle. This is Jeremy. Jeremy, my crazy sister Michelle."

"Wow, look at the two of you. You look exhausted, but you still make a handsome couple," Michelle said, brimming with too much energy. "Let's go out for breakfast and get some much-needed coffee."

She drove them to a small cafe near her condo, which was an old factory transformed into up-market housing in East Cambridge. "This cafe serves an excellent breakfast," she told them.

Emilie smelled the coffee as soon as they stepped through the doorway, and began to wake up a bit. They all slid into a booth and looked over the menu, sorting out what they were going to eat. The waitress walked over. "What can I get you?"

"Coffee all around," Michelle said.

The waitress scribbled on a pad, as they all gave her their food order. When she walked away, Michelle dug right in with questions.

"Okay – I am really glad to see you, but I need answers. And I don't want to pry but, Em, you have to tell me what the hell you're doing here. Why didn't you tell me you were leaving Memphis this morning to have breakfast here in Boston? We need to plan better."

Emilie smiled for a moment, and gave Jeremy an all-knowing grin. He was being a good sport.

"We're not arriving from Memphis, we just flew in from France," Emilie said.

"France. Get out! What the hell were you doing there? Did you two have a romantic fling? Tell me you didn't elope. Oh my God! And you didn't even let me in on the plan, your only sister. How could you do this to me?"

"Whoa, hold up there, Michelle. We didn't get married, and I have no idea why you jumped to that conclusion. I'd never do something major like that and not tell you."

Emilie hung her head, embarrassed. She wondered what Jeremy would think of that leap. "We needed to go to France last minute. It was business, family business."

"Well, thank you for that. Did you hear her, Jeremy? I need to know before you do anything like steal my sister away."

Jeremy held his hands up in surrender. "Okay, I heard. Don't even put me in the middle of this one. You'll be the first to know, once we decide anything. Satisfied?"

"Well, then why were you two in France?" Michelle gave Emilie that look, pleading with her blue eyes for more information. Emilie pulled her hair behind her ears, tugging a bit, as she tried to find the words.

"Okay, Michelle, here's the story. Just be forewarned, you're not going to like it."

"Wow, don't oversell it, Emilie," Michelle quipped.

"Remember the curse I told you about, the one we were asking Miss Boniverre about?"

Michelle nodded, her eyes intent. Emilie knew her sister wasn't going to believe her, but she had decided a while ago that she was always going to tell the truth.

"Well turns out . . ." she stammered, "well it appears the curse is real after all. So Jeremy and I went to Florida and then to France to end it."

"Excuse me?" Michelle said.

"We found out that the best way to end the curse was to burn the remains of the two men who actually made that pledge ages ago. You remember, Miss Boniverre talked about the chief and the sea warrior. The sea warrior turned out to be one of our ancestors, Captain Dominique de Gourgues. Father Eddie said we should cremate every last bone, and the effigies used in the ceremonies, too. To end the curse."

Michelle sat quietly and listened, blinking as she seemingly tried to make sense of Emilie's words.

"We went to Florida first, found the burial midden, and burned the chief's bones. Then we went to France, found the remains of our ancestor, the captain, and burned his bones, too. So, now the curse should be broken, and lifted off our family. No one will ever die from it again, like Mother did. Robert can get married without worrying about having his wife die on him. Father can stop obsessing over it all, and we can all go back to normal."

Emilie finished and sipped her coffee. They sat quiet a minute, as Michelle tried to absorb the story. She appeared to be having a hard time swallowing any of it; in fact, she looked stunned.

"You realize this is the most bizarre tale, like, ever. You two must be crazy, to go to such extreme lengths." She shook her head. "My sister and her boyfriend are out of their minds."

"Well," Emilie said, searching for some way to convince her. "Here's something you might like. Maybe this will help you believe."

Emilie pulled the antique brooch from her purse and unwrapped it. "This was in the mausoleum, on the captain's cloak."

"You took this off a dead guy?! You can't really believe in all this stuff? Guys, there's no such thing as curses. Listen, I'm glad you had some fun during this treasure hunt of yours, but really you can't believe that a curse existed in the first place, or that it was the reason for Mother's death."

She took a deep breath and looked as if she was trying to piece things together, frustrated by an idea she couldn't fathom.

"You two are lucky you weren't arrested with all the fires you started. Emilie, I think you need some serious help – you're out of your mind."

Expecting her sister to say something like this, Emilie didn't blame her for doubting, but she was determined to get her to understand somehow. "Yes, I do believe it. And so does Father, and Father Eddie, and Steve, too."

"Steve? That old anthropologist friend of yours?" Michelle asked.

"It doesn't matter. The only important thing to know is that we took care of it, finis! It is over, so no harm done," Emilie said. She waved her hand in the air as if she'd just finished a magic trick. Jeremy cleared his throat, ducking his head a tad as he mumbled a comment.

"Uh, no harm except that we destroyed some priceless anthropological relics and disrupted people's graves."

"Yeah, yeah, well, besides that. Whose side are you on, anyway?" she said.

Emilie smirked at Jeremy, and he smiled back. She loved it when he smiled at her like that. Her mind began wandering, dazed by his grin. Michelle just shook her head, noticing her sister's obvious infatuation. She snapped her fingers in front of her sister's face.

"Snap out of it, girl!" Michelle said.

"Sorry. I guess we're punchy from sleep deprivation."

"Okay then, you two will crash at my place the rest of the day while moi finishes a project at work."

"Sounds good, but we need to fly to Memphis this evening. I need to talk with Father," Emilie said.

"No problem. I'll arrange for the family jet to be ready, and will call Evans to have the car pick us up later."

"You're coming home?"

"I wouldn't miss this for anything!" Michelle laughed. "A good show is about to go down."

An hour later, Emilie settled into Michelle's spare bedroom for a well-deserved rest, snuggled up next to Jeremy. They slept soundly. Sleeping a good part of the day, she was exhausted by the constant flux between anxiety and relief. She woke just as Michelle returned home.

"Get dressed. We need to leave in thirty minutes," Michelle barked.

Emilie hurried and showered, feeling human again. With the heavy burden of the curse gone, she was in a wonderful mood. Jeremy and Michelle were packed and ready to go when she emerged from the bathroom. They drove to the airport and flew to Memphis, landing in time for supper. Emilie couldn't wait to tell her father the news, sure that he'd be relieved, too.

CHAPTER THIRTY

They landed at the Memphis airport, where a car awaited. Twenty minutes later, the limo pulled up the driveway of the de Gourgues estate. Evans and Nina appeared from the porch and pulled the bags out of the trunk before Emilie, Michelle, and Jeremy were even out of the car. Emilie was glad to be home.

They heard shouting when they stepped onto the porch. The three of them went through the foyer and into the front parlor, where they found Robert and Father arguing. The two men went silent as soon as the three of them entered the room.

"Wow! I sure know how to make a room go quiet," Michelle said. She walked over to her brother and gave him a kiss on his cheek. "Hello, big brother!"

Then she turned to Father and gave him a quick hug. "Hello, Father. It's nice to see you." She seemed nervous, and Emilie wondered if more was going on with her sister than she was letting on.

"Hello, Michelle," Pierre said. There was a look of indecision on his face. Emilie sensed her father was dealing with a lot of turmoil, and hoped her news would help lighten his load.

"Okay, tell me what you two are arguing about?" Michelle said.

Emilie wanted to tell her news, but figured she should find out what was happening first. She took Jeremy's hand and led him to the sofa, where they sat and silently watched the show. She looked at him, and noticed him smiling. He already knew enough to expect a spectacle when Robert was around.

"Don't you worry, Michelle. Father's just overreacting again. He seems to be blaming me for some unthinkably sinister scheme." Robert rolled his eyes, his patience clearly challenged. "It seems Father's imagination has gone a little wild lately."

"And just what is this sinister scheme?" Michelle asked.

"None of your beeswax," Robert retorted.

She was relentless. Being the youngest, Michelle usually got what she wanted and she used her advantage every chance she got. Robert adjusted his sleeve cuffs as he gathered his thoughts. He loved being center stage, and once again Emilie watched him turn his face into the mask he wanted them all to believe. Her brother cleared his throat and took a deep breath.

"So now, what brings you home again, Michelle? Of course it's a pleasure to see you again, just a little surprised, is all," Robert said. "But it's perfect timing." He scanned the room, and smiled. "Now that we're all here, let me tell everyone my good news."

Michelle clapped her hands. "I love good news."

"The other day, I told Emilie and Jeremy a secret. I planned on getting engaged to Rachael La France, and I asked them to keep it to themselves. We weren't ready to announce anything publicly. But, the truth is, we didn't want to wait. We were secretly married the other day. We eloped!"

Emilie gasped. "Rob, what the hell did you do that for?"

Robert smirked. "Relax, Emilie. We plan on having a big wedding party to share our happiness with everyone, but later when it's convenient."

"Well it's sudden, don't you think," Michelle snapped. "What's with all you people? Since when does everything have to be a big secret?"

Robert shook his head, a look of annoyance on his face. "I was hoping that my family would support me, but I guess I was wrong. Michelle and Em, please be happy. I love Rachael and I'm lucky she'd have me. And despite what Father seems to think, I'm not scheming something horrible. I don't know what his problem is, Rachael and I love each other, and I hoped someone would just be happy for a change." Robert rolled his eyes again and with exaggerated distress said, "Please, someone say congratulations."

Congratulations? Emilie felt like she'd been kicked in the gut. She twisted his words to find meaning, but could only form accusations. The reason for her hurried trip with Jeremy had been to break the curse quickly, before Robert married Rachael. *Now, the entire trip was for nothing.* One question flooded her thoughts: *Did Robert marry Rachael before the curse ended?* She was speechless for a moment. Jeremy reached over and placed his hand on her arm. Emilie took a deep breath.

Michelle hugged Robert, a wide smile plastered across her face.

"Well, congratulations. But, Robert, why all the secrecy? Why not wait? And Father, why do you think this is a horrible scheme?" Michelle backed up. "Why are the two of you arguing over this? This is supposed to be a festive occasion." She turned to Pierre and said with frustration, "Father, can't we just for once be a normal family? Tell us, please, why aren't you happy for Robert? What do you know that we don't?"

Pierre didn't say anything. The tension in the air was thick.

Emilie regained her composure and stood up. They all turned to look at her. A lump stuck in her throat. She swallowed and asked, "Why didn't you wait for us to get back, Robert? When did you and Rachael get married?"

"We were married a few days ago. Right after you left on your impulsive trip to Florida. I hope you enjoyed it, by the way," he said.

He smiled too much, a telling look that Emilie was beginning to recognize. It gave her little comfort as he continued.

"I guess you inspired us with your impetuous trip, Emilie. Rachael and I fantasized about a small romantic ceremony, so on the spur of the moment we did it. We went to a little chapel in the country and tied the knot, as they say. Then we took a couple of days off. You were right, Emilie, I needed a stress break."

"I said a vacation, not an elopement. Jeez, Robert, how could you?"

Robert ignored her question, took a swig of his drink, then cleared his throat.

"Anyway, then we came home and told Father. He was upset, but not because we eloped without the family," he glared pointedly at their father. "He didn't care about that, he was never one for celebration, as we all know. No, he was upset because he thinks Rachael will die because of that damned curse. That's all he cares about these days. He's obsessed!"

Robert turned around, addressing Pierre. "You really think I deliberately married Rachael so that she'd die from the family curse? As if I'd want my new wife, the most beautiful woman in the world, to die. It's absurd, old man. Why would I? I don't even believe in curses."

His voice rose contemptuously with each word.

Something was horribly wrong. She closed her eyes and reached out, trying to read his emotions, but she was blocked by a wall that surrounded her brother's heart.

"Robert, did you tell Rachael about the curse? Did she know?"

"Please, Emilie. I told you, I don't believe in that damned curse."

Emilie tried to understand his motivation. She looked at him candidly and said, "Well, just in case you do believe in it, don't worry. We took care of it."

Robert raised his head and looked back at her. He seemed hostile, and she watched as he broke out in a sweat. He loosened his collar. *What is going on in his head?* Once again, she was afraid of her brother, and what he was capable of.

"What do you mean, you took care of it how? What have you been meddling into now? Can't you just leave well enough alone? You are always trying to fix everything, fix everyone. Well, some things and some people just aren't worth fixing. What have you done, Emilie? You left home and went snooping around, meddling in things you weren't supposed to, it just causes more trouble whenever you go overboard."

"Don't talk to Emilie like that," Michelle blurted. Jeremy got up from the sofa and stood beside Emilie. Robert sneered at him, then stepped away, shaking his head.

Her brother turned on her, as if he had baited her and was waiting for his sister to respond. "Well, Emilie, what did you do?"

"It was real, you fool," she said. "So, we took care of the curse, of course. The curse is gone, and now you and your wife can live a long happy life."

"Ha! You too? There is no curse, at least not in the sense you're describing. Nothing looms over this family but bad luck."

He took a swig of his scotch and then swirled the remaining liquid. He stared at his glass and seemed to be in a moment of deep contemplation. His expression changed from angry to grief-stricken, and finally to disheartened. However, Emilie couldn't feel anything from behind his wall. Finally, he broke the thick silence.

"Unfortunately, I seem to be under that dark cloud right now. Just a few days ago Rachael and I were the happiest we've ever been. Then she suddenly fell ill." Robert harrumphed. "I'm afraid it's serious," he said. Robert's voice was flat, with no emotion.

"What the hell does that mean, Rob?" Michelle said.

Emilie wondered what he was talking about, as well. To her it seemed he was enjoying himself, putting on a big show for them all. Then a pinch of guilt made her regret her assumptions about Robert's intentions. *Maybe he is distraught.*

"Rachael is very sick, and it's not because of a damned curse. I'm upset and really need everyone's support right now, not accusations about some absurd plot."

He bowed his head, begging for some compassion. "Yes, I may have married her before you broke the damned curse, so technically she was cursed when marrying me, but none of that matters. The curse never even existed." Robert let out a bitter laugh. "You people are foolish to believe in such nonsense. Let's put the whole thing aside for now."

"She's in the hospital, getting tests done," Pierre said.

Robert turned around and gave more details.

"Something suddenly came over her yesterday when we returned. Nina and I brought her to the hospital right away. She's sick and so far the doctors don't know why, they can't explain it. Fools and medicine. It's just like when Mother got sick. That's why Father is blaming the curse, and why we're arguing. He's reliving his own past."

Emilie was sickened by the update, and frantic about Rachael. How were they going to help her now? It was the curse, what else could it be? Emilie felt so helpless again.

"Are you sure you don't believe, Robert?" Michelle asked with a skeptical look on her face.

Robert glared back at her.

"Well, I'm just asking. Others seem to believe in it, and she's loaded, after all. Even though you don't need more money. Still, the idea of a dying wife just terrifies Father, right? Do you want to terrify our father?" Michelle was taunting Robert now.

Robert's face fell with dejection. "You know, I thought we had a better relationship than that, I might expect that kind of accusation from Emilie, but how many years was I there for you in Boston? Father and Emilie never had a good word to say about me, but I expected more loyalty than that from you, Chelle.

"I've never made any secret of my indifference to Father. He must know in his heart why. He knows how he betrayed Mother, and that Tom Bennett was more of a father and mentor to me than he ever was!"

Emilie's heart shattered. It took a second for her to realize it was her father's emotions spilling over with another break-in. Pierre's spirits sunk and his heart cracked. So many pieces needed to be put right. She felt his guilt, all of his regret.

"Tom Bennett corrupted you, Robert. He wants to pit you against your own father. Don't you know when you're lied to and being used?" Pierre's voice shuddered in horror.

Emilie took a deep breath to pull herself together. She waved her hands and fanned her face. Tom Bennett, the same man who had stopped at her table in France. What was his game? Emilie remembered the awful feeling Bennett had given her, the evil she had experienced. *What is he doing with my brother?* She went to her father, and slipped her arm in his.

"It will be all right, Father."

Pierre shrugged. "No, you children don't understand. None of you know how bad this is, Tom Bennett is a cruel man. He traumatized your mother and me, and vowed to hurt us. He harassed us for years, then finally we thought it was over. Then your mother died. And now he's using you, Robert, as retaliation." He hung his head, and Emilie understood his profound sorrow.

"How could you, Robert? Trust a stranger over your own father?" Pierre sounded confused. "Whatever he said to sway you, they're lies."

Robert's face turned red with rage. His trembling hands yanked back his hair, and then in a raised voice, a pointed finger in the air, he screamed, "Don't tell me who I should listen to, old man! He was there for me, not you! And what you did to Mother—"

"I loved your mother with every fiber of my being." Pierre had tears in his eyes.

Robert ignored him. "I'm going to the hospital now to visit Rachael. I will bring my wife back to the house tomorrow, no matter what you people think."

"Now the truth comes out!" Pierre shouted in return. "You put too much stock in what Mr. Bennett tells you. Do you always believe strangers over your own father?"

Emilie knew Bennett was rotten. She reached out her hand toward her brother.

"Robert, I think you should listen—"

Robert turned and stomped off, slamming the front door behind him.

Pierre's brow rose, his eyes wide, still looking confused. He shook his head, as though trying to shake off the argument. Emilie was bewildered, as well. She looked over at Michelle, but she seemed to be the only one in control of herself. It appeared as if she had just found answers, not questions. Emilie had known her sister had information she wasn't sharing, and now Emilie was the only one out of the loop. Should she ask questions about what the hell had just happened? Watching her father, she decided to let things cool down first.

Tears persisted in the corners of her father's eyes. He pulled out a handkerchief and wiped them dry.

"I am sorry for that display. Jeremy, you must think we are lunatics in this house. The sad truth is we are a house full of agony, and sorrowful memories. It seems some dangers refuse to die and some scars never mend."

Pierre looked down at the floor, pausing for a moment. "Father Eddie told me what you were up to, and I can't say that I approved. You could have gotten into serious trouble, but I want to thank you for watching over Emilie. She would have been alone through the ordeal if you hadn't gone with her, so thank you for that. I'm glad that it's over and you're both safe."

Pierre patted Jeremy's shoulder.

"Thank you, sir," Jeremy said.

"Now, I have grave concerns about Rachael's health. I'm afraid it's too late. I think she's dying. I remember when she was a little girl visiting Emilie, and they read together, over there by the window. Why, I watched her grow up beside you, Em, as if you were sisters. I guess you two are sisters now. It seems like only yesterday."

Emilie was surprised that her father had even noticed them. Since Mother died, he had always seemed so obsessed with his own pain. She watched as he paced and wrung his hands, feeling the faintest comfort at the knowledge that he had taken notice all those years ago.

"Now this, this is what's left for her. Robert married her right after he heard what you were doing; he overheard me speaking with Father Eddie. And now that beautiful child is dying. He's my son, but I don't even know him. How could my own flesh and blood do such a cruel and selfish thing? What can I do now to keep that poor girl alive? I need to protect my family's future."

Pierre dropped his head. From the corner of her eye, Emilie watched as Michelle came to her father's side.

"Father, you're kidding, right? Cheer up, there is no curse." Michelle looked over to Emilie, giving her a stern glare, and then she looked at Jeremy. "Why do you all insist on this being real? Rachael will get better, you'll see."

Pierre snapped back into his familiar self, and mumbled as he moved toward the doorway. He wrung his hands as he left the room, absorbed with his own pain.

Emilie walked over to Michelle and hugged her, ignoring her protests. Then she motioned Jeremy to join her, and they shared a group hug, a moment of solidarity. Jeremy was the first to break away and kill the silence.

"Okay, girls, let's work this situation out. Everything will be all right. First, let's look at the facts." He squeezed them, and tried to lift the mood. Then he rubbed his hands together, and paced. "We eliminated the curse, but not before Rachael and Robert were married. Maybe the curse is still gone, maybe not."

Emilie nodded. "If the curse managed to stick around, it might have gotten to Rachael's spirit before it lost its power, you know, because we were burning the graves it was threatened and was in a hurry to get her into its grip."

"If you're right, and it took hold of her spirit because the curse was on borrowed time, that explains why Rachael got sick so quickly. The question is: was she actually cursed, or is it all a coincidence? Did we miss something else?" He laughed at himself. "Listen to me, I sound like some sci-fi nut! If only we could ask Doctor Who to use his TARDIS. Go back and change things a bit to help Rachael."

"Okay for real now, what can we do?" Michelle said.

"I know," Emilie said. "Let's have a talk with Father Eddie and ask him for ideas."

"It seems Father Eddie has too many ideas!" Michelle snapped back.

"I've got nothing else, Emilie, so I'm with you," Jeremy said. "Let's see Father Eddie. Michelle, you're coming with us, too."

"Oh no! Don't drag me into this."

Emilie took Michelle's hand and tugged.

"Hello, is anyone listening? There is no curse! This is ridiculous," Michelle said.

"Then you have no reason not to come and see him, right?" Emilie smiled as she pulled Michelle by the hand and led the way to the driveway. Just as they piled into Jeremy's truck, it began to pour.

"Great, is this an omen or what? I think maybe we should stay home, guys," Michelle said.

Jeremy turned the key without heeding her protests, started the engine, and drove off.

CHAPTER THIRTY-ONE

They drove to the rectory in silence as the storm outside pounded against the truck. Flashes of lightning illuminated the horizon. Finally, they arrived at the rectory and rushed to the front door. The rain poured down on them. They didn't waste time ringing the bell, but just plowed right into the front foyer. They hung their dripping coats, and noticed a light on in the parlor.

Father Eddie stood in front of the fireplace. The flames filled the rectory with warmth against the cooling storm. Hearing them enter, he turned to see who was there. A smile swiped across his face.

"Michelle, it is so nice to see you. It's been so long since you stopped here for a visit. Thank goodness Emilie and Jeremy dragged you back to Memphis. We miss you."

He turned to Jeremy. "So, tell me all about your travels. How did it go? You really haven't been gone long, I'm surprised you're back already. I thought you two might make a vacation out of your trip. Oh, and by the way, I received the packages you sent. Thank you."

"Things went very well, Father. With your help, we got lucky. We burned everything as instructed, even the effigies."

Father Eddie nodded, then sadly voiced his latest concerns. "If only it was that simple now. I'm afraid Pierre is troubled by Robert's sudden marriage, and now poor Rachael.

"I just came from visiting her in the hospital. They will let Robert take her home tomorrow. Her father wanted her to go back to his home but she insisted on staying with Robert, her husband. I assume you have all heard the news by now."

Everyone nodded.

"Anyway, the doctors have done all kinds of tests. They think being at the house will help her feel better, more comfortable, at least. Your father thinks that she's sick because of the curse. I am inclined to agree."

Emilie could feel Michelle's temper rising. A second later, she blurted her opinion.

"Father Eddie, I know that you're an educated man. How can you keep encouraging Father like this, and let him believe in this curse? These sorts of things just don't exist. It is physically and spiritually impossible to be cursed."

The priest grinned at her remarks, pacifying her.

"Ah, Michelle, if we only knew the whole truth. There are many things out there, real things that happen, that can't be explained away by religion or science, not yet, anyway. I know this all sounds strange, but it's real. Your family history points that out with every single wife who died before she was forty. After centuries, not one survived long enough to see a grandchild. It doesn't make sense statistically, but that is the fact, it is real. Yes, it is a curse.

"Read some of the references to curses straight from the Bible. In the Old Testament, Exodus 20, 'I, the Lord your God, am a jealous God, visiting the iniquity of the fathers on the children, on the third and the fourth generations of those who hate Me,'" he quoted.

"*This was a warning about the consequences of summoning other gods and worshiping effigies and false idols. If you don't want to call this a curse, then don't. Call it whatever you want. But, Michelle, I see a long, long line of death. To me that is definitely a curse!*"

Just as he finished there was a loud crack, and a thunderous strike hit the house. Michelle jumped.

"Okay, that was creepy. I forgot about these violent storms," she said.

The earsplitting noise brought everyone's nerves to the edge, and Emilie soaked them all in. The floors vibrated from the thunder, the wood slats rumbled under their feet, and the small trinkets that cluttered the shelves rattled. They all turned to the window when flashes of lightning came into view. The storm surrounded the rectory in a fury. The frenzy persisted as the storm pelted down a stream of heavy rain. One major strike hit, and zap, the electricity went out.

"Okay, that freaked me out," Michelle said.

"Thank goodness for the flame in the fireplace," Eddie said.

The blaze in the hearth cast their shadows against the walls as they herded to the middle of the room. The fire popped and snapped, and the rain slapped against the windowpanes in a pounding beat. Together they watched the storm, and Emilie was suddenly aware of an eerie silence.

"I think we're in the eye of the storm," Jeremy said.

Usually storms didn't faze her at all, but Emilie felt dread. She soon realized it wasn't her own fear, every emotion in the room had suddenly surged into her mind. She pushed the feeling away. *Remember why we're here, for Rachael. Get a grip.*

"Father, what can we do to help Rachael get well?" she asked. "There has to be something we can do. What about other ceremonies? Maybe you heard of other possible healing spells during your days in New Orleans?"

She pulled her hair back, uncomfortable, hot and sticky in the enclosed room. Her mind, tugged into the middle of a war zone. She knew the curse hadn't been extinguished, she felt it in her deepest core. They had gone through all that work, the travel, dealing with the graves, all for nothing.

Eddie paced the floor as he shared his meditations aloud.

"My guess is that she's cursed because she married Robert before the spell was broken. Simple. Unfortunately, Robert overheard me telling Pierre about your plans the day you left. Robert confronted me, and I warned him the curse was real, and asked him to be patient and to wait until you returned. The next day, your father called with the news about Robert's elopement. I don't understand why he did it, it makes no sense. Was he trying to prove it didn't exist? Why would he bother? Or did he hope it did exist, which is a terrifying possibility."

Michelle walked toward the fireplace and warmed her hands, then turned after a moment.

"Oh, it makes sense, all right. Robert wants to torment Father. His plan is finally exposed. A couple of months ago I met up with Jackson, and you wouldn't believe the things he told me about Robert. It seems his admiration for Tom Bennett goes a little too far. Talk about hero worship! Robert has been scheming something with Bennett for quite some time." Michelle shivered and then hugged herself.

"Why didn't you tell me this before?" Emilie spat.

"Sorry, Em, I wanted to when we were in New Orleans, but you seemed preoccupied. I didn't want to add more stress to your plate. Especially since I had no proof yet."

"You should have trusted me."

"I do trust you, Emilie. Please forgive me. Right now there are more important issues. Robert wants to take control of the company, all by his lonesome. He's so blind, and doesn't see that Bennett is pulling his stings. Damn him. Sorry, Padre."

"No problem," the Reverend assured her.

"If this is true, and he's being manipulated by that evil man, then we have to help Robert," Emilie said.

She thought of the deep pain Robert lived in, and knew that Tom Bennett had exploited that for his own purposes. There was nothing about that man that she trusted.

"Robert's not in his right mind. We need to be there for him."

"I agree, we should help him. He is your brother, after all," Father Eddie said.

Jeremy nodded.

"You can help Robert, of course, but first we need to be practical . . . A life depends on it. Rachael must be the priority. She's dying, she needs us now, more than anyone else. On my Uncle Thaddeus's grave, I promised I would finish this. There is no way anyone else is going to die. Let's see if we can come up with an idea, quickly. This poor girl has no clue what hit her. The sooner we intervene, the better. Time is running out for her."

Michelle drew in a deep breath.

"I'm still trying to accept all this," she said. "But if you're right about it being real then, of course, let's help her first. But everyone please remember, in the scheme of things, Robert is a grown man. He knows right from wrong. If what you're saying is true, then he deliberately married Rachael for revenge. Sounds to me like Robert might be beyond our help already."

Emilie didn't expect such harsh words from Michelle, but she knew her sister was right. Jeremy was right, too, no matter how much she wanted to save her brother, Rachael was the true victim here.

"What if we make the spell again?" Emilie brainstormed. "I'm talking about the old magic potion Miss Boniverre spoke of, that let people enter the spirit world. We could make the drink, and take it, and enter the other side to help Rachael. Father Eddie, what do you think? Is it possible?"

She watched Eddie as he rubbed his beads, his gaze distant, as if consulting with the other side for advice or permission.

"I considered that too, Emilie. I honestly think it could work, but think of the risks. Could it possibly kill someone, too? Could this cause another curse to begin?

"I remember something from my hoodoo friends down in New Orleans. They referred to this kind of ceremony as a divination. It's like a magical spell to summon the spirit. In this case, we need to go one step further. We need to enter the spirit world, and then see what's going on so we can get Rachael's soul back, and hopefully we come back, too. The question is, do we have enough information from the journal to be able to make the same drink used in the ceremony centuries ago? We also have to consider the talisman, the original carved owl and panther effigies were destroyed. You burned them. We would need something to create a link to another realm. There are too many unknowns. It would be too dangerous."

"I'll do it," a strong voice sounded from across the room.

They all turned and saw Pierre standing in the threshold.

He joined them near the fire.

"I'll do it, Eddie. I overheard the discussion about the potion, and the ceremony. I have faith in this plan, and we have to save Rachael. If I had only known sooner, but I couldn't save my wife.

"I will do this to make things right. Rachael is an innocent in all this. I can save her, and I can free my family from this deadly curse. If I don't try, I'll never be able to live with myself. I'd rather die trying than do nothing."

"No, Father! You can't do this; it's suicide," Emilie protested. "You heard Father Eddie. We don't even know if we can bring you back. The drink may kill you, it's poison. There's no sense in both you and Rachael dying."

Pierre put up his hand, his face stern.

"I know what the odds are, and I know what I'm doing, I'm not a fool. This is my destiny, Emilie. Just like you destroyed all the remains and idols, this is my part to play. As the head of the family it's my duty.

"Rachael will be at the house tomorrow. We will make the potion and I'll drink it and set her free before it's too late. It's my responsibility as the oldest living de Gourgues to do this to protect our legacy. No more arguments, it is settled."

Pierre turned and faced Father Eddie.

"Eddie, you're a true friend, and have been faithful to me for years. I would have gone crazy without your support after Bethany died. You were always there for me, and when I found out about the curse, you helped, and gave me the gris-gris bag for protection. I owe you more than I can ever repay. Friend, can you help with this one last thing? What do we need to get this done tomorrow? There's no time to waste."

"I'll get a list together," Father Eddie said. "I may have to go to New Orleans to pick up some of the ingredients, so I'll get moving straight away."

"We can get the ingredients, this cassava and yaupon holly, from Mr. Labue," Pierre said. "He approached me yesterday. He said that he'd had a dream, and he knew that we would be needing some things. He has what we need ready and waiting."

The room suddenly overwhelmed Emilie. *When will this end?* Her entire world was falling apart, her family disappearing into the cracks. Even Jeremy couldn't fix this. It was unbearable to think of her father dying by drinking the old magic. She broke down, tears rolling unrestrained down her cheeks.

"No, Father, please no. Don't do this. I sense this won't end well."

"I have to."

She lost it. Fear, the most potent of all emotions, pushed Emilie over the edge. It had been a long time since she was completely lost in a clairvoyant outbreak. Unable to catch her breath, she sobbed so fiercely that her body shook. Jeremy wrapped his arms around her and held her tightly, while she cried into his chest. Everyone, especially Michelle, worried about her, and all their concern added to her load to bear. It was a vicious cyclone of emotions.

"Emilie, are you all right? You don't have to hold back anymore or try to protect me. It's okay. Let it out," Michelle said.

Emilie kept crying, unable to pull herself together.

"Jeremy, can you take Emilie home?" she heard her father say.

"This is too much for her now. We'll take care of the details. You and Emilie have already been through so much. She must be exhausted."

"Good idea. I will, sir."

Jeremy guided Emilie to the truck and brought her back to the house. He was careful with her, as if she was a fragile doll. Emilie felt his tenderness, but he too was clouded with anxiety.

CHAPTER THIRTY-TWO

Jeremy led the way up the stairs. He washed Emilie in the shower and gently dried her off with a towel. Dressing her in clean pajamas, he rubbed her arms and legs to get her blood flowing and warm up her cold body.

Emilie wanted to smile, wanted to hug him, but she couldn't bring herself to do anything. The entire time, she stood numb as if sleepwalking, like a zombie. He tucked her in bed and wrapped the blanket tight around her, forming a small cocoon, no doubt trying to make her feel safe. She appreciated his tenderness, and was glad when he laid down beside her, but the emotional stress of everything that had happened was too overwhelming. Visions of death, and premonitions that she had been pushing away for weeks, now surged upon her.

She didn't understand the voices in her head, or how they got there, but the raw edges surfaced, engulfing her in shadows of the past, painful echoes and recollections. She was also afraid for Rachael, upset that everything they had done, all that destruction and struggle, had been in vain. She was angry with Robert, angry with everyone. *When will this deep dark veil leave my life?* She knew she couldn't bring her mother back, but to lose her father to this curse too . . . It was too much to contemplate right now. She wished she could turn off her mind with a switch.

Jeremy gently rubbed her arm and whispered softly.

"I love you Emilie."

Emilie drifted to sleep, but haunting fears of the curse's deadly reach dominated her dreams.

She envisioned Chief Saturiwa, standing tall with his massive body covered in dark tattoos of wild animals, to show his bravery to the world. He laughed at her, and at her family, who all seemed to be there, too.

In her dream, the chief chased her father down a long path. She ran alongside him, through overgrowth and marshes. Mosquitoes bit at her ankles and arms, and she swatted them away. The path was long and seemed never ending. All her deceased relatives were hidden in the scrub palms on the sides of the path. As her father passed, the ancestors reached out and tried to touch him. Their voices cried out in high-pitched screams that belonged to another world.

Suddenly, the chief stopped running and grew taller, while everything else distorted. His ebony hair matched his dark eyes, and he chanted with a thunderous voice as the sky flared with bolts of lightning.

Emilie became dizzy. Even though this was a dream, she felt the terror. The voices from the bushes, all her ancestors, cried out to her for help.

She sobbed in her sleep, while Jeremy held her tight.

CHAPTER THIRTY-THREE

It was an early morning start at the de Gourgues house. Emilie woke up to sounds coming from the kitchen downstairs. She saw Jeremy resting next to her, watching her. She could feel his warm skin against her own.

"How did you sleep?" he asked.

He brushed her hair back away from her face. She knew he was worried and she didn't want him to think of her as a burden that way. *Get a grip*, Emilie ordered herself. She swallowed. Her mouth was as parched as a desert.

"I'm fine, thanks. I think I finally got a little sleep and feel much better. I hope you slept."

He smiled. "No worries."

Emilie squeezed his hand, smiled, and forced herself to get up, heading straight for the bathroom. She splashed water on her face, brushed her teeth, and dressed. When she emerged, Jeremy was sitting by the desk, already dressed and looking ready for his day.

"My, you're quick. Morning person all the time?"

"I woke up earlier and washed," he said. "I need to work, remember."

"Come on, then. Let's give this working man a good breakfast."

Nina had made the coffee good and strong. Its aroma wafted up the stairway, and led them to the kitchen. A big breakfast was already on the table, with eggs and grits, biscuits covered with sausage gravy, and fresh-squeezed juice. The smell of bacon lingered in the air.

"Good morning, Nina. Nice breakfast. What gives?" Emilie said.

"We have a house full, so I decided you all need to have breakfast together. You don't have a problem with that, do you? Of course you don't," Nina answered for Emilie, and then hummed as she finished putting out the food.

"It looks wonderful, thank you," Jeremy said.

"I told you I like this one, Miss Emilie. Y'all could take lessons from him. Lord knows I have been trying for years to teach you children something about being happy. But now things seem dismal around here, more than ever. Y'all have so much to be grateful for, too." Nina shook her head and returned to the stove.

Michelle and Robert seated themselves for breakfast, too. Her sister didn't say a word, but kept looking at Robert as he sipped his coffee, and then back at Emilie. Emilie wondered what she was up to, Michelle looked uneasy. Nina came back to the table and placed a plate of pancakes in front of Michelle.

"Miss Michelle, here's your favorite." Nina smiled. "Now, tell me why you look like some deep secret gotz your tongue."

Michelle grinned a familiar, crafty smile. "Nina, you have a vivid imagination."

"You're trouble, no doubt about that, but a nice kind of trouble." Nina smiled and left.

Robert didn't joke with Nina. Instead, his eyes roamed from one sister to the other, then to his father, and back again. "I'm picking up Rachael after breakfast, and bringing her back to the house. Does anyone have a problem with that?"

"Of course not, we'll be happy to see her, Robert," Emilie said.

"I have a nurse coming also, to watch after her. So there's no burden on anyone," he added.

"No one thinks she's a burden, for God's sake," Pierre said.

"I'll help the nurse take care of her, you know, maybe I can read to her," Emilie said. "I have fond memories of us reading together in the library. It will be nice to see her again after all this time."

"That's right," Michelle said. "The two of you were inseparable when you were kids. Sounds like boring times to me, though. Does she still have that beautiful long auburn hair?"

"Yes, she does, Michelle," Robert said. "And thanks for your support, Em. Just please don't tire her out more than she can stand."

"My, you're protective," Emilie said

"Do you need help picking her up at the hospital?" Jeremy chimed in. "I'd be glad to lend a hand."

"That's nice of you to offer, but I'll be fine. I'll have Evans with me." After a swig of coffee, Robert stood. "Come on, Evans, time to go," he bellowed down the hallway.

As soon as he left the room, Jeremy spoke up. "That was awkward."

Michelle snickered until she looked over at Father. She immediately stopped.

"Father, any second thoughts about today?" Emilie asked. "It's not too late to change your mind. We can find another way to help Rachael. Maybe if we just keep a good watch on her health, she'll be okay."

Pierre put down the paper he had been reading and looked at his daughters intently. "The decision was made, Emilie, and we are going through with the plan. There's no time to lose. I need both you girls to be strong for me today. No matter what happens, we go through with it to the end. Don't let me down. Promise me." He rose from his chair, and excused himself.

Emilie heard the doors to the library close behind him. She didn't begrudge him his alone time today.

Jeremy turned his head to the side and lowered his voice. "Emilie, I'll do it. When Father Eddie arrives later today, I'll take the drink instead of your father. I promise to return, so don't worry, everything will be fine."

"You can't do that," she replied softly, almost in a whisper. "Father won't let you. Once his mind is made, there's no changing it. Besides, I don't want you hurt, either."

"Don't worry about it. Years ago the captain survived because he was strong. I'm younger and stronger than your father. Surely he'll understand that I stand a better chance of making this work."

It was silent again. Michelle looked at Emilie and Jeremy. "Keeping secrets, Em?"

"Of course not. You trust me, don't you?"

Michelle guffawed. "Emilie, the two of you are the only people I trust in this entire world."

They finished breakfast and Jeremy left for work, promising to return when called back for the ceremony.

The nurse arrived an hour later. A rigid woman, she stood straight and looked around the front hall with probing eyes. She handed Evans her papers from the health agency that had sent her, and they exchanged a few words. Emilie sat on the stairs and watched. It didn't take her long to decide she didn't like the nurse.

Evans showed the newcomer to the front bedroom that had been prepared for Rachael. Moments later, attendants brought Rachael in, rolling her on a stretcher to the bottom of the stairway. They folded the legs up and carefully carried her to the upstairs front room. Emilie followed behind.

Everyone fussed around the bed, while Emilie stood back and watched. They carefully laid Rachael's fragile body onto the massive king-sized bed. She looked ashen, a ghostly figure on the verge of death. Emilie almost didn't recognize Rachael with her sallow face and sunken cheeks. Even her hair lacked its usual vibrance. Michelle walked in and patiently waited with Emilie, in the corner of the room

Robert had made a good choice putting his wife in the front guest room instead of his own. From here she'd be able to see people come and go, which would be good for her. The southern sun filled the room, making it the most cheerful of the house. The wallpaper was a blue print of ancient maidens garbed in flowers, beautifully matching the Wedgwood lamps and vases on the bedside tables. The French doors opened up to the porches that encased the front of the house, and overlooked the estate's entrance. Beautiful, cerulean satin drapes hung down the sides of the panes of glass, complementing the blue sky and enveloping the room in soothing tones, exactly what Rachael needed to feel better.

Robert walked into the room, and the nurse stepped back from Rachael's bedside. He sat on the bed close to Rachael and spoke softly to her, gently running his fingers down her long strands. He smiled at Rachael and Emilie swore she felt a warm tenderness coming from her brother, a special feeling she had never felt from him before. His wall was down as he gazed at his wife, adoring her. Rachael managed a smile for him before he left. "I'll see you later this evening sweetheart," he said softly as he left her bedside. He nodded to Emilie as he left the room.

Emilie stood back, and watched as Nurse Ratchet fidgeted with the monitoring instruments and equipment. Finally, the nurse settled down in a chair beside the bed, and the two sisters went to Rachael's side. She looked so small and helpless, and a memory from years ago struck Emilie.

Her welled-up anger bubbled to the surface. She forced herself to hold back her tears, determined to put on a strong, comforting face for her friend. *This is not Mother.* Emilie forced a smile, her face ready to crack at any moment. "Rachael, don't worry, we'll take good care of you. Would you like me to read to you?"

"I'd love that, maybe later, when Robert goes to the office."

Rachael had forgotten that Robert had already left the house. Emilie hung her head. Rachael had always been the bright one, the whiz who knew everything and was on top of any situation. Now look at her...

"Of course," she said. After a moment, "Look, Michelle came all the way from Boston just to congratulate you and Robert on your marriage. You know, we won't be happy until we can all celebrate together."

Rachael smiled up at Michelle. "I am so happy you're here, too. I promise we'll all go shopping together for the wedding reception." Rachael winced. They stepped back and the nurse injected her with some pain medication.

"She'll sleep now, for a while."

The two sisters sat near Rachael on the bed, giving each other concerned glances and then smiling at Rachael, holding her hand, until Emilie's old friend drifted into a gentle sleep. Emilie wiped tears from the corners of her eyes. She couldn't help thinking that someone she loved would soon be in danger of dying in order to save Rachael. The plan was sketchy at best. Her misgivings weren't just because of that, though, she felt a premonition about her father. He was too willing. Emilie knew something was wrong.

Her vision blurred, so she rubbed her eyes with the back of her hand. Instead of seeing normally again, she saw a hazy mirage of the Chief Saturiwa. She squeezed her eyes shut tight, frightened by the image. *It appears in my dreams and again now? What is my subconscious saying to me?* She pushed the illusion into a corner of her mind.

Michelle leaned her head toward Emilie, looking concerned.

"Don't worry, Emilie, things will work out." She whispered, to avoid disturbing Rachael as she drifted off.

"A lot has happened, Em, and I'm trying hard to understand all the revelations that have been dumped on me in the span of a day. It's a lot to comprehend, yet something like this was inevitable, wasn't it? You already knew and tried to warn us years ago. And these problems between Robert and Father have been going on for months now. I knew something was wrong, too."

Emilie heard Michelle's words but was more interested in what was going on in her sister's mind. She carried a burden. Emilie sensed it, but what? She grabbed Michelle's hands in hers. "I'm glad you're trying to understand this stuff. I know it's not easy for you," Emilie said. "But I feel like there's something you're holding back. What aren't you telling me? Is it about Robert?"

"You're right, there is something. I'll explain it all to you, but first I need to talk with Father. I promise, I will tell you everything very soon." Michelle rose from the bed and quietly left the room. "I'll be back soon, Emilie," she said over her shoulder.

Emilie nodded. After Michelle had gone, she got up and went to the desk across the room, where a familiar-looking book lay amidst other novels. She opened it to a dog-eared page and read aloud.

"'With every day, and from both sides of my intelligence, the moral and the intellectual, I thus drew steadily nearer to the truth, by whose partial discovery I have been doomed to such a dreadful shipwreck: that man is not truly one, but truly two.'"

Her heart ached as Robert Louis Stevenson's words hit home. When they were children, the book had been one of her brother's favorites, now, it seemed oddly appropriate that he should have such fondness for *Dr. Jekyll and Mr. Hyde*. The passage brought a tear to her eye, thinking of Robert and his dual personalities lately. He could be so good and yet, so bad. Then she mulled over the two men who had started this curse, Captain de Gourgues and Chief Saturiwa. They had truly started a shipwreck, two men's spirits colliding into one.

Something clicked in her brain. Emilie put the book down and went downstairs to her father's library.

CHAPTER THIRTY-FOUR

Emilie walked into the library. Her presence must have surprised her father and sister, because they both looked up like startled deer. She knew something was going on between them.

"Can I help you with something, Emilie?" her father said.

"Sure, you can help me. You can be straight with me for a change, and tell me what's going on. No more putting me off under the guise of protecting me. I want the truth, now."

Michelle smiled. "Father and I were just making plans, that's all." She walked over to Emilie, took her hand, and led her to a chair, then sat down in the chair beside her. "Listen Em, I understand. After you left last night, Father Eddie and I went over your notes. Then, when I held that old book in my hands, and turned the pages, well, suddenly the concept of the curse made sense to me. I mean, I get it now. Anyway, we made plans for today, and listed the ingredients for the damn potion.

"That's when it really hit home," she continued, "and I started to worry, too. The drink Father's going to take is toxic. No wonder you broke down and begged him not to do it. But, Em, we have to go through with it. There's no other option."

Emilie pulled her hair back behind her ears, and started twisting the ends around her finger. "Father's chances of surviving this ceremony are slim." She closed her eyes a second, holding back her tears.

Michelle drew in a deep breath, then let it out. "I asked Father to reconsider, too. What we are about to do is dangerous, and I'm not just talking about the poison he's about to ingest. We're attempting to hop into the other world. You know how I hate supernatural stuff like this. Besides that, we already lost our mother. I don't want to lose my father, too."

"Don't talk about me like I'm not in the room," Pierre said.

Michelle suddenly dropped her head, and for a moment Emilie thought she was going to cry. But Michelle cleared her throat instead. "You know, I regret all the time I lost with Father." Michelle turned around and looked at Pierre. "All these years I've stayed away, ever since I left for school. I guess I just want you to know that I do love you, Father. Even though you aren't the most nurturing man in the world, I know that you want what's best for us, out of love, and I appreciate everything you've done for the family, and for me."

Pierre stood behind his desk, shifting his weight from foot to foot. He seemed like he was searching for the right words. The vacant stare was gone, and that observation gave Emilie a small lift.

"Michelle, you're right. I've never been a supportive father. Ever since your mother died, I felt there was nothing left inside of me to give. I'm a selfish man, I didn't want to be reminded of her, and you children remind me of her all the time. Especially you, Michelle, you have the same blue eyes."

Surprised by his words, Emilie was relieved that he had finally shared his feelings. The room was silent for a moment. The clock in the hallway bonged the noon hour. Pierre stepped closer to them.

"I thought you were better off, thought it was best to keep my distance. It was the only way I knew how to survive in this world. I hope someday the three of you will forgive me. I'm afraid that I've hurt Robert beyond repair, and that is my hell to bear. I should have paid attention to what he was going through. I know from experience that it's not easy for a boy to lose his mother."

Pierre smiled at his daughters. His face transformed, and suddenly Emilie wanted to know more about him. She had never dared dream of this kind of conversation with Father.

The day Mother died, it was as if she'd lost both parents. All these years gone by with only sad indifference between them, she hadn't felt a connection to him the way a daughter should with her father. Emilie imagined it was even harder for Michelle, being younger and away for so long.

Michelle had tears in her eyes. She wiped them away quickly and turned away. Emilie felt her sister's remorse. She, too, wished their relationship with Father had been different. Neither of them wanted to lose him. But he had made his choice, and seemed willing to die if it came to that. If he didn't make it back from the other world, at least they'd had this last chance to let him know how much they cared about him.

"Father, you look like you need a hug," Emilie said. She looked at Michelle, who stayed in her chair with no intention of moving. Pierre opened his arms. Emilie got up and embraced her father, feeling the warmth and comfort.

"I made my choice and don't want you girls to worry anymore. We're doing this, so let's move on. We have more important things to discuss."

Michelle harrumphed. "Like what?"

"This is critical, so please listen to me seriously, especially you, Michelle." His tone was urgent. He looked at his watch. "I'm going to get right to the point, we don't have much time. I take no pleasure saying this, but your brother isn't in his right mind. He's been manipulating things at the company. When I realized what Robert was doing," he shrugged, "well, I've known changes were required for some time now."

Pierre paced the floor in front of them, speaking as if dictating a letter. "Emilie, the other week when you helped me to my office..."

"You mean when I called Doc?"

"Yes, and thank God you did. He came and checked on me, and said he didn't like how I looked. He ran some blood tests. I asked him not to say anything because I didn't want you to worry, but it turned out I'd been drugged over an extended period of time."

Emilie drew in a breath. "How? Why?"

"That's what I wanted to know. Once I realized what was happening to me, I took action. I have some loyal employees, thank God, who brought to my attention certain things when I started asking questions. Then I had security install video surveillance in my office. Before long, I had proof. My secretary was drugging the coffee with low doses of lysergic acid diethylamide."

"Father, that's LSD." All the pieces started coming together for Emilie. Robert's strange moods, the conversation Laura had on the phone, *he likes his morning coffee*. The bizarre behavior her father had displayed at work. She gulped back her surprise.

"Father, I am so sorry. I didn't realize."

"I know. You believed I was crazy, like everyone else. But it doesn't matter now. Once I found out, we did more digging. I had the accountants audit the books quietly, and that's when we uncovered that Robert has been stealing company funds. The money was traced to fake aliases, all hiding Tom Bennett. You heard Robert yesterday evening; he seems to care more about that man than me, his own father. I have no idea what he was thinking, and he has no idea who he's dealing with. Tom Bennett is a monster."

Emilie shivered. She remembered the way Tom Bennett had glared at her with those threatening dark eyes, and the horrible feeling she'd experienced when he had touched her hand. *The audacity*. Surely it wasn't an accident that he had bumped into her in Tours. He must have been behind all the spying. *But why?* She was horrified to think that her brother was involved with that man, and that he had drugged their father. *No, it has to be a mistake, is Robert capable of this?* Nothing surprised her anymore.

Michelle had been listening in silence, but at mention of Tom Bennett, she gasped. "Jackson Bennett says the same thing," she said. "Remember him, Rob's college roommate? He approached me a few weeks ago, and told me things about his father. He gave me a heads-up that something fishy is going on. We've been working on it together ever since."

Michelle took her sister's hands in hers, and pleaded. "Emilie, like I said last night, I wanted to tell you the other week in New Orleans, really, but decided to wait for proof. We finally got our hands on some documents that prove the embezzlement." She let go of Emilie's hands and turned to their father. "I planned on showing everything to you, Father. That's why I came home with Em…except you already know."

Michelle's face pinched with worry. "Father, you have to stop Robert. Tom Bennett hates you. Jackson told me how his father is obsessed with you, talking about bringing your legacy down. Sounds dramatic, but obviously he's doing it, taking your money and using Robert. The traitor! I'm so disgusted with Robert for going along with this crazy man's plans. Sorry I waited to tell you, Father, but I have proof now." She reached for her bag, on the floor near her chair, and pulled out a manila folder. "Here's what Jackson and I came up with." Michelle held the folder out to Father.

He took it. "Thank you. Yes, I know all about it," Pierre said. "Tom Bennett has been a threat for many years. Your mother despised him, he had evilness about him."

Emilie shivered, knowing the feeling.

"Your mother had a gift much like you, Emilie, and she knew things. I truly thought we had heard the last from Tom Bennett after she died. Did your Aunt Victoria tell you about him, Michelle?"

"No, why would she?" Michelle said.

"No reason. I just assumed she might have shared the story since you've spent so much time with her up in Boston."

"She didn't mention it," Michelle said. "I'm so sorry that he's bothering you after all these years. We've got to stop him, even if it means stopping Robert, too."

"Well, my fate is sealed," he said. Pierre stood quiet a moment, his head bent as if praying. "I'm just upset over Robert, I didn't see it coming. I was so absorbed with myself that I never noticed what was happening to him. I wasn't even aware they knew each other, Robert and Tom. Or that his roommate Jackson was Tom's son." He hung his head. "Oh, will God forgive me?"

Emilie's father's guilt weighed on her, and a cold thought crossed her mind. *Will Robert go to jail for all he's done?* She looked at Michelle, who was caught up in the drama of it all.

"Robert had me fooled. I thought he genuinely wanted to help me with the company so he could take over. I believed in him." Pierre stared absently a moment. "Robert's failure is my sin, and I will have to do penance for it. I hope you girls will forgive me somehow. I never meant to neglect you."

He dropped his chin to his chest. The room stayed quiet until he cleared his throat. "Listen to me, we don't have much time. I've changed my will. The estate is in your hands, both of you. The changes have been made, and the paperwork is already signed and sealed. It is up to you two to protect my legacy. Make no mistake, Robert will be furious that he's excluded. He's under the impression everything is his, as a birthright, but I will not allow Tom Bennett to use my son any longer."

Pierre stopped pacing, and stood in front of Michelle. "Your brother will fight you for control, no question. After I die, you'll have a battle on your hands."

Emilie hated to hear him talking like this. His anxiety was unsettling. Pierre started pacing again. He walked to his desk, kneading his hands together, his brow wet with perspiration. "Father, you talk as if you want to die," she said.

"We all die, Emilie." He waved a dismissive hand at her and continued, talking faster now. "The accountants have straightened things out as much as possible while Robert's been occupied. He's involved in a Trojan project I invented to keep him busy. Officially, he has no control over any funds.

"If I survive the ceremony today, then I'll confront him and deal with the whole situation myself. But we all know there's a chance I won't survive, and make no mistake, I'm willing to take that chance if it means saving Rachael's life and my family's future. It doesn't matter if you agree or understand, be brave, and let me go through with this to the end. Promise me, girls."

They nodded half-heartedly.

"If I die, you will have to enforce things. I'm leaving the final business decisions to Michelle." Pierre looked at Emilie. "Do you understand, Emilie? One person needs to be at the helm."

She shook her head, terrified at the thought of her father dying today.

"Promise me." He dropped his hand on his desk. "Make sure Robert has no access or control, not the slightest. You will have to be strong. Can you do this? Are you up to the challenge?"

"Yes, of course, I'll do my best," Michelle said.

"Robert will make your life hell," Pierre continued. He hung his head for a moment, in deep meditation, before he looked at them again. "You still need to promise me one thing, both of you: live with your brother in the house. It's the only asset left with his name on it. I just can't take that away, too. The house will be his legacy."

"Thank you for trusting Emilie and me," Michelle said. "Don't worry. I'll take care of things, and Emilie, too, the same way she always took care of us. Though I have a feeling she won't be in Memphis long." Michelle smiled. "You and Jeremy make the perfect couple, and you're destined for more than Memphis."

Pierre nodded his agreement. "Emilie will always watch your back, Michelle, no matter where she is. Never underestimate the help your sister can provide with the business."

"You're right," Emilie said. "We'll watch each other's backs, right, Chelle? Though no more secrets, no more doubts."

"There's just one more thing. Robert has already proved his deceit runs deep. Don't trust him again until he proves himself, I'm afraid he may have lost his soul already, so pray for his redemption. Father Eddie says it is never too late. I hope he's right."

Emilie still had reservations about all this. If her brother had done such horrible things, then why not go to jail? She knew the answer before she even voiced the question aloud: her father wanted to avoid the scandal of it all. Knowing her father, there wouldn't be any jail time. She asked the question anyway, already anticipating the answer.

"What about criminal charges against Robert?" she said.

"Promise me, both of you. No charges, ever. This will be handled privately, no one is to learn of this. I owe your brother that much."

Emilie went back upstairs and read to Rachael for the remainder of the afternoon. Her voice comforted herself as much as it did her ill friend. With everything going on in her family, secret agendas and her brother's inexcusable behavior, it was almost more than she could bear.

What I need is time, to sort it all out in my head.

Unfortunately, time was limited. She looked over at the big bed and considered Rachael's weakened body. Then, she remembered her mother and the days before she died. Emilie didn't want that suffering to happen again. This plan had to work, for everyone's future. Her Father was right, and she'd do her best to support his decision.

While Emilie read, Michelle sat at the desk in Rachael's room quietly working on her laptop, reviewing some information Father had given her about the new will. Michelle fidgeted, and Emilie sensed her sister's anxiety, but she kept reading and thinking. Somehow she had to find a way to make sense of everything happening, while trying to understand what her brother had done. *But how does one reconcile the drugging of one's own father?*

Nina came into the room with lunch, and left sandwiches on folding tray tables. Emilie was in no mood to eat. The room was quiet, but turbulent theories pounded within her brain like a drum. Never had the silence been so loud. She concentrated on the sound of the hallway clock's ticking, back and forth. The movement helped to keep the emotions in a steady rhythm, instead of pulling her mind apart.

Late in the afternoon, Emilie's phone rang. It was Father Eddie informing her that he'd be there soon. Emilie made a quick call to Jeremy; Michelle nodded as she heard the conversation, acknowledging the update. A few minutes later, the front doorbell rang. She heard Father Eddie bustling into the foyer, and he was escorted straight to Pierre's library.

"Ready, Michelle?"

Emilie and Michelle went downstairs and found their father and Father Eddie headed for the kitchen.

"I just called Jeremy. He's on his way," Emilie said.

"Good, we need him here for support," Pierre said. "And to help make the drink and perform the chant in the ceremony."

Eddie nodded as they entered the kitchen.

"Nina, you're dismissed for the evening. Go to your sister's house. We need quiet here tonight," Pierre said.

She turned and gave him a stern look. "There's a house full of people and I got dinner to prepare. Now that Miss Rachael is here, everyone will be needing to eat to keep up their spirits."

"We don't need a big dinner. Go, I insist."

Nina's brow pinched in anger. "This time you've gone too far, Pierre. If their mother wuz—" she stopped mid-sentence, noticing Father Eddie standing in the kitchen doorway. "Are you going to have one of those Catholic masses for Miss Rachael? Well, fine then, why didn't you just say so." Nina turned around, grabbed her stuff, and left in a huff.

"Let's get going. We have to make the drink and perform the ceremony before Robert gets back from the office. We don't have much time left," Eddie said.

Michelle popped into the room. "I dismissed the nurse for the day, so now the house is clear of potential witnesses. Rachael had an agonizing day and she's weak. The effects of the medication the nurse administered before she left should keep her knocked out. Hopefully that will last for a while, but we need to make sure her vitals remain stable until we're finished."

"Of course," Eddie said.

Emilie heard the front door open, and immediately the barest sense of calm swept over her. A moment later, Jeremy walked into the room.

"Good, we're all here. Let's get started," Pierre said.

The three men took over the kitchen and prepared the drink, according to the specifications of the Timucua legend. Father Eddie had acquired the cassava plant from Mr. Labue. Emilie hated to think that such a kind man had been pulled into the middle of this mess. She kept her hopes high that it would all be over soon.

The men used holly leaves to make the white tea, which ironically turned out very dark in color, just as described in the journal. So far all looked well, and they prepared a second drink using some of the white tea as a base, and then added the poisonous cassava. Once brewed, they carefully carried the potions upstairs and placed the pots on the table at the end of Rachael's bed. Father Eddie acted as the coordinator.

"Okay, folks, listen up. First, we need to make the altar. Michelle, use this sand mixed with the ashes from the chief and the captain, and please draw this out on the floor here, in front of the hearth." Father Eddie indicated the area and handed her the paper with the diagram. "Take this diagram we copied from the journal. Have it fill the entire area here, so we have room to move around."

"These ashes are dead people? I'm not good with dead people or art," she said.

"Do your best," Father Eddie said.

She studied the drawing and then started marking it out on the floor.

"Okay, now," Father Eddie continued. "Let's see . . . We're using the ashes sent back from the burial sites, those will have to suffice for the idols they used. In essence, the idols of the panther and owl are there in the ashes. Emilie, I heard you have a brooch that was on the captain's cloak, can you get that? We will use that as our new talisman, just to make sure we have a connection with the captain." Eddie nodded, checking off a list in his head.

Emilie returned with the brooch, and placed it in Father Eddie's sizeable hand. He bent over and placed it with care in the center of the altar that Michelle had drawn on the floor.

"I wrote out the words of the chant as the author of the journal had understood them. Everyone, take a copy and see if you can make sense of the phonetics."

He handed each of them a slip of paper with the sounds written down, broken out like in a dictionary. They all looked over the words, pronouncing them softly to themselves.

"Now, this is how it will happen. I will act on behalf of Chief Saturiwa, and your father as Captain Dominique."

Father Eddie turned to speak to them face to face. "First, your father and I will drink the white tea together to purify our spirits and then, Pierre, you will drink the second potion as we recite our parts. I will use this knife and slice your arm, and drip some blood into the potion in this wooden bowl. When you drink again, hopefully it will bring on the trance."

Eddie turned and spoke to his friend in a tender voice. "Pierre, once you enter the correct state of mind and travel to the spirit world, see if you can locate what is holding onto Rachael and then set her free. And friend, please return to me."

He turned and finished, speaking to them all. "Your father will then free Rachael and return her to us. Understood? Are we all set?"

Jeremy cleared his throat and spoke up. "Father Eddie, I want to do this instead of Pierre. No disrespect, but I think I stand a better chance. I'm stronger, younger, and I will have the best chance to survive the potion."

Pierre objected. "No, this is for me to do. I'm the only de Gourgues here who is cursed, and it's my responsibility. Thank you, Jeremy, but it's not possible your way."

Father Eddie placed a hand on Jeremy's shoulder. "I'm in agreement with Pierre. He is our best chance. Now let's do this before it's too late."

Emilie felt a twinge of relief. She had never wanted Jeremy to take the poison, and thankfully, he dropped the subject. The priest lit a fire in the hearth just beyond the altar of ash Michelle had drawn. Then, he placed some of the captain's and the chief's ashes into a wooden bowl. He placed the brooch from the captain's cloak near the bowls. They were ready to begin.

CHAPTER THIRTY-FIVE

Father Eddie and Pierre drank white tea from a smaller bowl and recited words in the Timucua tongue, fumbling the foreign syllables. After repeating the ceremonial incantation, they took a second sip of the white tea and Emilie watched her father turn pale, sweat dripping from his brow. Strength appeared to drain out of him. Emilie handed him a towel. He took it, gave her a nod, and patted his face dry.

"Let's continue," the priest said. He sounded exhausted, but started the ritual again. Father Eddie then took Pierre's upper arm while holding a knife in the other. A streak of light cut through the dimness and Emilie flinched. It was a hunting knife, the worn handle made of a warm chestnut-colored wood, honed smooth, and the blade was wide and sharp. It fit snug in Eddie's hand. He sliced Pierre's arm and Pierre winced, watching his blood drip into the bowl.

Emilie felt the echo of hot searing pain as the knife cut into her father's arm. She was confused. Her body clenched against the pain, as if she had also been cut. She pulled up her sleeve and examined her arm, expecting to see blood. Her skin was unscathed.

This troubled her. It was bad enough that she experienced her father's emotions, but now she also felt his physical pain too. This was a new aspect of her clairvoyant gift, revealing itself at the worst of times.

She swallowed back her fear. Emilie had promised her father she'd be strong, and she meant to keep her word. As if he sensed her distress, Jeremy reached over and touched her arm. Just as before, her balance was restored. She gazed up at him and nodded to show her appreciation, and that she was okay and had pulled herself together.

The priest mixed Pierre's blood with some of the ashes, then added some potion from the second pot, the brew with the cassava.

Emilie glanced over at her sister. Michelle's eyes were wide as she mumbled the words. Realizing her sister was scared to death, Emilie reached over and held her hand. Michelle looked down at their hands and smiled. She found some spunk, and her chant grew louder.

Father Eddie recited as Pierre drank from the bowl. Emilie turned her attention to her father, watching him swallow. The bitter taste of cassava and coppery metal lingered on her tongue. Her father grimaced but forced himself to swallow more of the deadly mixture. As he guzzled the brew down and consumed the poison, Emilie shared his agony.

Pierre choked and dropped the bowl, clutching his throat with both hands. Father Eddie, still chanting, filled the bowl again and handed it to Pierre. He took it, nodded, and drank another swig, forcing it down in a big gulp. His face reddened. Eddie took the bowl, and moved it aside.

Pierre was shaking as if cold, but still dripping with sweat. He swayed a little, and Emilie felt herself sway in response. Eddie reached out to help Pierre steady himself on his feet and one squeeze from Jeremy's hand calmed Emilie as well. He joined the priest in the mantra. The two men chanted, louder by this time. Emilie suddenly became woozy herself as their song vibrated in her head, pounding like her worst migraine.

Then the room transformed. A force hovered above them, and everything became surreal. Things blurred and distorted. The furniture seemed to bend and the bedpost looked crooked. Her father rocked back and forth as if to balance himself against rough seas. Groggy and out of focus, Emilie's head spun. Then the invocation stopped and there was no sound at all, as if a vacuum had sucked up all the noise.

Thud! Silence was broken when her father collided with the floor.

"Ouch!" Emilie felt the beginning of a bruise.

"Are you all right?" Jeremy's voice was faint, as if it came from a great distance.

Emilie heard herself scream. Pierre was on the floor, his eyes bulging and his face fixed in a grimace of pain. She reached out for him, but was constrained. She turned and realized Jeremy held her back. She was vaguely aware that he continued to recite the ritual words. Emilie looked into his eyes, searching for the strength she needed. She rubbed her forehead to massage the spiking headache away. She breathed deep, drew in her resolve, and regained her self-control. She joined Jeremy and Michelle in the chant.

"No onoromota holatamaqui."

Her father convulsed, his body jerking painfully. His face burned crimson as the cassava potion overpowered his body. He continued chanting despite his pain. They all recited the verses together, the words sounding more like a song with each zealous refrain. Emilie swore she heard her father howl, like a rabid animal.

The fear and superstition, the horror, the pain, images and emotions spilled into Emilie's head with no way for her to control the flow.

Then she realized that something major had changed. There was an underlying shift in the room. She went with him, as Pierre soared into the spirit world beyond the veil.

The world around Emilie changed, distorted like in a fever dream. Small things, like the book on the table were larger, while things like the bed shrank. A rotten smell accosted her nostrils, reeking like the decomposition of corpses. The stench leached into the room.

The lamps blinked on and off, then the room plunged into darkness. Only the flames from the fireplace provided illumination. A flash of light blinded them, as if a star filled the space between them. Emilie covered her eyes, and she heard unnatural, guttural noises streaming from Pierre.

Pierre was split in two—existing in his comatose body lying on the bedroom floor, and at the same time in another dimension of time, a different space and state of being. Emilie saw his face spark with enlightenment. She understood, he could see everything and everyone. Pierre's soul possessed an understanding of who he was, and he was content. His spirit attracted the others from his lineage, and they connected with him. In this realm, he experienced his family history, and now possessed the knowledge of all of them within himself. He turned and gazed at Emilie, who was by his side, and smiled. She felt fatherly warmth, which she had never known before. Emilie's spirit glowed alongside his.

His mood swung like a clock's pendulum. Now, on the opposite side of the veil, doom was near. He bravely opened himself up to determine its origin. Emilie knew Rachael's spirit was close but remained enslaved. Rachael struggled to go back to earth, back into her shell, but was paralyzed by some power stronger than herself. The power was sinister in nature, and held her so tightly in a grip of evil that she couldn't project an uttered sound from her soul.

Pierre went to Rachael, moving through space and time by sheer will. Emilie soared with him, feeling the sense of wind blowing through her very soul, and knew when her father had finally found her. Pierre raised his arms up in protest, and laid hands on the evil veil that possessed Rachael. He pushed back against the wickedness, commanding it to leave her. Emilie pushed and wielded her strength as well. A vague image appeared through the mist, and she could see her father's determined expression, with clenched teeth and raised brow. She felt his fortitude; no resolve had ever been so pure.

However, the malevolence was strong, and possessed deep-seated power. Pierre couldn't push it away from the girl, its hold was too tight, even with Emilie's most fervent attempt to help. Pierre knew what had to be done. He cried out with his essence to all the family members in this veiled space and summoned them to gather. Emilie became aware of many spirits—her father, grandfather, great grandfather, and many more. All of the spirits throughout the centuries, belonging to the de Gourgues lineage were now there, united as one strong force of nature. It was an intense sensation, and Emilie surged with inner strength from the reinforcement.

In her heart, Emilie acknowledged that this moment was Pierre's destiny. All along, it had been his role to free his family from the curse. He opened his soul and with his life force appealed to the other spirits. He led the way, knowing that together they could defeat the evil, breaking the cursed bonds with one united will.

A heavy fog appeared; Emilie's breathing became labored, somehow hampered by the humid air. She heard water splashing, as if someone was trudging through a swamp, forcing their way through murky waters. She saw a figure emerge, Captain Dominique de Gourgues, the strongest of them all. When he materialized into the light, standing by his side was the tall and brave Chief Saturiwa. His ebony hair and dark eyes no longer seemed menacing like in her dream. His stare was fixed, determined, as he matched the Captain's dignified stance. Both ghosts conveyed a sense that a mutual mission was about to happen, and that they were on the same side and at peace with each other.

Using Pierre's soul as a guide for moral strength, and the Captain's and Chief's spirits as the compass, together the ancestors joined their forces and banished the evil power away from the girl-child named Rachael.

Emilie sensed Rachael's release. Freed from that realm, she returned to the earthly space. Rachael's spirit fell, racing rapidly back down the path of the veil, in a blur. She swirled down the tunnel back to her shell, filling her body once again. Rachael's spiritual being melded with her physical, and Emilie envisioned herself falling too, to the point of nausea, yet she felt so liberated.

The lineage was emancipated, and their souls set free.

Pierre's spirit soar, feeling light as air, in a euphoric high, his burden of earthly beliefs gone. He was one with the spirit world, and he knew this was where he wanted to remain. He would not return to Earth. She watched his spirit fly by in bliss.

Emilie was heartbroken, even though she understood her father's experience of total happiness, his nirvana. Pierre was finally at peace, but she knew this was the last time she would sense him. Her father had chosen to die, and now she'd be without him.

She turned, detecting someone powerful close by. It was her mother. Bethany slowly revealed herself, and Emilie could see her mother's delicate face, heart-shaped like her own, with her freckles and soft pink lips. Bethany joined her father, and together they filled each other with deep love and peace. Emilie sensed their happiness.

They forgot Earth. Her parents' suffering was erased and replaced with love. This was their eternity, their forever after. Together, Bethany and Pierre melded their spirits, appearing as a single bright light in the vast universe. Emilie was alone, her parents' spirits gone from her, forever.

CHAPTER THIRTY-SIX

Seconds went by in the physical world, after Pierre's body went limp on the floor. Only a moment passed as everyone stared at his lifeless form.

Emilie was in a tailspin, filled with her own anxiety and processing her father's last experiences as well. Somehow, she'd connected with him in a way she had never done before. She had seen and felt everything in the other dimension, and she was confused by the bizarre wonder of it all.

Emilie heard Rachael, gasping and wheezing for air, like she had just escaped from drowning. She watched as Michelle rushed to her side. Rachael sat up, her face glowing, her beauty restored. She looked healthy, her cheeks filled with color and her hair lustrous. She had been saved.

"She's okay. It worked!" Michelle called out to the others.

The lights came back on. Emilie turned her attention back to her father on the floor, unresponsive. Jeremy was at his side, trying to resuscitate him, pounding on his chest and counting. He pumped her father's chest in even thrusts, fiercely trying to save him. Jeremy refused to give up, until Father Eddie edged him aside minutes later.

"It's over. Now he needs his last rites," the priest said.

Kneeling near her father's body, Father Eddie took out a purple cloth and wrapped it around his neck. He held a bottle of holy water and some blessed oils and made the sign of the cross over her father's eyes, ears and mouth, mumbling prayers and absolving Pierre of his sins.

She wondered if it mattered whether her father received the sacrament before or after he died. She knew her father was gone before anyone else realized it, and she couldn't feel any hint of his lingering presence. Even though his last emotion was jubilance, she still mourned.

The fire in the hearth had died down to coals. The room smelled smoky, and Michelle was spraying air freshener at Rachael's request. She stole a look at their father lying on the floor and Michelle almost buckled. Emilie watched as her sister drew in a deep breath and then returned to Rachael's side. Father Eddie continued to sprinkle holy water over Pierre's body and kept reciting prayer after prayer for his friend.

Dazed, Emilie sat on the floor next to her father's body, with tears sliding down her cheeks. She tasted the saltiness and wiped her face with the back of her hand. Emilie felt drained and unable to speak, which didn't matter because she had no clue how to explain her experience on the other side of the veil. They wouldn't believe her anyway, especially Michelle.

The emotions in the room were erratic. Emilie attempted to sort them out, weaving her way through, but they were layered too thickly. Echoes of the spirits from the other side lingered in her mind, too. She was afraid things had gotten beyond her control. Jeremy placed his hand on her back. It helped to know she wasn't alone, but his confusion only added to the burden.

Rachael appeared grateful to be alive and well, smiling and looking gorgeous as ever. However, she also seemed confused, as she searched the room for Robert.

"Emilie, call the doctor, please," Father Eddie said.

She mindlessly pulled out her phone and dialed Doc Hannigan's number. She heard Eddie ordering the others in the room as she waited for the doctor to pick up.

"Quickly, let's get these things out of here. Dump what's left and wash everything thoroughly. Jeremy, take the knife and all the ingredients and dump them in my bag. That's right. Here are my keys, lock them in my car," Father Eddie said. "No one can know about the potion. There can't be implications of foul play."

A voice answered the call. "Hello this is Doc—"

"Doc Hannigan, this is Emilie de Gourgues. Come to the house now. My father . . . he's dead."

"I understand. I'm on my way." The Doc hung up, not sounding surprised to hear the news. Meanwhile, the others were straightening the room. Jeremy grabbed the keys and did as instructed. Father Eddie wrapped a bandage over the knife wound on her father's arm and rolled down his shirtsleeve. Michelle had grabbed a vacuum from the closet in the hallway and swept up the sand on the floor. Emilie had never seen her sister clean house before, and for a bizarre brief second she was amused. The only thing that remained from the ceremony was Pierre lying there, dead on the floor.

The doorbell rang. Michelle escorted Doc Hannigan up the stairs to the front bedroom. He nodded at Rachael when he walked into the room, then went to Pierre's body.

Doc Hannigan was an older gentleman, and took his time bending down to be close to the body. He pulled a stethoscope out of his bag and inspected her father, checking his vitals for heartbeat and pulse, then opened his eyes and shined a light into the orbs. When finished, he pulled his phone from his jacket pocket and called for a transport to the morgue. He smiled, but the smile seemed foreign on his soft and humbled face. "I'm sorry for your loss, girls. I know how much your father loved you both. It looks like he went painlessly; look, he has a smile on his face. It's better this way."

"What does that mean?" Michelle snapped.

"Oh, I'm sorry. I didn't mean to be insensitive. It's just that going fast like this is often a better alternative than having your father drag things out and suffer through chemo and all."

"Chemo! Em, did you know about this?" Michelle spun around, outraged.

"No, of course not." Emilie leaned toward Father Eddie. He shook his head, obviously also unaware of Pierre's true state of health. "I wonder why didn't he tell us?"

"Maybe this was all done to spare us?" Michelle said.

"Let's not worry anymore. He's with Mother now." Emilie was uncertain about a lot that had happened, but her parents' happy ending was the one truth she felt confident about.

A few minutes later, Jeremy led the paramedics into the room. They recorded the time and particulars on a paper form snapped onto a clipboard. Doc Hannigan signed the paperwork for the death certificate, and the two men prepped the body to be carried out.

"I tried CPR, but unsuccessfully," Jeremy said.

Doc Hannigan nodded. "It's a shame. He was just in my office the other day, too. He wasn't much for appointments, so I knew he wasn't feeling well. Almost like he sensed it was about to happen."

"Well, at least I was able to give him his last rites," Father Eddie said.

Eddie said more prayers, asking God's blessing on the family in this time of sorrow. The attendants did a side-glance each time Eddie made the sign of the cross in the air, as if the priest was a crazy man. Many in the South were suspicious of Catholics. If only they knew how wayward this priest had gone. Emilie watched as the scene played out, remaining distant, like it was all an old movie and she was in the back row.

"Emilie, are you all right?" Doc Hannigan looked concerned, as if he had asked the question a few times already. He stared at her, checking the pupils of her eyes.

"Yes, Doc, I'm fine."

Everyone in the room knew it was a lie.

CHAPTER THIRTY-SEVEN

Emilie sat in the corner chair and watched the others. The transport men were just leaving, along with the Doc Hannigan, when she heard a car roar up the driveway, then the car door slammed. She was sure it was Robert. There was a commotion downstairs before he dashed up the stairs, racing toward the front bedroom.

Robert burst into the room, and immediately looked at Rachael. He jerked his head back a second and looked confused when he saw her sitting up in bed, looking healthier than ever. "Oh my God, Rachael. I had such a fright. I thought that something was wrong. Why is there an ambulance in the driveway? What's going on?"

Rachael shifted her gaze and Robert followed. He saw everyone crowded around their father, who appeared dead on the gurney. Men were strapping the last belt, and preparing to leave.

"What happened here?" Robert said.

"Sorry, Robert," Doc Hannigan said as he held out his hand. "Your father has passed away. Sorry for your loss, son."

"How did this happen? What did he die from, heart attack?"

"Yes, it looks like his heart gave out, but the fact is that he was riddled with cancer. Looks like he was spared a painful and long road of suffering. Someone was looking out for him." Doc raised his eyes.

"Yes, indeed." Robert looked around the room, taking in every detail. He froze, staring as the men passed by him, wheeling out the body.

"Robert, Father had a heart attack, he was gone before we could help him. Jeremy tried to resuscitate him, but it was hopeless." Michelle choked the words out between sobs. It seemed as if the reality of the situation was beginning to take hold for her.

Emilie watched as Robert scanned the room. Everyone else was sending out many emotions, mostly dark. A jumbled mix of sadness, remorse, and confusion.

The negative vibrations unleashed from her brother shouted more loudly than all the others in the room. Robert glared as if he was angry, and she figured it had nothing to do with Father's death. Something else was eating away at him.

He recovered his poise in an instant, pulling himself together like a true performer. He moved to sit at Rachael's bedside. "Are you all right, sweetheart?"

"Robert, it's as if a weird miracle happened in this room."

Emilie overheard Rachael and wondered if she'd spill something about the ceremony.

"Your poor father died, right there on the floor, but I feel perfectly well. It's as if he gave me his life." She averted her eyes. "I am so sorry about your father."

Robert pressed his lips together tight, and inhaled short breaths. After a moment, he leaned over, gave Rachael a kiss on her forehead, and absently began playing with her thick hair. "You look wonderful, Rachael. It's as if you were never ill."

Emilie noticed he had something in his other hand, which he covertly slipped into his pocket, and then he held Rachael's hand in his.

What was he hiding? She was vaguely aware of more commotion as people began to file out of the bedroom. Emilie got up from the chair, not able to remember how she'd gotten there in the first place. Jeremy offered his arm, and as they left the room she heard Michelle suggest that Robert and Rachael sleep in Robert's room, since Father had died here.

Robert followed them out and then turned down the hall toward his own room. He pulled out his cell phone as he opened his bedroom door.

Emilie tugged on Jeremy's sleeve and mouthed,

"Wait a minute."

They stopped and she listened. Her brother was on the phone with someone, and she wanted to know what he was up to. Emilie turned around and walked closer to his room in order to eavesdrop.

"Do you freaking believe that! Right there on the floor. It blows . . . Yes, I can still get the money but things will be shut down for a few days now . . .

"Yes, it's in the charter. But . . . Let me check . . . Okay, we'll meet up in a couple of days."

There was a rustle, as if Robert was pacing the floor.

"What? Oh, she's fine. Like a miracle, I just don't get it. I didn't even have to use a dose . . . Yes, well I guess it all worked its way out of her system on its own . . . Uh huh, you too." He stopped talking.

Emilie turned and ran away from Robert's door, pulling Jeremy along as they fled down the hall toward her own room. Once there, she listened and waited until Robert walked out of his room. He went into Rachael's room for a moment and came back out saying, "Yes, let me get a bite to eat first. I'm famished. I'll be right back and help you to our room."

Robert blew Rachael a kiss.

Emilie scooted back into her room and closed the door quickly.

"What was that all about?" Jeremy asked.

"Didn't you hear him? Robert was talking to someone on the phone and I bet it was Tom Bennett, or maybe Laura, my father's secretary. Hmmm."

She went back to the door and peeked. "He's gone downstairs. Hurry before he comes back up."

"Hurry and what?"

"I need to check something. Come on."

Emilie pulled Jeremy back into the hall, and led the way to Robert's door. She went in and looked around for his jacket. It was flung over the desk chair. She dashed over and checked the right pocket, pulling out a small bottle and a packaged syringe. She opened her hand and showed Jeremy.

"See, look at this." She read the label. "It's sodium thiosulfate. Why the hell would he have a syringe and this in his pocket? Do you think he'll notice if I take it?"

"Hell, yes," he replied.

"Do you know what it's used for?"

"A dose of this can work to dechlorinate tap water. I've used it before in the field to stabilize water before is flows into rivers. It kills ringworm, and it also reverses cyanide poisoning, if caught in time." Jeremy's face suddenly went pale. "You don't think that your brother . . ."

"Let's get out of here," she said.

The two of them went back to Emilie's bedroom and sat a moment, taking in the new discovery.

"They did tests on Rachael, right? They would have known if she was poisoned, wouldn't they?" Emilie said.

"You would think so, but the tests they performed might not pick up ataxia if it wasn't something they were looking for. The human body already has some trace of cyanide, so maybe nothing triggered an alert in the bloodwork. Besides, it's not a common thing here in the States, it happens more often in third-world countries where they eat staples like yuca that produce cyanide naturally. If prepared incorrectly, they can actually die. Wait, Em, yuca is also called cassava," he said.

"You don't think that Robert gave Rachael cassava? As in the same plant we used in the magic drink that flipped my father into some hallucinated dream state and ended up giving him a heart attack? Oh, I can't even imagine that my brother would do that. I mean, I think he loves her."

Jeremy shrugged. "Well, maybe it was innocent. Maybe what we found in his pocket was there only to help her. You know, like a last-resort kind of thing."

"So, Robert just happened to be armed with the antidote, sodium thiosulfate, to help Rachael detoxify. But the question is, how did he know she needed it? I don't like this twist," Emilie said.

"Well, thank God she's better now. Who knows, maybe Robert had ringworm."

Emilie punched Jeremy in the arm.

CHAPTER THIRTY-EIGHT

Three days of calling hours were held at the funeral parlor, a long, consuming ritual. Business associates paraded past the family to pay their respects, most also trying to gain an edge for future deals. People from all over the world sent their condolences if unable to attend. With a successful enterprise comes a responsibility to the community: family obligation kept them standing in place, like sentries at a gate, accepting the kind words. Hour after hour, people swept by the three siblings. For Emilie, their faces blurred into one massive silhouette, and she blocked out as much as possible. She was still struggling to sort out all the echoes left in her mind from the blitz that had happened in the other world.

Jeremy stood by her side, which helped her to be brave, but he worried about her too much. She certainly wasn't about to tell him everything she was experiencing. She wanted to protect him, and was afraid too much information might send him packing. It was bad enough just knowing that her brother stood beside them playing at being a good son, when they all knew he was somehow behind so much of this drama.

There was another reason Emilie spared Jeremy her burden. She knew he still grieved for his Uncle Thaddeus; his funeral wasn't much more than a month ago. Jeremy talked about the promise he'd made, and planned to keep it. Jeremy would have no rest until he discovered who had paid Mr. Pierce to steal the journal from his Uncle Thaddeus in the first place. While he and Emilie had been chasing down burial sites, he had hired someone to track Pierce. To that end, Jeremy had received a call the day they returned to Memphis. His sources reported that Mr. Pierce was once again staying at the Peabody Hotel. Jeremy planned on paying him a visit soon, after the funeral business was over.

Each night after calling hours, they went back to the house, where Emilie crashed after taking a sleeping pill. This was not how she wanted to deal with things. Her worst nightmare was happening to her. She was losing control, and was afraid she may lose Jeremy, too.

On the fourth day, a Catholic Mass was scheduled. Barely conscious of her surroundings, Emilie walked down the aisle flanked with oak pews. Jeremy escorted her to the bench where Michelle, Robert, and Rachael were already seated. She smelled the heavy fumes from the incense as the altar boy swung the thurible over the coffin, its clatter rattling her nerves. Memories of her mother's funeral haunted her, and she slipped into depression. She wanted to be left alone, but everyone's emotions scratched at her mind, threatening her with another possible clairvoyant break-in.

When the somber Mass finished, a long procession of cars drove to the cemetery to lay Pierre's body to rest in the plot next to his beloved Bethany. A large pecan tree shaded the area and a breeze skipped across the wide lawn, giving them relief from the hot, late-morning sun. Emilie stood beside Michelle, holding her hand as they cried. Jeremy stood behind them, his hands on their shoulders. Rachael shed tears too, and gently dried the corners of her eyes with a Kleenex. Emilie was happy her friend was alive and well.

Robert stood alone without remorse.

The casket lowered into the ground, the last flowers strewn on top of the grave. Emilie made the sign of the cross, then turned to walk back to the limo.

"Thank God that's over," Robert said just before they reached the car.

Emilie wiped her eyes. "We have no more parents to bury, Robert."

He shrugged and walked faster to catch up to Jeremy, who had gone ahead to open the car door. Her brother leaned toward Jeremy and said, "What's your game, Englishman?

Are you a sap in love with my sister, or just another purse chaser?"

Emilie was behind them and heard the taunt. Her face burned. "Robert! What the hell are you saying?"

"Never you mind. I need to get out of this place and have a drink. Let's go already."

On the fifth day after Pierre's death, John Lawson, Esquire, was expected at the house to read the last will and testament. All the people concerned mingled in the front parlor. Robert played host to those who had an interest in the will. Emilie watched him sway as he crossed the room. He obviously had a few drinks under his belt already. He gave no indication that he felt their father's loss. His sedated smile looked foreign, and Emilie wondered what had happened to the brother she knew and loved. He was a tragedy. She hoped Rachael hadn't noticed his inebriation.

"Would anyone care for a drink?" he called out.

"I'll pass," Jeremy said.

"Me, too," said Emilie.

"Make that three, none for me," Michelle said. Emilie watched her sister. She looked anxious, and who could blame her? Soon Robert would learn the truth, and they had no idea how he'd react.

"Well, aren't you like the Three Musketeers, or would that be the three stooges?" Robert chuckled. "Sober little mice, aren't you all? Maybe you should lighten up a little, Emilie." Robert laughed, thinking himself clever.

Emilie turned away, and felt her face turn red.

"Robert, really, don't you think you've had enough?" Michelle said.

"I'm just getting started," he replied.

"We need to talk," she persisted. "Listen to me, Rob, please. There's something you need to know about Tom Bennett. It's important. The sooner we talk the better."

"Oh please. Michelle, when I want advice from my baby sister I'll ask. Until then, shut it," he said.

Robert smiled, but Emilie sensed his fury toward his own sisters. The funeral had been a huge affair, and during the drama, Robert publicly played the dutiful son and the honorable new husband, with Rachael by his side. Important people attended, people of influence that Robert wanted on his side. He was a born manipulator. Emilie knew that, having watched him in action on many occasions. He put on a good show; Robert had everyone fooled except the family. His sisters knew his true feelings about Father, even though misguided.

Robert turned his head when a voice from across the room called out. "I'll take a scotch and water, please." It was Tom Bennett, Emilie recognized his evil smile as he sauntered closer to the bar.

"Well, hello again, Miss de Gourgues," he said.

A cold shiver trickled down her back, and her skin crawled. Emilie glared at him and turned to leave, disgusted that he was there.

She heard her brother say as she walked away, "One scotch and water coming up. I wasn't expecting you here today, Tom. I'm surprised, but it's always good to see you." Robert handed Tom Bennett a glass and raised his in a toast.

"Thank you, Robert," Emilie heard Bennett say. "I just wanted to lend you my support. I don't have an interest in the will, but I'm hoping we can speak after you're finished here, if I'm not imposing." The man grinned. "Could you stop by the Peabody, at your convenience, of course?"

He stood there chatting up Robert, brazen and dark, so smug in her father's house. Tom Bennett was not a good man; others in the room looked over at him and whispered amongst themselves as he attempted feeble jokes. He and Robert laughed, as though they'd forgotten the somber reason for the occasion. Bennett was trouble, and Emilie wished he'd crawl away into some dark corner, somewhere far from them.

Afraid she was going to be sick, Emilie left before she had to hear any more. In the foyer, Michelle caught up to her.

"Emilie, wait," she called. "Do you believe his gall? And Rob standing there yakking with him, and Father only dead a few days. Already the vultures are circling."

"Father was right about Tom Bennett. He's evil," Emilie said.

A moment later, Tom Bennett walked past them on his way out, sauntering as if he owned the place.

"Michelle, restrain your anger, please. You're giving me a headache."

"Sorry, it makes me seethe to see that arrogant man here. Robert was already so bitter, now there will be no turning him back to the family. It would take a miracle. And in a few minutes he'll hate me more than ever, as soon as the truth is revealed."

"Don't worry, Michelle. It will be all right."

"Easy for you to say, Em. Secrecy was necessary to save Robert from criminal charges, so not many people know the entire story. They'll think I'm the gold digger. Top that off with the fact that in order to keep Robert from jail, everything has to remain quiet. Unfortunately, that means Tom Bennett walks free, too. Stew over that a minute."

"There you two are," Jeremy said, joining them in the foyer. "After seeing Bennett here, I thought you might need this." He handed them each a glass of wine.

"Thank you, sir." Jeremy always made her feel better. She reached into her pocket and rubbed the small shell that she'd kept with her since he'd given it to her.

Emilie checked her watch. While they waited for the will to be read, the replacement security locks and codes to all the offices were being installed. Pierre's secretary Laura had been given a pink slip the day before, and she had signed a confidentiality agreement in return for immunity to prosecution. Laura had happily signed, but she never implicated Robert. Not that it mattered, Emilie reflected. She and Michelle knew the truth.

John Lawton, their lawyer, had followed her father's wishes and drawn up the necessary paperwork after their last meeting. Father wanted to avoid slander around the family name, at all costs. Now, it was up to Michelle and Emilie to finish the last part of Father's plan. Emilie stood there, her stomach in knots, waiting for the other shoe to drop.

Mr. Lawson passed by her in the foyer and entered the parlor. "Can I have everyone's attention, please? As acting attorney and executor of Pierre's last will and testament, I'd like to begin. First, I would like to go through some wishes that concern the staff and friends, and then I ask that the children and Reverend Eddie, please meet with me in the library afterward."

He read the part of the will covering various charities that Pierre had remembered with contributions. Then, the staff and longtime loyal employees from the company were given various lump sums of money for their loyal service. A final statement of thanks was read and then most of the room emptied out, except for Nina, of course. She stayed on and started cleaning up the mess left behind. The family converged in the library to finish the reading of Pierre's will.

CHAPTER THIRTY-NINE

The three siblings, Robert, Emilie and Michelle, as well as Rachael, Jeremy, and Father Eddie, filed into the library. There were six chairs taken from the dining room and set up facing the desk for this occasion. The sun shined through the windows and made the room feel a bit stuffy. Emilie and Jeremy seated themselves at the farthest end.

Mr. Lawson followed them in and closed the doors behind him. He marched rigidly across the room and sat behind Pierre's desk. He was facing them all, and did a quick visual inventory as if he were a teacher taking attendance. His fresh-pressed dark suit and starched white shirt offset his silver hair. On most days, he appeared to Emilie as a confident man, but today he looked cautious as he sorted through the pages in front of him. Emilie knew he must have reservations about doing this task, having dealt with Robert before. From this day forward, Robert would consider him the enemy, after the reading of the will, and her brother was not the kind of man one wanted as an enemy. Clearing his throat, Mr. Lawson began.

"Good afternoon. Let me start by giving my heartfelt condolences. Pierre was an exquisite man and my dear friend for many years. I will miss him. He loved you children, and he carefully planned his will to ensure the best outcome for each of you. He tried to give you each what you needed to succeed in becoming good people . . . happy people. Your father hoped one day you'd be content in life, as your mother had been."

Robert's face was red as he shifted in his chair. He was seated on the other end of the row, and clearly agitated already with Mr. Lawson's sentiments.

"Please, Mr. Lawson," he interrupted, "can we get on with it? I need to check on things at the office."

Rachael tugged at his sleeve. "Please, Robert, let him continue as he sees fit."

Robert rolled his eyes, letting everyone know his patience was thin and he was only appeasing them for now. The room fell quiet and Mr. Lawson continued.

"Well, as I was saying, Pierre wants you all to succeed. The family estate is a large responsibility. Because of this, he wanted one person to be at the helm, to prevent . . ."

He reflected for a second.

"To prevent confusion between you siblings. "

He turned and looked directly at Emilie.

"Miss Emilie, your father knew how much you cared for the family. Always there to support everyone, you were a rock for him, staying in Memphis and by his side over the years."

Robert let out a loud sigh. Emilie frowned and then glared in his direction. He dropped his head into his hands.

"Because you were such a devoted daughter, Pierre felt that tying you down to run the company full-time wasn't in your best interest. You've already given enough of yourself."

A big grin broke across Robert's face. Emilie knew he was relieved that she didn't have control over the company, now he probably thought he was guaranteed to inherit that honor himself. He was in for a big letdown.

"Emilie," Mr. Lawson continued, speaking directly to her now, "your father wanted you to be able to expand your horizons. You're free to do what you want, to be yourself. Running the company on a daily basis would only tie you down here. You still own half of the business interests, and you can assist when needed, but that's where your obligations end. You won't need to stay in Memphis any longer, if you choose to go elsewhere."

She smiled and nodded.

"So, Emilie, be free and discover what you need in life." Mr. Lawson smiled.

Emilie leaned toward Jeremy, and they shared a smile. Their future had just gotten a little easier. Unfortunately, she still had to deal with her clairvoyance, which lately seemed more like a curse than a gift. Her heart was held hostage by ugly emotions that didn't even belong to her.

Mr. Lawson cleared his throat and then addressed them all.

"Pierre gave a great deal of thought to the remainder of the estate," he continued. His hands began to shake, and the paper he held onto rattled.

Robert picked up on his uneasiness and looked puzzled. He shot a glance at Emilie, but she turned away.

"For this reason, he left the other half of the business interests of the estate to one person, who will have full control over all daily business transactions. This person will be the chief executive, overseeing the board of directors." He wet his lips. Emilie remained poised at the edge of her seat, waiting for him to deliver the final blow.

"Pierre stipulated that his youngest daughter, Michelle, would take over these duties immediately. Michelle, we can go over things in more detail at your earliest convenience—"

Robert jumped from his chair in protest. He was visibly shaking in anger. "Wait one damn minute! I am the rightful heir. Michelle is no businesswoman; she doesn't know the first thing about our company. For God's sake, she's been in Boston for the past ten years. You've got to be insane to think this is Father's wishes! I am the one who knows the business, I am the one who will run the businesses. This is a fraud and will be contested. Clearly, there's been a mistake."

Everyone in the room reacted to Robert's outburst. Mr. Lawson tried to appear calm, gesturing for Robert to sit, but Emilie knew that even he was intimidated.

"Now just hold on there, Robert. Simmer down and let me explain," he said. "Your father's will was well thought out, as I have already said. It was notarized, and witnessed by upstanding people. There are no grounds to contest his request, I assure you. Let me read exactly what he wrote concerning this, word for word if need be."

Robert stood unmoving, like a freight train ready to head down the tracks, steaming with rage as Mr. Lawson began to read Pierre's words.

> "The businesses owned by the estate will be under the direction of my daughter Michelle, with whom I have every confidence and trust. She will enact the best interest of the businesses, as well as the best interests of the family. This choice has weighed heavily on my mind, and has been well conceived and thoroughly evaluated. In my sound mind, I know this is the only course to protect the family interests and its legacy . . ."

Mr. Lawson mumbled, "There are a few more lines here, as it goes on . . ."

"Read them," Robert demanded.

Mr. Lawson picked up the document from the desk, stood straight, and began to read again.

> "There have been troubling issues in recent months and I am concerned by my son's involvement. To keep the company and the family protected from unlawful events in the future, I remove my son Robert from any affiliation with the family business interests in any capacity. Prior illegal activity on his part, that had been monitored, will not be revealed to anyone outside a small circle of trusted advisers and friends—"

"You have got to be kidding!" Robert shouted. "I am his only son and the rightful heir. I will fight this in court, and I promise you will regret this day. My father was the one acting crazy for months. He wasn't in his right mind. Many witnessed it, including Emilie."

Robert waved his hand toward Emilie, his eyes pleading for her to speak up. She shook her head at her brother, and refused to look away.

Waving his hands downward, Mr. Lawson again tried to calm Robert. A few moments later, it was quiet in the room.

Robert sat back down. No one else dared to speak up. Rachael patted Robert's arm, but he jerked it away in anger.

"Can I finish, Robert?" Mr. Lawson continued. "In a nutshell, your two sisters will each own half the business interests of the estate. Michelle will be the one managing the day-to-day business of the companies and its affiliates. Emilie will be there as a support, of course, and can step in at any time if need be. However, Robert, you're not left out in the cold, not by any means. A sizable inheritance is set up for you to receive, as well. You have the mansion. The house belongs to you with only one provision: that you allow your sisters to live here too, if they wish."

Mr. Lawson sorted through some manila folders that lay flat on the desk, and pulled forward the one he sought. He talked quickly, and his hands trembled as he opened a thick binder filled with white pages.

"There is also a very generous trust set up for you and your lovely wife Rachael. You will inherit it jointly with conditions that its compounding wealth and interests be passed on to your future children. No transfer can be made into other accounts. I have all the detailed documents here, and we can go over them together."

"So, let me get this straight," Robert interrupted. "My father is still controlling me from his grave, making sure I stay in line. He's keeping an eye on his legacy, still pulling the strings, with no regard for my feelings, his only son. All he cares about is the damned family name and legacy. I've been reduced to nothing more than a token son, a headdress, name and title but with no real power. Well, thanks a lot, Father."

He rubbed his fingers against his forehead, massaging out the tension. "Even from the grave he can't show me one sign of affection." Robert swallowed hard and turned away. A moment later Robert spoke again. "Okay, then. Is there anything else we need to know right now?" he asked.

Emilie was surprised by his sudden transition from rage to apparent acceptance. Mr. Lawson moved back to the desk and produced additional paperwork from his Italian leather briefcase.

"I will leave a copy of the will for each of you to review in your own time. I also tailored a financial breakdown for each of you, to help answer any questions. Later, I'd like to meet with you each individually, but not until after you have had a chance to review the paperwork. Please don't hesitate to have a lawyer of your own choice review it, if you deem that appropriate." He laid out the folders on the desktop, each marked with their names in black ink.

"All of you are very lucky, and have complete financial security. The only thing left in the will is your father's wish to make a sizable donation to the Church. Pierre requested his friend, Father Eddie," he nodded in Eddie's direction, "be in charge of the trust set up for the Church in his and Bethany's names."

Robert stood and looked pointedly at the lawyer. "I want you all to know, I am not so willing to give up all the power of the company dealings without a fight. Don't forget, I work there already. I know the deals and the business, all of it.

"Mr. Lawson, you need to give me a few days to look into this will in more detail, and then we can discuss things. I am sure there will be more questions for you, too. So, Mr. Lawson, for now let's leave all as is," Robert said. "You don't need to enforce the will yet, it can wait until we are all sure of what it really means. Michelle may decide it's too much for her, anyway. I can meet with you to discuss this in a couple of days. Right now, I need to check on business, the rest of you may have forgotten, but we are actually open today."

Michelle stood up.

"Not going to happen, Robert. You can't go back to the office, and about you working there . . . Well you did work there, past tense."

She turned and faced her brother, looking him in the eye. "Your desk has been cleared out, and your things are being delivered here, later today. As of right now, you're not allowed to set foot in any of the company buildings."

Robert's face instantly turned red. He tensed his body into a tight knot. "You can't do that," he screamed. "I'm going to the office right now."

"Don't even try. Security has been alerted. The codes have been changed. I took the liberty of going through your papers last night, and I came across quite a few documents that I need to discuss with you, in private. You have some serious explaining to do."

Robert's temper flared out of control. "How dare you speak to me in this manner! You have no right to go through my desk. You're a crazy bitch. I want you arrested."

Michelle moved across the room, until she was face to face with Robert.

"Maybe I am crazy, but no worse than you. Go ahead, Robert, call the police," she taunted in a haughty voice. "You can explain how you were stealing money from the company. I believe the term for that is embezzlement."

Emilie watched her brother, like everyone else in the room. It was the first time she ever remembered him looking terrified. Robert swallowed hard. Sweat appeared on his forehead.

"My, my, you are the snake in the grass," he said. His voice sounded off.

Michelle stared at him with insolent eyes.

"How do you know such things, cheeky little sister? I think you're misinformed."

"Oh come now, don't play the innocent with me. I know what you've been up to," she said. "Stealing, cheating. Funneling money into Tom Bennett's copious funds. Let's not forget drugging our father, and my personal favorite low, paying people to steal ancient books and journals from old English scholars!"

Jaws dropped. The room went silent. Emilie turned to Jeremy, worried about his reaction. His face paled in front of her eyes, his smile erased. It took only a second for the meaning of Michelle's words to incite him. Jeremy leaped up from his chair, crossed the room, and grabbed Robert by the throat.

"You're the one responsible for my Uncle Thad's death? You hired that piece of rubbish, Mr. Pierce? Bloody hell! I should kill you!" Jeremy released his hold on Robert. He glared at him with contempt. "No worries, I won't lower myself to your standards. Drugging your father, too. You're insane." Jeremy pushed Robert away in anger, and Robert tumbled to the floor.

He managed to get back to his feet, his face livid. Robert straightened out his sleeves and brushed at his jacket, his hands shaking violently. "Well, I hope you feel better now that you have shown your true colors."

Jeremy raised his fist, but restrained himself before he took a swing. Emilie hurried to Jeremy's side.

"It's not worth it," she said to him. "Look at me, not him." Emilie pulled on his arm. He turned to face her and immediately calmed down. "It's not worth it, Jeremy. We know what he's done. It's all over, we stopped the curse and fulfilled your Uncle Thaddeus's wishes. We saved his Aunt Rose's spirit."

"What's this? You think you stopped the curse, that Rachael was cursed? Wake up, people!" Robert hadn't missed a beat. He flung his arms up in the air in exasperation, then turned and drummed a nearby tabletop, tapping it as if it were a bongo drum. He had everyone's attention. "There are no such things as curses, fools! Well, at least I got back at Father with that one. I did scare the shit out of him with that curse business." Robert spun around and glared at Jeremy. "You have your precious book back, so why don't you just leave us, Englishman!" Robert pushed his hands away as if swatting a fly. "Go home and stay away from my sister. You're not part of this family!"

"Enough!" Father Eddie said.

The priest stood up so fast that he startled everyone. "I've had it with your disrespect. Robert, your disloyalty disgusts me." He didn't say anything else, but he didn't have to. His stance spoke volumes.

"You will regret this, Robert," Jeremy blurted out. "You disgraced your father, and your scheme led to my uncle's death. You think that hurting anyone in your way is okay? Well, it's not okay, and I'm not going to let you hurt Emilie anymore. You should know that there was a curse, you fool. Your father died saving you, saving Rachael, saving your family legacy from that curse. He sacrificed his own life. You sulk like a spoiled child, when you should be grateful instead that you have a family that cares about you, even when you don't give a damn back."

The room was dead quiet.

"What are you talking about?" Rachael said. "I vaguely remember something happened in the room that night. Was there really a ritual? I thought it was a dream."

"You were sick, Rachael, and just dreaming," Robert said. "My father died from a heart attack."

"No, I remember, I was the one dying. Then something happened and I woke up feeling strong again, only to see Pierre on the floor and then he died, right in front of us all. Do I owe my life to Pierre?"

"Yes, Rachael," Michelle said.

Rachael stood, her face pale with shock. She searched the room, looking at each of them, and she seemed ready to cry. She turned and sailed out of the room.

Emilie watched her leave, relieved as some of the anger in the room went with her. Robert stomped out next, *probably going to have his nose wiped by Tom Bennett at the Peabody.* Emilie felt no sympathy for her brother. She also understood that there was more drama ahead for them all.

CHAPTER FORTY

Robert entered the gracious lobby of the historic Peabody Hotel. The marble floors gleamed down the side spaces that surrounded the sitting area. The center space was covered with a high exotic ceiling made of carved wooden panels, adorned with gold leaf and colorful painted shields.

Clusters of people sat comfortably on the soft sofas below, immersed in the warm decor. The sound from the overflowing fountain was white noise in the busy hall; it was made of black marble that held a pool of water that was frequented by the famous Peabody ducks in a celebrated spectacle twice each day. The pool had a centered urn of carved children in stone, holding up a heavy potted flower display.

Robert paid little attention to his surroundings, however, too consumed with everything that had just happened. He searched the space for Tom Bennett. Looking around one of the large columns that bordered the room, Robert finally found his mentor, chatting away with a blonde stranger at a bar in the corner. Robert headed across the span but was intercepted midway by one of the very last people he wanted to see.

"Well, hello there, Mr. de Gourgues. I think we have some business we need to finish."

Hugh Pierce smirked at him as he stood barring Robert's way, waiting for a response.

"Mr. Pierce, I believe we're finished. There's nothing more to be done." Robert was tired of this pesky man. He stared down at him, trying to intimidate, but unfortunately, the man was persistent.

"Sir, please come with me to discuss this privately. I assure you, our transactions are not completed yet."

Robert looked at his watch and sighed theatrically. Out of the corner of his eye, he noted the security camera mounted in the corner of the room, and took an extra moment to ensure he'd been seen. "You go ahead and I'll follow you up. The third floor, right?"

"I will see you soon," Pierce said, nodding, and then he walked away.

Robert roamed the walkway that flanked the expanse of the huge lobby, not wanting to be seen following Pierce to the elevators. Specialty shops lined the perimeter. Robert window shopped and then walked into a men's clothing store and bought a golf shirt for five hundred dollars. Satisfied that enough time had passed, he grudgingly went up to the third floor hotel room. He made a conscious choice to use the stairs rather than the elevator. He didn't pass any hotel staff in the hallway, and Robert knew this older section of the hotel, which contained cheaper, smaller rooms, had no security cameras. He knocked on the door.

Hugh Pierce opened the door and with a wide arm, he bowed, as if letting in royalty. Robert entered the lilac-colored room, ready to put an end to things. Pierce closed the door and walked over to the small desk that he improvised as a bar, and poured them both a drink from a bottle of Highland Park whiskey. He handed Robert a small glass. Robert took a swig of his favorite smoky malt, trying to cover up his annoyance.

"So, Pierce, what business do we need to discuss?" he said, holding back his contempt for this man.

"I want one more payment," Pierce said. "It's only fair considering everything I have done for you. Plus, there is one more piece of information I have. I know it will be of some interest to you."

Pierce swirled the drink in his hand confidently, waiting for a response. "Just tell me what you know, I'll be fair if I think it warrants payment. I've been more than generous with you already," Robert said irritably. After everything else that had happened in the past twenty-four hours, the last thing he needed was Hugh Pierce continuing to milk him dry.

Pierce obviously picked up on Robert's frustration, and sped up his story, nervously crinkling an envelope he held in his hands. "Agreed, you have been. The thing is, while I was researching some of your family's history, I took the liberty of searching some public records on your mother's side, as well. Some very interesting information came to light, and I know it will be of interest to you."

"Please, I really don't care about my mother's family. I'm not really impressed by any of them." He let out a deep sigh, trying to stay patient.

"Believe me, Mr. de Gourgues, you want to know about this. It concerns your sister."

Robert's mouth curled up with a smile. "Well go ahead, tell it all."

Once Robert was indeed interested, Pierce unloaded the information willingly.

Robert listened to the whole story. Intrigued, he grabbed the yellow envelope from the man's hands and scanned the documents inside. Robert lingered over a photo for a moment, studying a familiar face. *Well, well, baby sister,* he thought, *what have you done, Michelle?* A smile touched his lips.

Robert agreed to pay for the information without hesitation. They reached an agreement of five thousand dollars, and Robert handed him the cash from his inside jacket pocket. Pierce shuffled the money, then made a snapping noise with the bills and shoved them into his own breast pocket.

"Done deal. Nice doing business with you, Mr. de Gourgues. Let's have one more toast and seal the deal," he said.

Hugh Pierce took Robert's glass, and turned to top it with more booze. Robert extracted a small vial from his pocket and covertly poured its contents into Pierce's glass, which rested on the table in front of him. Pierce turned around, handed Robert his glass, picked up his own, and raised it to toast their business conclusion. Clanging glasses, they gulped the smooth scotch. A few scant seconds after a brisk swig, Mr. Pierce gasped.

His glass fell to the gold carpet. Pierce grabbed his throat, his mouth gaping wide as he fought for air. He dropped to his knees, choking, and then toppled over.

Robert smirked as he watched Pierce's body contort as the man convulsed. He took a sip of his beloved scotch. The struggle ended, and Pierce's body went limp in death. Robert bent down and verified that his pulse was gone. He picked up the empty glass from the floor with a napkin, and placed it in the bag with his recent purchase. He grabbed the money from Mr. Pierce's front jacket pocket, and returned it to his own. Then, Robert strolled to the door and, after one last glance, he left the room still sucking down the scotch in his own glass. He was happy to be rid of that pest.

Robert took the stairs down to the lobby. Looking across the open span, he gazed up to survey the second-story balcony, decorated with ornate black wrought-iron railings. Satisfied that no one was tailing him, Robert ambled over and joined Tom, who still sat waiting at the bar, his glass in hand.

"Barkeep, a drink—make it scotch, a double." Then Robert placed both glasses from the room onto the black slate counter, to be cleared off and cleaned. The hotel had the best service. No evidence would be around to connect him with Pierce's death, even if authorities could determine it was from cyanide poisoning. Robert smiled at his cleverness. Tom Bennett raised his eyebrows.

"You seem pleased with yourself. So, how are things?" Tom asked.

"Some things are fine, some not. The Pierce matter was taken care of. No more loose ends," Robert said.

"Good."

"I just need to discuss with you some bumps I ran into regarding my father's will."

Tom frowned. Robert knew Tom expected everything to be smooth sailing now that his father was gone. Tom had already made commitments with anticipation of a payday soon. Robert had hoped that his inheritance would be his golden ticket into Tom Bennett's secret society. He wanted in, hoping to prove he was the right material by handing over money to fund various projects. Tom had promised him a spot. *This change in the will better not blow my plans apart.*

"Okay, Robert, tell me what happened?" Tom said.

He noticed Tom's sharp angled nose, and a dangerously worried look. Robert cleared his throat. "The old guy screwed me, even in death. He changed his will and left the business and the accounts to my sisters. Do you believe that? What an ass. Even in death he's killing me!"

Tom Bennett took a long swig, then slammed his glass down. "Contest it. Robert, you have a copy of the original will. Just play up his senile mind that you so boldly induced. Judges see crazy old people dragged into court all the time."

"I can't. Somehow, my family knew I drugged Father, and they knew about the stolen money, too."

Burning with anger, Tom Bennett's face tuned dark. Robert drew in a deep breath. He understood no one crossed this man and lived, he had too many demons and influential followers, some even more dangerous than himself. All the monies that had been funneled into Tom Bennett's accounts were needed for his great master plan, and it was only part of the fee Robert had to pay, to be accepted as a member of one of the most influential societies in the world.

"Tom, please check your accounts to see if the money is still there," Robert said.

"You make sure you cover your tracks," he replied, pointing his finger at him. "No fucking way is Pierre going to squeeze me from his grave. You have no idea how much I hate that man."

"Okay, okay. Then make me a part of the society, and then we can bring in your big guns. What I need is something to stick on my siblings, something to use as blackmail, in order to get control back, the sooner the better."

"Robert, why didn't you tell me about this sooner?"

"I just found out myself. They locked me out of all the buildings, too. Unbelievable! I am at a loss here."

Part of Robert worried Tom Bennett was going to blow him off; another part hoped he would. He wanted Tom's confidence, and to please his mentor. But there were times, like right now, when Robert was afraid of the man. He looked like pure evil. Robert looked up at him, giving away his vulnerability.

Tom smiled at him. "Don't worry, buddy." He slapped Robert on the back. "It's time for me to call in other friends for assistance. We'll take care of things, don't worry, we can still play together. Count on it. I will find a way to get you back in charge of things. We have to gain control over those business accounts. Remember, there's no way to back out now."

Tom Bennett's face distorted a bit, and for a split second he reminded Robert of an animal, a dark wolf maybe, marking its territory and establishing dominance.

"It was a life commitment you made in our deal. Those are the rules," Tom said.

Robert shivered inside for a split second before he nodded. "Yes, we are in it together," he said, to reassure himself as much as Tom. "Let me know when I need to do something for the cause."

Tom left the Peabody. Robert sat and had a couple more drinks, thinking about the secret society. He had wanted to join for a long time now, ever since Tom first talked about its existence. Tom Bennett ran the show, and he needed the money to fund things.

Robert was okay with that, as long as he was part of the plan. This was his destiny, just waiting for the day he'd be inducted as a full-fledged member of the Black Wolf Society. The society offered power and protection, and most of all, brotherhood.

CHAPTER FORTY-ONE

Emilie and Jeremy hadn't spoken much with each other since Pierre had died. Concentrating on anything proved difficult for Emilie, with the stew of emotions boiling in her head. Jeremy was patient, knowing she had to deal with her loss in her own way and time. He gave her space, leaving each day to work on the project, and returning in the evening to see her.

Every night, he slept at the house. Emilie wanted him near, cuddling her and calming things down in her head. In a way, she was using him. That thought made her even sadder. She didn't want him to think that was all she wanted from him. Emilie loved him more each day, but couldn't deal with happiness while a cloud followed her.

Ten days after her father's burial, Jeremy left for work. Emilie watched as he drove away. She crossed the front porch, slipped into the wicker chair, and closed her eyes. The warm morning breeze soothed her skin. She could hear the swooshing of the leaves in the rolling wave of the wind, their tips rattling in the breeze. She reached into her pocket and found the small spiral shell. Emilie rubbed her finger over the smooth surface and began to remember.

In this brief stolen moment of tranquility, Emilie remembered Florida: the warm sunny day spent with Jeremy. They had been happy that day, as they searched together. There were no loud voices in her head, no turbulent emotions, just a calmness as they paddled up the stream. She needed that peacefulness now.

The silence was broken by the roar of a motorcycle, its hum lingering in the background before it faded away. That sound was replaced by the cawing of a bird, again fading away but replaced by the many shrills of different birds all squawking and singing out at once. Their calls bombarded her peace. She pushed the sound from her mind, flexing her telepathic ability like a muscle as she moved the images in her head in and out, hoping to teach herself how to control all of her senses. More than anything right now, she wanted to learn how to shield herself properly, and maybe even block other's turmoil from her mind trap. She pushed again, stretching. It took all her energy, but if she wanted a normal life she needed to learn how to use this shield.

It was a hot Memphis summer evening. Jeremy walked across the front porch and sat next to Emilie. He knew that she had been here all day, almost motionless, deep in reverie. Nina, concerned about her apathy, had called him. Emilie heard her tattling on the phone in the foyer. If it was a Dream Barbie Jeremy was after, it would never be her.

Jeremy reached over and touched her face with a gentle hand, brushing his fingers across her skin. Emilie immediately lost some of her negativity. She felt his love; it seeped into her soul with warm joy, and she knew he'd do anything to help her get better.

"Em, look at me," he said.

She turned and gave him a faint smile, but part of her was still far away. She hurt inside, knowing he could feel her distance.

"Emilie, I've finished my work here. My part of the project is completed."

He was quiet a moment. Emilie knew what was coming next, before he even said the words. She rested her head on his chest and waited for him to finish his thoughts.

"I want to go back to Guilford, just to stop in and see my family for a bit. Please come with me. Before you answer, just take time to think about it. I think it's a good idea to get away from here for a while. Come with me, and meet my family. They want to meet the girl I'm in love with, the girl who stole my heart."

A tear ran down her cheek. She had dreamed of meeting his family many times, envisioning them in her head. Even so, there was no way she could handle it right now. Every day she woke up in tears, depressed to the point of not trusting herself. Jeremy wanted them to meet the girl he was in love with, but that girl was missing.

Someday she would meet them, but not when she was like this, all broken inside. She loved Jeremy too much to begin their life together while she was so messed up. Jeremy would understand, just like she understood his need to go home and check on his loved ones. She raised her head and turned to face him.

"Jeremy, you should go home and check in with the family. I want you to go. But I can't yet. Soon, but not yet, not like this. I need to figure out how to get out of this hole I'm stuck in, and I have to do it by myself. Do you understand?"

Jeremy dropped his face and looked away. "I was afraid of this. You always need to control things on your own terms. All I want is for you to accept my help without feeling obliged or, worse yet, guilty. Let me share your emotional burden. Then someday it will be gone, I know it. I don't understand your gift completely, and probably never will, but I can still help you."

"That's just it, Jeremy. You can't help. It is up to me."

He turned back around and looked at her. She searched his hazel eyes, trying to find the reason that she felt sorrow coming from him, now mingling with her own.

"Okay, I trust you," he said. "You know what's best. I can wait. I'll stay here with you until you're ready, and then when you're feeling more like yourself, we'll visit the family together."

Emilie stared at the floor, afraid to look him straight in the eye any longer, scared he'd see her true intention. She needed to be alone and sort things out for herself.

"No need for you to wait. I think you should go home now. Believe me, I will feel better knowing you're doing what you need to, for yourself. Allow me to go off by myself and get my head together. I promise, we'll talk with each other every day. You're still stuck with me, Jeremy. I just need some alone time . . . to learn how to manage this gift I'm cursed with."

Jeremy's eyes watered, and his smile disappeared. Emilie watched as he swallowed back his regret, and wiped the corner of his eye with his hand. Despite his bronze tan, he looked pale.

"Wow. I don't know what to say. You've surprised me, Emilie. I thought my being around helped you. I don't like this."

"I don't like it, either."

The big clock in the entry hall chimed, calling the family to dinner. Emilie and Jeremy went to the dining room. Everyone was there, Robert and Rachael, and Michelle of course. They all ate in silence. One of many uneventful meals, they each sat in their own world, with their lone and peculiar ideas. The only sound was the tinging of silverware against the china.

Emilie noticed her father's empty chair and she felt vacant. She heard his voice in her head. His last feeling was happiness, being with Mother. Emilie hoped she'd feel right inside soon, so she could give her love to Jeremy the way she was meant to, with abundant joy.

After dinner, Emilie and Jeremy strolled on the porch together. She motioned for him to sit on a bench and she leaned against him, looking up into his face.

"Jeremy, you know I love you with all my heart."

"I know."

"You know I need you and want you, right?"

"I know."

"I want you to understand. These emotions . . . they pound in my head so hard, every day, unrelenting. I think I can teach myself how to control the empath in me, but it's going to take time."

Emilie looked at him with pleading eyes until the tears were ready to spill over. Jeremy drew in a deep breath.

"What do you need to do, and how can I help?" he asked.

"I'm going back to the coast, to Florida, near the ocean. I need time to sort out all the craziness in my head. I never felt at peace until I was there, with you. I hope to find peace there, again, but this time without relying on you." Emilie grinned. "I don't think you realize how powerful your touch is for me. You basically help me balance out the clairvoyance and make it manageable."

"See, Emilie, that's exactly why we should stay together."

"No, that's not right. Sure, I need to come to terms with the things I've experienced already and find a way to let go of all the havoc tied to them. But it's more than that. I have to know that I can handle this gift on my own, and not be afraid to be myself again. I hope you understand. I don't want to lean on you, Jeremy, I want to love you."

"I'll go with you," he said, "if you want me to."

"Please understand." She hung her head. "One day I'll function like a normal human being again. It won't be for long, just long enough. Promise me you'll enjoy your family for a while."

He respected her enough not to argue the point any longer. "Take the time you need. I'll be there as soon as you ask me to join you, I promise."

He took her in his arms, and poured his feelings into his embrace. She basked in his tenderness and hope. She felt his apprehension, and fear of loneliness, too.

"Please don't be sad," she said.

"You ask a lot from me." He held her even tighter.

They spent the night together in passion. Their bodies meshed in complete surrender, their souls in abandonment. Emilie let herself become vulnerable, open to Jeremy's touch. His understanding of her need to retreat actually made her feel closer to him than she had ever imagined possible. Knowing she was free made Emilie all the more bound to him. Love's last kiss found peace in sleep.

First thing in the morning, Jeremy left for England. Emilie said goodbye to him, then she said farewell to her sister, too. She boarded a plane and headed for Florida, searching for peace in the last place she had felt tranquility. She was chasing nature again, but this time hoped to break the bonds that kept her a prisoner in her own mind.

CHAPTER FORTY-TWO

Emilie left Memphis and stayed in a hotel near Jacksonville while searching for a house. She found a small bungalow, a ranch built in the 1980s, nestled on the coast with the beach as the backyard. The house had gray cedar siding with a coral pink front door. A weathered deck wrapped the house, with a ramp that led down to the beach's sand. Located in Vilano Beach on Coastal Highway, it was a quiet place south of Jacksonville and north of St Augustine. She paid cash for a quick sale, the furniture stayed as part of the deal, and the sellers had been ecstatic getting rid of it after it had been on the market for so long. She closed on the property almost overnight, and moved in immediately. Emilie had her own private getaway within a week.

Some problems can be solved with money, she reflected, *just not the important ones.*

She acquainted herself with the local town and ventured into the shops, mingling with the crowds. Most of the time, she was alone at her house or on the beach, and she used the solitude to discover more about herself. She sorted the mixed-up emotions that had caused her so much pain, and slowly gained power over her gift, instead of it controlling her. She was beginning to understand her ability and how to use it properly. Testing her strengths daily, she went downtown and allowed other people's emotions in, and exercised her reaction. She learned how to use her shield, stretching it and understanding its boundaries.

The summer heat had blasted the beach during the tourist season. Emilie had enjoyed the warmth, but after weeks of it, finally the autumn promised some relief from the scorching sun.

She looked out at the ocean, gazing across the blue-gray turmoil as the thunderous waves crashed at her feet. The wind blew through her hair, and she pulled it back behind her ears as she walked along the shore. Her feet, warmed by the wet sand, cooled when the waves washed over her toes. Sometimes, she felt like a child, here alone on the beach, amazed at such simple things. She watched as the dirty white foam that edged the water settled on rocks that lay near the surf.

She brought herself back to the real issues, ready to analyze the past few months and her progress. This had become a morning ritual, tracking the headway she'd made. She had finally achieved closure regarding her parents' deaths. Understanding the reason why her father stayed in the beyond, love for the family, helped her accept everything. Sorting through the emotional currents that troubled her during her father's otherworld experience took time, but with reflection came understanding. He'd given up his life out of love for his family. Now, the little girl inside her knew her parents were together again. She had experienced it while Pierre was in the trance. She'd felt exaltation, that was the last sensation she had shared with her father, when Pierre joined Bethany in spirit. Her mother and father finally had the happy ending that their love deserved.

Emilie no longer carried her family's burden of a guilty conscience. Living away from them made it easier to realize they were not her responsibility. Sorting through all the chaos that had bombarded her, now her mind was in clearer waters.

Time had passed with the changing tides, in and out, in and out. Still she was depressed, but now for different reasons. She was herself again, but missing a piece—Jeremy. He called her early every morning, but that wasn't enough anymore.

Her phone rang. She looked at the caller ID, it was her sister, who called for short check-ins often. She swiped open her phone, and stood still. Her feet sank into the soft warm sand, as more waves washed ashore and splashed against her legs.

"Michelle, good morning. You're calling early."

"You know what they say about the early bird. Besides, I have lots to do today, so I thought I'd give you an update now about everything going on here. My conversation won't trigger any bad feelings for you, will it?"

"No. I'm clairvoyant, but I need to be near someone to sense their emotions."

"Yeah, right. Sorry, Em, but that still sounds creepy to me. Guess I'm not very empathetic, you tapped everything from that vein."

They both laughed. "So tell me, what's up?"

"Well, I had a day full of meetings yesterday. Em, I'm learning the business and keeping up with the men. There was a lot to unravel after Father died, but things are running smooth now."

"That's wonderful, Michelle. I want you to know how proud I am of you. You're a natural at running the estate, and a great businesswoman. Just a few months and already you have things running smoothly. Father's faith in your abilities was on target."

"Thank you for your support, Em. There's still more to clean up around the mess Robert made, and knowing that Tom Bennett is getting away with the embezzlement is frustrating as all hell. They can't pursue him without revealing our brother's part in the scheme, and we promised Father to not expose Robert's crime. So, my hands are tied there."

There was a moment of silence over the line, until Michelle burst out in excitement. "I almost forgot to tell you. The police came to the house the other afternoon. They questioned Robert about the death of Mr. Pierce."

"No! Pierce died? What happened?"

"The guy was murdered. Poisoned. They asked Robert a bunch of questions about being at the Peabody that same day.

Get this, Rob just happened to have his lawyer here at the house when the police showed up. It was as if he knew."

"You don't think he had anything to do with the murder? Michelle, that's our brother you're talking about."

"I don't know what to think when it comes to Robert. Anyway, it was a brief encounter. They asked what he and Mr. Pierce had talked about in the lobby. Evidently the guy just asked for the correct time, they've got Rob on one of the hotel security tapes checking his watch for Pierce. Robert answered the police's questions, and they left. So, I guess there's no evidence that he was involved after all. Still, I think it's odd. But I'm not about to stir up any more trouble with Robert."

Emilie thought Mr. Pierce's death far too coincidental, and now Jeremy would never have a complete account of his Uncle Thaddeus's death. Maybe it was for the best. Of course, Robert claimed he knew nothing about Uncle Thad's heart attack. Only time would help Robert see the impact of his actions on others. That wasn't Emilie's responsibility.

"What's that supposed to mean, not stirring up more trouble? Still problems in paradise between you and Robert?" Emilie asked.

"You know he's not talking to me," Michelle said.

"Yes. He won't answer my calls, either."

"Emilie, I try to talk with him, honest. Robert pretends I'm not in the room. I try to say things about Tom's grudge against father, but he refuses to hear me. He thinks they're lies I'm making up!"

"Why on earth would you even want to lie about that? He needs to wake up and grow up," Emilie said.

"He doesn't know about the inconsistencies we caught when the results came back from the accounting audit. Robert refused to listen. It's so stressful at home right now."

Emilie knew it was getting to Michelle, she didn't have to feel it, she heard the angst in her sister's voice.

"Maybe I should get a house of my own?" Michelle said.

"That might be a good idea, to help you keep your head straight."

"Yes, it sounds good, except then I'd worry about Rachael being alone with Robert."

"He's her husband, he won't hurt her. How is she doing since she returned to the house?"

"Rachael is friendly when Rob's not around. Living in the big house again, trying to keep the marriage on track. Still, I worry about her. Being with Robert is challenging, dealing with his moods and extravagances."

"Yes, I remember it well," Emilie said. She pulled her feet out of the sand and started pacing the shoreline as she listened.

"Father Eddie has been a pillar of support, as usual. He's helping Rachael come to terms with what she saw on the day of the ceremony, and also counseling her and Robert. Eddie hopes they can develop their marriage and get over their trust issues," Michelle said. "After everything that happened, I don't know why they decided to try to make it work."

Emilie didn't want to know Robert's motivations about anything. She was stepping back from the situation. Her brother could be so secretive, and a marriage without trust would have many burdens.

"Everything will be all right eventually, I guess. These things take time. Speaking of which, I have to go. I'll call tomorrow, though."

"Okay, kid, have a great day," Emilie said.

Emilie ended the call and slipped the phone into her pocket. She padded across the sand and headed back to the house. She thought about Robert, but then stopped herself. Emilie didn't want to experience that emotional turmoil, even if she still had concerns for Rachael. She needed to draw her lines and not cross them if she wanted to keep her sanity.

She and Father Eddie had had a few conversations, too. He'd known about her empathic talents, even as a child. He'd warned her over the years to only take responsibility for her own feelings. She practiced disassociating herself from outside influences. This was a fine line to walk. She didn't want to become a cold person, but to survive, she needed to pull back and block some of the emotional ties. Breaking the bonds without losing her compassion, that was her elusive objective.

Emilie still dreamed of Jeremy, and wanted to start a life with him. She refused to block anything from him, and swore to always share her feelings and be open to his. They respected each other's needs and were honest. She loved and needed Jeremy more than ever.

As she neared the house, her hand went to her neck. She found the small shell she'd had a local jeweler turn into a necklace for her. She rubbed the red spiral shell between her fingers, remembering Jeremy's warm smile. Now, after months of independence and sorting of things in her head, she was alone and miserably missing Jeremy. She wanted to be the proper friend and lover he deserved.

Each morning, as the sun rises over the ocean's horizon, washing light onto the beachfront, they talk. Today after she'd spoken with him on the phone, things felt off. Something was wrong. He was still in Surrey enjoying his family, and she didn't have the heart to ask him to leave them, in order to be with her. Emilie felt like the most selfish person in the world, but she wanted him with her so badly. Chances were good that on the next call, she'd be begging him to leave England.

Someday she'd be in Surrey too, but right now her place was here, near the ocean. Watching the tide come in and listening to the thunder of the waves, it soothed her soul. Near the ocean, Emilie felt close to God and was happy, but her heart ached for Jeremy. She needed to find a way to ask him to come back to her. *Why are the simple things in life still so hard for me?*

CHAPTER FORTY-THREE

Jeremy was frustrated. He'd never intended to stay away from Emilie more than a couple of days, or a week or two at most. It had been months. On the call this morning, they spoke about being together soon, but there'd been no mention of an actual date. In the back of his mind, he wondered if her feelings had changed toward him. *Did I dream her love up?* He'd begun to question too much, that was when he realized he had stayed away long enough.

Jeremy booked a flight, needing to see her right away. The frustration of being apart had to end. The next sunrise, he was determined they'd share together. He grabbed his luggage and was on his way back to Emilie. He would find out where he stood, one way or another.

The red-eye landed at the Jacksonville Airport. Jeremy was too excited to be tired. Only four in the morning, and everything was still dark. Sprinting to the rental car lot, he found his reserved car and plugged in his preprogrammed GPS. He longed to see her face, to touch her and love her. He wasn't going to waste a minute, excited to see Emilie in her new house.

Squawking gulls woke Emilie, as they flew by her window on their way to the morning meal. She tried to go back to sleep, but even the pillow over her head couldn't block their noise. The window had been open all night, letting in the cool ocean breeze. The lulling sounds of the surf had eased Emilie into a peaceful sleep, but now she was wide awake. She rubbed her eyes and reluctantly tumbled out of bed. She looked out the window and sighed, realizing she was up early; it was still dark.

The predawn hours of the morning were often her most satisfying. Emilie liked the quiet, and didn't usually get woken by flocks of birds. She skidded her slippered feet into the kitchen and reached up for the makings of her morning brew. She fumbled as she made the coffee, grabbing the filters and struggling to get it straight in the contraption. She measured, filled, and pressed the button. Every morning she drank her coffee on the deck, while watching the sun rise over the water. That was her favorite time of day, because that's when she called Jeremy, and imagined they were in the same room talking. It was the only way she wanted to start her day.

The coffeepot puffed, as the last of the steam pushed through the grounds. The smell of fresh-brewed coffee filled her small kitchen, and woke up her senses. She'd never get a single-serve brew maker. She'd miss the aroma too much. She pulled a mug from the white laminated cupboard, and just as she was about to pour herself a cup, someone knocked on the door.

An adrenaline rush shot through her body. No one had ever visited her at this house. *Is that even my front door?* Another knock. She wasn't just wary, but a little frightened by the unexpected interruption at this early hour. *Can't be a lost tourist at this hour, maybe someone's car broke down.* A fleeting memory of an old movie she had watched years ago flooded her with images of a home invasion. She remembered why she had wanted to carry and learn how to use a gun, but it was too late for that now. Grabbing a knife from the kitchen was too scary a risk for her. Slowly walking to the front door, on her guard, she picked up an umbrella on her way. She imagined using it to poke someone's eyes out, better than nothing. She meekly answered the knock. "Who is it?"

"Is it too early to get a cup of coffee from you, Miss Emilie?"

Her heart leaped to her throat. Excitement surged through her entire body, her blood rushing in her veins from head to toe. A happiness that had been floating in limbo awakened, and she was in heaven. She dropped the umbrella.

Frantically she yanked off the chain lock, twisted open the bolt, and pulled open the door. Without waiting another second, she jumped into Jeremy's arms. Their bodies collided and he embraced her lovingly, longingly, kissing her until they ran out of breath. When Emilie was confident this wasn't a dream, she pulled him into the little house and closed the door.

His hazel eyes reflected her love, and his dimples were deep set in a joyful smile. Jeremy, more handsome than she'd dreamed, stood in front of her and for a moment she had a hard time believing he was there. Moments ago, she'd been excited anticipating their morning call, this face to face was overwhelming, but desired. She could feel his excitement, a sensation of his deep love matching her own feelings. Emilie hoped this ecstasy would never end.

"Good morning, beautiful." His accent stirred her in a sinful way.

Emilie leaned forward on her tiptoes and landed a gentle kiss on his warm, wet lips. "Good morning, handsome."

Jeremy gave her a long tight embrace and then let her go. Taking a small step back, he pulled a box from his pocket, and stood silent a moment.

"Emilie, I love you. Please marry me."

She reached up and kissed him again, but more urgently this time. The euphoric feeling of floating on air filled her spirit.

"I take that as a yes," he managed to say when he pulled away for air.

She giggled. "Yes. Yes, of course. I'm so happy to see you. I love you. I missed you so much, and yes I want to be with you forever."

Emilie closed her eyes a second. Her feelings mingled with his. So many emotions were running through their minds, mirroring each other's succinctly. Her clairvoyance was in high gear, but this time she let it flow. It felt good, and natural.

They had a whole life to plan and to live. They had a marriage to arrange and a family to build together, a future to discover. Time would bring them many adventures, good and bad, but they'd always stay honest in their love, together. A love bond, replacing all cursed ones.

Jeremy placed his hands on her shoulders.

"Hey, don't you want to see what's in the box?"

He opened the small black velvet case. Inside was an antique Edwardian diamond ring. Emilie gasped, it took her breath away, it was so stunningly beautiful.

"It belonged to my Aunt Rose Riley many years ago. My Uncle Thad kept it, then he left it to me," Jeremy said.

Emilie looked up at Jeremy and smiled, and wiped the back of her hand over her eyes. Tears blurred her vision, as she took the box and stared. The design was unique; Emilie had never seen such an exquisite piece. A floral burst design with a bezel set, it looked so lacy and airy. It reminded her of the intricate design they had admired together when visiting the old cathedrals. The ring's center encased an old mine-cut diamond that sparkled as she turned the box. It was encircled with a floral halo, studded with small rare-cut diamonds that twinkled and extended down the side.

"Jeremy, this is gorgeous. It's even more special because it was Aunt Rose's."

He blushed. "I can buy you a new one of your own too, it's just that this ring reminds me of you."

"This is perfect—just like you."

Jeremy took the ring out and slipped it on her finger. It fit perfectly.

"How about some coffee? I always give handsome men who propose to me a cup." She smiled and took his hand, and led him into the kitchen.

"Cute place you have here."

"It was nothing until you arrived." She smiled and grabbed a cup, filled it with coffee, and led the way to the back. She slid open the door and they both took a deep breath, letting the sea air fill their lungs.

"Beautiful. Emilie you belong here, near the ocean. The waves match your energy."

They drank their coffee and talked a little, then walked on the beach. Basking in their moment of happiness, they watched the new day begin, together in an embrace, as the warm sun filtered its way over the sandy beachfront. The sun rose above the rolling waves of the eastern shoreline like a golden dome. They took the moment to meditate and accept their good fate.

The gulls started up their noise and the local joggers began to show up. Emilie and Jeremy left the beach and soon ended up in the bedroom to share their built-up desires.

They made up for the lost time, taking turns satisfying each other. Hours later, smiling deliriously, they were ready for lunch. Emilie grabbed a robe, and they trotted into the tiny kitchen and searched the cupboards for some soup. Then, the phone rang. Reluctantly, Emilie answered. She put it on speakerphone, so they both could listen as she searched for the can opener.

"Emilie, I need you to come home right away. Something strange is happening."

It was Michelle, she sounded frantic.

"Good morning, what's up, sis?" Emilie said.

"Good morning? It's afternoon, girl. I know that tone of voice. You're not alone are you? Is Jeremy there, too? Hello, Jeremy."

Jeremy laughed aloud. "Yes, I'm here. You're on speaker. What's up, Michelle?"

"Seriously, I need you and Em. You know how Robert has been giving me the cold shoulder, right? Well a bombshell just exploded in front of me!"

Emilie dropped a can of soup onto the rose-colored laminate. It clanged on the counter, and Jeremy jerked his head up to see the commotion. "Here we go again. What do you mean exactly, Michelle? You said he's not talking to you. You're not making sense."

"Robert dug up something that happened to me when I lived in Boston. He threatened to use it as leverage against me. Don't you understand? He's trying to get me overthrown by the board. I need you here to help me talk sense into him. Are you coming?"

Emilie looked over to Jeremy, and saw his face twitch. He was such a warm-hearted soul, and she knew he'd put her sister's needs above their own. He was right, too: she couldn't be selfish and hide away anymore. It was time to face reality.

"Yes, of course, we'll be there if you need us. Can you give us a few details?"

There was silence on the line, and then Michelle mumbled as if covering up the phone. "It's hard to discuss like this. Someone might be listening," she whispered.

Emilie had hoped to enjoy some peaceful time alone with Jeremy, but she had to help her sister. There was no other option.

"We will get there as soon as possible," Jeremy interrupted, speaking her same thoughts aloud. "As long as you think it will help. We've got your back, kid."

"Good, thanks, both of you. Come soon. I need you both here." The line went dead.

Jeremy and Emilie stared at each other, wondering where this was going to lead. They would be there to help, because that's what family did. Once the situation was under control again, they could get back to their own personal business. The two of them were bonded for life, Emilie knew that now. Together, they would face Robert and weather whatever storms were brewing. After everything they'd already been through, this time Emilie had no doubt that their bond would last forever.

<>>

This is the end of book one.
The next story, **EXPOSING SECRET SINS** is available at
your favorite book distributors.

Acknowledgments

My never-ending gratitude goes to my husband, for his constant love, support, patience, and faith in me. I am blessed and thankful for my children. Each has a unique place in my heart forever and is the life in my soul no matter how grown. I am also beholden to my mother and siblings for their lifelong critiques. A special remembrance to my nephew who inspired me to write - Dana, you will always be in my heart.

A special note of thanks to my original Beta readers, especially: MaryLou Paquette, Janice Paquette, and my friends Rita and Gil Oats, who have given me confidence to continue on my writing journey. Thanks, goes out to my new beta readers Virginia Duval and Barbara Lipe, their keen eyes and hearts are appreciated.

To my local writer's critique group – thank you for your camaraderie Memphislores. I've also received help from a number of fellow authors, who have shared their experiences and have given their support in many ways. My heartfelt thank you goes out to a great community of Indie writers. Indie Authors have big hearts, willing to share everything, and are true champions of empowerment.

A good story needs an author but a great book needs an editor. Thank you, Caroline Smailes for your help fleshing out the story thread. Thank you Jen Blood of Adian Editing for your insights and final editing touches.

Thank you George Hodan for your spectacular photography used on the original book cover. Discover his art at these places: HodanPictures.com

From the Author

I hope you have enjoyed reading
BREAKING CURSED BONDS

Your feedback is helpful and means a lot to me, so if you have a few minutes to spare, I'd be honored to have a review by you. Leaving a few short words about your reading experience at the store or distributor where you bought the book, or Goodreads or similar book review sites, will help other readers find the story, as well.

Reviews bring life to a book, especially in today's digital markets. Your feedback is important and very much appreciated.

Thank you for spending your time getting to know the de Gourgues siblings. Look for book two of the serial:

EXPOSING SECRET SINS

You can sign up for updates by using the 'subscribe to my newsletter' button at my websites:

http://elisabethzguta.com/
http://ezindiepublishing.com/
http://ezindiedesign.com/

Let's Connect with social media:

https://twitter.com/zguta
https://www.linkedin.com/in/elisabethzguta
https://www.facebook.com/ElisabethZguta
https://plus.google.com/+ElisabethZguta/posts
http://www.goodreads.com/author/Elisabeth_Zguta

I hope to connect with you there!
Thank you for reading **Breaking Cursed Bonds** –
I appreciate your support.